D1593282

FLOATING CLOUDS

JAPANESE STUDIES SERIES

COLUMBIA UNIVERSITY PRESS   NEW YORK

FLOATING CLOUDS

HAYASHI FUMIKO

TRANSLATED BY LANE DUNLOP

Columbia University Press
Publishers Since 1893
New York   Chichester, West Sussex
Originally published in Japan as *Ukigumo* by Rokko Shuppan, Tokyo, 1951.
Translation based on the edition published by Shinchosha, Tokyo.
Translation © Lane Dunlop, 2006
This edition © Columbia University Press, 2006
All rights reserved
Japanese Studies Series

This book has been selected by the Japanese Literature Publishing Project (JLPP), which is run
by the Japanese Literature Publishing and Promotion Center (J-Lit Center) on behalf of the
Agency for Cultural Affairs of Japan.

This translation is dedicated to Ce Roser.

Library of Congress Cataloging-in-Publication Data

Hayashi, Fumiko, 1904–1951.
  [Ukigumo. English]
  Floating clouds / Hayashi Fumiko ; translated by Lane Dunlop.
      p. cm. — (Japanese studies series)
  ISBN 0–231–13628–5 (cloth : alk. paper)
  I. Dunlop, Lane. II. Title. III. Series.
  PL829.A8U5513   2005
895.6'344   2005051851—dc22   2005051795

Columbia University Press books are printed on permanent and durable acid-free paper.
Printed in the United States of America

c 10 9 8 7 6 5 4 3 2

CONTENTS

I AM BY FATE A WANDERER. I have no native place. My father was a man of Iyo in Shikoku, an itinerant peddler of dry goods. My mother was a maid at a hot springs inn in Sakurajima of Kyushu. Since she had married an outlander, she was driven out of her hometown. The couple came to rest in a place called Shimonoseki in Yamaguchi Prefecture. That Shimonoseki is where I was born.

—Hayashi Fumiko (*Diary of a Vagabond*, 1928)

Hayashi Fumiko was born on the last day of 1904, on the second floor of a tinsmith's shop in the Shimonoseki neighborhood of Tanaka-cho. Her father, Miyata Sentaro, was twenty-two, her mother, Hayashi Kiku, was thirty-six. At the time of their marriage, Kiku had already had two husbands and borne three children, two boys and a girl. Public censoriousness apparently existing at even the lowest levels of Japanese society at the time, the fact that her husband was not a local was sufficient to drive the couple out of Sakurajima. The marriage lasted only six years. In 1910, Miyata Sentaro, having achieved success in the dry goods business, took in a geisha of Amakusa. One snowy day, Kiku and her daughter Fumiko fled the house. Fumiko's mother remarried the same year, this time to a man twenty years her junior, Sawai Kisaburo, the eldest son of a farmer of Okayama Prefecture. In the spring of this year, Fumiko entered grade school at Nagasaki. It was the first of more than ten grade schools she attended during the peregrinations of her family as itinerant peddlers throughout the coalfields of northern Kyushu. Hayashi remembers this as a happy period. She has written: "I was a child brimful of life at that time. . . . It was a pleasure to be praised by my mother for being such a good peddler" (*Diary of a Vagabond*).

Left to tend the house while her parents were out vending their wares, Fumiko would borrow books from the local library and read them avidly. Later, because of the extremely straitened circumstances of her parents, Fumiko was sent for a while at age ten to live with her grandmother in Sakurajima where she was made to do the cooking and tormented by her elder sister.

At age fourteen, Fumiko entered the upper girls' school at Onomichi. In order to earn the tuition fee, she worked at night at a twine-making factory and during vacations as a housemaid. Without any close friends at school, she secluded herself in the library and read at random among foreign and domestic literature. At eighteen, she began writing fairy tales. In March 1922, she went up to Tokyo with Okano Gun'ichi, a Meiji University student she had loved since upper-school days, working among other things as a minder of footwear at a public bathhouse. Her parents followed her to Tokyo, opening a night stall first in Hibiya and then on the Kagura Slope, the Naruko Slope, and the Dogen Slope. Fumiko would spell her mother minding the shop.

In 1923, Okano, who had graduated from Meiji University and returned to his native Innoshima, giving as his reason the strong opposition of his family, broke his promise of marriage to Fumiko, a great blow to her. In September of that year, the great Kanto earthquake occurred. After visiting her parents in Juniso to make sure they were all right, Fumiko on a whim boarded a sake freighter sailing from Shibaura to Osaka, to visit friends in the Kansai area. After her return to Tokyo, Fumiko worked variously as a trainee nurse at a maternity hospital, as an employee of a trading company, and doing odd jobs at home. From this year on, she began keeping a diary, which was later published as *Diary of a Vagabond*.

In 1924, taking such jobs as a maid, a factory worker, a salesgirl, a waitress, and a public letter writer outside a local ward office, Fumiko contrived not only to make her own living but to send money to her parents, who had returned to Onomichi. She also sold many children's stories and poems to various magazines. This year, falling in with a band of anarchist poets who frequented a restaurant in Sakana-machi in Hongo, she moved in with one of them, a fellow called Tanabe, for two or three months before learning that he had an actress sweetheart. While visiting the writer Uno Koji (1891–1961) and questioning him about story-writing methods, she was told to write as she spoke. This dictum, stunning in its simplicity, was to exert a decisive influence on Fumiko. She was also assisted financially at this time by the writer Tokuda Shusei (1871–1943).

In Taisho 14, or 1925, Hayashi Fumiko turned twenty-one and married the poet Nomura Yoshiya, who knew how to value her literary talent. At about this time, Fumiko worked as a waitress at a café in Shinjuku.

The following year, Fumiko, having separated from Nomura Yoshiya, went to live in a rented room atop a sake dealer's shop in Hongo with the female proletarian writer Hirabayashi Taiko. That December, Hayashi married the painter Tezuka Ryokubin.

In October 1928, on the recommendation of Mikami Otokichi, a writer of the time, twenty-two installments of Hayashi's *Diary of a Vagabond* were published in "Women's Arts," edited by Otokichi's wife, Hasegawa Shigure, and received favorable comment. Frequenting the Ueno Library all during this year, Hayashi read at random and ravenously. There is a frontispiece photograph in the Shinchosha edition of her works (1961), showing Hayashi at this time, seated by her worktable and stirring the coals in a brazier while passionately poring over some text.

In the summer of 1929, Hayashi, in a red bathing suit (having sold all her bathrobes and dressing gowns),[*] was doing her laundry in the entryway of her lodgings when a representative of the Kaizosha Company called to request a manuscript. Hayashi gave him the book-length first part of *Diary of a Vagabond*. Published in July 1930, the book was an instant best seller. Together with two sequels published in November 1930 and January 1931, it sold 600,000 copies in two years. What apparently captivated the hearts of the general reading public was its simple-hearted good spirits and optimism in the face of dismal and discouraging circumstances. Despite the author's own occasional self-pity, sentimentality, and despair, the strong and single-minded energy behind the pathos spoke to the hearts of many lonely people, as the critic Togaeri Hajime has remarked. Hayashi celebrated by taking a trip to

[*]It should be noted that the factuality of some of Hayashi's autobiographical details has been questioned by recent scholarship. Cf. Joan Ericson's *Be a Woman: Hayashi Fumiko and Modern Japanese Women's Literature* (Honolulu: University of Hawai'i Press, 1997). Trans.

China with the royalties from the book for two months in the fall of 1930. In the following fall she made an overland trip via Siberia to Europe, where she lived mainly in Paris enjoying the cultural life and writing furiously. In January 1932, she went to London on a herring boat, for a stay of a month or so. Upon her return to France, owing to overwork and malnutrition, Hayashi was temporarily stricken with night blindness. In May, with money sent to her by the director of Kaizosha, Hayashi embarked on the long return to Japan in a Japanese mail-boat, making stops at Naples, which very deeply impressed her, and Shanghai.

In September 1935, Hayashi published "Oysters," a long short story about life in the lower depths, in the literary journal *Chuokoron*. The title is a trifle mysterious, as there is no mention of oysters in the text. Perhaps it is meant to imply that weak, ineffectual characters such as Shukichi and Tama, the protagonists of the story, are swallowed up by the society that ultimately consumes them as easily as oysters on the half shell.

As the clouds of war gathered and darkened over East Asia, Hayashi was accredited as a special war correspondent for the newspaper *Mainichi* in December 1937, in time for the fall of Nanking. In September of the following year, Hayashi was dispatched to Shanghai by the information bureau of the Home Ministry as one of a group of writers (the PEN unit) to follow the army in China. Later, on her own initiative, Hayashi visited an army hospital; then, catching a ride on a *Mainichi* truck, she entered the recently fallen city of Hankow. In October, returning to Japan on a company plane, Hayashi gave talks in principal towns and cities on what she had observed at the front. All during this decade, she kept up a steady stream of publications of poems, stories, and novels.

In September 1941, Hayashi, Osaragi Jiro (whose novel *Homecoming*, telling of postwar conditions, was translated by Brewster Horwitz and was the first Japanese novel to appear in English after the war), and the proletarian writer Sata Ineko were sent by *Mainichi* to visit and encourage the troops in Manchuria.

The following year, as a member of an information-gathering unit, Hayashi was sent to the Japanese-occupied areas of Singapore, French Indochina, Java, and Borneo. Her trip lasted approximately eight months, a prolonged contact with other lands and peoples that provided material for her postwar novel, *Floating Clouds*, and *Borneo Diamond*, a tale of comfort women in the South Seas.

In December 1943, Hayashi adopted a newborn baby boy called Tai. In April of the following year, for the sake of the child's survival, she left famine-ridden Tokyo, with her aged mother, who had been cast off by her father for a younger woman. Settling in the hot springs town of Kadoma in Nagano Prefecture, she went back to writing fairy tales, which she read aloud to the children of the town. She returned to Tokyo in October 1945. In June of the following year she published *Borneo Diamond*, and in January 1947, the story "River Gobies." "A Late Chrysanthemum," the story of an aging geisha fighting a gallant rearguard action against the ravages of time and the disappearance of lovers (except for one, who shows up to sponge money off her), was published in November 1948 and won the Women Writers' Prize a few months later. The story "Ashes" was published in February 1949; "Beef" and "Tokyo" in April 1949; and, finally, "Blindfold Phoenix" in March 1950. These stories, detailing the almost incredible hardships and deprivation that ordinary Japanese matter-of-factly endured during the five years after the war, are in such stark contrast to the affluence of present-day Japan that reading them might be a depressing experience were it not for the old Japanese mindset, the sweetness in adversity that they convey despite everything.

In the winter of 1949–1950, Hayashi contracted pneumonia. From this time until her death the following year, she experienced a gradual decline in health. Her hard life was finally telling on her. *Floating Clouds*, the story of a woman faithful to her lover from the idyllic days of their meeting in occupied French Indochina to the sad, deprived days after their return to defeated Japan, his abandonment of her, and her eventual death, was serialized from November 1949 to August 1951.

Floating Clouds is unquestionably Hayashi's major work. Although it is not an autobiographical novel, it contains more of Hayashi and her life than any other work, even than *Diary of a Vagabond*, which employs the autobiographical form. Though other stories render into fictional form particular passages or aspects of her experience, *Floating Clouds* treats Hayashi's whole life, lived through, transformed, and transcended by art in one of the great Japanese novels of the twentieth century.

On June 28, 1951, while Hayashi was writing up a walking and sampling tour of famous Ginza food shops for *The Housewife's Companion*, she consumed a small amount of sardines at the Miyagawa establishment. Returning home at 9:30 that evening, she was taken violently ill an hour and a half later. Emptying her stomach with her husband's help, she died the same moment of a heart attack. Services were held in her own house on July 1, with Kawabata Yasunari, the Nobel Prize–winning author of *Snow Country* (1947), officiating as chief mourner. In addition to this tribute from a fellow writer and admirer of her work, ordinary people from faraway neighborhoods came to stand outside her house as a sign of respect and affection, testifying to the sway her work held over their hearts. Even in her later wealthy years (attributable exclusively to her writings), Hayashi remained a daughter of the people.

Near the end of "River Gobies," this passage occurs:

> Chioko felt lonely. Unable to bear the feeling, Chioko went out at the back door. In the partly cloudy, partly clear skies, the gentle noonday sun of late spring shone upon the waters of the river. Chioko went down to the river's edge. Already she felt as if she had been chased to her last hiding place. There was nothing she could do. "I'll die," Chioko murmured to herself. Although she couldn't die, her heart said that kind of thing. Her body had the confidence of its strength, saying, "I'll live," but her weary heart, like a fretful child, called to her: "I'll die."

Tamiya Torahiko, a fellow chronicler of Japanese folklife as it existed before the present regime of affluent consumerism, has said of this passage that he knows of no other that expresses as deeply and poignantly the pain involved in going on living—the pain not just of the character Chioko but of the thousands and hundreds of thousands of ordinary Japanese people, who also bore it.

There is little to analyze in Hayashi's work (except, of course, that it is beautifully well written). Her work draws on the feelings of the common people, and as long as such feelings (or a memory of, or an imaginative sympathy with them) survive, so, I think, will her work. Late in her life Hayashi remarked that she did not think her work would outlive her. Her forecast has proven inaccurate by fifty years so far, and it is at least possible that the best of her work, like that of Higuchi Ichiyo (1872–1896),* another female chronicler of hard times, will last as long as Japanese literature does.

---

*Recently commemorated on the new Japanese 5,000-yen banknote. Trans.

Outside the hot springs inn in Sakurajima of Kyushu, where Hayashi's mother worked as a chambermaid, a literary marker is engraved with a poem that Hayashi once wrote on a piece of colored paper for a restaurant proprietress who requested a sample of her calligraphy:

Hana no inochi wa mijikakute
Nigashiki koto nomi ookariki

The life of a flower is short
Only bitter things are many

These words of hard-earned wisdom, dashed off in a lighthearted moment, might well memorialize the brief but fully lived and fruitful career of Hayashi Fumiko.

Lane Dunlop

ACKNOWLEDGMENTS

THE TRANSLATOR WISHES to acknowledge, gratefully, the help of Elizabeth Floyd of the Japanese Literature Publishing Project, and Susan Heath and Anne McCoy of Columbia University Press. Their expert editing—the excision of unnecessary words or phrases, the rewriting of accurate but awkward English and the occasional felicitous touch, to name just three services they rendered the text—has made this a better book.

L. D.

NOTE TO THE READER

WHERE NECESSARY, slight abridgment of the original text has been made. Names appear in the traditional Japanese order, of surname first.

FLOATING CLOUDS

1

SHE WANTED TO CHOOSE a train that would arrive late at night. So Koda Yukiko spent the day just wandering around the town of Tsuruga, after leaving the repatriation center where she had spent the last three days. She had parted from the other sixty or so women who had also returned to Japan from overseas and had completed several days of physical examinations. She found a house near the customs warehouse that had a small general store in it and some rooms for rent. There, Yukiko was able to stretch out by herself on the tatami-covered floor, something she had not done in a very long time.

The owners of the lodging house were kind and had heated the bathwater for her. There must have been few boarders, because they did not seem to have changed the murky water. But for Yukiko, who had been traveling for some time by boat, the water, saturated with the oils of human skin, felt good. Even the drops of icy rain that bounced up against the dirty window of the bathhouse evoked waves of feeling in her. The wind was blowing. Yukiko opened the window and looked up at the leaden sky. It was not much of a sky, but it was the one over her own country, which she had not seen in so long. She held her breath and looked.

Yukiko spread her arms along the sides of the oval bath and was surprised again by the sight of the thick scar—thick and raised like a worm—where her left arm had been cut by the sword. As she poured hot water from her cupped hands over the scar, she suddenly lost herself in pleasant memories of the past, even though she knew full well that life from this point on would be a constant struggle to survive.

It was tedious. How tedious everything is once you have missed your chance, Yukiko thought as she ran the dirty hand towel slowly over her body. It seemed unreal that she was even sitting in this sooty, cramped bathhouse, washing her body. The chill wind, piercing her skin, blew in from the window. Yukiko felt the change of seasons all the more keenly for not having felt this kind of cold wind spraying on her skin in a long time. When she left the bath and returned to her room, bedding had been laid down on the reddish brown tatami and a fire had been kindled in a small hibachi in a wooden box. Beside the hibachi was a tray and a small bowl filled with vinegary shallots. Yukiko picked up the aluminum teakettle that was just beginning to shake and boil over and made some tea for herself. She ate a shallot greedily, stuffing her cheeks with it. Along the corridor outside the sliding paper door, she could hear the voices of two or three women as they crowded into the room next door. Yukiko pricked up her ears. Separated from them as she was by a single thin sliding screen, Yukiko easily recognized the voices as those of several geishas who had been on the boat with her.

"It's good to be back. But more important than getting back to Japan . . . I've got to think about myself."

"It's so cold, it's depressing. I don't have any winter things. I don't know what I'm going to do for clothes from now on."

Despite their words, the women sounded surprisingly cheerful. They were giggling as they spoke. What was so funny? she wondered.

Having nothing else to do, Yukiko lay down on top of the bedding and let her mind go blank for a while. Her spirits sank. She couldn't help feeling depressed. Meanwhile, the noise in the next room did not let up. It felt good to fling her body, warmed from the bath, against the damp coolness of the old bedding. But there was still another long journey, this time by train, awaiting her. The thought of seeing the faces of her relatives was beginning to lose all its appeal. Yukiko wondered if it wouldn't be better to go right to Tokyo and look for Tomioka. Luckily, he had left Haiphong in May. He had promised that he would go first and make all the arrangements and wait for her. But now that she had arrived in Japan and was faced with this cold wind, his promise was somehow harder to believe. But of course there was no way to know until the two of them actually met. As soon as the boat had first docked in Japan, Yukiko had sent a telegram to Tomioka's place. Like everyone else, she had spent three days being examined at the repatriation center. Then everyone from the boat had left at the same time for various parts of the country. There had been no response from Tomioka during those three days. Thinking that even if he had written, her situation right now might be pretty much the same, Yukiko more or less resigned herself to it. She dozed for a while, but when she awoke, not much time seemed to have passed. The paper door had darkened and a light had come on in the room. It sounded like it was mealtime next door. Yukiko realized she was hungry. Pulling her knapsack out from under the pillow, she took out the rations that had been distributed on the ship. Four Camel cigarettes, tissue paper, dry bread, powdered soup, canned pork, and Irish potatoes were neatly arranged in a little tea-colored box. Taking out some chocolate, she lay on her stomach and nibbled at it. It was not the least bit delicious.

The reddish yellow waters of Doson Bay floated up to her closed eyes, bringing a pleasant feeling. The white lighthouse on the cape of Doson, the dense greenery of Hondo Island—with the thought that she would never see them again, Yukiko had fixed her eyes on them from the ship, as if to burn them into her memory. But already the colors of that foreign scenery were starting to fade. It was an effort to recall them. The ladies in the next room—perhaps they were leaving on the night train—seemed to have finished their meal and were settling the bill with the proprietress. Yukiko, while listening to the commotion, emptied a packet of powdered soup into a mug, poured some boiling water over it, and drank. She ate the rest of the shallots. Pretty soon the women, unanimously chorusing, "Thank you for all your trouble," bustled along the corridor in the wake of the proprietress. Listening to their voices, Yukiko felt lured by the thought that these women, too, were returning to their various parts of the country. According to what Yukiko had heard on board the ship, the geishas had worked at restaurants in Phnom Penh on a two-year contract. Although politely referred to as geishas, they were in fact comfort women summoned by the military. Among the women who had assembled at the reception center in Haiphong, some were army nurses, typists, or office girls, but most were comfort women. A surprising number of Japanese were among the comfort women who had come from the towns and villages of Indochina to gather there. Koda Yukiko had worked as a typist at the Pasteur Research Center—with its plantation for growing quinine, used in the treatment of malaria—midway between Dalat and Dulan.

She had arrived at Dalat in the fall of 1943. This area was sixteen hundred meters above sea level. Temperatures ranged from about twenty-five degrees Celsius—very summery and warm—to a chilly six degrees. Perhaps because it was an upland region, it was an extremely pleasant place to live. There were many tea plantations administered by the French. In the clear upland atmosphere, the sweet sounds of the French language were, to Yukiko, very exotic.

Yukiko suddenly thought of writing a letter to Tomioka. Although she didn't know what to say, perhaps her feelings would take shape as she wrote. The thought that she was in the same country as Tomioka caused her spirits to pick up a little from the forlorn, empty feelings that she had had at the center in Haiphong. Yukiko bought some letter paper and an envelope from the boy at the shop.

YUKIKO CHANGED HER MIND. She would go straight to Tokyo and call on Iba. Unless the house had been burned out in the firebombing, she would stay at Iba's until she was able to see Tomioka. Although she had nothing but unpleasant memories of Iba, there was nowhere else to go. Since she had not sent word to Shizuoka, her family would not be expecting her.

Yukiko left Tsuruga on the late-night train. On the platform, she spotted two men who had been with her on the boat, but Yukiko deliberately distanced herself from them and boarded a car at the back of the train. People were milling about on the platform and swarming onto the train through the windows. With great effort, Yukiko, too, was able to climb on through a window. She felt conspicuous and out of place. Upon seeing Yukiko—obviously back from the south, with no winter clothing—the people around her stared at her out of the corner of their eyes. These were certainly the faces of defeat, Yukiko thought, looking all around her while being pressed and jostled by the crowd. Perhaps because it was night, every face was drained of spirit, every face was pale and drawn. Faces that seemed to have no resistance left were crammed up against one another in the narrow car. It was almost like a slave transport. Little by little, Yukiko was getting an uneasy feeling from these faces. What had happened to Japan? The faces of the soldiers, sent off earlier in a wave of flags, were nowhere to be seen. Even the mountains and rivers ranged all around in the dark train windows were a tangible sign of the fatigue that gripped the country.

The train reached Tokyo in the evening of the next day. It was raining. Yukiko got off at Shinagawa. From the platform of the metropolitan railway, the back windows of a dance hall could be seen. Under faint lights, the heads of a number of dancing couples were swirling and circling around. In the gleaming drizzle, strains of jazz flowed out. Cold and shivering, Yukiko glanced up at the dance hall that sat atop a bluff. A couple of tall military policemen, in shining white helmets, stood at the end of the platform. The platform was jammed with slightly grimy humanity. As she listened to the jazz, Yukiko's keyed-up nerves relaxed and she began to feel like leaving everything to chance. And at the same time her heart was cold with fear about how she would support herself at all. Most of the people on the congested platform had knapsacks over their shoulders. Now and then, she would catch sight of a woman walking down the stairs, wearing deep red lipstick and arm in arm with a foreigner. At the sight of them, Yukiko would stare at the flashy woman, as if at something remarkable. The life of the old Tokyo had completely disappeared.

By the time she got off at Saginomiya on the Seibu line, it was the last train of the night. Crossing the tracks, Yukiko walked along the wide avenue toward the power station, a building she remembered. Three young women, walking quickly in the rain, swept past her. All three of them had gaudy pieces of cloth wrapped around their cheeks and the collars of their long overcoats turned up.

"Today I saw him off at Yokohama. He probably has a wife back home. But people—they live for the moment. It's all right, I suppose . . . But he introduced me to a friend of his. Very strange, I thought. Passing his woman off on one of his friends. It's hard for us Japanese to understand . . ."

"Isn't it better that way? After all, once you split up, you know you won't be seeing him again. So you change your feelings. In my case too, he'll probably be going home soon. It's a nuisance to have to go out to the army base at Atsugi. I'm starting to think of looking for someone else . . ."

Yukiko hurried after the lively women. Their voices were loud and carried easily. As she listened to their conversation, Yukiko thought, Has Japan really changed that much? It gave her a strange feeling.

Presently, the women turned off to the right, at a mailbox. Yukiko was soaked to the skin by this point and utterly weary. Around here, it seemed, things were exactly the way they were when she had left for the south. She turned in to the left at the signboard advertisement for the midwife Hosokawa, and the Ibas were the second door in at the end of the narrow alley. When everyone saw how wretched she looked, no doubt they would be shocked. Yukiko stood before the stone gate for a moment, tidying herself up under a dark streetlight. Her hair and her shoulders were drenched. What a spectacle she was, Yukiko thought. As she pressed the bell, she felt as if her time in Indochina had been a dream. A light came on in the glass door of the entryway. Suddenly the shadow of a large figure appeared on the earthen floor at the doorway. Yukiko's heart raced. It was the shadow of a man, but it was not Iba.

"Who is it?"

"It's Yukiko . . ."

"Yukiko? Yukiko who?"

"Koda Yukiko. I was in French Indochina . . ."

"I see . . . who did you say you wanted to see?"

"Is Iba Sugio here?"

"Ah, Iba-san? He hasn't come back yet from the evacuation area."

The shadowy figure slowly slid the door open, as if greatly inconvenienced. The man, who was still in his nightclothes, was clearly surprised to see a young woman standing at his door, drenched to the skin, without an overcoat, and with a knapsack slung over her shoulder.

"I'm a relative of Iba's," Yukiko explained. "I just got back today . . ."

"Oh, please come in. Iba-san left for the country when it became too dangerous here. He went to Shizuoka three years ago."

"You mean he's completely evacuated this house?"

"No, I've been living here in his stead. But his bags arrived recently, so we're expecting him back."

Hearing their voices, a woman who was apparently the man's wife came out to the entryway, holding a baby in her arms. Yukiko told them about the circumstances of her return from French Indochina. It seemed there had been some trouble between the man and Iba, over something to do with the house. The man did not seem too happy to see a relative of Iba's, but he was kind enough to say that it was cold in the entryway and to come into the living room.

Aside from a ball of rice, which the people at the inn in Tsuruga had made especially for her, Yukiko had had nothing to eat or drink on the train. Her body felt as if it were floating. As she passed along the corridor, she bumped into a sewing machine. When she entered the living room, the six-mat room that Iba had always slept in was filled with so much piled-up, crated, and baled baggage that even the firm, springy tatami mats sagged under it. When she heard that Yukiko had just come back from Indochina, the wife—feeling sorry for her, perhaps—made some tea and gave her a dried sweet potato. The man, who was about forty, had the large physique and the brusque manner of an ex-soldier. His wife, slightly built and pale, had a freckled face, but when she smiled, charming dimples appeared.

That night, borrowing two futons, Yukiko was able to bed down in a cramped space among Iba's heaped-up baggage. Taking out two boxes of rations from her knapsack, Yukiko presented them to the man's wife as a gift.

She climbed in between the futons and, as she lay there, she poked her finger into the straw-wrapped baggage. It was a tightly nailed crate, so she could not tell at all what was inside. According to her hosts, Iba would be coming back to Tokyo by the end of the year. They had been asked to clear out of two of the rooms, the wife said. There were six in their family, so they were still unsure about which of the rooms to vacate. Although they had guarded the house with their lives during the air raids, now they were suddenly being told to get out. There was nowhere for them to go. It was unfair, the wife said. Iba, on the other hand, could not stay in the countryside indefinitely. He must be getting impatient. Yukiko could well imagine the feelings of the Iba household, who had quickly sent their baggage on ahead. It was clear that all of them were in good health. Yukiko, for her part, had a feeling that was like disappointment.

3

KODA YUKIKO HAD ARRIVED in the town of Dalat in French Indochina in the second half of October 1943. The typists assigned to the team of the engineer Mogi, who was with the Ministry of Agriculture and Forestry, had first arrived at Haiphong in Vietnam. Mogi had been dispatched by the army to inspect forestry conditions in French Indochina. Recruiting typists who worked at the same ministry, he'd assigned one to each official in the group. There had been five candidates, one of them Yukiko.

After arriving at Haiphong in a hospital ship, they had gone on to Hanoi in army automobiles. Three of the typists were to work there in Hanoi. Koda Yukiko was assigned to Dalat in the highlands. The one remaining typist, Shinonoi Haruko, obtained a post in Saigon. The one who had drawn what was considered the least desirable assignment was Koda Yukiko. Perhaps it was her modest, unremarkable appearance that had relegated her to such a place. In contrast to her wide forehead, her eyes were narrow and her skin was pale. Lacking in obvious charm, nothing about her features, indefinably tinged with sadness, drew people's eyes. Her photograph, pasted to her army identification card, made her look older than her actual twenty-two years. The one distinctive thing about her was that she looked nice in clothing that had a white collar, but other than that, she always appeared to be wearing the same clothes, no matter how she dressed. Shinonoi Haruko, who was going to Saigon, was the most beautiful of the five. Her features resembled those of a popular actress of the day. The existence of the likes of Koda Yukiko drew no one's attention.

The party left Hanoi in two military cars. Driving through Tanoa and Fuki, they spent the first night in Vinh, in the southern part of French Indochina. It was a 350-kilometer drive from Hanoi to Vinh. They took rooms at the Grand Hotel in Vinh. The hills and fields along the way were smoldering blackly, with the remnants of brushfires. In places, the fires were still burning, giving off a murky yellowish smoke. There was almost nothing to be seen but plantations of oil-paulownia trees and pines. Perhaps it was because of the endless forest landscape that Shinonoi Haruko, heaving a number of deep sighs, deliberately assumed a forlorn air. Yukiko felt utterly exhausted from the long, unfamiliar journey. After leaving Tanoa, the cars sped along the long road in the dusky twilight. But as they neared Vinh, swarms of white moths fluttered up from the darkness around them. Attracted by the cars' headlights, they came toward the illuminated road in countless numbers, like scattered scraps of paper.

To the left of the hotel—was there a canal there?—the voices of Annamese boatmen echoed over the water. Bullfrogs were croaking noisily. The group parked the cars in a space bordered by betel palms and Burmese silk trees and were then shown to their rooms. Shinonoi Haruko and Koda Yukiko were ushered into a tidy room downstairs with a view of what was indeed a canal.

Haruko opened the window. She could hear the sound of the water in the canal. On the table there was a lamp with an orange lampshade.

The two women's insignificant-looking suitcases were set side by side on the table. The pink, flower-patterned wallpaper, the soft blue blankets on the double bed, typical of French taste, were neat and appealing. For the two women long accustomed to the poverty of wartime Japan, it was very nearly a fairy tale world.

When they'd freshened up and gone out to the dining room for a late supper, a soldier with the white armband of the military police came by, asking to see their identification papers. For the young policeman, the two Japanese women must have been an unusual sight, bringing thoughts of home. That night, both Yukiko and Haruko had difficulty getting to sleep. Although it had been slightly cold when they had left Japan, as they'd headed south from Haiphong, Hanoi, and Tanoa, the season suddenly reversed itself, back toward summer. They just could not fall asleep on the soft, yielding mattress. The bullfrogs thrummed heavily, like notes from a thick-necked three-stringed guitar echoing in their ears all night.

The situation at the Iba house, the farewell parties with friends, the hectic days of vaccinations at the army headquarters just before she left Tokyo, all came floating back to Yukiko like mirages. The idea that her fate would be to come all the way to French Indochina seemed so strange. It was something she had not imagined she would ever do.

Iba Sugio was the younger brother of Iba Kyotaro, who was married to Yukiko's older sister. Sugio had both a wife and a child. Since they were the only relatives of hers who had a house in Tokyo, Yukiko came to stay at Iba Sugio's house as soon as she had graduated from her girls' school in Shizuoka and had lived there while attending a typing school in Kanda. Sugio, who worked in the personnel department of an insurance company, had a reputation as a decent man. But one night, the very first week after Yukiko arrived, she had been violated by him. Yukiko was sleeping in the three-mat maid's room. Unable to get to sleep, half dozing and half waking, she heard Sugio going to the kitchen for a glass of water. Presently, the paper door of the maid's room slid open. Yukiko listened to it dreamily. The paper door quietly slid shut again. There was the sound of stealthy footsteps on the tatami. A man's body settled down on her, pressing heavily against her chest. Startled, Yukiko opened her eyes in the pitch darkness. There was a smell of leather, and Sugio said something in a low voice that Yukiko could not understand. A rough-skinned leg was thrust between the futons. At first, Yukiko thought she would cry out. But then something inside her said that she should not, and she stiffened up her whole body and was silent.

After the event of that night, Yukiko had the feeling that she could not face Sugio's wife, Masako. But when night fell, Yukiko began to feel extremely impatient, knowing that Sugio would be coming for her. Each time, Sugio would stuff a handkerchief in Yukiko's mouth. It was strange to Yukiko that Sugio, neglecting his beautiful, intelligent wife, should display this violent lust for an unremarkable woman like herself.

Yukiko lived with the Ibas for three years. After graduating from typing school, she found a job at the Ministry of Agriculture and Forestry. Masako did not seem to have any idea what was happening between Yukiko and Sugio. Occasionally, taking the child with her, Masako would go to stay for a few days at her parents' place in Yokohama. On these nights, Sugio would go to bed early and summon Yukiko. There was nothing Yukiko could do but submit to what he wanted. Sugio never talked about the future and behaved toward Yukiko just as he might with a prostitute. What hardened her resolve to go to Indochina was a desire to extricate herself from this kind of immorality. But until she was sure that she would be going, she did not mention the possibility either to the Ibas or to her mother in Shizuoka or her brothers and sisters. Only when it was definitely settled did she inform her relatives and the Ibas. Sugio greeted the news with barely a change of expression.

At seeing Sugio's unexpectedly impassive demeanor, Yukiko was overcome with a sense of humiliation. But she took pleasure in the idea that by leaving the Iba house she would drive a thick nail through Iba's heart. Toward Masako, too, Yukiko had begun to feel a certain hostility. From time to time, Masako would say such things as, "Yuki-san, you get sulky all of a sudden these days. We'll have to marry you off soon." This could be taken either as a joke or a caustic remark. When Sugio heard that Yukiko would be leaving for Indochina in two or three days, he bought her some medicine, a handbag, and some underwear. It mortified Yukiko to have Sugio make those sorts of purchases for her. Masako, as usual, thought that Sugio's solicitousness toward Yukiko was strange. She seemed to be repelled by it.

4

AT DAWN, YUKIKO HAD A DREAM about Sugio. Perhaps because she had
come all this way by herself, Yukiko felt a curious yearning for the
warmth of a human body. She felt a loneliness like that of slipping down
into hell. Although she had come this far, she wanted desperately to go
back to Japan. She could not stop thinking of the busy way that Sugio
would pant for breath as he stuffed the handkerchief in her mouth.
Although all along she'd thought that she detested Sugio, suddenly, at
this distance, he had started to seem dear to her. It was very strange,
she thought. Surely Sugio must be lonely for her, too. But he was a man
of few words, and so he had not said anything much even though their
relationship had continued right up to the day of her departure. It had
lasted three years. Why hadn't a baby been born? During those same
three years, Masako had given birth to another child, a boy.

The endless tangled memories became almost unbearable. Yukiko
quietly got up. When she opened the glass door that led onto the veranda,
the canal shone right before her eyes. It was lined with tall Burmese silk
trees, and the air was filled with the noisy warbling of small birds. On the
surface of the canal—hazy with a faint mist—a number of Annamese
small craft were moored. Yukiko leaned against the edge of the stone

veranda and let the morning breeze wash over her. The feeling was indescribable. She had had no idea that such a dreamlike country even existed. Listening to the cries of the little birds, Yukiko gazed out over the canal. A flock of swallows flew past. The murky sea at Haiphong was a boundary beyond which everything faded into empty distance. Yukiko had little idea of what kind of life awaited her.

Everyone ate an early breakfast, got back into the automobiles, and left, heading for Hue, the ancient capital in southern French Indochina. Between the *mokumao* trees lining the road, they could see smoke wafting up from cooking fires built outside the huts that stood alongside the canal and were roofed and walled with rushes. Along the wide colonial road the yellow Citroën sped on its way with a swishing sound, as if the tires were sticking to the asphalt. The men were talking about how Vinh, with its population of more than twenty-five thousand, was a rather important town in northern Annam. Presently, the colonial highway branched off into two roads, one leading to the uplands of Laos. Now and then, smoke rose from the forests on the right-hand side of the road. After they drove for some time along the colonial road to Hue, at the heart of a large forestation district a pale light began finally to color the air, and it was dawn. As the sun rose, the air turned completely dry. Under the high sky, the landscape was one of cool, refreshing summer.

They passed their second night in Hue. Here again they stayed at the Grand Hotel. There were considerable numbers of Japanese soldiers stationed in Hue. In front of the hotel, the broad Hue River flowed past. The Clemenceau Bridge was nearby. Yukiko had a sense of disbelief that the Japanese Army was occupying even a place like this. She had the feeling that the Japanese soldiers had pushed things along too far by advancing this far. Their luck had been too good to this point, she thought. But Yukiko had no leisure to ponder whether the Japanese would be able to hold on for long to this treasure-house. There was nothing to do but give herself up to what the others did—travel only with simple thoughts and yield up her body as the car raced along. The Japanese soldiers that one saw around here looked poverty-stricken. Wearing uniforms that did not fit them at all, their figures, with battle helmets jammed down over their big heads, looked like those of soldiers who had come from an imperfectly civilized country. The Annamese walking the streets, the occasional Frenchman or -woman, were perfectly matched with their surroundings. The Chinese merchant quarter, too, had a cultured air about it. Along the streets in the heart of the city, the camphor trees were bright and fresh looking. In the morning sun that blazed down, they shook off their pollen like gold dust and put out new buds. Around the red brick palace, young Annamese schoolgirls, wearing checkered socks, were playing soccer. For Yukiko this was an unusual sight. Fire trees and canna were in bloom along the promenade by the river. The swollen yellow river sent a fishy smell through the town.

Perhaps because they were traveling under foreign skies, the party of seven behaved rather freely. There was an atmosphere of release about them. An older man called Seya, from the Mining Corps, had ridden in the women's car ever since Hanoi. It became a custom for him to sit next to Shinonoi Haruko. Deliberately jamming his body against Haruko's shoulder and knee, sweating stickily, he brazenly told dirty stories. Hearing that Saigon was so much like Paris that it was called Little Paris, Yukiko felt envious of Shinonoi Haruko. She also would have liked a posting in a beautiful city. Since it had already been decided, there was nothing to be done. But Yukiko was well aware that, for a woman, the type of assignment given was determined by her beauty or homeliness. It seemed somewhat cruel to Yukiko that she should be consigned to a humdrum job in some place called Dalat, deep in the highlands, that she had never seen or heard of. For a young woman, there is nothing worse than the completely ordinary. It was oppressive to think that she would have to work there for a year.

At the time of her departure from Tokyo, Sugio had said jokingly that if Indochina was a good place, wouldn't she please invite them all to join her. At least they would be liberated from the oppressive conditions back home. Yukiko fantasized that maybe Sugio would decide to leave the insurance company and volunteer to come to Indochina.

Staying one night in Hue, the party boarded the Saigon-bound train at the station by the seaside. The cars were narrow and attractive. The second-class cars had unexpectedly luxurious accommodations. There was a sofa, a little table, and a small fan that kept busily circulating the air. Beside the compartment was a shower stall. This was much more comfortable than the automobile journey. When they ordered coffee, the Annamese "boy" brought it in deep teacups that looked just like flower vases. Here, for the first time, Yukiko was able to settle down together with Shinonoi Haruko, just the two of them in the same compartment. The train vibrated violently. It now became clear that these vibrations were the reason for the device of the vase-shaped teacups. Yukiko and Haruko were flabbergasted at the sandy dust that blew in from somewhere, not the least bit different from the automobile journey. No matter how luxurious the accommodations, this train, with the yellow dust blowing through it, was still unclean. Haruko—how and when had she contrived to get them?—was wearing silk stockings and shoes with fashionable rubber soles. Ever since they had climbed onto the train, Yukiko had been bothered by the fact that Haruko was wearing a sweet-smelling perfume. Yukiko, feeling miserably defeated, had on trousers that had been retailored from her schoolgirl's blue serge uniform and soiled black shoes, in which the tips of her toes bulged. On the long journey, her trousers had gotten somewhat dirty. Gazing enviously at Haruko's thick makeup, Yukiko said, "You're lucky to be stationed in Saigon, Shinonoi-san."

"Oh? Whether it's a good place or a bad place, I won't know until I get there. But Koda-san, the quinine plantation of the Pasteur Institute, isn't that top-notch? Since you're a student, you'll soon learn French and Annamese both. It's a high-class place, no? That's what I think. It sounds like a good place."

Yukiko knew perfectly well that Haruko was being kind and consoling her.

"But I hear that there is hardly anyone there. It'll be lonely. First of all, to leave all of you who have also been through hard times and to go to the mountains where I don't know anyone, it'll be so lonely. It'll be dull."

The train, rattling violently, ran on and on through the hills and vales.

It was night when they arrived in Saigon.

5

YUKIKO, PERHAPS BECAUSE she was not used to this kind of travel, was completely exhausted. She also had inexplicable bouts of fever, which recurred several times a day. They were to stay in Saigon for five days. Here again, army procedures took a good deal of time. There was no leisure to explore the city by oneself. At Saigon, they stayed in army-designated quarters that, for the first time since Haiphong, were suited to their subordinate status. On the fourth day, Shinonoi Haruko, accompanied by a man who worked in the Army Information Section, went to lodgings at her workplace. The place where Yukiko and the others were staying had evidently once been the private residence of a Chinese merchant. In the empty rooms, which were stripped of all ornaments, there were only fold-up cots. Two Annamese women did some listless housekeeping. The group going on to Dalat comprised the engineers Mogi and Kuroi, the elderly Seya, and Yukiko. In the dining room, this group always sat together in a corner. There were several large, crudely drawn maps on the walls. Three sandalwood tables stood in a row. People who were staying here on some business or other had their meals in this room. The assortment of people in the rest of the dining room was always changing. In this dining room, with its continual meetings and partings, one person whose face never changed sat in a cool seat by the window. Suddenly, Yukiko took note of this man. Even as he ate, he was always reading a book or newspaper. He didn't seem to have any particular companion. The length of time he sat there was as precise as if stamped with a seal. He was dark-complexioned and had bushy hair. As he sat, reading on and on, his long, thin face, seen in profile, had a spiritless expression like that of a dead man. In the evening, coming back from somewhere or other, he would set a bottle of whiskey before him in the deserted dining room and have a drink. In his half-sleeved shirt and tan trousers, he looked Annamese to Yukiko. Since she had a fever, Yukiko would now and then go to the dining room for ice. This man, always sitting with his knees drawn up in an unbecoming manner, would be there again, drinking his whiskey. Even when Yukiko entered the dining room, he didn't seem to pay any particular attention to her. With a faraway look in his eyes, as if he was savoring his solitude, he sat and had his drink.

Not far from here there was a street in the Chinese merchant quarter lined with places to eat and drink. Into the night, it was alive with the sound of gramophones and radios. Sometimes the wind would carry strains of Japanese patriotic wartime songs such as "Father, You Were Strong" into the dining room. As she drank her medicine in a corner of the room, Yukiko was suddenly captivated by this particular song. For no reason that she could name, she wanted to talk to the man who was having his drink. An adventurous feeling came over her. Yukiko thought that all men must have the disposition of a Sugio. Perhaps because they were under foreign skies, she had a sense that the man wouldn't mind if she even started talking to him without being introduced. Picking up one of the Japanese newspapers that lay scattered about, she looked it over intently. With the sort of nonchalant bad manners that took no notice of anything around him, the man read his book and drank his whiskey. As he drank, his skin began to take on a reddish tinge. His long arms, visible beneath a white short-sleeved shirt, caught Yukiko's eye. Was he perhaps thirty-four or thirty-five?

Later, lying alone in her narrow cot, Yukiko could not get him out of her mind, and she thought that she would part with him without ever learning his name or where he worked.

On the fifth day, there was a truck going to Dalat. Yukiko and the others made travel preparations once more, this time to leave Saigon.

In the old days Saigon had been called Pre Nokoru, a name given it by the Khmer people that meant "city of trees." Indeed, the avenues of Saigon were lined with lofty, towering *yo* trees. Beneath the trees, cyclos, reminiscent of the bicycle taxis of Tokyo, raced about like insects along the sleek asphalt pavements. On bustling Kachina Street, the French children playing underneath the tamarind trees in their blue school uniforms were like a picture. The tamarind trees, covered with pearlike fruit, gave the feeling of a garden park. The clothes of the Annamese and the Chinese merchants under the rows of tall trees, as they strolled along the spotless streets, seemed amazing to Yukiko, after the drab colors that people wore in Japan. She felt envious of Shinonoi Haruko yet again. She was jealous of the good looks that allowed Haruko to be stationed in a beautiful city like this. Under foliage so dense that it blocked out the sun, Japanese soldiers were on patrol. They looked as if they lacked the backing of any homeland or military organization. Looking almost forlorn, they walked the streets in small clusters or, rather, they wandered about as if they had been abandoned there. The faces of her party, too, perhaps because of fatigue from the long journey, were greasy and miserable. Yukiko felt a stab of loneliness, as though she had become a coolie-girl with no self-respect, hired by the day. She wanted to go back to Japan. She no longer cared what kind of place Dalat was. She longed to be with people. She was sure she couldn't live all alone in the uplands of Dalat. Old man Seya of the Mining Corps, once deprived of Shinonoi Haruko, turned his attentions to Yukiko as easily as turning his hand over to show its palm. He beamed at her.

"You seem strangely depressed. Let's see some good spirits. Wherever we go, the Japanese Army will be there. There's nothing to worry about. What's more, as the only Japanese woman, you will have a great many responsibilities. You will be working hand in hand with the Imperial Army. Isn't that so . . .?"

6

SIXTY KILOMETERS FROM DALAT, when they had reached a village called Prenh, the winding road began to ascend the long slope of the Ranbean highlands. The truck gunned its engines as it made the twisting ascent. Although it was evening, every now and then a white peacock would suddenly fly up from the roadside shadow of the trees, startling everyone.

Evening mist trailed across the highland. Here and there, lines of early flowering cherry trees brushed against the truck. The terraced forests were dotted with large villa-style structures. There were villas where the peony-colored bougainvillea grew profusely and others where mimosa trees had been planted around the tennis courts. The mimosas, with their golden blossoms, gave off a subtle, scarcely perceptible perfume that wafted into the truck as it passed by and put Yukiko into a dreamy mood. She felt something sublime in this upland that Saigon, "the city of trees," could not compare with. Annamese farm women in their three-cornered sedge hats, balancing burdens at the ends of poles placed over their shoulders, stood aside to let the truck go by.

Dalat, in Yukiko's eyes, was like a mirage. With the Ranbean Mountains behind and the lake in front of it, the terraced town completely conquered Yukiko's uneasiness and fantasies.

When the truck entered the garden of a white-walled building that was said to have been the town's police substation, Yukiko saw that a Japanese flag was hoisted high on a pole in the middle of the garden. A new signboard reading Local Forestry Office had been fastened to the stone gate. Beneath the sign, boards had been attached on which the same legend was written with India ink in smaller letters in Annamese and French. In the reception room, with its view of the lake, the party met Makita Kizo, who was the section chief. It had been settled that Yukiko would work here for the time being, and an Annamese maid showed her to her room at the end of the corridor on the second floor. Although her room did not have a view of the lake or the town, the Ranbean Mountains came down close in front of the north window. The bougainvilleas were in full bloom in the garden, and a furry white dog was gamboling about on the lawn.

The long trip was over at last, and Yukiko finally settled down in her own room. The absence of carpets on the teak floor provided a refreshing, cool feeling. There was a crude bedstead—where had it been brought from?—and a table and chair. A narrow Western-style wardrobe that had been painted white seemed out of place in the dusky room. Small birds in search of their roost warbled noisily in the twilight dusk. Mogi, Seya, and the others departed in Makita's car for the Ranbean Hotel, the only first-class hotel in town. Makita was said to have started his career in the Tottori Forest Bureau and to have moved on from there to the Ministry of Agriculture and Forestry. He was a short, stout man in his forties. At the end of 1942, he had been posted to Indochina as a civilian employee of the army. He had four subordinates, but they all seemed to be away on research trips. There were two Annamese interpreters, a government forester, and a female office worker who was said to be of mixed race.

Yukiko was so tired. Although invited with the others to dinner at the Ranbean Hotel, she did not feel well enough to go. When she sprawled out on the bed, she could feel the train's vibrations continuing, and the insides of her ears felt as if something were pressing on them. She wanted to fall into a deep sleep. When she closed her eyes, the noises of the forest, like the sound of cicadas singing, remained as loud as ever. The paint smell of the wardrobe assailed her nostrils.

That evening, Yukiko, alone in the spacious dining room, ate a Japanese meal that the Annamese maid had kindly prepared for her. In the middle of the room there was a chimney built like a rock formation, and a black, shiny piano stood near the door. When she placed her hand on the white starched tablecloth, Yukiko felt that her yellowish hand was even more unclean looking than the Annamese maid's. A bougainvillea blossom floated in a glass finger bowl. The style of soup served and the reddish-black fish pâté shaped like a sausage were unusual to Yukiko. Although the maid seemed to be already past thirty, she had pretty eyes. Her smooth face, the color of tanned persimmon paper and with a high hairline, had a fine dusting of powder, and she wore blue paste earrings. She spoke a little broken Japanese. On the big window screen, masses of white moths were clustered. When Yukiko had finished her meal, there was suddenly the sound of a car engine pulling into the yard in front. Had Makita, the section chief, returned? Yukiko wondered, but surely it was too early for that. She pricked up her ears. The maid ran outside and in a soft voice called out, "*Bonsoir,*" toward the garden entrance. Presently there was a man's voice, a confused sound of footsteps, and talking. A tall man abruptly entered the dining room. It was the same man Yukiko had seen reading in the dining room in Saigon. His footsteps echoed as he entered the dining room. When he saw Yukiko, he seemed slightly surprised. He gave her a brief glance of recognition and went briskly out into the corridor again.

Even after Yukiko had finished her meal, the maid still did not come back to the dining room. Earlier, Yukiko had reddened and returned the man's greeting, and then he had simply left the room. Yukiko grew irritated at there being no sign of his coming back. Suddenly she felt a painful emotion, as if her deathlike fatigue had returned. Flustered, she stole out of the dining room and upstairs to her own room. She peered into the mirror of the wardrobe and applied several coats of lipstick. She combed her hair, powdered her face, and hurried back down to the dining room again. But everything was empty and quiet except for the frantic wings of the white moths beating against the window screen. After a while, the maid brought in coffee. But she served it quickly and left the room again. No matter how long Yukiko waited, the man did not come back. A bit depressed, Yukiko went back to her room. Someone was coming up the broad staircase. Yukiko put an ear to the door. When the sound had died away, she went downstairs again. Feeling bored, she raised the lid of the piano and picked out, with the fingers of one hand, the tune of "Song of the Seashore," which she had played often as a child. On the wall hung a chart of forestry statistics framed in glass. As she traced the illustrations of samples of such trees as the *kacha* pine, the *merukushi* pine, the *yo* tree, the oak, and the *kuri* oak, Yukiko felt, as if for the first time, that she had really come, alone, to a faraway place. Since it didn't seem as if anyone would come to the dining room, Yukiko went out into the garden. Stars glittered clearly everywhere in the sky. The transparent night breeze ruffled the skirts of Yukiko's heavy silk poplin dress. From nowhere in particular came the fragrant scent of flowers. From the direction of the path, a woman's voice was heard calling, "*Bonsoir.*" Thin clouds floated through the sky, dodging the stars. The lake could not be seen. Returning to her room, Yukiko leaned on the windowsill. After a while, a telephone rang noisily somewhere on the first floor. Soon after, Makita's car must have returned—there was a sudden commotion downstairs, and Yukiko could hear several laughing male voices.

7

AT DAWN, YUKIKO LAY LISTENING to the mountain breeze blowing through the pines. She had been dreaming a moment before that she was playing tennis with that same man on a wide grassy lawn. It had been a sweet dream, but when she tried to remember more of it, she lost the thread. In any case, he would probably be leaving here soon . . . And yet she took pleasure in the thought of this chance encounter of two people who had been brought together twice under the same roof, as if blown there by the wind. Before going down to the dining room, she put on her makeup carefully and selected a dress that, while plain, was made of white silk. He and Makita were there, sitting over by the large open window, drinking coffee. Although Makita turned to Yukiko and smiled, the other man did not even glance at her. He had his feet up on the windowsill and he was looking out over the lake, which was covered with mist. His nonchalant manner—clearly a kind of pose he was striking—seemed to her like the stubbornness of a junior high student.

"How are you? Come over, Koda-san. It was a long trip. You must be tired. Tomioka here tells me the two of you stayed at the same place in Saigon."

Yukiko looked uneasily in the man's direction. Makita said to him, in a low voice, "Yukiko will be working here for the time being as a typist. In six months or so, we'll have her go off to the Pasteur Institute."

For the first time, the man turned toward Yukiko. Still seated, he said, by way of greeting, "I'm Tomioka."

"What, you're meeting for the first time? I was sure you'd already been introduced. This is Tomioka Kengo. He's also from the main office. About three months ago he was transferred from Borneo. It's unusual for us to have a Japanese woman around here, so you'll have to resign yourself to people making a fuss over you. Since it's just you out here."

Yukiko sat down, a distance away, on a leather sofa. The night before, in the hotel lobby, Seya had been saying that Yukiko was a plain young woman and therefore probably good at work. The woman called Shinonoi, who had been left in Saigon, was something of a beauty, and Seya had worried a bit about possible problems. But seen at a distance like this, Koda Yukiko did not seem as plain as Seya had made out. Even the fact that she did not wear her hair in a permanent wave, the way most women did, was attractive. First of all, she was modest. Her bare legs, neatly arranged and protruding plumply from the hem of her dress, would probably have been made fun of back home in Japan and called "turnip legs." But here there was a dearness about them that reminded one of tatami mats and paper sliding doors. Her sloping shoulders and the clear white skin of her nape made one feel how good it was to have the same blood—one almost wanted to pray. Her forehead was slightly broad, but even so her appearance was somehow far more pleasing than that of the maid Niu. It was good, too, that she did not wear hexagonal glasses, like Marie, the office worker who was of mixed race. Section Chief Makita could not believe his good fortune in having this young Japanese woman come all the way to these highlands. In the past, he had not thought very highly of women who went abroad. But Koda Yukiko made an extraordinarily good impression on Makita. Her makeup was very skillful. It made Makita happy that she was not the sort of woman that Seya said she was. On the large table there was an arrangement of canna flowers. In an extremely good mood, Makita talked over some technical matters with Tomioka. Absentmindedly, Yukiko looked toward the bright window. She had so many different feelings at once.

Tomioka, smoking a cigarette, his hands clasped behind the chair, leaned his head back against the headrest. He was wearing a crisply ironed brown summer suit and a wristwatch with a slender band of cool-looking plastic that resembled glass. A red second hand circled around the black numerals of the dial. His neck was freshly shaven, and his nape gleamed a pale color. Soon the bell rang in the dining room, and Makita went out first, followed by Tomioka and then by Yukiko. At the center of the white tablecloth was a glass bowl heaped with unusual white and purple flowers. The meal started with miso and tofu soup, served with red aluminum utensils. Then delicious-looking dishes, including omelets and salted fish were brought to the table, one after another. Yukiko sat next to Tomioka, across from Makita. Mogi, Seya, and Kuroi, who were also staying at the hotel, had not yet put in an appearance at the office. The ceiling fan made a disagreeable scraping sound. Makita, slurping up his miso soup, began talking with Yukiko.

"They say life back home is getting to be quite difficult. This must seem like paradise to you."

Since Yukiko had never before been blessed with this kind of life, it was even more than paradise for her, but at the same time it made her uneasy. She felt a sense of emptiness, as if she had broken into a rich man's house.

From time to time, Tomioka would talk about things such as the research being done by the Ministry of Agriculture and Forestry in Saigon. He criticized the high-handed Japanese way of dealing with the French section chiefs in the French forestry bureaus.

Makita, chiming in, added quietly that it was unseemly for Japanese officials to be strutting around places like the Continental Hotel when there was so much poverty at home. To convert that sort of big hotel into lodgings for a supply depot was wrong, even during an occupation. Wasn't this thoughtless takeover by the Japanese military, on the contrary, sure to arouse animosity? He said, "We're lucky, though. No matter what the military may be planning, as long as we just do our duty and take care of the forests, we'll be all right. We should be grateful for that, anyway."

Tomioka had stayed in Saigon about ten days to do research at the ministry's laboratories on Rousseau Avenue in connection with charcoal-based fuel. Tomioka was having bread for breakfast. Yukiko reached for the butter dish, to pass it to him, and he looked at her hand. The sight of a Japanese woman's firm, fleshy hand seemed wonderful to him. It was a beautiful, gentle hand, covered with downy, baby hair, he thought.

'I was thinking I might go to Ranhan in four or five days, to have a look at their work on bamboo-reinforced concrete. Kano-kun sent me some information on their project on charcoal forestation. Have you seen it? The idea of charcoal-powered cars is not a bad idea, either. Back home, too, I hear they're converting over to the charcoal automobile. That's because we've been doing it here since the beginning. Could you have a look at Kano's report? I've also been thinking I'd like to go to the research center at Trangbom and see Kano . . ." Tomioka spoke rapidly and then left the room, heading back to the lobby before the others.

"What a strange man . . ."

Without meaning to, Yukiko let this comment slip to Makita.

"He's a bit eccentric. But at the same time he's a man of deep feelings. Every three days, he writes a letter to his wife. I wish I could do that. He has a strong sense of responsibility. Once he takes something on, he does it right."

The fact that Tomioka wrote to his wife once every three days was a sharp blow to Yukiko.

8

IN THE EVENING OF THE SECOND DAY, Section Chief Makita left on an urgent business trip that would take him to Saigon and Phnom Penh for about ten days. It happened that the old man Seya was leaving to go back, so the two of them left together in the same truck. Mogi and Kuroi set out with an Annamese interpreter to survey their district. Tomioka and Yukiko were the only ones remaining behind. Tomioka had the best room—facing east midway down the corridor on the second floor. Yukiko had a curiously bleak feeling about Tomioka, the man who wrote to his wife once every three days. Whenever they would meet in the dining room, Tomioka greeted Yukiko offhandedly with a "Morning" or "Hey" or the like. Anything that needed typing, he gave to Marie. When Marie grew tired of her work, she would go to the dining room and play the piano. The piano had a fine tone that was probably helped by the upland atmosphere. Although Yukiko didn't recognize the melodies, from time to time she listened entranced. Tomioka, who also seemed to like music, would sit at his work desk, simply listening. Marie was apparently only twenty-four or twenty-five, but maybe it was her glasses that made her look older. She was said to be from a good family. She had graceful legs, and she always wore navy-blue socks and white shoes. The contours of her waist and her hips were just right. Viewed from behind, her figure was elegant and beautiful. Her hair, a light reddish brown, was cut in a bob with a slight wave and swung heavily back and forth. Each time Yukiko, who had no accomplishments to speak of, heard Marie's piano playing, she felt inadequate by comparison. Marie spoke good English, French, and Annamese, and worked quickly and efficiently. Yukiko sometimes wondered why it had been necessary to summon a woman like herself to this remote upland in French Indochina. Yukiko's job was to type up things on a Japanese-language typewriter. Consoling herself with the fantasy that the information she typed might be used in important secret documents, Yukiko whiled away the empty hours.

Because of Makita's sudden departure, Tomioka's trip was put off. But on the fifth day, Kano Kyujiro suddenly came back to Dalat from Trangbom, together with an Annamese assistant.

As soon as he walked into the office and saw Koda Yukiko, he blushed. Tomioka introduced them. Evidently an earnest young man who devoted all his energy to work, Kano pulled up a chair and began talking with Tomioka about business.

"Can't you stay for a while?"

"I keep getting diarrhea, and I don't feel too well. I was just a bit nostalgic for the civilization of Dalat. I didn't think you'd even be back here, Tomioka-san . . ."

After they had talked for a long time, the two had the maid bring in some coffee. Apparently they were close friends. Kano seemed younger than Tomioka. He was short for a man, and fair-skinned.

He wore a dark blue open-necked shirt and white Western-style shorts. He had an athletic, nimble quality about him. But despite his build, there was something nervous and timid in his eyes. He seemed to have a weakness of spirit that kept him from holding anyone else's gaze.

The atmosphere at supper in the dining room was lively for once. Before the meal Tomioka uncorked a bottle of white wine that he'd gotten in Saigon. Yukiko also was offered a glass.

"So, Koda-san, are you from Chiba?" Evidently feeling the effects of the wine, the normally taciturn Tomioka abruptly asked Yukiko if she came from the rural area just outside Tokyo that people in the city considered provincial and unfashionable.

"No, I'm not from Chiba. You're rude . . ."

"Oh, really? I thought you were the Chiba type. Where *are* you from?"

"Tokyo . . ."

"Tokyo? You're lying. People born in Tokyo don't look like you. If you are from Tokyo, it must be from somewhere right near Chiba—Katsushika, maybe Yotsugi . . ."

"Oh! That's awful."

Yukiko grew sulky, and Kano decided to step in. "Tomioka has the world's sharpest tongue," he said. "Please don't mind him. It's just a bad habit of his."

"Is that so? Tokyo, huh? For someone who claims to be a Tokyoite born and bred, you have the wrong accent altogether. How old are you, Koda-kun?"

"Old enough."

"Twenty-four? Twenty-five?"

"No. I may not look it, but I'm only twenty-two. You're awful."

"Twenty-two, huh? Well, they say that women who look a bit older are intelligent. It's foolish to want to look young."

Tomioka reached for a bottle of Cointreau this time and pulled out the cork. Kano had graduated from the same Tokyo agricultural school as Tomioka. Tomioka and the well-known Professor Yasunaga had backed Kano for the post in forestry research in Indochina. Both Tomioka and Kano were fond of literature—Tomioka being a fan of Tolstoy and Kano a fan of the novelist Soseki and the humanist writer Mushanokoji.

"Let's have a toast. To Koda Yukiko, who has come all the way to Dalat on occupation duty!"

So saying, Kano pushed a glass toward Yukiko. Yukiko was in tears, and wanted somehow to fight back. Quite drunk by now, Tomioka looked at Yukiko's glittering eyes and saw a strange beauty in them. It was the same glittering light that he sometimes saw in his wife's eyes. Bewildered by something he could not understand, he downed his Cointreau in a single gulp. Yukiko quietly slid her chair back and left the room. It was too beautiful a night outside to go back to her room on the second floor. She went down the broad path that glittered with the evening dew and then wandered on, aimlessly.

"Look, you've made her leave."

Kano went upstairs to Yukiko's room and knocked, but there was no answer. The door wasn't locked, so it opened when he turned the handle. On the bed, lit brightly by the lamplight, was a pair of discarded black panties, the kind that a schoolgirl might wear. Kano stood in the doorway for a moment.

Even after he returned to the dining room, the image of the black panties remained.

"She's kind of stiff and conceited, isn't she?" Tomioka said, spitting out the words. Kano thought that Yukiko must have gone outside, and he wanted very much to go and look for her.

"Doesn't she look like that actress Miyake Kuniko?" Kano said to Tomioka.

"I wouldn't know. All I know is, it's no good for a young woman to come to this sort of place."

"Well, that's very old-fashioned of you. As far as I'm concerned, Dalat seems like a better place than I remembered."

"Koda Yukiko is not your type, Kano."

Kano poured some more Cointreau for himself and gazed with bloodshot eyes at the white blades of the unmoving ceiling fan. Tomioka, looking bored almost to death, put his feet up on the sill of the screened window and leaned all the way back in his chair.

"I wonder how long we'll be out here," Tomioka said with a sigh. "We can't win," he continued, as Kano turned toward him with a questioning look. "At least that's what they were saying in Saigon. Of course this is just between us, but I think by next spring we'll know more."

"When you're out in the interior like this, it's hard to get any news. Are there any signs like that? Is there any news?"

"People are saying we can't win. That's all."

"Oh, really? I actually believe that everything will be all right. What is the Japanese Navy doing, I wonder?"

"Well, perhaps they have a plan . . . it does seem as if they've been getting results."

Still bothered by the image of the black panties, Kano got up and went to the doorway to push the switch for the fan. The white blades spun into action with a low humming. The flowers on the table trembled in the draft.

9

TIME PASSED, AND STILL Yukiko didn't come back. Tomioka dozed in the draft from the fan.

Kano turned the fan off. He quietly left the dining room and went outside to look for her. From the dense darkness of a row of early flowering cherry trees came the cry of a crow. The air was moist, as if all movement had stopped. A faint light flickered among the trees. Right beneath the forestry office, there was a scraggly-looking house built in the style of a Chinese merchant villa. Apparently no one had lived there for some time. The garden was overgrown, and some plants that looked like South Seas roses had put out small flowers. Someone was singing behind the hedge. The song was Japanese. Ah—Yukiko's in there, Kano thought. He went in behind the hedge. The air was loud with insects. On a wooden bench with a comfortably curved back, Yukiko sat and sang.

Yukiko knew that it was Kano. She stopped her song and stood up, as if peering through the darkness.

"What's the matter?" Kano asked. "Were you angry?'

"It's nothing."

"Please come back in. It's not good to expose yourself to the night dew. Around here you can get sick from just a mosquito bite . . ."

"I'll go back in later."

"Tomioka's a good person. But he has a sharp tongue. And I think his nerves may be shot, too."

Kano put a hand on Yukiko's shoulder. The feeling of her soft, womanly skin beneath the thin silk dress made him flush all over. He had had several glasses of wine and, perhaps because he was drunk, it was a particularly bitter effort to control himself. Two or three times he tried to grasp the soft flesh of Yukiko's shoulder, but she twisted away. Yukiko herself was feeling a painful tightness in her chest that she could not control. A spirit of rebellion welled up in her, and she instinctively wanted to make the acid-tongued Tomioka suffer. She had no interest at all in this pale-skinned man. She stood there silently. Once more Kano came clumsily to her side. In the distance, they could hear the faint sound of the engines of cars pulling up to the hotel.

He had only arrived here today. Was this feeling of attraction to Yukiko merely physical? The thought crossed Kano's mind. But he sensed that this might be his only opportunity with her, so he drew close to her again. Yukiko looked at him hard, her eyes glittering. The night air was heavy with the scent of flowers and the foliage of many plants.

"Kano-san, it was because conditions at home had become so terrible that I volunteered to come out here. Do you know what I mean? I'm a young woman—how could I go on living every day, surrounded by war and still believe the talk of the 'honorable death of the hundred million'? I didn't come to this country as a diversion. I wanted to float away somewhere. Then to have Tomioka-san make one nasty comment after another. Of course I would be hurt by it. All three of us are Japanese. Asking me if I was from Katsushika or Yotsugi, I don't need that kind of thing. To have struggled through all kinds of difficulties to get to this point, and then be laughed at and condescended to . . ."

Yukiko was starting to speak in a high-pitched voice. His own emotions were strong, but he set them aside and looked into her shining eyes. Hearing that she had come here to escape a hard life made him try to imagine the life that she had left.

"Tomioka was drunk, you know." Kano faced Yukiko, and gripped her by the arms.

"Stop it! You're drunk yourself, Kano-san. I'm not like that . . ."

As she spoke, Yukiko stiffened. She closed her eyes, but she didn't especially try to throw off Kano's hands. Then Kano's lips were brushing against her cheek. She instinctively turned her face away.

Just then a voice called, from the roadside. "Hey, Kano-kun!" It was Tomioka. Kano said to Yukiko in a low voice, "Please come back after me."

Then, picking his way through the grasses, Kano went out toward the road. When Kano emerged silently from the grasses, Tomioka suddenly had a disagreeable feeling. Without offering any explanation, Kano simply matched his pace to Tomioka's and, bathed in his companion's displeasure, went back with him toward the office. The night air was cool, and the asphalt was slippery.

"It will be snowing at home pretty soon," Tomioka said with a yawn. "Ah, I'd like to go back," he continued. "Just once would be enough. I want to go back."

Kano remembered Yukiko's words—that hardship had sent her away from Japan—and he didn't answer.

"Is Koda Yukiko upset?" Tomioka asked, lighting a cigarette.

"Yes, she's angry."

"Oh, really?"

"She's a nice young lady."

"A nice young lady, huh? Is she a lady?"

"She's a good girl. She's had a hard time of it."

Kano thought that this was as good a time as any to tell Tomioka how he felt about Yukiko. For a while Tomioka just walked along silently, smoking his cigarette.

'Didn't you have anyone you liked back home?"

"Well, sure, I guess, maybe."

"Hm."

At a bend in the road, Kano turned around and looked for Yukiko, but she was not to be seen at the foot of the slope.

"Hey, do you want to take the car to Fuimon and fish tomorrow?"

Fishing was a preoccupation of Tomioka's. There were four waterfalls in the area, and he often went to Fuimon. Kano didn't feel like going fishing. He had finally come back here after a long time away, and he wanted to see people. It was a pleasure to see Tomioka again after so long, of course, but he was surprised by the strength of his response to Yukiko. The feeling he'd had when he had ventured into her room—he couldn't do anything about that. Rather than answering, Kano just gave a quick whistle, the kind used to summon a dog. From the direction of the automobile shed, a dog barked faintly.

"Makita has done well for himself. After all this time, Saigon and Phnom Penh will seem like oases."

"Hm."

"Tomioka-san, did you have any interesting experiences in Saigon?"

"I don't know. Do you think there's anything really interesting there?"

"But you must have been interested."

"You, too, should go to Saigon once, anyway, before you return to Trangbom. You'll come back feeling refreshed."

"Saigon? I haven't been there in a long time."

Kano didn't care one way or another about Saigon. He could not forget the glitter in Yukiko's eyes that he had seen earlier by the light of the stars. He was anxious to talk to her again and to dispel that loneliness of hers. There was a soft night breeze, and it seemed to calm him somewhat—he was beginning to regret the brusque way he'd treated her before. When he thought about Yukiko saying that she had not drifted out here as a diversion, this touched something in him as well. Being here was better than serving as a soldier. Her words pained Kano, as if someone had suddenly touched an old, forgotten wound. For a moment he recalled the dismal wartime conditions when, as a draftee of the Akabane Engineers Corps, he had gone to help with the occupation of Nanking. One dark night, on some lake or other, sneaking a woman aboard a boat, he had taken his pleasure in a furtive, hurried manner. The memory floated up behind his eyes, its outlines clear as a shadow picture.

10

TOMIOKA WAS FEELING BORED, so he said good night to Kano outside the dining room and hurried upstairs. According to the luminous dial of his watch, it was well past eleven o'clock. When he entered his room, the maid Niu was folding up his laundry and putting it away on the shelves. She was tidying up the room, with her usual sluggish movements. Somehow watching her at work gave him a feeling of unbearable loneliness, and he went down the back stairs to the specimen room. He turned on the light and sat down in a chair made of logs. Glancing over the dried samples of wood arranged in the display case, it became unclear, even to him, just what it was that had brought him to this strange place.

He thought of writing a letter to his wife, Kuniko, which he had not done for some time. During his trip to Saigon, he had not communicated with anyone back home for more than ten days. He felt that his wife was the only one he could confide in about his deep loneliness. The figure of his wife, who he was sure was suffering alone through indescribable hardships in Japan, appeared before him as if in a dream. He wanted to tell her that he would find a good way soon to send her the Michel lipstick and the face powder he had bought in Saigon.

His throat was dry. He left the specimen room and went back to the dining room. Kano was still there, lifting a glass of what was left of the Cointreau to his lips.

"Has Koda-san come back?"

"Yes, she's back. She's gone to her room."

Tomioka had a glass of water and went back upstairs. Niu was no longer in his room. Tomioka locked the door and lay down on his back on the bed. The springs squeaked a bit as they settled beneath his weight. He stared at the frosted glass globe of the light fixture on the ceiling. There was no motion at all in his heart. Loneliness weighed on him, and the idea of writing to his wife felt like an insurmountable chore. He got up and changed into a pair of yellow pajamas. His nightclothes, meticulously laundered and ironed by Niu . . . There was something sad about her thoughtfulness.

Kicking back the blanket, Tomioka stretched out at ease on the sheets. He could hear the door of the dining room creak open on the first floor, and the sound of Kano's footsteps slowly coming up the stairs. That Kano, that Kano, Tomioka muttered to himself. Koda Yukiko's willowy figure reminded him a little of his wife, Kuniko. First of all, the curious discovery that they both sometimes had the same light in their eyes resonated in Tomioka's heart. In this remote place, Koda Yukiko had reminded him of the fact that there was an affinity of words and of lives that only men and women of the same race can share.

Tomioka realized that Kano was having trouble getting to sleep. From the next room, he could hear Kano agitatedly dragging a chair across the floor and opening the door of the wardrobe.

Tomioka could not fall asleep either. He had a feeling he'd forgotten to turn off the light in the specimen room. Getting up again, he went out into the corridor. When he went downstairs, Niu was standing, in her water-blue bathrobe, in the doorway of the specimen room.

"I forgot to turn the light off, so I came downstairs," Tomioka murmured in Annamese.

"I came to turn the light off too."

So saying, Niu, holding her bathrobe closed in front of her, stood on tiptoe, reached up, and shut off the light switch on the wall. Tomioka grabbed her and held her tight as she collided with him. Niu seemed about to say something, so Tomioka hastily pressed his lips over hers. He gave her a long kiss, leaving the slightly built woman standing as if propped against the wall. Tomioka went up the back stairs. He had the impression that Niu was somehow laughing at him. Walking slowly and deliberately, Tomioka went back to his room.

The night was quiet.

At times the pines would make a sighing sound as the wind blew through them, but tonight they were silent. Tomioka summoned up an image of the forests that he had hiked in South Borneo, looking for *merukushi* pines. The forlorn-looking long needles of the horsehair pines, the broomlike shape of the *merukushi* pines, and the pale *kacha* pines appeared and disappeared in his mind's eye one after another. He had been surprised at the flowing masses of water plants resembling hyacinths, which spread over the width of the muddy yellow river. Was it all part of a dream that had vanished? Plants, unless they were suited to their soil, did not grow well. In fact, the Japanese cedars that had been planted in the garden of the forestry office here in Dalat were not doing well at all. Applying the observation, Tomioka thought that just as plants are firmly rooted in their native soil, the same principles applied to people and to differences in race. On the chart, the area of distribution of the *merukushi* pine in Dalat was given as 35,000 hectares. How could one stupid Japanese forester understand the statistics of this foreign land that he had barged into? How did they hope to sell off, to other parts of the world, these great forests of *merukushi*, with their beautifully shaped trunks and the fine grain of their wood? Were not the Japanese—who were suddenly rummaging about among the treasures of other people that had taken them centuries to develop—nothing but robbers? How on earth were the Japanese going to administrate so many sublime forests? People's hearts always remain free. Tomioka was assailed by drowsy, random thoughts. It was impossible to sleep.

He turned off the light.

Just at that moment, he heard Kano's door open stealthily and someone start to make his way downstairs. Surely he was not . . . Tomioka silenced that thought, and pricked up his ears. After a while, like drops of water dripping down into a deep well, came the sound of a musical scale being played on the piano in the dining room. The life of abstinence during his research trips in the mountains must be driving Kano crazy, Tomioka thought. He quietly sank his head into the pillow. He was suddenly disgusted at the memory of his secret kiss with Niu before. Both he and Kano were in love with something that was not love. Both of them had lost the spirit of camaraderie they had had in Japan. They were becoming just like the Japanese cedars that had been transplanted to the uplands of Dalat and had begun to wither. We are getting too much of that South Seas sun, Tomioka thought.

11

"BONJOUR . . ."

He woke to the sound of Marie greeting someone on the landing downstairs. Lifting his heavy head from the pillow, Tomioka looked at his wristwatch, and saw that it said nine o'clock. So that's what time it is, he thought, slowly sitting up in bed and smoking a cigarette. His head throbbed. What should he do? His body seemed to have no desire to move. Everything felt vague. He could hear little birds chirping. When he slowly slid the window open, the clear upland sky and the greenery everywhere below reflected each other in a remarkable harmony. The air was cool and refreshing. Niu, who was wearing a shiny, persimmon-colored dress, stood in a large flowerbed in a corner of the garden. The way that women were always healthy and never tired was hateful to Tomioka. The heart of someone like Niu, who had snickered after their long kiss, was a mystery. Tomioka stretched out his entire body for a moment and then sat back down on the bed. He felt that there was something meaningless about moving at all.

On his way to the bathroom to wash his face, Tomioka rapped on Kano's door. There was no answer. He put his hand to the knob, and the door opened easily. The window was wide open. Lying on the bed in nothing but a pair of light-brown striped underwear was Kano. His clothes were strewn about on the floor. He was sleeping facedown, his naked flesh as smooth and pale as a peeled egg. His mouth was open, and he occasionally emitted a snore that sounded like water gurgling through a wastepipe. Dead to the world, Tomioka thought as he roughly shook Kano awake by his cold shoulder. Kano opened his eyes dully. His eyes were bloodshot and unfocused.

Tomioka left him like that and went to take a cold shower. It was morning now—nothing had happened, right? The ghostlike apparitions of the night before had receded with the dawn. Wrapping himself in the large bath towel, Tomioka found the energy to sprint up the stairs. Putting on a neatly ironed white, half-sleeved jacket and a pair of long brown gabardine trousers, he set about the disagreeable task of shaving himself in the mirror. The fragrant smell of coffee reached the second floor. A church bell began to ring.

Tomioka went down to the dining room. Over by the window, Koda Yukiko was having breakfast alone.

"Good morning," he said.

Her eyes were puffy and red. Yukiko just smiled in response to his greeting. The gentleness of her expression made Tomioka feel embarrassed. He turned away as if angry and went over to his own table. When she brought him his breakfast, Niu was like a different person. Her face was impassive and Buddha-like as she set down his coffee and toast. From the office came the sound of Marie busily typing.

While finishing his breakfast, Tomioka decided to walk to Mankin, about four kilometers away. There was a forestry inspection substation there, near the royal tomb district of the Annamese kings. He was feeling out of sorts and thought it would be good to spend time in the forest. There were many sawmills, large and small, in the villages of Dalat. Tomioka silently walked along the winding hill road, listening to the earsplitting, shrieking sound of logs being sawn asunder. By the roadside, groves of enormous oaks and pines of every variety—their leaves and needles overlapping—shut out the morning sun. The sky, where the forest had been cleared, flowed blue like a river. Suddenly hearing footsteps behind him, Tomioka turned around. It was Koda Yukiko. She was hurrying after him, her white skirt fluttering.

Tomioka thought his eyes must be deceiving him. He stopped. Yukiko approached, short of breath.

"What's the matter?"

"What should I try to get done today?"

"Work, you mean?"

"Yes . . ."

"What about Kano-kun?"

"He's still sound asleep."

There must be an Annamese forestry employee around, Tomioka thought, but the newly arrived Yukiko would not be able to understand him.

"Didn't Makita-san leave any instructions behind? "

"No, he didn't say anything . . ."

The two were walking along the road toward Mankin. Neither one spoke. Now and then, an army truck or a car would pass them, and the soldiers driving turned back around to look at the unusual sight of a Japanese woman. Yukiko deliberately walked at some distance behind Tomioka.

Tomioka remained silent. Finally Yukiko asked once more, in a small voice, "What should I do?"

Tomioka turned slowly around and said, "Up ahead are the tombs of the Annamese kings. How about doing some sightseeing?" His voice sounded as if he were angry.

Tomioka was walking in very long strides. Yukiko had no idea if he was even a kind person. Viewed from the back, he looked as if he was in a very bad mood. He was dangling his helmet from one hand, and he was wearing rubber-soled shoes that looked comfortable. Yukiko was wearing the white shoes she had purchased at a good price and with such care in Saigon.

The road split, and they entered onto a narrow footpath. At some point, Tomioka slackened his pace, and soon they were walking shoulder to shoulder. She realized that he must have been taking such long strides before because army vehicles were passing by.

Suddenly he broke in. "I understand you were angry last night?"

"Hm? What?"

"Kano said that you were really angry at me."

"Yes, actually, I felt hurt."

Tomioka put on his pith helmet, reached into a pouch at his waist, and pulled out a forestation chart. He spread out the chart as they walked along. Nearby in the woods, mountain doves began to sing. The white chart reflected up in his face, and Tomioka pulled out a pair of pink-tinted sunglasses from his chest pocket. When he put them on, the chart was suddenly tinted pink. From narrow openings here and there in the forest canopy, the strong, glittering sunlight poured down on the path. A bit embarrassed to be walking with a Japanese woman, Tomioka kept a wary eye on his surroundings. The customs of Japan, even here, this far away from home, intimidated Tomioka's conventional Japanese soul.

12

THERE WAS A FEELING OF FREEDOM in walking along through the forest like this, even though all around them were dense stands of giant rare deciduous and evergreen trees. Sweetish, sticky pollen dust hung thick in the air. There was also a suffocating feeling in the way they were walking along without speaking. Unseen airplanes droned overhead. Forested land surrounded the royal tomb district. Towering *kacha* pines and Chinese black pines grew together in the forest. At the very end of this forested area, a zone of twelve or thirteen hectares devoted to *kacha* pines began. Charcoal-burning ovens stood outside the small houses throughout the area.

Yukiko was tired of walking. She had not slept well the night before—the walking made her breathless, and her back tingled painfully. But when she did pause to take a deep breath, her lungs filled with the cool, bracing air. Yet Yukiko didn't have the slightest interest in her surroundings. Her heart was solely and continually attracted by the tall figure of Tomioka up ahead. Yukiko walked with a feeling of lonely sweetness that made her desire to grow more intimate with him. Fantastic emotions made Yukiko deliberately wear an expression of melancholy. Whenever Tomioka turned back toward her, Yukiko showed him a face marked with pathos, with the loneliness of an uprooted woman. Beneath that veil Yukiko was feeling a solitary excitement. She gave a heavy sigh.

Tomioka turned around. "You must be tired," he said.

"Yes."

"Walking twelve kilometers in half a day is nothing to me. No matter how long I walk in the forest, I never seem to get tired. And I sleep well at night."

"By the way, will Kano-san be staying here long?"

"He may be here for a while, yes."

"I have a bad feeling about him."

"Why? Because he has a rough manner?"

"Last night, he was terribly drunk. I was frightened."

Tomioka quietly walked along. He was thinking of the difficulty he'd had getting to sleep the night before, and wondering if it was connected. He suddenly felt a sort of hatred for Kano. Tomioka stopped short so that Yukiko, who had been walking close behind, would come alongside of him. When she did, he grabbed her shoulder and then embraced her under a big dusky Chinese black pine. Yukiko, too, was surprisingly natural about it. Breathing heavily, she pressed her face against Tomioka's chest. He pulled his face away so that he could look closely at her fleshy lips. He was struck by how good it felt to hold a woman of the same race as himself, who shared nuances of speech with him—so different from his kiss last night with Niu. He felt free just to gaze at Yukiko's flushed face. With her eyes closed, her face very much resembled that of his wife. Tomioka could do nothing about the fact that, as he actually cradled Yukiko's head in his hands, his feelings were rushing a thousand leagues away, desiring something completely different. He had the feeling that his ability to love a woman cleanly had been dulled here in the south. As he kissed Yukiko, he could not escape the feeling of having traded a forest habitat for a small, cramped cage. He kissed her for a long time. Yukiko was digging her fingernails into his shoulder impatiently. But already Tomioka's passion had started to fade. A small wild white peacock flapped through the forest, and was gone.

The two walked for a while among the woods, villages, and spacious plantations, and did not return to the office until considerably past noon. Tomioka went immediately to his room, got a towel, and went off to take a shower. Yukiko casually looked in at the office. Kano was there alone, leaning over a desk near the window, writing something. The fan was not on, so the room was hot and stuffy. Without even a glance toward Yukiko, Kano propelled his pen over the paper. The cover was on the typewriter, so Marie must have finished her work and gone home. Yukiko went upstairs to her room, only to find that the door had been left open. It gave her an unpleasant feeling, as if someone had been looking around. Yukiko stared at her bed and her table. There was a deep hollow in the bed, as though someone had been sitting there. It made Yukiko somehow unbearably uneasy. Locking the door, she lay down quietly on the bed, but this brought her no feeling of rest. Nothing but blue sky could be seen through the open window. A sense of pointlessness descended on her. The situation back in Japan, of course, was a restless one of being hounded from place to place by the war. Here it was different—a loneliness ponderous as a millstone, a solitude that ate into the core of the body. Now and then, a smile rose up to her lips. It had not gone so far as a pledge of love, but the idea that she had won a man's heart gave her a sense of wealth. Her situation with Iba seemed far away and less important. There was a glamour about Tomioka, who seemed always on the verge of some uncontrollable emotion. Yukiko felt that it would be love to the uttermost, that tears would flow like a river. This man, who feigned coldness but was not cold at all, had crumbled, and it gave Yukiko a good feeling. That such a cynical, sharp-tongued man who was faithful to his wife should nevertheless be won over so easily was for Yukiko a source of great pleasure. She felt she had had the last word over his cold-hearted manner. She thought that the strength she had shown in refusing to succumb to Kano's passion last night must have earned her today's happiness. A feeling of gratification crept over her as she fell deliciously asleep.

When he had showered and changed into fresh clothes, Tomioka went down to the dining room. Kano was sitting idly in a wooden chair facing the veranda. Tomioka picked up the heavy volume of Chevalier's *Botanical Encyclopedia*, and sat down in the chair next to Kano's. He looked out at the Ranbean Mountains directly in front of them and at the lake sparkling below. In the empty room behind him, the fan made a clattering sound as it revolved. At Tomioka's bidding, Niu brought them some cold beer and a plate heaped with slices of cold duck.

"How about a drink?" Tomioka asked.

Kano listlessly reached for a glass. Little birds were singing noisily all around them. As they drank their beer and looked out at the scenery, the colors of the mountains changed gradually with the changing angles of the rays of the sun. It pleased Tomioka that Kano was kind enough to silently drink beer with him. The mountains, the lake, the sky—they were those of a foreign country, but one that the French had been able, calmly and easily, to assimilate. And yet there was a broad resistance here that the narrow, lopsided thinking of the Japanese could not encompass. Even though they acted in a lordly way, Tomioka and all his fellow Japanese were no more than small intruders. Tomioka had begun to feel keenly the strangeness of outsiders being set down in this place, without any thought given to whether or not they had any real ability. It was nothing but a cheap trick that would soon be seen through. Yet the image of the lake was one that would remain in Tomioka's heart. In this land belonging to someone else and where no one paid any attention to them, the Japanese people were busily scurrying about like so many ants. Their cleverness at assuming a practical demeanor had helped them advance this far. The *kacha* pines must already be fifty or sixty years old, but the Japanese were felling great numbers of them all the time, with no idea of what to do with them. All they did was to report the numbers, and nothing but the numbers, to the military. The numbers were mocking them. They employed the Moi tribe to transport the lumber along the Danimu River or by rail. In Tomioka's opinion, however, the felled timber was not moving well at all; it was accumulating in freight cars. And as for the Danimu River, the big trees, such as *kacha* pines, *oburikasuto*, and Chinese black pines, simply lay tumbled about on the riverbanks, their freshly cut ends exuding sap. Only the statistics traveled, from desk to desk. Treating the simple, clumsy Moi people as lazy slaves, the military assiduously exploited them. Tomioka drank his beer and began reading the encyclopedia. These works on the products and plants of Indochina, compiled over many decades by the French scholars Crevaux and Chevalier, who had lived here for many years, had been rather difficult for Tomioka to obtain. But for learning about the forestry of French Indochina, these were immortal works of scholarship.

Kano, looking relaxed, and less ill-humored than before, said in a loud voice, as though he had just thought of it, "Is Miss Koda asleep?"

"Hm, I wonder."

"You took her to Mankin earlier, didn't you?'

'No, no, she followed me, so I just took her along to see a few sights."

"I'm in love with her. I thought you should know."

"Oh?"

"I'm not complaining, but a while ago an officer from the Engineers' Corps came and asked me who the Japanese woman was who was walking along nice and proper with Tomioka-san. You're a quick worker, I thought."

"This is getting much too complicated. We were just walking. Was it the second lieutenant from the Transport Division? The one who said that . . ."

"I went to Mankin right away, myself. I searched all over, but couldn't find anything . . ."

Tomioka stealthily turned his eyes toward the lake. What would Kano do if he knew that he'd deliberately entered the footpath leading into the woods? The thought made Tomioka's blood run cold.

"Everyone is pretty quick to appreciate women around here," he said casually.

"Well, I was surprised by how quick you were. Going off to Mankin with Koda-kun while I was still asleep, that wasn't fair. With a woman, you know how it is—the atmosphere of a moment decides everything. I can't even trust you, Tomioka-san, even though you sound as if you're so blunt all the time."

"She followed me. The section chief left without giving people any instructions and you were asleep, so she came to ask me what she should do. So, thinking that it would be good to do some sightseeing, I took her around. That's all it was. We didn't make a special date to go there or anything of the sort."

"Well, that's all right, then. I'm in love with her. It's only a matter of time before I come to grips with her, somehow."

Kano gave a bashful smile and poured some more beer into their glasses. Tomioka lit a cigarette and thought, It may already be too late. But then he thought perhaps it was not. He was more deeply weary than he had been before. His trysts with Niu, which had continued every night until the day he went to Saigon, had kept him from the fierceness of desire that Kano had clearly felt. His intimacy with Niu, also, was a passing affair. His own heart was, he thought, incapable of putting out any shoots of love toward anyone other than his wife, Kuniko. Section Chief Makita seemed to have some idea of what was going on between Tomioka and Niu. But Makita was not the sort to report the misbehavior of his subordinates if it reflected poorly on his own management. Tomioka had taken full advantage of Makita's laissez-faire attitude.

At some point, the sun, rimmed with orange, had begun to set toward the Ranbean Mountains. On the lake there were delicate ripples, like inlaid golden needles. A smell of oil heating came floating out from the back of the dining room. The beauty of the evening made both men thoughtful.

"It is peaceful here, but back home things must be hard. Falling in love is such a luxury, I know," Kano said.

"Do you think we'll win this war?"

"Sure, we'll win. After all we've been through, defeat is out of the question. To come all this way just to lose . . . we can't even think about that. I don't think about defeat. Makita and you are uneasy about it, but if worse comes to worst, I'll cut myself open on the spot . . ."

"You can't just cut yourself open. I don't like to think about defeat either, but there is the possibility, you know. I don't like to touch on the subject if I can avoid it, but the news I've been hearing is not altogether good. The people around here are sensitive to what's going on. In the usual Japanese way, we're pressing ahead by force, but we don't have any gold or silver, and no winged chariot. The Japanese emblems of authority have all faded. The sun is going down on us before our work is done. We're lost, but we're still bustling about arrogantly. We're pondering all kinds of plans to fight more efficiently, but we have no ability to carry them out. It's like handing a sword to a monkey."

"Don't say things like that. There's no way to know if we'll win or not, at this point. In the worst instance, there's always the 'honorable death of the hundred million.' It will be good to die . . ."

"That's irresponsible," Tomioka said, irritated.

He got up and went to the bathroom. Just as he left the dining room, Koda Yukiko, as if she was his replacement, came into the dining room, looking well rested. She was dressed in a red-checkered gingham dress and had bound up her hair with a thin blue ribbon. Startled, Kano turned around and looked at her for a long moment.

"You haven't had any lunch, have you? You must be hungry," he said, offering her a chair. Yukiko seated herself demurely in the chair beside

Kano's and crossed her bare legs. In the rays of the golden sun, her face was suffused with a rosy color. Her lips had a blood-colored sheen. There was a Japanese perfume about her. Feeling nostalgic and wondering what scent it was, Kano paused for a moment. Oh, it's camellia oil, he thought. Yukiko's hair gleamed lustrously. Kano, taking a bulky envelope out from his pocket, placed it on Yukiko's lap.

"Please look at it later."

Yukiko quickly wrapped the envelope inside a white handkerchief. Tomioka returned from the bathroom, his footsteps heavy. Deliberately not giving Yukiko even a glance, he gazed for a while at the sun, as if dazzled. Kano brought the beer and a glass out from the dining room, poured out a beer, and handed the glass to Yukiko.

An uncomfortable silence hung over the group for a while. Presently Tomioka, cradling the weighty Chevalier volume, silently left his chair and the dining room. Kano thought that Tomioka was at last exercising tact.

13

THE RAIN HAD BECOME A DOWNPOUR.

The sound of the rain coursing along the eaves became as loud as a waterfall. Yukiko was recalled to reality. She was not able to fall asleep. Brightly colored memories of Indochina, like scenes on a revolving lantern, appeared and disappeared in her mind. There was a sharp late-night chill, and she was cold with just one blanket. Although her body was heavy and tired, she also felt keyed up. She lay with her eyes open in the dark, listening to the sound of the violent rain, overwhelmed by a loneliness against which there was no defense. It was a blessing that Iba was not here in the house. It wasn't that she was reliving memories of the past, but she was glad that the events with Iba were now four years behind her. She was bedded down in a place where no one knew her, not even by sight. Yukiko had experienced that before, in Indochina. She had not seen Shinonoi Haruko at the repatriation center in Haiphong, nor had she met with anyone there who knew about Haruko's circumstances. Before the end of the war, Kano had been taken away to Saigon by the military police. Tomioka, who had stayed on until the end, had fortunately been able to return to Japan in May, ahead of Yukiko. Although she did not know how Tomioka's feelings might have changed between May and today, Yukiko was confident that if they could only meet, everything would be resolved. Her confidence also came from her peace of mind.

The next morning, the rain stopped. The clear early winter sky blew away the dampness after the rain. On the persimmon tree in the narrow, ravaged garden, wrinkled persimmons were ripening. Yukiko could see from the tree's growth that years had indeed passed. The wife of the man who was staying here invited Yukiko to the breakfast table, saying that although they were only having black barley rice, she was welcome to join them. The woman's husband had apparently left the house at the break of day. She said that he had gone to Nagano to buy apples. He was from Nagano and had recently begun dealing in apples. Sooner or later, though, everyone knew the controls on the fruit market were going to break down. So he was thinking now of going to Shizuoka to buy salt, taking the salt to Nagano to sell it, and then bringing miso back to Tokyo.

"If only he were on better terms with Iba-san, he could ask him for help getting some salt, but for some reason he doesn't have much good to say about Iba-san. Would you happen to know of anyplace that he could buy some salt?"

Yukiko knew nothing about that sort of thing. An eight-year-old boy, a seven-year-old girl, a three-year-old boy, and a little baby were at the table with the woman. The husband's younger brother was also staying with them, but today the two men had gone to get apples, the woman told Yukiko.

Yukiko was willing to try working at anything, but she wanted to decide what to do after she had seen Tomioka. The woman was kind enough to say that if she didn't mind the room where they were storing Iba's baggage, Yukiko was welcome to stay there for the time being. Yukiko accepted gratefully.

It was not clear at this point whether Yukiko would be able to return to her former job. She had little desire to return to it, though. After breakfast, she got directions from the woman and went to use the telephone at the neighborhood sake distribution center. She made a call to Tomioka's office at the Ministry of Agriculture and Forestry. However, the woman who answered the telephone informed her that Tomioka had resigned from the ministry. Yukiko decided then to go see Tomioka at his address in Upper Osaki, and she set out in that direction. Getting off at Meguro Station, she walked along the excavated area for the railway, where the trains ran by below, asking people for directions as she went. She passed the mansion of Prince Fushimi and walked through the burned-out residential section, peering at the house numbers. From the train, the area looked like a field of ruins. And indeed, nearly everything of the old neighborhood seemed to have been destroyed. Finally locating the house with Tomioka's street number on it, she stood at the door but felt a curious sense of diffidence. Tomioka's name card was affixed to the door, and there were two other name cards as well, evidently of people who were sharing the house. All the windows of the badly damaged house were held together with thin strips of tape. An uprooted bamboo plant, washed out of the ground by the rain, stood leaning against the ramshackle board fence. She did not like to come face-to-face with Tomioka's wife, but no answer had come to her telegram and she could not telephone him either, so Yukiko had little choice but to visit. Steeling herself, she slid open the latticed door and called out to the people inside, announcing herself as a messenger from the ministry. A refined-looking older woman of about fifty came to the door for a moment and asked her to wait. And then suddenly, the tall, kimono-clad figure of Tomioka appeared in the entryway. He did not seem surprised to see her. He stepped into a pair of sandals and came outside. He began to walk along silently, and Yukiko followed. When they had turned the corners of a number of small alleyways, they emerged onto a wide, lonely avenue lined with ruins. For the first time, Tomioka turned around to Yukiko.

"You look well," he said.

"Did you get my telegram?"

"Mm."

"Why didn't you respond?"

"I thought you'd come up to Tokyo anyway."

"So you quit your job?"

"I quit in July."

"What are you doing now?"

"I'm helping my father in his work . . ."

"That person at the door—that was your mother?"

"Mm."

"I can see the resemblance—I thought so."

"Where are you staying?"

"With some relatives in Saginomiya."

"Could you wait here for a moment?"

"Yes, I'll wait."

Tomioka, saying that he would come back after he had changed into street clothes, went back the same way they had come. From behind, in his dark blue kimono with a white splash pattern, there was a strange air about Tomioka, as if the man was somehow different. Yukiko sat down on what was left of a stone fence that had been largely destroyed and waited. The wind was cold. In her black serge trousers and a blue worn-out jacket, which she had borrowed from the woman at Iba's place, she fit perfectly into the desolate environment. This is a dangerous visit, Yukiko realized only now. Her face burned.

About half an hour later, Tomioka came back, wearing Western-style clothing. He was wearing an old, shabby winter coat, which contributed to a general sense that he looked older and worn out. He had also become very thin.

Looking at Yukiko from a distance as she sat on the ruined wall, Tomioka felt nothing at all. In the completely changed setting of these ruins, he had no desire to try to revive the dream of Dalat. Controlling his feelings of irritation and already determined that this was the end, Tomioka walked to Yukiko's side. Once more, automatically, he said, "You look well."

"Yes, I came back with the one idea of seeing you, so I had to be well."

As though to emphasize her words, Yukiko looked up steadily at Tomioka, as if dazzled by him. Tomioka smiled slightly but did not reply. No doubt Yukiko, just recently repatriated, did not see the inevitable conclusion of the separation that wedged itself between them. Since reading her telegram, Tomioka had not had a very good feeling about the whole thing, but nevertheless he at least had to fulfill his responsibility. He had been worrying about seeming like a scoundrel, but now that he had actually seen Yukiko again, that worry no longer seemed necessary. He suddenly felt that he had the strength to make a clean break, after this evening. "Where shall we go?" he asked Yukiko, although he quickly realized it was unlikely that she would know of any place. Recalling that he had heard from somebody that little inns were opening up these days in Ikebukuro, Tomioka headed for that part of town. Any number of inns built with thin, unseasoned wood had begun to go up. Houses had been constructed here and there, seemingly at random. There were markets and eating places. The confusion of the rapid development of the area made it quite a suitable place to take women for secret assignations. Tomioka slid open the front door of a small wooden inn with just a sign saying Hotel and went inside. A pale-faced woman with disheveled hair stood in the entryway. She was chewing noisily on a wad of gum and wearing shoes that had not been laced properly. As she went out, she bumped against the doorjamb. Yukiko felt a chill go through her.

The room they were taken to was a four-and-a-half-mat room on the second floor, right over the market. The soiled tatami was pocked here and there with cigarette burns. There was no ornamental alcove or anything. The walls were painted green and covered with scratches. In a corner of the room, two sets of soiled bedding—solid-color red quilts— were piled up. On top of these, two calico pillows without their slips gleamed with hair oil.

Taking out some money, Tomioka ordered some wonton soup and sake. In the empty room without either a table or a brazier, the pair felt as if they had been abandoned. Leaning against the wall, long-legged Tomioka sat with his knees up, clasping them. Yukiko, with her elbows propped up on the quilts, was scratching almost violently through her clothes at her full breasts.

"I didn't realize things had changed this much."

"We lost the war. How could things help but change?"

"I suppose. Still, I wanted so much to see you. You're acting so cold. Don't you have any fellow feeling for a repatriate?"

"Don't talk nonsense. I'm a repatriate myself. You're not the only one. There are a lot of others in our situation too."

Yukiko's accusations and her dramatic way of talking, as if only her experience was remarkable, made Tomioka uneasy. He could not get used to her familiarity. Yukiko, for her part, was waiting for Tomioka to show a strong emotion of any sort. She could not understand why, even though they were now completely alone, he was still as formal and aloof as when they had first met. Had the sympathy that had developed between them been an illusion? Yukiko pulled herself across the floor toward Tomioka, and rested her chin on his knees.

"Why do you act like you don't know me?"

"What?"

"Don't you like me?"

"What are you talking about? You women have things so easy."

"It's not easy. If I had thought that I was going to be discarded, I wouldn't have come back like this. I would have come back with Kano-san. But I understand your feelings."

"Don't say foolish things. Kano is Kano. It's your fault too, to have acted that way. Women like to wag their tails at everybody. For a woman, a place like that is paradise. It must be nice, knowing that everybody wants you."

"I can't understand why you're talking this way to me now. You don't have any love for me anymore, do you? All right, I'll show you. I'll wind up just like that woman we saw before, in the entryway. I won't care what anybody thinks. I'll wallow around in the mud."

"It's nothing to get hysterical about. I myself, now that I've come back to Japan, cannot live a life without any responsibility, the way I did in Dalat. I just mean that it's unreasonable to try to continue the life we had at Dalat, here in Japan. But I do want to be of any help I can to you. I'm willing to take on that much responsibility."

"What sort of responsibility?"

14

AS HE CONTINUED TO DRINK THE SAKE, Tomioka's mood grew brighter. He was freed from the troublesome tangle of feelings he had had before, and he regained the nerve to plunge into the same dangerous relationship. Even while he indulged in fantasies that were far removed from the messy reality of such things as his household or the matter of Koda Yukiko, the human core of loneliness within him made him want to stifle these thoughts and take in his arms the woman who lay weeping by his side. When he had come back to Japan, he had continued to deny his memories of Yukiko, and little by little they had started to fade. But when he saw her before him like this, he had the feeling that without warning he was being shown a fault line that would divide his past from his future, and settle his fate. This time, he pulled himself over toward Yukiko, and pressed his shoulder up against hers.

Yukiko said, "I remember. All kinds of things . . . Back then you and I were like crazy people. The time you went to inspect the reserve forest of Chanbo, with Makita-san and that lieutenant commander—what was his name?—who had come from Japan, when you were getting in the car, you said suddenly: 'Isn't Koda-san coming too?' And the lieutenant said, 'Yes, yes, let's take Miss Koda,' and the four of us went to Chanbo.

And we stayed at an Annamese hotel, and there were lamps on the tables at dinner, and all of us drank sake and got drunk and fell asleep. I'd found out that your room was the farthest one out, so in the middle of the night I went to you in my bare feet. There was a marsh in front of the row of rooms, and a strange-sounding bird was singing out in the forest. The door was unlocked, and when I turned the knob quietly, the Annamese caretaker was standing in the garden. I was startled . . . That was the first time with you, wasn't it?"

While she talked, Yukiko took Tomioka's hand and wound her fingers between his. Tomioka thought, Oh, yes, that's right, isn't it? While soldiers had been shedding their blood and dying, he had been fooling around with a woman. The insanity of everyday life at that time now seemed to Tomioka like the events of a dream.

The flimsily built rooms in this hotel had walls almost as thin as sliding paper doors. Any sound in the building could be heard as clearly as if from next door. But as soon as they closed their eyes, memories that only they knew about rose to their minds' eyes. On the floor of the *kacha* pine forests, pampas grass and *alang-alang* flourished. Here and there, peonies, arbutus, and eugenia dotted the forest floor.

Tomioka remembered the forest of Chanbo particularly. Felling and cutting the trees into rounds took a team of two laborers a whole day for four trees. Many of the sawyers in the area were Moi tribesmen and Annamese. All of them were afraid of malaria, though, and even when recruiting notices were posted, there were not many who wanted the work. Tomioka took the initiative then—he had often recruited his own day laborers before setting out for Chanbo. Cutting the trees into boards and small squared pieces at little sawmills in the mountains, the sawyers sent the lumber to Dalat by army truck. The laborers were worked to the bone for ridiculously low day wages. They took a liking to Tomioka however, and although they were faintly aware of Japan's defeat, they had worked hard for him right till the end of the war.

"It's already too late to go back to those secluded mountains of Indochina, isn't it? We talked about becoming laborers and making a living by cutting wood out there, just the two of us, for the rest of our lives."

"Hm."

"You did say that."

"Well, we can't go back again."

"That's right. We can't go back. If Kano-san hadn't made that trouble, the two of us might have fled into Chanbo at the end of the war. But it's not true that people can live anywhere. I don't really know that people can live in harmony with nature."

Even Tomioka did not want to live out a life in this squalid and defeated Japan, gasping with the effort simply to keep his head above water. He could hear something like the voice of nature calling to him once in a while, deep in his heart. Just as Jesus' hometown had been Nazareth, for Tomioka his soul's heartland was the forests of Indochina. There were times when Tomioka felt pulled by a longing that was like love.

Before they knew it, it had become evening.

The market beneath the window was uproariously noisy. Yukiko had gone out alone and bought some sushi and a beer bottle full of sake made from lees. Yukiko, who had no place to go home to, wanted to talk with Tomioka a little while longer. As the two grew drunk on the cheap sake, they fell into a feeling that all was lost.

It seemed the natural thing, for Tomioka to touch Yukiko. With no feelings whatsoever, the pair snuggled together in the bedding that had been laid down earlier in the day. For them, mating had become a habit. Tomioka tried to give himself over to another self—the one who, like Christ in the garden of Gethsemane, had suffered and been abandoned. If God is for us, who can be against us? Tomioka even thought that he should go with this woman. He had the feeling that his parents and his household could be to him nothing more than a temporary protection. In his drunkenness, Tomioka heard a voice telling him that he should climb over that fence one more time and live his life with this woman. The time of Japan's flowering has already passed, he thought drunkenly. He embraced Yukiko and kissed her passionately for the first time in a long time.

All around them, the hotel was growing noisier. At one point, a rude and boisterous lady of the night, getting the room wrong, slid open the door of their room. The two did not even bother to separate their bodies. The wind and the thunderous sound of the cars of the national railway also burst into the room regularly.

Yukiko, though warmed by Tomioka's body, wanted something more violent. She worried that, for him, this was a makeshift measure, meant to meet an immediate need. Yukiko remembered that in her three-year secret relationship with Iba, there had also been this feeling. Tomioka, on the other hand, felt a loneliness—even while holding Yukiko—like that of a fire burning itself out into ashes. He reached out now and then to pour himself another small cup of sake. Yukiko nibbled at pieces of sushi. They had many private memories, but their hearts had grown almost completely opposite. They succeeded in igniting their passions, but they did not talk of the future.

"You've gotten awfully thin," Yukiko said.

"That's because I haven't been able to get anything good to eat."

"I've gotten thin too, haven't I?"

"No, you haven't."

"You can tell me. When you hold me, which of us is plumper, me or your wife?"

Tomioka reached out for the small cup.

There would be no more eruptions of feeling between them, he thought. They had both misread each other. Both of them were spiraling into a sense of defeat. They no longer had the fire to break through. They were merely forgetting.

"You know, I think I did something cruel to Kano-san. Because you were making so much of me, I ended up teasing Kano-san. And yet he would have gladly died with me. He never had any feelings of doubt. Even the war—no one believed more strongly than he did that Japan would win. He was a good person. He was the perfect accompaniment for us."

"You're a terrible woman."

"Perhaps, but don't women have that side to them?"

Tomioka wanted as much as possible not to think about Kano. Yukiko, on the other hand, seemed to use talk of him as a way to revive Tomioka's feelings of love. He was exhausted, but she did not seem tired in the least. Taking in her fingers a blackish, discolored slice of tuna, she calmly chattered away. Her primeval female strength was hateful to Tomioka. The face of the woman who looked up at him from the red quilt—flushed and shiny as if it had just been washed—looked vulgar.

"What are you thinking about?"

"Nothing."

"About your wife?"

"You idiot!"

"Yes, I'm an idiot. A lot of women are. All of the men are wonderful, right? It's pathetic, having responsibility for a fool. Not thinking about the future, clinging to you just because you're here now with me, anybody would agree it's foolishness, I know. But still, coming back from so far away and then being able to meet you, I'm completely happy. That's all I wanted. But at Haiphong, I hated to think that you would be meeting your wife . . . What kind of person is she? She's a beautiful woman, isn't she? Educated, graceful . . ."

Yukiko vaguely tried to imagine Tomioka's wife. She imagined her to be slender, faultless. While Yukiko chattered, Tomioka was dozing off.

"You lied when you said that when I got back you would have set it up, and then you'd split with your wife and be with me, all free and clear. Men lie. They trick women and keep their own world neatly to themselves. It's terrible, bringing me to a place like this and letting me realize that. You said that when we got back to Japan, everything would be fine, like in the past, and that we could even live as day laborers . . ."

Closing her eyes, Yukiko stroked Tomioka's skin. His hipbones stuck out. The roughness of his skin, which was probably also due to lack of nutrition, was pitiable. Yukiko, placing her hand on her abdomen, felt something mysterious, in the smooth, sleek touch of her skin. It was strange that the skin of a woman who had lived this kind of life should still be so velvety smooth. Even when a country had lost a war, did the skin of its young women suffer no change? Once more, stealthily, Yukiko put her hand on Tomioka's abdomen.

"Tomorrow we'll go our separate ways. Then, sometime, we'll meet again in a place like this, and you'll get drunk and fall asleep. It doesn't mean anything to you, that I've come back from so far away. Don't you think it's a miracle that I've been able to come back? I hate the way you worry about all sorts of things, but still don't treat me the way you did in Dalat! Wake up!"

Yukiko pinched Tomioka's skin, hard.

Although he had been dozing off, being pinched made Tomioka open his eyes. He looked around at the unfamiliar room but was overcome with drowsiness. Closing his eyes again, he said, "Be quiet. You're tired, yourself. A little sleep will do you good. It's no use thinking about the past all the time."

"You don't feel anything, do you? The things of the past are important, you know. If we lose them, we're nowhere. I don't want to become like an old person—undernourished, without any energy, feeling tired all the time . . . Don't people say that Japan has become free now? They're not feeling all sorry for themselves in the next room. Get up, and stop acting like an old man. If you don't, I'm going to your wife's place tomorrow for a talk, all right?"

15

THE AFTERNOON OF THE NEXT DAY, Yukiko went back, alone, to Iba's house in Saginomiya.

Although they had not exchanged any firm promises, Tomioka had told Yukiko that even if they did live together, things would not go well unless they waited for a while.

So it can't be helped, Yukiko thought. Tomioka had said that, at any rate, he would soon find her a place to stay and bring her a good sum of money as well. She could of course see that these were makeshift solutions, but she had no choice but to believe him.

She had parted from Tomioka at Ikebukuro Station, and he had quickly disappeared into the crowd. Forlorn, Yukiko had spent some time leaning against a pillar on the platform, looking at the people disgorged by the train cars and the waves of people getting on. The faces of a badly nourished people who had been exploited to the utmost throughout the long war jostled past and flowed around Yukiko.

Yukiko had no destination.

Although she'd returned to Saginomiya, there was no one in particular waiting for her there. Yukiko considered returning to Shizuoka, but her heart was too caught up with Tomioka to leave Tokyo. By and large, she was happy that she'd been able to see him. Even so, something in her secretly realized that, with things as they were, she was an encumbrance to him. Thinking that she too would have to enter the life of the masses and look for a job, Yukiko suddenly thought of the dance hall she had seen at Shinagawa Station. Maybe she would try being a dancer, she thought idly. She tried placing herself—a transformed version of herself, with her face made up—amid the flow of the lively music, but given the way she looked now, it was impossible to make the idea seem at all realistic.

Since she had received just a little sum of money from Tomioka, Yukiko headed for Shinjuku. Shinjuku, which she had not seen in many years, was as crowded as ever. The fact that she did not see one face she knew made Yukiko feel that she was walking the streets of a foreign city. New models of automobiles raced past. On the cold, wet pavements, the crowds, bulky with winter clothing, walked along. Yukiko came to a large building with its windows blown out. She recognized this as what had been the Mitsukoshi Department Store. When she turned right alongside the building, she came to a series of alleyways where the wares of one roadside vendor after another were lined up. Sardines by the handful were fished out of kerosene cans and offered for sale. There was bean-jam candy in little glass-lidded boxes. There were vendors selling tangerines heaped up in pyramids, vendors selling rubber-soled shoes, vendors who laid out rows of frozen squid at five yen apiece. Along every alley, such roadside markets overflowed into the roadway. In the desolate rubble left by the firebombing, dirty street children clustered, taking long drags on cigarettes. Yukiko bought some tangerines at twenty yen a pile, clambered up atop the rubble, and sat down. She peeled a tangerine and ate it. All the troublesome old ways of life had been smashed to bits, she thought. This gave her a cool, refreshing feeling. More at ease here than anywhere else, she spit the pips of the sour tangerines out on the ground.

Would the revolution Japan had experienced actually change people's hearts? she wondered. The faces in the crowd all seemed as dear to Yukiko as family.

It was amusing to think that, right about this time, Tomioka would be returning home and giving his wife some explanation for his overnight absence. What excuse would he offer? Knowing Tomioka, he would no doubt handle it smoothly. The members of his family probably felt no uneasiness about him. The sweetness of the fantasy she had had before—that when she came back to Japan she would meet Tomioka and they would move to a new house—was bitter now to her.

In the afternoon, Yukiko returned to Saginomiya. Giving the two remaining tangerines to the children, she went into the room where Iba's baggage was stored. The room was cold and lonely.

As if she had just thought of it, Yukiko, looking at Iba's baggage, felt suddenly that she would like to rummage about in it, find something valuable to sell, and live on the proceeds for the time being. She thought that this would be fitting revenge upon Iba. Even if she opened up the baggage, saying that she was searching for something of her own, most likely the people of the house wouldn't suspect anything. And even if Iba came back and learned that his baggage had vanished, since it was Yukiko who did it, he surely would not take her to task, Yukiko thought.

When night fell, Yukiko was given a sweet potato by the people of the house and allowed to steam it with theirs.

Eating her potato, Yukiko looked out at the narrow garden through the small glass window of the sliding paper door. In among the dirty azalea shrubbery, a skinny tricolor cat was watching something intently. Yukiko remembered the azalea that had bloomed with peony-colored flowers in the early spring, and the past came rushing back to her. After a while, the cat, slowly and with an air of languor, passed under the loquat tree next to the hedge and out of view.

Yukiko slid the door open, stepped onto the long wooden porch, and called out to it. But the cat did not come back.

16

ALTHOUGH TOMIOKA DID THINK about Yukiko for two or three days, he quickly began to forget about finding a place for her or raising some money for her. Rather than trying to help her, he was more inclined now to simply break off the relationship. These chance encounters were difficult to the point of suffocation. He prayed that she would simply decide to go her own way.

Tomioka was trying to launch a venture with an acquaintance in the lumber business, involving buying up lumber wholesale in the mountains. They had been planning to set off quite soon for the northern countryside of Nagano and lay in supplies of cedar boards. However, the acquaintance's efforts to raise capital were not going well. There were problems too with getting the lumber rafted down from the mountains. The trip kept being put off, from one day to the next. If the deal would only go well, it would mean a substantial profit. Right now lumber was selling for fantastically high prices on the black market. Tomioka was filled with the desire to take a risk. Since returning to Japan, he had developed a powerful aversion to the life of a government clerk. He thought that by seizing this opportunity he could change the course of his life.

He had put in a telephone call today to his acquaintance, Tadokoro, at his shop. But when he was told that it would take four or five more days for the capital to come through, he had returned disappointed.

As soon as he got home, his wife announced that a woman had come calling. When he heard that the woman had left a message that she wanted to see him tomorrow at the Hotei Company, Tomioka realized it could only be Yukiko.

The "Hotei Company" meant the Hotei Inn, where he and Yukiko had stayed in Ikebukuro. Tomioka's face was glum, with a trace of irritation. Kuniko, seemingly oblivious, said, "She asked me if I was your wife. Who is she? Does she have something to do with Tadokoro-san's company?"

"No, no. I wonder if she's not the wife of the head of the Hotei Company. I met him recently on business."

"I see. Even so, she didn't give me a very good feeling. All kinds of people are emerging now, since the end of the war. She's the type of woman I just can't feel friendly toward. Where were you, when would you be back?—she was familiar to the point of rudeness."

Women's intuition must instantly reflect back to the other person, Tomioka thought. In his heart, he formed a secret fear. It was no doubt through intuition that Kuniko had gotten a certain feeling from Yukiko. Tomioka thought that it would almost be better to tell Kuniko now, before it was too late, about the affair with Yukiko. But how could he? She was sitting before him in her baggy wartime trousers, mending their winter quilts, with her sewing spread out over her knees. He thought it would be too cruel to announce his love affair in a foreign land. Making such a confession to Kuniko and wounding her deeply—Tomioka could not bear to do it. Kuniko had stayed with Tomioka's parents and waited faithfully for her husband, while enduring patiently a poverty-stricken existence.

The next afternoon, Tomioka went along to the Hotei Inn and found Yukiko waiting for him there. Leaning against the brazier in a maroon overcoat and with her hair falling far down on her forehead, she presented an almost unrecognizably splendid appearance.

"Yesterday, I called at your place," she said.

"Yeah."

"Your wife seems like a very gentle sort of person."

"You've become terribly fashionable."

"Yes, I bought this coat. Do you like it?"

"Where did you get the money?"

"I sold something that belonged to a relative, although I didn't tell him about it. I was awfully cold, and lonely too. I couldn't help it."

"Is that really a good idea?"

"I couldn't help it."

Tomioka took a long look at Yukiko's new, flashy appearance. Her transformation from the languid, listless person she had been seemed sad. He thought of a scene he had seen a long time ago in a Kabuki play—all he remembered was a lamenting and deranged woman standing on a pier, clutching a stake. If he were to thrust this woman away here and now, wouldn't she sink into an abyss of loneliness and ruin? He could see it happening.

"What are you thinking about?"

"Nothing in particular. But it's going to be hard for both of us from now on."

"Do you think there's no solution? I'm becoming resigned, myself. When I saw your wife, it made me so sad. The whole time I was walking around the area afterward, I thought about it. She's a wife who trusts her husband. She's a neat and clean and attractive woman. I'm afraid to bring misfortune on a good person like that."

Wondering whether she meant what she had said, Tomioka looked hard at her. He could readily imagine her loitering outside his house. Yukiko took a handkerchief from her overcoat pocket, and wiped her eyes. Unexpectedly, the handkerchief was one that Tomioka had used at Dalat.

"You want to get rid of me, don't you? That's what I think. You don't care one way or the other about me, I can tell. I've become a burden. But if you abandon me, I'll slip down into hell. I'll become ashes and blow away. I can't go on living seeing nothing but your shadow, and I don't want to receive the leftovers of your love for your wife like a beggar . . ."

"What are you talking about? You're a fool. It's very strange that you bring up love right now. I've been thinking about all sorts of things that are a lot more important right now. If I don't think of a plan, it will be difficult for you too, I imagine. That's why I came here today, even though I was busy."

"Don't put the blame on me. I can't make you understand what I want. Why can't I depend on you as much as I want? Aren't you thinking of something else right now? But I'm not even asking for anything unreasonable. Find a place for me somehow, and come and visit me sometimes . . . I want to go to work right away. I was never meant to be your real wife."

Sipping some cold tea, his knees nervously shaking in the chilly air of the room, Tomioka listened to Yukiko's hysterical entreaty. Yukiko had been left by herself for three days, and now, just seeing Tomioka's face, she wanted to talk about everything at once.

"Are you looking for a room for me?"

"Yes, I'm looking. You probably think, It's just one room, so why is it so slow? But with everything burned out like this, it's hard to find anything. Even if I do find something, I need many tens of thousands of yen for the deposit. Just wait a little bit longer . . ."

"You're living in a house, so you can be calm about it but I'm a homeless person. The place where I'm staying now, it's not somewhere that I can stay as long as I like because of family obligations . . . My relatives evacuated, and the people living there now don't know about their future. I'm just borrowing a room for a few days. I want a place of my own."

"I'll find you something soon. It's not as if I'm just putting it off. In a time like this, there aren't many houses to be had. By the way, don't they supply any fire in this hotel? I'm freezing to death."

"You're right. Why don't I go borrow a beer bottle from the hotel, like before, and come back with some cheap sake?"

Yukiko—her mood seeming lighter—drew her handbag to her and began rummaging about in its contents. Finally fishing out a coin purse, she clambered to her feet.

"Just a little is all right. I don't want to drink a lot," Tomioka said.

"Are you going back early today?"

"No, I don't have to go back especially early."

"Won't you stay the night? I have some money."

"I can't stay tonight."

"Oh, how dull. Why? Were you scolded, last time?"

"I'm not a child. Nobody scolded me. Today is no good for me."

Not wanting to force him, Yukiko left the room. The room was a different one from the one they had stayed in last time, but it too was frigidly cold, and the dirty, loosely woven tatami mats were depressing.

Tomioka lit a cigarette and, as he smoked, remembered the things his wife had said about Yukiko. He began to think that instead of meeting with a woman in this desolate hotel room, it would be more pleasant to be sitting in his tearoom, listening to the sound of the water starting to boil, casting an eye over the newspaper, Kuniko at his side. Somehow or other, he even had the dreadful thought that perhaps Yukiko could have been kind enough to die in French Indochina. He had a memory of having read somewhere that in every human heart, at all times, two opposing prayers existed side by side, and that one of them was addressed to Satan.

Watching the smoke of his cigarette trail away, Tomioka fixed his eye on Yukiko's bulging handbag. He reached out and drew it toward him. Inside the dirty felt handbag, there was a hard object wrapped in a purple carrying cloth that seemed to be a bolt of fabric. Other than that, there was some makeup, a Parker fountain pen with the blue diamond trademark that Tomioka had bought in Saigon, a pack of Peace cigarettes, a hand towel, and a cake of soap all tumbled together. There were also two letters addressed to her relatives in Shizuoka. After a while, Tomioka, putting the handbag back as it had been, stubbed out his cigarette in the ashes of the brazier. But now he was feeling bad toward Yukiko. He thought of Kuniko and her calm ways. Just by being here in this kind of place, entangled with Yukiko, he was trying to escape the loneliness of his present life and sacrificing his wife in the process.

He thought back to the time when he had eloped with Kuniko, who was then the wife of another man, and made her his own wife. His selfish heart that heaped new sins upon the old now seemed like his fate. The maid Niu, whom he had left in Dalat pregnant with his child, had gone back to the country. The idea that he had settled everything by giving Niu a round sum of money was strangely painful. From time to time, he dreamed about her. No doubt Niu had already given birth to the baby. It would be a mixed-race child, Tomioka thought, and he wondered if she was feeling ashamed.

After a while, her cheeks reddened perhaps by the cold wind, Yukiko came back.

"I bought some sushi again. Sake too—I got a whole bottle."

Yukiko held the beer bottle up against the light of the window, so that Tomioka could see it. Carelessly emptying the cold leftover tea into a corner of the brazier, Yukiko filled the cup with sake.

"I'll test it for poison." Yukiko put her lips to the cup and tossed off half of it in a single gulp.

"Ah, that's good. My chest and my stomach feel like they're on fire."

Tomioka poured himself a cup and downed the contents in a single swallow. Yukiko poured more sake into his cup.

"Will you stay tonight? Can't you do it? Just this once—I don't ask for much. If you don't like this place, we can go somewhere else. If you need money, I have a couple of nice things we could sell, so we can stay somewhere more pleasant."

Tomioka gripped Yukiko's hand. Yukiko was not able to keep her emotions to herself, and there was something almost primitive about her heart that was lovable. Freed from his sense of being crushed by the weight of circumstances and of family—invigorated by the sake perhaps—Tomioka kissed and nibbled at Yukiko's fingers.

"Bite me harder."

Tomioka gave her fingers a series of sharp nips. Yukiko put her face down into his lap and began to weep. Had he actually hurt her?

"Even I don't understand how I became this sort of woman," she said. "Please do something. Anything."

As she wept, Yukiko rubbed Tomioka's knees with both her hands. The room was beginning to grow dark. The lively voices calling out from the markets were clearly audible. Tomioka put his lips to Yukiko's hair, but in his heart he felt it to be an empty, theatrical gesture. He began to recognize the primitive feelings of a woman, which were missing in his wife Kuniko and which Tomioka became aware of only when he drank.

"I shouldn't have gone to see your wife. I can tell she's a good person. And yet, when I thought of her being your wife, her face seemed hateful to me. After visiting your house, her face comes back to me all the time, as if to stab me in the heart . . . Your wife must certainly know about me. Has she said anything?"

"She hasn't said anything."

"That's a lie. I made a very bad face and glared at her. She gave me a strange look, then looked me over, from the top of my head to the tip of my toes, and smiled unpleasantly. An eerie, unbearable smile. Her gold teeth were gleaming. Why does she have gold inlays on her front teeth?"

Yukiko raised her face and grinned at Tomioka as she spoke. Her weeping face, as if washed, was bare of makeup. It looked fresh. The hair she wore down over her forehead was disheveled. It gave her a charming, coquettish look. Perhaps because he was drunk, he thought he saw Yukiko's face wavering nearer and farther, darker and lighter.

"But she's much older than me . . ."

"Do you have something against her?"

"That's right. She can't have you all to herself. A wife with gold teeth at the front of her mouth. How do you kiss her? It makes me shudder."

Tomioka did not like having his wife's defects bluntly pointed out like this. Dragging out one of the quilts piled in a corner of the room, Tomioka placed it over his knees. It was a dirty, sticky quilt with a chilly feel to it.

"You're like a foot-warmer. Do you mind if I put my feet in from here?" Yukiko sounded drunk.

"You say you're going to find a job? What are you planning to do?" As he asked this, Tomioka threw back his third and then his fourth small glass of sake.

Yukiko said, her expression growing slightly serious, "I'd like to become a dancer, but is that all right with you?" She looked at Tomioka with a coquettishness that shone up from the depths of her eyes. Tomioka, while thinking that being a dancer would be all right, did not say whether he approved.

It was getting on toward ten o'clock.

Tomioka mumbled, "Well, I should be getting back." He took out a roll of bills from the inner pocket of his overcoat and deposited it on Yukiko's lap.

"Here's a thousand yen. Before it runs out, please get yourself a job, anyplace. As soon as I find a room, I'll let you know. Tomorrow evening, I'm taking a little trip to Nagano. I won't be able to see you for ten days or so. In the meantime, please give some of the money to the people of that house so that they will let you stay there."

Yukiko, taking the roll of bills in her hand, felt as if she had been thrust away, just like that.

"I don't need the money. Can't you stay the night instead? Going to Nagano for ten days—you're leaving me, aren't you. That's it, surely. Tell me the truth."

Tomioka gulped down the rest of the sake and said, "No, that's not it. I don't know how to apologize to you, but frankly, we've been dreaming ever since we lived in that beautiful country. You won't like this, but coming back to Japan and seeing this completely different world, I thought it would be atrocious to make my family suffer anymore.

Although everyone has been through a lot, they have borne up under it. I can't come back to Japan just to leave the people who waited for me. It seems like I've broken my promise to you, but until you're happy I'll do anything I can. I'm trying to think . . . I like you. Yet it's my weakness that I just cannot live with you. Even tonight, it's not that I cannot stay with you, but I had a bad feeling about not telling you the truth. It's true that I'm going to Nagano. I was planning to talk to you about all this after I got back from my trip, but then I decided to tell you now, instead. If we do part for good, I know that you'll have a hard time. But it's impossible for me to leave my family. Because they have no one else to depend on."

Yukiko covered her ears with her hands and shook her head. She glared at Tomioka, her eyes glittering.

Quietly pushing the quilt aside, Tomioka said, putting his hands on Yukiko's knees, "There's no other way."

"You mean that it's all right, whatever happens to me, as long as you and your family are happy. I don't need this kind of money. I don't think that taking money from you is happiness. If you don't mind me saying what I want to, your wife and I are one and the same. You probably think that it'll work out somehow for me, as long as you make your wife happy. Well, why didn't you think of that the first time I visited you, in the entryway?"

Yukiko's drunkenness came out all at once. She was not thinking a great deal before she spoke, but she knew that she could not stomach Tomioka's selfish way of talking. The same man who had been so relaxed and expansive in Indochina had suddenly withered upon his return to Japan. Yukiko did not like the weak-mindedness of his newfound scruples toward his house and family. She took Tomioka's hands in both her hands and tugged on them. Then she abruptly rolled up her left sleeve and showed Tomioka the long, thick vertical welt on her arm. She said, "Do you remember this? It was all because of your lying to Kano-san. I know all about your affair with Niu, too. You think people's innermost feelings are crazy. Everybody immediately trusts a person like you. Whereas people like Kano-san or me, we're not trusted; we're thought to be abnormal. But back then, you didn't seem like a fake to me. Now you want to make your house splendid, make your family happy—in order to build that happiness of yours, you'll sacrifice any number of people. And that innocent look you put on, it's hateful. If your house and your wife are so precious to you, why weren't you cold to me from the start? I don't want to chase your wife away. But I've spent too much time, I guess, imagining all sorts of good things. I'm staying here tonight, so you can go back whenever you want."

Her eyes were fixed on Tomioka. Then she wrapped herself into the quilt from head to toe, and rolled away from him on the tatami. Tomioka simply sat there, watching her.

17

ABOUT FOUR DAYS LATER, Iba unexpectedly returned to Tokyo.

Yukiko had been on her way out when she saw him coming along the alley, walking purposefully. At first she thought that it was not Iba, but his older brother. Iba seemed to be surprised to see her as well.

"Oh, is that you, Yuki-chan?"

Yukiko blushed, with the suddenness of it all.

"When did you come back? Why didn't you go back to Shizuoka first? So it is you, after all."

Iba had aged tremendously in the four years since she had last seen him. Even the expression on his face had changed.

"How did you know I was coming back?"

Iba turned up the collar of his black overcoat and said, "I can't tell you about the family in detail here. How about going somewhere and relaxing with a cup of tea?"

He headed toward the wide, dusty avenue, where the wind seemed to blow colder. Yukiko, watching Iba from behind as if she was looking at something completely unfamiliar, followed. Iba crossed the railway tracks but did not enter the station. Instead he went straight along the street and ducked in under the curtain of a buckwheat noodle shop diagonally across from the station. There was no source of heat inside, and the tables lined up in the concrete entryway were coated with dust. The two sat down in a corner, facing each other, but they both were so cold that they drew their knees up toward their bodies and rubbed their legs for warmth. At their corner there was a glass door covered with fine latticing, which made it especially gloomy and cold.

"Do you have buckwheat noodles?" Iba asked.

The waitress, wearing a gauze mask over her face and her hair in an old-fashioned upswept style, said that things were still difficult, so they didn't have any soba. When asked what they did have, she said there was black tea, adzuki bean soup with dumplings, and soda water. Remarking that they could hardly drink soda water in this cold, Iba ordered two adzuki bean soups. The old-fashioned noodle shop had exactly the atmosphere of an eating place in one of the old post towns. Taking a pack of Peace cigarettes from his pocket, Iba lit one up and then put the pack back in his pocket. Yukiko, shaking a bit from the cold, said, "Let me have one, too."

"So you smoke now?"

"It's just so cold, I want to have a little smoke. Inhaling makes me feel warmer."

After lighting her cigarette, Iba asked about various things. He asked so many questions that it became annoying. The waitress brought over two bowls of muddy soup flavored with *dulcin*. The lids were sweaty inside when they removed them from the bowls, and the soup was a light brown color. Two little dumplings were afloat in each bowl.

"You went ahead and opened up my luggage?"

Iba spoke with his face lowered, picking up a dumpling with his chopsticks. Yukiko was silent. She also started on her soup, and thought, The people of the house must have informed on me.

"I understand you purposely opened my bags. Why would you do that? If you needed money, you could have just asked me, and I would have come up with something somehow. But even more than that, it's odd that you came back to Tokyo and didn't tell your people in Shizuoka. Someone sent me a letter to tell me about it—is it true you sold off some of my things?" Iba relit his cigarette, which had started to go out, and drew the smoke in with powerful inhalations.

Yukiko now had no sympathy for Iba whatsoever. "It was so cold. I just opened your bags, and I borrowed two or three items."

"And sold them."

"I know it was wrong, but there are people whose homes have been burned out, so I thought that you wouldn't miss just a few things. I thought you'd forgive me. I bought this overcoat with the money."

"Why didn't you go straight to Shizuoka?"

"I didn't want to go back. Also, there was a friend who came with me from Indochina, and I wanted to start looking right away for a place to work. I meant to go see everyone after I'd gotten settled."

So saying, Yukiko took from her handbag two letters addressed to her family back home and showed them to Iba. They were letters she had written four or five days ago and forgotten to send.

"What did you sell?"

"Two pieces of silk gauze, and there was a small bolt of cloth too."

"And you think it's right, to do something like that? Since going to Indochina, you've changed."

Yukiko was silent.

"I gave up my job at the bank and went to be a farmer in the country. But a person who has lived in the city cannot settle down in the country. I meant to have my family come back by the end of this year and sent the baggage on ahead. Valuable items fetch a high price now. I meant to sell them and supplement my business. Didn't you have an overcoat stored away in the country?"

"Yes, so please sell that one. I don't care if all my things are sold. I was planning to get married. That's why I came to Tokyo first."

"Oh? When are you getting married?"

"It didn't work out. He has a wife. When I came back to Japan, everything went wrong."

"What does he do?"

"He was at the Ministry of Agriculture and Forestry. I worked with him over there. Since he came back, he says he's doing something in lumber."

"How old is he?"

"Much younger than you."

"You've been deceived."

'No, I haven't. But we separated."

It was strange to Iba how Yukiko, who had been a meek, reticent girl, had changed completely. She had become adult, with an assertive way of speaking. Since it was cold, Yukiko had wrapped a purple carrying cloth around her cheeks. The whiteness of her skin set the purple off nicely.

"Will you be staying on here, then?" Yukiko asked.

"No, I'll just be staying three or four days, going here and there, seeing friends and looking things over, and then I plan to go back. You can come with me."

"Without your bags?"

"Yes, I'm leaving them at the midwife's on the corner. It was she who wrote to tell me about you."

"Oh."

They left the soba shop, but having nowhere in particular to go, they loitered outside the station, talking.

"I'm going to Shinjuku from here, so check up on me to your heart's content."

Yukiko spoke with no appearance of timidity.

Iba, standing with his back to the wind as if he was cold, said, "I'll go with you." He entered the station with Yukiko and bought two tickets.

They took the train to Shinjuku. It was a day of soft sunlight but extremely windy. Most of the train windows were broken. It was as cold as if they were racing along in a refrigeration car.

"It's been bombed all to hell around here."

Iba was eyeing the burned-out ruins that lined the areas between the stations.

"I'd like to become a dancer. Is that all right with you?" Yukiko said suddenly, with a casual air.

Iba did not answer immediately. Then he asked, "You don't want to be a typist?"

"I'm tired of that kind of work. And they say the salary is not too good. I've heard that at the halls for the American soldiers, there are all sorts of ways to make money."

"That's probably so, but are you going to be in it for a long time?"

They arrived in Shinjuku, where they started walking around, aimlessly. At the Musashino Theater, a film about Madame Curie was showing, so they went to see it. Yukiko wondered how many years it was since she'd seen a foreign film. The two sat down side by side in the damaged plush seats. In the theater too, it was freezing cold. The squalid little theater no longer had any of the charm it had had before the war, and it seemed very strange to be watching an American film here, in this situation.

Yukiko felt Iba grip her hand in the darkness. What on earth did he have in mind? His hand was hot. Yukiko found the hand unpleasant, but she endured its hold on hers. In the reflected light from the silver screen, Iba's face in profile reminded her of a corpse. Yukiko felt teardrops welling up as she thought about her recent parting from Tomioka and about the loneliness that had followed.

By the time they left the theater, it had grown dusky outside.

The roadside stalls had vanished, and the area looked abandoned. The streetlights on the corners only made one feel the misery of defeat all the more sharply. A wind as cold as ice was blowing. The two came out onto the avenue where the trolley ran. It was lined with small, rickety shops that looked like chicken coops, but these too had closed early. These days, burglars and pickpockets roamed the streets, so by the end of the day all the shops were shut tight.

Yukiko took Iba to a little, shacklike Chinese noodle shop that she had been to a couple of times, on the trolley avenue. It was growing dark, and Yukiko wanted to drink some strong sake. She felt that she could not bear it unless she poured a powerful drink into her devastated heart. They ordered soba noodles topped with bamboo shoots and sat down next to the small stove. Wondering how many years it had been since she had watched a busily burning stove like this, Yukiko cautiously reached out a finger to touch the gleaming tin chimney.

"I don't want you to become a dancer," said Iba, smoking a cigarette. Yukiko, still resenting his audacity in holding her hand earlier, did not answer.

Iba went on, speaking quietly and gazing at Yukiko's flashily made-up face. "I've been worried about you all along. I was worried whether you would make it back all right. Japan is in bad shape right now. All the prominent people have been caught, and things have been turned upside down. People who looked down on others in the old days are at the bottom of the heap now. I think some of these changes will be to the good."

"The whole country was acting crazy," Yukiko replied. "Just the fact that from now on there will be no war is a relief. How did you avoid the draft?"

"I was worried about that all the time. I was working at an army factory in Hamamatsu, so I escaped the draft. But when I think about it now, it all seems like a dream. Hamamatsu was bombed too, and after that I worked as a farmer. It's a mystery to me why I wasn't drafted, actually. After the war, the thing I worried about most was you. I didn't think you would get back this easily."

The steaming buckwheat noodles arrived. They ate, cradling their bowls in their hands. The bamboo shoots were tinged an unusual red.

"Delicious . . ."

"Yes, this place is really good. It's run by foreigners. You get really large portions, and it's cheap."

Yukiko felt that it would be too disgusting to return with Iba to Saginomiya where they would sleep next to each other in that cramped room. She had the feeling that everything she wanted was being withheld, and that what she didn't want was being forced upon her, as if it was her fate.

"Are you staying at the house tonight?" she asked.

"Yeah."

"You probably don't have a room set aside?"

"What room were you sleeping in?" Iba said.

"In the tearoom. It's full of baggage."

"We can sleep together."

"There's nothing to eat."

"I brought back about six liters of rice. It is my house, after all. We'll use the kitchen and cook some. There's nothing to be shy about. There's a nice set of quilts in the baggage. Let's go back and open it up."

"I'm staying at a place in Ikebukuro, so I'll go there."

"You're being very careful."

"It's not that. It's just that tonight I have to meet a friend. It's too much effort to deliberately set out in the morning . . ."

"But it's good to see you, after such a long time. We still have a lot to talk about. Please come back with me. I don't know what clothes you've sold, but I won't scold you."

"Yes, well, I don't care how much you do scold me. I want to go to my friend's place, to talk about a job."

The very idea of sleeping with Iba made Yukiko shudder.

18

TOMIOKA'S TRIP TO NAGANO was put off. The talks at Tadokoro's place were going nowhere. Unless one moved quickly, market conditions kept changing so fast that it became too late to act. Rumors were flying about that the currency was going to be completely revalued. Tomioka wanted to order large quantities of lumber right now. Hearing that the sale of paper on the black market was roaring these days, he wanted to have a hand in that also. But when he was thrown out into the world on his own, he realized his own powerlessness. Everyone might look as if they could be trusted, but in fact, when they lowered their voices and spoke quietly about business, each was thinking only of what would benefit him. Nobody seemed really worried about the new situation produced by the war. People wanted to think that everything would be all right and that out of this chaos, something good—something they could rely on—would come to them alone.

More even than the war, people were enjoying this thrilling, revolutionary period. Human beings are easily bored, and prefer change to monotony. A time of vicissitudes, with everything going around and around like a carousel, stimulated people.

Tomioka thought that he had no choice but to raise capital for his venture by selling his house. If he could just put together five or six hundred thousand yen in ready cash, he was sure he could somehow get the rest later. He could not bear to simply let a chance like this go by.

One morning, over breakfast, Tomioka's wife, Kuniko, asked, "Remember that woman from the Hotei Company, who came to visit recently? Well, I saw her in the neighborhood yesterday evening. Do you think she knows someone around here?"

Tomioka had been close to forgetting Yukiko. Now, as he silently sipped his soup, he could easily imagine her loitering in the neighborhood, even down to the anxious expression on her face.

"Since she asked when you were coming back from Nagano, I didn't know what to say. I thought it would be awkward if she met you on the way back, so I said you had returned yesterday . . . When I said that I'd take a message for you, she said she'd come all the way to this neighborhood, that she was staying permanently at the Hotei Company, and that you were by all means to visit her, even at night. 'Please tell him that,' she said. 'If you tell him that I want him to return the money I loaned him the other day, he'll understand,' she said. Then she briskly walked away. She was wearing a lot of makeup."

Tomioka found it difficult to breathe. It seemed to him that she had probably settled in at that hotel because she had nowhere else to go. When they were alone together earlier, she had thrust his thousand yen back at him, saying that she did not need it. But her accusation—that he was sacrificing others to his own happiness—even now weighed on him.

In Indochina, Tomioka had made Yukiko his own, enraging Kano—who was a gentle and straightforward person—to the point of insanity. Because of that, Yukiko had been wounded by Kano. But at that time, the two had casually supposed that they would be able to marry and had been allowing their feelings to develop with that end in mind. Tomioka had lost his appetite, and he set down his chopsticks. Although Tomioka imagined for just a moment that, perhaps, if he were to sell the house, he could divide the money between his wife and his parents and live penniless with Yukiko, the fantasy brought him no comfort whatever.

"Did you borrow money from that company?" Kuniko asked in an uneasy tone.

"What time was it last night?"

"It was about seven. I was on my way back from shopping. You came back late, so I forgot to mention it to you. But this morning, on the missing-persons program on the radio, the name Hotei came up and I remembered. What kind of business does the Hotei Company do, I wonder."

Tomioka did not answer. Since they always had breakfast late, his mother and father were in another room. Kuniko, folding the newspaper, asked: "May I go now?"

As if in a trance, Tomioka just looked at her slender face. He wanted to explain everything to her. He was dead tired.

He wanted her to uncover his secret. Despite the fact that he lacked the bravery to continue in this uneasy situation for long, Tomioka was also well aware of his selfishness toward Yukiko. This was entirely his fault. Since returning to Japan, he had assumed a hard mask and had become averse to showing how he really felt. He knew he must seem like a completely different person. Kuniko naturally sensed that his relationship with that flashy woman must have something to do with it. Intuitively, her thoughts had become dark and uneasy. These days there was a restlessness in Tomioka's eyes, even while he was caressing or embracing his wife. At some point he would just stop and sigh. In lovemaking, even before he had spent his powerful sexual energy, there were times when Tomioka would give up, coldly pushing Kuniko away.

"You've changed completely since you came back from Indochina."

Kuniko had said this, wonderingly, soon after Tomioka's return. Tomioka, too, was well aware of the transformation. Every morning, when he shaved, his own face in the mirror—a bit swollen and distended these days, no doubt from his drinking— reminded him of the character of Stavrogin, in *Demons*. It was not that he had ever been delicate looking, nor indeed did he have coral lips, and his face was not gentle and interestingly pale. But he couldn't shake the sense that there was a growing resemblance.

"I don't like to have that kind of woman prowling around the house. Is there something going on? Your behavior has changed completely."

"No, no. Nothing has changed."

"Should I go and repay that loan?"

"There's no need to bother yourself about men's business."

"But I don't understand."

"I'm telling you not to worry, and I'm the one concerned. You should believe me."

"Right, but aren't you in some kind of debt to her? As soon as the subject comes up, you get all touchy."

"I'm just preoccupied. There's no telling how the business venture with Tadokoro will turn out. It might be best if you kept your unnecessary doubts to yourself."

Tomioka dearly wanted, one more time, to set out for the mountains and forests of French Indochina. He was beginning to believe there was no work—other than in the mountains and forests—that would suit him. His parents, his wife, the house—they all seemed like so many burdens. To live his whole life as a laborer in those great forests seemed a far happier prospect than his present existence.

An image of mangroves, their tangled roots protruding from the mud of the shore, grappling with and anchoring one another, floated back up into Tomioka's mind. Even at the mouths of the harbors of Haiphong and Saigon, there had been walls of mangroves, with their oily leaves and their roots like tentacles. He was filled with a desire to go to the south again.

Kuniko looked at the cold face of her husband, who had fallen silent. Suddenly her tears overflowed.

"What are you crying about?"

"Lately I've been thinking that this is my punishment—that you want to separate from me. I feel that I'm being punished for various things."

"Life is hard, so of course you're a bit nervous. I'm not thinking in the least about a separation."

Tomioka could not tolerate this self of his who was telling a lie. It was as if all his lies together were arrayed before him, like seeds of a pomegranate sliced open.

19

UNABLE TO CONTINUE PAYING the hotel bill in Ikebukuro, Yukiko drifted back to the Iba house in Saginomiya. Iba, however, who had returned to Shizuoka, had sent word that he would be moving back to Tokyo in two or three days. The six-mat tearoom and the four-and-a-half-mat reception room had been emptied for him. Although it was called a "reception room," the roof consisted only of red tiles, and the tatami in the room was worn smooth. There was neither a cupboard nor an ornamental alcove.

Yukiko stayed there for one more night. Iba had left a letter for her. He had inspected the bags. He was not particularly angry, but he would be distressed if she caused him any further inconvenience. The rooms were cramped, and he could not have her staying on after his return. She should go wherever she liked. If she had no place to go, he would have her return to the countryside, to discuss her future with all the relatives. If, while he was away, she laid hands on the baggage again, he would have to think about what he wanted to do.

Every piece of baggage was trussed up like a wild goose. There were paper seals affixed. Yukiko thought it was hilariously funny. She felt like snipping all the cords with scissors.

Men had a knack—an instinct, almost—for escaping ties with others, Yukiko thought. She felt there was something hateful in the way they coveted material possessions. It seemed right to deprive them of those possessions. Yukiko stayed just one night this time, and then had a neighborhood forwarding agency deliver Iba's quilt wrapper to the Hotei Inn in Ikebukuro. The people in the house did not particularly object. Since they were not on good terms with Iba, they looked on silently, their faces stony. Their expressions actually seemed to say, Do as you like.

When Yukiko opened up the quilt bundle at the hotel in Ikebukuro, out tumbled Iba's padded kimono, a rather worn Inverness cloak, and a bag containing almost ten liters of adzuki beans. Also in the bundle were two futons, a wool blanket, and a comforter made of *meisen* silk. Feeling bold and audacious, Yukiko immediately sold the cloak and the beans at the market outside the station. Stealing things was rather enjoyable, Yukiko thought. It made no great difference if these few items vanished from Iba's baggage. When she thought of the way he had played around with her for three years, she still felt a huge surge of anger. She believed it would have been all right if she had stolen everything.

The next day, through the kindness of the proprietor of the Hotei Inn, Yukiko was able to rent the old storage shed belonging to a kitchenware dealer in the neighborhood. The dealer had built a new shed right alongside his house. It was about thirty meters square. A roll of new tin-plate was being stored there. There was just one window, in the ceiling, and no water or electricity. The kitchenware dealer kindly put down two old tatami mats. For a woman sleeping alone, this was enough. Now that she had found a room where she could live by herself, Yukiko suddenly wanted to see Tomioka again. She sold one of the futons to the Hotei Inn and used the money to buy pots and pans and a portable clay cooking stove. For the first time, she was also able to buy almost two liters of rice and a small amount of charcoal on the black market. Steaming the rice in the new, metallic-smelling aluminum pot, she put the remaining embers into the heater for the table over the *kotatsu* (sunken hearth). As she ate the hot, steaming rice with a raw egg broken over it, Yukiko experienced the pleasure of cooking for oneself. After she had eaten her fill of the white, polished rice, she sat for a while, doing nothing, at the *kotatsu*, and a loneliness that would not be satisfied by food alone began to spread through her. Counting the seams in the quilt, she looked at the wall made of roughly cut wood. The flame of the candle wavered in the draft that came in through the chinks between the boards. Sometimes it almost went out. Bleak and forlorn, Yukiko wondered how long she would be able to endure this kind of solitary existence. The bucket of water that she had pumped earlier stood coldly in a corner. That it was possible to live on this little gave Yukiko a certain measure of happiness. But it was an unreliable happiness that was no help in understanding what to do tomorrow.

The next morning it was raining.

Yukiko got up late and went out to mail a letter to Tomioka and to stop at the public bathhouse. On the way back, she stopped at the station and bought a newspaper. She tried opening it to the Help Wanted columns, but all the advertisements seemed to be for typists. On the one hand, she thought that she would like to start working somewhere tomorrow, and on the other she lacked even the energy to look through the ads. She spent the whole day dozing in the dark shed.

She spent four or five days this way. Tomioka still did not come. She realized that he had probably returned from Nagano, but she wondered if perhaps her letter had not reached him.

She decided to go to Shinjuku and walk around a little. It was evening, and a cold wind was blowing. Most of the roadside stalls had already shut down, so the area felt deserted. Yukiko tried to walk along briskly, as if she were on an errand, and at the same time she started to think about what she should do from this point on. She was not averse to going back to Shizuoka, but now that she had managed to find a place to live, maybe she should try taking care of her own needs there for a while. She had walked as far as the Isetan department store when a tall foreigner called out to her. He asked where she was going, and on the spur of the moment she smiled and stopped. He began walking alongside her. Yukiko became bold and adventurous. The foreigner had begun speaking rapidly. Yukiko silently drew near him. She had the sense now that her fate was advancing toward a destination.

The foreigner leaned over every so often to touch Yukiko's face before continuing to chatter away. Yukiko, recalling the time when she had spoken a mixture of French and English with the Annamese, was able to come up with a sentence here and there.

"We are just walking, with no place," Yukiko ventured.

"That's all right. I was walking along myself with nowhere to go."

At some point, she had linked her arm through his. Although there was nothing to laugh at, Yukiko raised her voice and laughed away as if she were drunk.

Arm in arm with the foreigner, Yukiko entered Shinjuku Station and boarded an unusual national railway train reserved for foreigners. Overawed by the splendid surroundings, Yukiko shrank into herself and clung to the man's arm.

Yukiko took the foreigner back to her miserable shed. He was so tall that his head nearly touched the ceiling. He clumsily inserted his long legs under the quilt of the fireless *kotatsu* and gazed wonderingly about him. In the faint, wavering candlelight, Yukiko started to kindle a fire in the portable clay oven. The smoke swirled densely, hanging heavily in the air of the shed. Yukiko, pointing at the skylight, commanded the foreigner, in English, "Window get up." Obligingly, the foreigner opened the skylight. The cloud of smoke was quickly drawn upward and out.

20

THE NEXT AFTERNOON, the foreigner came to see her again. He entered the low-ceilinged shed, toting a green Boston bag. He opened it up and pulled out a series of gifts one by one, talking rapidly the whole time. He set out a big pillow, a heavy little box, rations, and candy. The little box was a battery-powered radio. When he turned the dial, sweet dance music flowed out. Putting the little radio to her ear, Yukiko showed a childlike happiness. It seemed to her that a new transcendental fate flowed out from the tone color of the music. True, they did not speak one another's languages well, but there was a sense of common humanity, an ease of spirit in which they understood one another in the flesh. Yukiko felt as if she had gained the self-confidence to set forth in life, afraid of nothing. Resting her head on the clean pillow slip, Yukiko grew tearful.

She thought that the sensibility of a man who brought her a pillow was beautiful.

> My dearly beloved, now it has withered,
> but this flower that yesterday was the color of lapis lazuli,
>   bright and vivid,
> today is like a pleasant memory, telling me of past days
>   spent with you.

The foreigner said his name was Joe. Quietly humming the song with the radio, the foreigner said she should learn the words by the next time he came. He wrote them out on a scrap of paper and handed it to Yukiko. Slowly going over each word, Yukiko learned the pronunciation and tried singing the song aloud. She was struck by the magnanimous spirit of this American soldier. His was not an island spirit like that of the Japanese but something broader. She felt in him a racial characteristic of acting freely wherever he found himself—something bright and optimistic that was not in Tomioka. There was no loneliness piercing her heart. There was not the intense feeling over something unclear and unfocused. Maybe it was because they were able to act freely that they felt no need to search one another's hearts.

That evening, after Joe left, Yukiko went to the public bathhouse with some soap that he had given her. It was Palmolive, a brand she had bought before, in Saigon. Yukiko had a new self-confidence. She thought it would be pleasant to live this way, rather than with a man who plunged her feelings into disarray. But she was not sure that even simple pleasure could be trusted.

One evening, more than ten days after she'd moved into the shed, Tomioka came by. Thinking that it was Joe, Yukiko went straight to the door. She pulled it open and was very surprised to see Tomioka standing there. Tomioka was surprised too, at the change in Yukiko: her hair gleamed lustrously with oil and was done in an upswept style. She had shaved her eyebrows and applied kohl under her eyes. She was wearing earrings of artificial diamonds, but she had simply thrust her dirty bare feet into a pair of sandals.

"You've moved to an interesting place."

"Well, it may not look like much, but to me it's a palace."

She had covered over the wall with white paper and hung a vase with an arrangement of chrysanthemums from a nail. On a small tea table, a candle flickered. The little box radio was on. The silver foil wrappers of a brightly colored carton of chocolates glittered in the candlelight. Not even sitting down, Tomioka, looking around him, calculated the change in circumstance that she had undergone in the last few days.

"Pretty stylish around here."

"Oh, you think so?"

The radio was playing a dance tune. Looking up at Tomioka as he stood there, Yukiko, like a child caught misbehaving, inserted her legs under the *kotatsu* quilt.

"When did you get back from Nagano?"

"Two days ago."

"Did you get my letter?"

"That's why I came."

"How about coming in under the quilt?"

Pushing his hat back on his head, Tomioka plunked himself down and put his legs under the quilt. The big white pillow was unpleasantly conspicuous, in the place where Joe always sat. Tomioka fixed his gaze on the pillow.

"You seem happy."

"Do I? All I know is I haven't starved to death yet."

Tomioka fell silent and just looked at Yukiko's face. Illuminated by the light of the candle, her features resembled Niu's. In her face he could see the innate strength that all women seem to possess, as sturdy as the roots of a tree. He felt a mixture of envy and jealousy as he stared at Yukiko and took in her new way of living. She seemed to be influenced by no one. Far from thinking of Yukiko as an encumbrance, he was starting to feel a renewed hunger for her.

"I envy you." He spoke without really thinking.

"What are you talking about? What's enviable about this kind of life? Do you just keep changing your mind about everything?"

"No, and I'm sorry if I've offended you. It was just the way I felt. If things are going badly, it's easy to envy other people."

"You're making a fool of me. Men are all like you. Japanese men are selfish through and through. They only think of their own convenience."

Tomioka picked up the little box radio and spun the dial around any number of times. Yukiko went outside. Thinking that if Joe were to come, she would ask him to stay away tonight, Yukiko stood outside the station for a while. But even after thirty minutes, Joe had still not appeared. Yukiko went to buy a beer bottle filled with rotgut sake and returned to the shed. Tomioka was drowsing at the *kotatsu*, his head down. Seen from behind, the man cast a curiously thin shadow. Utterly gone was the masculine power of the man who had lived in Dalat.

"I've brought some sake. Do you want some?"

"Are you treating me?"

Exchanging the candle with one she'd bought, Yukiko filled two glasses to the brim. She touched her lips to her glass.

"How is your work going?"

"It's not really going the way I want it to. I'm going to sell the house and risk everything."

"How is your family?"

"My aunt has a house in Urawa. Everyone's moved there. I'm going to try on my own. I can no longer depend on other people's money."

"That sounds very difficult."

"You're very formal tonight. I admire how calm you are, carrying everything off in style."

"Are you being sarcastic?"

Yukiko decided that she didn't care if Joe came tonight or not. Not knowing what would happen tomorrow, living in what amounted to a shack—this was her real life. Yukiko looked closely at Tomioka's face. He had a dusty, old smell that was almost pathetic. Yukiko began to realize just how much people could change with circumstances. She felt as if she had found a new spiritual pride, and for the first time found herself looking down on Tomioka.

Tomioka had managed to raise a little money. Fumbling in his inside pocket, he drew out an envelope of money and nonchalantly tossed it onto the *kotatsu* coverlet.

'It's just a little, but I thought you might need it."

Yukiko, looking at the brown paper packet, did not appear particularly moved.

"Since returning to Japan, it's taken me some time, but I've come gradually to understand various things. I understand now that Japan really did lose the war. And so, because of that, I don't really hold anything against you, Tomioka-san."

Yukiko added some charcoal to the portable clay oven and grilled some squid. When it was done, she put it on a plate and tore it into small pieces. She felt that the room was made cheerful, with the fragrant aroma of the roasted seafood. Even the aroma seemed to say, I'm living my life well. How about you?

The ground trembled as a train roared by. Yukiko got up to lock the door.

"What if we'd stayed in Dalat and lived out our lives there?" Tomioka asked.

"I think it's good that we came back, after all. Even if we had stayed on in Dalat, we wouldn't have been happy. To live there with no money, as the people of a defeated country, I don't know that we could have stood it. Here, on the other hand, we are just suffering like everybody else."

Perhaps it was so. But thinking over her own words, Yukiko felt that they were not completely honest. Maybe the problem was that people always tried to say that things were going well, no matter what. She thought dispiritedly of the brave front she'd put up since returning to Japan.

Tomioka, drawing the radio to him, fiddled with the dial, turning it to a new program. But the news was gloomy.

As if unable to bear listening, Tomioka switched the radio off. He said, as if he'd just thought of it, "Apparently Kano has come back."

"Really? When?"

"Recently, when I met a friend from the Tottori Forestry Bureau, he told me."

"My! Is that so? Is he well?"

"Would you like to see him?"

"Yes, I would. Kano-san, at least, is a good man, an honest man."

"You're right."

When she heard that Kano had come back, Yukiko realized that he had been the indispensable third party in the relationship between herself and Tomioka. Abruptly there was a knock on the door. Quickly getting to her feet, Yukiko opened it and went outside. Joe was standing there. Making as if to push Joe away, Yukiko told him that some relatives had come from the country today and asked him to please make it tomorrow. She escorted him as far back as the station.

Tomioka felt oppressed by the sounds of the English they were speaking at the door. He wanted to know how it was that Yukiko had gotten to know a foreigner. Looking at the large white pillow, he began to feel the strength to finally break with her. After about an hour, she returned.

"I was in the way, wasn't I?"

"It's all right. I sent him back."

"How did you get to know him?"

"It doesn't matter, does it? He's lonely too. It's the same feeling you had for Niu."

"Don't talk about that."

"I want to be different from now on."

"That's so. That's good. I'm not saying a word against it."

"He's young, and he's kind. He even teaches me songs."

"I see."

"He's a very good person. He's going back to his own country in two months or so."

"So then you'll look for someone else?"

"Well, that's an unpleasant thing to say . . . He's a person I met when I could have gone either way, between life and death. That's probably what you think of women, though, isn't it?"

The candle had gone out, but the light coming from the skylight was quite bright. Yukiko lit a match and reached for the candle.

"Have you been trying to say that now would be a good time to pull out?"

Yukiko seemed to be getting angry, so Tomioka, downing the remainder of the sake, took off his hat and set it on the tatami. He didn't feel like going back home. His drunkenness gave him a temporary courage. The strength to toss aside convention swelled up inside him.

"May I stay tonight?"

"Didn't you come with the intention of staying?"

"Yes, I did."

"You're lying. You suddenly wanted to stay, right? I understand. I've become slightly more intelligent, you know."

"If you don't want me to stay, that's fine, I won't. You're getting all riled up. I can't handle you."

Yukiko began fiddling with the dial of the radio, and Tomioka said emphatically, "Turn on something foreign. Isn't there some dance music? Japanese programs depress me. We don't have to listen to it, do we? Turn it off."

The radio was broadcasting the war-crime tribunals. Spitefully, Yukiko set the radio on top of the *kotatsu*. Tomioka seemed to lose his temper— he switched off the radio and set it aside roughly on the floorboards.

"What are you doing?"

"I don't want to listen to it."

"You should, though. It concerns all of us. They're talking about us. That's your problem—you don't want to think about such things."

Yukiko put her lips to her glass and glared at Tomioka. The furious seas that they had ridden during the war had calmed now to this abject flatness with not a single wave in sight. Tomioka took off his smelly socks and lay down in his overcoat. Ignoring the big, white, plump pillow, he rested his head on his arm instead.

"After all," Yukiko said, "we aren't going to get far on your efforts, are we? If we can't live together, I'll have to make my own living. I hope you can resign yourself to that."

"I won't stand in your way. But it's all right if I come over occasionally, isn't it?"

"No! You were in the way tonight, even."

"In the way of your business?"

"So, is that how you feel about it? You always want to be the good boy and stand on the sidelines, smirking at other people's weak points, don't you? Kano-san and I were caught in that trap of yours."

"Are you saying I deceived you?"

Yukiko didn't answer. She realized that their feelings were not equal, and that she had been the one who loved more passionately. She said, "I was in love with you. That was the problem, wasn't it? I'm a nuisance."

Yukiko spit out a piece of squid she'd been chewing on and tossed it into the portable clay oven. It smoldered and smoked there, in the blue flame of the fire.

Late that evening, Tomioka went home. Holding her breath, Yukiko listened to Tomioka's steps recede into the distance. She pushed open the door and went outside. The sky was dusted with stars, and frost glittered on the road. Passing the back of the darkened marketplace, Yukiko ran toward the station. Tomioka was nowhere to be seen.

Yukiko made her way back to the shed. In the deserted room, the third candle had now burned down to a stump and was flickering. Yukiko felt remorse at all the things she'd said. She had not meant to blame Tomioka alone. But the things she'd said had seemed to make him feel worse and worse. He had slowly put his socks on and gotten to his feet. Yukiko had looked up at him, startled. She wanted him to stay, so her loneliness would be shared. But she could not hold him back with her words.

Yukiko blew out the candle. She sat at the *kotatsu*, pulling the quilt over her. She wrapped her arms around herself and cried.

21

TOMIOKA RETURNED HOME, but he could not get the disagreeable parting with Yukiko out of his mind. Apparently Kuniko had stayed up late, packing. If he had to sell the house in which they had lived so long, it would have been better for it to have burned down. It would have been a refreshing, clean break, Tomioka thought.

Everything that had constituted his familiar surroundings was vanishing. For a person improvising his life from day to day, even this much family was oppressive and suffocating. Yukiko's way of living, on the other hand, was enviable. Yet it also seemed quite sad. His weakness was that he was unable to stand behind this woman and shelter her. He needed to meet with her again soon and break with her more formally, he thought. Meeting in this furtive manner would not lead to any conclusion. He felt that since returning to Japan, he had for the first time observed the subtle workings of a woman's heart. Yet there was no denying that his emotions had changed. Occasionally, infected by its environment, the human soul could change utterly. Tomioka thought that although it would be well if they parted like this, it was not too late to meet one more time and speak with her.

Toward dawn, Yukiko had a dream about the official residence at Dalat. In it, she and Kano were sitting on the veranda, in each other's arms.

Even after she awoke, the memory of a day when they had all gone to see the tea plantation at Aurpuru Proi came back to her. It was New Year's Day, and upper-class Annamese, wearing black jackets and white silk trousers, went to a church halfway up the low hill of Hontore. The hamlet of Hontore, surrounded by great forests, was beautiful and picturesque.

The area was red earth of basaltic origin. It sat sixteen hundred meters above sea level and had a temperature range of from twenty-five to six degrees Celsius, All this, Tomioka had explained to her and Kano-san, made it a good place to grow tea. Perhaps because the temperatures here in the uplands tended to remain low, the trees grew sideways much faster than they grew upward, he said. Yukiko, wearing a white dress trimmed with lace, walked along the paths of the spacious plantation, leaning on Tomioka's arm. Kano stopped now and then, and looked around with an unhappy expression.

"I've been feeling sick. I think I'm going to have a nosebleed."

"What's the matter? Is something wrong?"

Both Tomioka and Yukiko stopped and looked at him.

"What's the matter, Kano-san?"

"Yukiko-san, you're awful. Did you bring me out here just to make a fool of me?"

"What are you talking about?"

At that, Kano said, with a strange smile, "I would rather that you not be arm in arm with Tomioka."

Flustered, Yukiko took her arm from Tomioka's.

Tomioka burst into loud laughter. The Annamese guide, startled by Tomioka's laughter and thinking that perhaps he had made some mistake in his explanation, looked uneasy.

The three of them began walking again, this time with a healthy distance between each person.

"We plant the healthy seedlings after eighteen months have passed. We weed them, and we fertilize them five or six times a year with thirty kilograms of nitrogen, forty kilograms of phosphoric acid, and fifty kilograms of potassium as our standard per hectare. Fertilization is done every other year. We pick the leaves two years after planting. We make back our operating expenses for the cultivation of the tea crop beginning in the sixth or seventh year. When ten years have passed, the plants achieve their maximum yield . . ."

As she listened to the guide's explanation, Yukiko began to feel afraid of the continental spirit of the French, who, over a long period of years, showed constant devotion to the cultivation of tea. The long history of these tea fields that had been carefully managed for so many years made her feel ashamed of the high-handed tactics that the Japanese had used to take over everything—even these fields—in a short amount of time. She obviously lacked sensitivity herself if Kano needed to come right out and ask her not to walk arm in arm with Tomioka. It did not seem to Yukiko that the Japanese would be able to inhabit French Indochina for long. As a matter of fact, she sensed that, in some form or other, a terrible retribution was coming.

"Even though the soldiers of the Imperial Army have pushed their way in here," Tomioka said, "Japan will not be able to take over these vast tea and quinine plantations in a day. The most we can do is steal them, ruin them, and spit them out."

Kano did not answer but simply ripped the official ivory badge from the chest of the Annamese guide and then pinned it on his own chest instead. Yukiko was not sure what to make of the scene. That was the night she was stabbed in the arm by the drunken Kano.

That day too was now part of the past. And the Japanese, who had been rushing across that beautiful country, had been chased back to Japan.

It served us right, Yukiko thought. She opened her eyes wide and gazed through the skylight at the dark, cloudy skies.

Yukiko was fiddling with the dial of the radio when there was a knock on the door. She was not expecting any early-morning callers, so she thought it might be someone from the Hotei Inn. When she stood up and opened the door, she was surprised to see Iba, with a furious expression on his face, standing there. A maid from the Hotei Inn had followed him but had already retreated halfway back along the alley.

"I thought this would happen."

Removing his shoes, Iba stepped briskly up into the shed. Yukiko could not think of a thing to say.

"You probably didn't think I'd come after you like this, did you? You certainly have changed."

"Don't talk so loud."

"Don't tell me how to talk."

"Why are you so angry?"

"Doesn't it figure that I'd be angry? I located the forwarding agency. Am I not supposed to be angry, when you rob from me, and then sell my possessions on to a hotel? I hear you're a prostitute these days."

Yukiko's lips were paralyzed with anger. Iba's aggressive attitude disgusted her.

"I couldn't help it. I have to live. Anyway, what's a futon to you?"

"You mean if you don't have a futon, you can't make any money?"

"Well, what did you expect me to do? And keep your voice down. Even if I do have a futon of yours, is that so bad? What about the way you treated me as a plaything for three years? If you want it, just take it."

"It's dirty, but I'll take it. Once I've laundered it, I can use it again. It's a valuable item."

Iba took out a pack of cigarettes and put one between his lips. Looking around for a match, he smiled cynically at the radio and the big pillow. When she saw his smug expression, Yukiko felt something flare up in her chest. He could think whatever he liked. She didn't want him sitting here one more minute, though. Iba said casually, "Your business seems to be going pretty well. You seem to have some nice things. How about it? You've hit on a nice line of work here, eh? If you give me a cut, I'll lend you the futon for the time being."

Yukiko was silent. Why had the men around her turned out so vulgar and broken-down?

"So you must have some connections from all this. Don't you get cigarettes and clothes and whatnot from it?"

"What are you talking about? Please take your futon and go. I don't need anything."

Yukiko began to cry, not caring how she looked to him. It was dreadful just to see Iba's face there in her room. Iba pulled the radio toward him and turned the dial. The music of a samisen flowed into the room.

"Oh? This works on batteries? Very convenient."

Iba removed the back cover of the radio. There were lots of little vacuum tubes lined up in a row, like toys. Yukiko, standing, looked down on them. Then, she reached down, took off the tabletop, and pulled up Iba's futon, which she had been using as a coverlet. She folded it briskly and thrust it down at Iba.

"Well, you don't have to hand it over right this minute."

It was as if she'd been cursed by this little radio since the day before. At the sound of the samisen, Yukiko felt lonely.

"By the way, I've brought along sixty or seventy pounds of dried sweet potatoes—would you know a place where I can sell them?" Iba spoke while putting the cover back on the radio. Yukiko didn't answer. How should she know of a place to sell dried sweet potatoes?

"This radio must have been expensive."

"It's not mine."

"I wonder if we couldn't do something like this in Japan, and take out a new patent on it. I think I might be able to make some money out of this . . ."

Iba held the radio up right next to his ear and listened to the notes of the samisen.

22

TOMIOKA WANTED TO MEET YUKIKO one more time, so he sent her a letter by special delivery. He didn't want to meet at her place. He had no desire to sit there again, feeling intimidated. He asked her to meet at the Yotsuya-mitsuke railway station, letting her know the day and time.

The day, when it did arrive, was rainy. Christmas also had passed. But people didn't seem to mind the rain, perhaps because they were busy getting ready for the New Year's holiday.

Tomioka waited at the station for about ten minutes. People of every social class busily came and went through the turnstiles as he watched. For no particular reason, he began to feel a kind of despair. He had sometimes had this same feeling in Indochina. It was a sense of unease, of not knowing what to do next. He could feel it settle in his heart.

Tomioka nervously tapped the toe of his shoe on the pavement and looked up the sloping street. A wet mongrel staggered along the gleaming pavement. It seemed to be wandering around in search of someone.

Looking at his watch, Tomioka thought, She's not coming. He decided that he would wait just a little longer. He tried whistling to the dog. The dog turned quickly in the direction of the whistle and gazed at Tomioka.

Then it gave a melancholy look, as if to say, That's not the right person, and trotted off, toward some roadside shrubbery.

"Were you waiting long?"

Yukiko came to his side and bumped against his shoulder as he stood under the eaves of the station.

"I was thirty minutes late, so I thought that you probably wouldn't be here. I was thinking of going back."

Yukiko, her head wrapped in a red silk scarf tied tightly under her chin, looked up at him with a lively expression. The idea that she had thought of simply going home because she herself was late seemed presumptuous and far too casual. He felt that he was being manipulated. The time to separate had come, he thought.

Tomioka started to walk. Following him, Yukiko stepped straight into a puddle. Tomioka walked briskly ahead, but the whole time he was imagining Yukiko's face as she splashed through the puddles behind him. He felt that she would be a good companion to share his loneliness. Yet he felt dogged by a sense of guilt about even walking along with her.

But with absolutely nothing to his name, Tomioka was not sure that he could continue to endure this new reality. Even the soul within him that usually gave him comfort was now filled with an empty desperation. He lacked the self-confidence to go on living.

It occurred to him that the two of them could commit suicide together. He recalled an incident in which a young Japanese had eloped with a foreign woman. When they learned that they were being pursued, they had drunk poison at a suburban railway station.

The incident demonstrated the separate and isolated condition of human beings, who are like so many floating clouds.

With nowhere to go, the two of them wandered as far as the municipal railway station.

"It's so cold. Shall we go have tea somewhere?"

"Hm."

"You seem unhappy."

"Unhappy?"

"Yes."

"That's only because you've been saying such unpleasant things."

"Yes, you're right. And then of course, when we're alone, we go over these things we said, again and again. I am becoming less sensitive, I'm afraid."

"Do you think so? And yet you seem so relaxed and happy."

"Really? That's surprising. I don't feel the least bit relaxed. You yourself have changed completely. You know? I think I've come to the point where I have no idea what's ahead for me."

Tomioka stood in the rainy street and looked down the beautiful avenue of trees within the grounds of the former crown prince's palace. It was not clear now to what use even this building would be put. The entire estate was striking: beyond the iron palisade, the pale gray structure of the palace was wrapped in dark masses of trees that gave off a smokelike mist.

Tomioka walked dejectedly along the street, Yukiko now at his side.

"Back then, you and I were good people. We were just our real selves, living naturally."

"Hm. But who knows if what we had was real happiness. Here, look at this palace. In some way it's more beautiful now, now that it's lost everything. No one knows what it will even be used for. But once it was a palace. There's a vestigial charm that lingers over it. Somehow it's very moving."

Yukiko looked up vaguely at the earthen wall of the palace. The place gave off a faint odor of mud. She was not sure she could follow Tomioka's feelings to the same conclusion, but certainly she too felt the sadness of things. The rain and cold, especially, gave the scene a certain melancholy. An expensive, cobalt blue car went by swiftly just then, its tires sending up a spray of rain.

Tomioka wanted Yukiko to become his companion on the road to death naturally, of her own accord, without him forcing her into it.

The people of this lonely country had been nailed up on crosses, Tomioka thought. No matter what the war, defeat itself seemed a sad and pitiable end. Tomioka envied the simple fighting spirit that he had observed in women, and he was irritated by their easy flow of feeling. He looked down at Yukiko as she walked along beside him. What was frightening was that not just this woman, but also all women, had come through the long suffering of the war without, apparently, a single mental scar.

"Where are we walking to?"

"Are you tired?"

"I can't bear walking in this rain. I'm going to catch a cold."

"We could go to Akasaka and then from there by trolley to Shibuya."

"All right. So what was it you wanted to talk about?"

'Talk about? Oh, nothing especially."

"Changing your mind again, I see."

"No, I just wanted to see you."

"You're a smooth talker. So, you wanted to meet me? Not the first time I've heard those sorts of affectionate words."

"Is that all that women think about—affectionate words?"

"I would say so."

Tomioka could not bear the way these conversations went. No matter how often they met, there was never any result. Yet it was strange even to Tomioka—this shallow, selfish desire to drag Yukiko, who knew nothing, into his egotism, wanting to make her his companion in death. He seemed to himself a deceitful person.

23

IN SHIBUYA, they went into a Chinese restaurant under the girders of the railway overpass. They sat down facing each other, alongside a charcoal briquette hibachi. The blue flames gave out puffs of air through the lotus-hole vent. In a corner of the empty room, where there were no other customers, three waitresses in shabby white coats stood idly waiting.

Yukiko held her hands over the hibachi and set her muffler on the wire netting to dry.

The waitress came by to take their order, and Tomioka asked for chow mein.

"We'd like a bottle of sake as well," he added.

Yukiko, grinning, took out a pack of Western cigarettes from her green plastic handbag and made Tomioka take one. Tomioka took a long drag on his cigarette, with obvious relish, but still he felt fatigued from wandering around in the rain. He had asked her to meet him, but now he could think of nothing in particular to talk about.

"When are you moving?"

"My folks have moved out. I'll be celebrating New Year's in an empty house."

"Oh? All alone?"

"Well, my wife will probably stay."

"Ah, quite the ladies' man."

Yukiko's disappointment showed. Presently, the sake was brought.

"I know where Kano is staying," Tomioka said. "Do you want to see him?"

"Oh, you know his address? Where is he?'

Taking out a small notebook, Tomioka riffled through the pages. He wrote out Kano's address in pencil on the back of his own business card and handed it to Yukiko.

"He's in Odawara?"

"Yeah, I hear he's staying with his mother. Apparently he's still single."

Yukiko's eyes blazed in response to Tomioka's thoughtless remark. Nostalgia and a desire to meet Kano as he was when they separated in Indochina flamed up in her.

The sake was warming. Yukiko drank two or three cups along with Tomioka. He said, "It's just three days from now, huh?"

"What is?"

"New Year's."

"Oh, right. New Year's? I hadn't even thought about it.'

"What do you think? Should we go, right now, someplace far away, like Ikaho or Nikko?'

"Hmm, I've never been to Ikaho, but it sounds good. I'd like to soak in a bubbling hot spring for a while. Can we really go?"

"If it's just for one or two nights, we can go. Do you want to?'

They were adrift anyway, so what did it matter if they went wherever their trivial human emotions took them, Tomioka thought. He wanted, when it came down to it, to end his life with Yukiko in the mountains, surrounded by bare winter trees.

Tomioka watched Yukiko as she hungrily ate her chow mein. Gilt earrings trembled in her little earlobes. Her black hair was cut short at the neck.

"Isn't it cold at Ikaho?"

"It'll be nice even if it's cold."

"That's true."

They were like a newlyweds making plans for their honeymoon. Yukiko, with a buoyant expression, put the card with Kano's address written on it into her handbag. Casually taking out her compact, she checked her reflection in the small mirror.

Tomioka was fantasizing the scene in which he killed her. She was bathed in blood, just like a character in a silent movie. The audacity that allowed him to entertain these thoughts was exhilarating. I'll kill her. I'll also die, right on top of her. No one will have any reason to reproach us. Ordering a second flask of sake, Tomioka absentmindedly gazed at Yukiko's flat-planed face as she applied her makeup. Was this a face desired by foreigners? The thought seemed very odd to Tomioka. It was a vulgar face. Flattish, jowly, a mediocre face with no redeeming features. Only, when one looked at it closely, it was almost a primitive face. The forehead, the eyebrows, the area around the eyes were like an image of Buddha.

"Is it all right if you stay out?"

"Yes, I locked up when I came out. Even if someone comes, they'll just think I'm away."

"Did Iba come to take the quilt?"

"Oh, you got my letter? That's right. So now I'm sleeping with a blanket."

She seemed cheerful enough, though. Yukiko took up the flask of sake and poured some into Tomioka's cup. Tomioka drank, occasionally eating some scallions and bamboo shoots that he'd scattered over the chow mein as relishes. How petty and to be pitied was this day-to-day existence. The actions people performed were nothing but a series of farces. Timidly, furtively, human beings lived out their lives in petty farces. Morality too was a farce. It might be that at the edge of death people would finally wake up, with a start. Then, for the first time, true tears might flow.

Tomioka carried out his plan to take Yukiko to Ikaho. They arrived late at night and were taken by the hotel car to a hotel called the Kindayu. The town was full of steep hills, and the hotel was at the top of a hill as narrow as an alleyway. The fusty smell of the hot springs water was everywhere. Yukiko walked along, peering wide-eyed into the houses on both sides of the sloping road. Ikaho was surprisingly simple, a very romantic place. They had arrived late at night, and the sound of the water and the wind from the mountain felt especially cold on their skin. When they entered their room at the back of the inn, they saw that a large *kotatsu* had been installed and a board laid over it. Yukiko put her legs in beneath the quilt cover. They warmed up quickly.

"What a nice place. How did you know about it? Have you been here before?" Yukiko spoke in a coquettish tone.

"I came when I was a student."

"Such a nice place. It's just like Dalat. If I had some money, I'd like to stay here forever."

"But you'd get tired of it if you stayed for a long time. Two days is probably the most you can enjoy it."

"Yes, maybe so."

The room was small, but there seemed to be a stream running below the window; they could hear a murmuring sound of water. A maid entered, bringing tea and dried persimmons. Small chrysanthemums were arranged in a basket-shaped bamboo vase hung in the ornamental alcove, together with a lithograph landscape scroll. The room was commonplace, but they were on a journey and had come to a hot springs town. Perhaps that was why the loneliness Tomioka had felt earlier in the day had lifted. Despair was real, but it was also true that dark moods lifted and gave way to more pragmatic concerns. His thoughts of suicide were beginning to seem ridiculous, even to him. In order to die with Yukiko, he had deliberately sought out a stage for a very theatrical death. Meanwhile, in the ocean of the entire universe, this incident was nothing but a fleeting speck of foam. Tomioka, still wearing his overcoat, had his legs sprawled under the *kotatsu* quilt. Resting his head on one arm, he stared up at the sooty ceiling.

The maid entered again, saying, "Would you like to change into a padded kimono?" She set down a pile of kimonos and other items. Yukiko, quickly changing in the next room, asked the maid for a hand towel. Tomioka thought it was too much trouble even to take a bath. Just moving his body was a bore and a chore. If he could pass out just like this, he would have liked to have sunk into the depths of the earth, then and there.

"Aren't you changing?"

"Well . . ."

"Let's change and order supper right away. I'm starved."

"It's too much bother. Let me rest a while. Why don't you take a bath?"

Yukiko, tossing her discarded clothes into a corner of the room, came over to the side of the *kotatsu*. Sniffing at the sleeve of her padded kimono, she said, irritably, "I can smell other people in this . . ."

24

TOMIOKA WAS RATHER DRUNK. For the first time in so long, his heart felt at ease and liberated. Leaning against the alcove post, he sang in Annamese:

> Your love and my love
> That first day only, were real
> Your eyes were true eyes
> My eyes, too, that day only
> That hour only, were true eyes
> Now, both yours and mine
> Are eyes of doubt

It was a popular folk song. Yukiko was becoming rather drunk too. As she followed the dimly remembered song, she felt a deep longing for the life they had led in Dalat.

Yukiko stretched out a leg and felt around with it for Tomioka's leg beneath the *kotatsu* quilt. She located the sole of his foot.

"Tomioka-san, I do wish you well. Now and then, when you think back on our time in Dalat, please give me a call. All right? I've resigned myself now. It will be enough if we can meet like this when we have a chance. That will be good. Our story is like that song . . . I understand."

Tomioka, closing his eyes, quietly hummed the Annamese song. Yukiko stood up for a moment, went over to Tomioka's side, and slid her legs under the coverlet, right beside his. Even so, Tomioka kept humming, without opening his eyes.

"What are you thinking about? Let me in on it. Please, just half of what you're thinking."

Tomioka opened his eyes.

Yukiko was adorable. The woman's words, coming straight from the heart, were like a rainbow appearing in the sky. Tomioka, feeling drawn to her, took her fingers and put them to his lips.

Suddenly she cried out, "I'm lonely, lonely."

He was taken aback by her sudden loss of self-control. A woman's heart, he could only suppose, was carried along on the flow of the moment, like the flow of water beneath the window,

He started thinking of methods of suicide. He considered what might be the best way to kill the woman and then artfully dispose of himself afterward. Two lovers at a hot spring—after their deaths, no one would be small-minded enough to wonder whether it had in fact been a double suicide. That also would be just as well, he thought.

The electric lamp was reflected in the large red tray on top of the *kotatsu* that held the remains of their dinner. On the red lacquer, little pines had been engraved in gold. These were some of the last things that he would see . . . The thought made everything look lonely and beautiful.

He noticed that the rain had cleared.

Yukiko said, "How is your business coming?"

"Business?"

"Yes, your lumber deals."

"Oh, that? I'm sure it'll work out somehow."

"Have you sold your house yet?"

"Yeah, I did. I've already gotten half the money. Next year I'll register the sale, and by the end of January I'll vacate the house and hand it over."

"How much did you get for it?"

"Does it matter?"

"No, but it's all right to ask, isn't it?"

Now she was over her temporary hysterics, Yukiko stared intently at Tomioka. How on earth had she been drawn to this kind of man? It was funny even to her. They were like two people who simply met from time to time. She stood and went down to the bath area again, taking her towel with her.

When she'd descended the narrow stairs and gone in, there were two young women already sitting in the bath. They had long, disheveled permanent waves and were chattering away quite loudly.

The reddish muddy water lapped over the tiles along the edges of the bath. Yukiko silently dipped one leg into it, near where the two women were sitting. Perhaps because she was drunk, her legs were wobbly, and she first staggered, then jumped, with a great splash, into the water. As the spray flew up, the two women glared at her, leaping aside in an exaggerated way. Clicking their tongues, the two started for the edge of the bath.

"I'm sorry," Yukiko said.

The two women did not give her so much as a smile. Irritated by their silence, Yukiko stretched her legs out leisurely in the hot, red water and watched them. Both of the women were from the city, no doubt, but they had big, sturdy hips, like large-boned farm women.

Yukiko, proud of her willowy nakedness, was stirred by an impulse to display herself alongside the two women.

The two women sat down heavily on wooden stools in the rinsing-off area and resumed their conversation.

"When he left, Tami-chan said to him in English, 'Come again.' Because that was the only English phrase she knew. After that, they told her to stop looking for Americans and switch to something like working in an office. And then she immediately began swimming around with the men again, so she was no help. But she said she wouldn't be able, because she couldn't even stand the sight of a Japanese man."

The two broke out into loud snickers.

Ah, so they're that kind of women, Yukiko thought. She cast her mind back to her shack in Ikebukuro. At this moment, perhaps, he had come for a visit and was knocking on the door. The two women, using fragrantly scented soaps, were combing each other's hair with big plastic combs.

The attitude of the two young women—at least to Yukiko's drunken way of thinking—seemed to be challenging her. All but saying, We are of a different order from dirty creatures like you, they flaunted their fashionable large jars of skin lotion and their big towels. Yukiko was using a thoroughly boiled little Japanese hand towel she had borrowed from a maid at the inn and a cake of soap that had an unpleasant, fishy smell.

"When I go back tomorrow, I'm going to a Western clothes store. Do you want to come with me? I just got a bright red suit there, with gold buttons on it."

"Oh, really! And did your 'sweetheart' have it made for you?"

"That's right. You know how generous he is."

Yukiko giggled. One of the women, her lips painted scarlet, glanced over and said, "What are you laughing at?"

"What? I was just laughing to myself about something I remembered. That's all."

"Hm! I think you're laughing at us. Even though it was you who was drunk and came crashing into the bath."

"I said I was sorry."

The other woman chimed in, "Being drunk doesn't give you license to snoop in other people's affairs."

The pair grabbed their things and headed for the dressing room.

"She's wearing earrings in the bath, and using a dirty towel—what sort of person is she, anyway?"

"Isn't that obvious?"

She could hear the two of them snickering. Yukiko, splashing up the hot water, sang in a loud voice:

> Your love and my love
> That first day only
> Were true . . .

She sang in Annamese. Unexpectedly, her voice was soft and voluptuous. The laughter stopped.

> Your eyes were true eyes
> My eyes, too, that day only
> That hour only, were true eyes
> Now, both yours and mine
> Are eyes of doubt

As she sang, Yukiko had a wild, ravaged feeling, as if at the utmost bounds of debauchery.

25

TOMIOKA AND YUKIKO whiled away two days in Ikaho. It rained on both days. As might be expected, on New Year's Eve there were no other guests. The large inn was hushed and deserted. Despite their leisure, Tomioka was unable to come to a better understanding of anything or to make a clear decision.

He felt a deep self-distrust, a distrust he suspected was probably shared by everyone who had returned from the war efforts around the world. However, the country as a whole was so small and so densely populated that each person simply responded to the situation by holding himself apart in some way from all others. To pursue any wider truth, in this small, broken country, seemed impossible.

Everyone was being difficult. The members of his family had simply holed up, each in a separate loneliness.

"Do you have a cigarette?"

"No, I don't."

"What are you thinking about? Hey, why don't we spend New Year's here instead? If you're short of money, you can pawn my overcoat. Or this watch. If you're ashamed to, I'll go into town and sell the watch . . ."

So saying, Yukiko picked a cigarette butt out of the ashtray, stuck the little remnant into a Japanese pipe, and lit it.

Tomioka, lying on his stomach at the *kotatsu*, had been rereading yesterday's newspaper. Now he turned around and, propping himself on one elbow on the tatami, looked up into Yukiko's face.

"What?" she said.

"You know, the world has become a pretty terrible place."

"What do you mean? How, exactly?"

Pressed for something more specific, Tomioka felt as if his cheeks had gone numb. Looking hard at Yukiko's un-made-up face, with its wide-open eyes, he said coldly, "Life itself has become a bore."

Yukiko was not quite sure she understood what Tomioka meant.

Playing with a button on Yukiko's shirt that seemed about to come off, Tomioka said, "Our situation is hopeless."

"But I don't know if it's really hopeless. You've certainly touched bottom in your thinking."

"That's one way of putting it. You haven't touched bottom, anyway. You probably still think the world is an interesting place."

"What's so interesting about it?"

"That things have come to this pass . . ."

Little by little, Yukiko began to understand what Tomioka was thinking about. She felt as if sweet tears were about to overflow to the bottom of her throat.

"Shall I try telling you what you're thinking about?"

"No, you don't need to."

"You're thinking about leaving me?"

"No, no, that's not it."

The button came off. Holding it in his fingers, Tomioka lay down on his side in a fetal position, as if he was trying to make his body no bigger than the *kotatsu*.

"Shall I go sell the watch? I would like to spend New Year's here."

White rain streaked the windowpane. Yukiko stood up and slid open the glass-paned door. The mountains and sky were a milky white and streamed with mist.

"It'll be a rainy New Year's."

Shutting the door, Yukiko crept back under the *kotatsu* quilt. Tomioka, abruptly sitting up and placing the button on the top of the coverlet, muttered, to no one in particular, "I've come to want to die."

Yukiko picked up the button and tried placing it against her chest. She heard him but let his words go by. But then, plucking at the bits of thread that remained where the button had been, she said, "I'd like to die too."

"You? Don't just go along like that. You should develop your life in all sorts of new ways. Enjoy life more . . ."

"What do you mean, develop my life? Don't be ridiculous."

"Have you really thought about death? I mean, seriously. It's no good to just lightly say, 'Oh yeah, I want to die too,' if you haven't."

"No, I have thought about it seriously. I've been thinking about it all along. Even at Haiphong, I had the intention of dying. And at Dalat, when that incident happened with Kano-san, that's what I was thinking. I'm not scared of death."

"That just shows how far you are from being able to die. Saying that you're not afraid—that's taking a rose-colored view of death. Death is frightening, and it should be frightening. Unless you allow your mind— bang, just like that—to go blank, you can't die. If you were to decide to die, what method do you think you would choose?"

"They say potassium cyanide is the easiest way, right?"

"And if you wanted to commit suicide and didn't have any?"

"I wouldn't know until the time came, would I? And if I do make my mind blank, I won't be able to think about my method of death, will I?"

"What about a case of two people committing double suicide? If one of them doesn't make their mind a blank, things won't go smoothly, will they?"

"That can't be right. Rather than suddenly going blank, we need to pass through and carry out our plan silently, with our hearts cold. Otherwise, it won't work, will it? If death is frightening, certainly thinking about how to do it is frightening too. So in order to die together, we would need to plan things carefully."

"I've fantasized about climbing Mount Haruna with you and dying there."

"That's funny. I've been thinking about doing that sort of thing lately, too."

In this exchange of their feelings, little by little, the consciousness of death began to take shape—a dusky shadow there in the room with them.

26

ULTIMATELY, THERE WERE TWO STYLES, Tomioka thought: to die in a moment of intense pleasure, or to die in a moment of despair. The way of despair seemed to him like a pretense for the world's benefit. Basically, if someone did choose death, for whatever reason, there was in fact no despair at all in that person's mind.

Beneath the quilt next to him, Yukiko seemed to be having terrible dreams. He listened to her moaning for a while, and then, unable to bear it any longer, he groped about for the ashtray, stubbed out his cigarette, and switched on the light of the paper-covered lamp by his pillow.

"What's the matter?" he said, tugging at Yukiko's pillow. Yukiko flipped over in bed to face him and opened her eyes.

"Oh, I had a bad dream. A strange and frightening dream."

"So it was a nightmare?"

"It was; a horrible one. I was being pursued by a bloody horse whose skin had been flayed. No matter where I fled, he chased me . . . Somehow or other, a person in pale clothes and with no face was riding the horse. Even though I was in such trouble and tried to say, Help me, help me, I couldn't make a sound."

Tomioka stretched his legs out under the *kotatsu* coverlet. Yukiko, looking toward the light and blinking hard, said, "Today is New Year's."

Although it was in fact only three nights, the two had the feeling that they had been living at this inn for a long time. Tomioka felt a deep sense of fate. Were it not for the war, he would not have gone to a distant place such as French Indochina and would probably not have met this woman. By now, he would have been living out the bureaucratic life of a dependable clerk. Gazing at the sooty ceiling—so stained that it looked like a map of the world—he recalled the city of Hue, remembering how, along the road from the railway station into the heart of the city, the buds on the young camphor trees gave the trees a soft, golden hue.

On the promenade along the city's river, the blooms of canna and clematis were as brightly colored as printed silk. Coconuts, betel palms, and sweet osmanthus flourished everywhere. Tomioka remembered the Moi tribesmen, clad only in their red loincloths, lined up along the promenade to sell the two or three parakeets in their cages.

Tomioka's life in Dalat was becoming a single design, like that of a splash-pattern kimono, printed indelibly on his memory.

Monsieur Marcon, the bureau chief of the Forestry Bureau at Hue, had probably returned to that Hue by now and might very well be leisurely smoking a cigar at this moment on the outside balcony. He always seemed to have a good-natured expression—although he must have had unpleasant thoughts about the Japanese Army. Marcon had crossed the seas in 1930 to Indochina as a department chief in the Forestry Bureau. He had graduated from a forestry college in Nancy, France. Although he must have thought of Tomioka and his ignorant colleagues—young men from the countryside with no sense of proper procedure—as comical figures, Marcon always maintained an extraordinarily grand manner, even when he was handing over the bureau. Paying special attention to Tomioka, Marcon used to tell the younger men that they should think of their work with the mountains and forests of Indochina as being akin to grappling with a great tiger. Tomioka and his colleagues, understanding nothing about those mountains and forests and with no background knowledge, had invaded the area on the orders of the military, with the idea, derived from maps alone, that it was a flat region forested sparsely by pines.

When he had been invited to Marcon's residence in Hue, Tomioka was asked whether he knew the names of all the trees in the garden.

He had been unable to identify even the betel palm. The *rimu*, the *tagayasan*, the *bode*, the *kyenkyen*, the *sao*, the *yo*, the *benben*, the banyan—Monsieur Marcon had pointed them out one by one and had described to Tomioka the distribution and distinctive features of each. In the mountainous forests of French Indochina, the rains were heavy and the forests magnificent, Marcon would say. He had been here for a long time, but the research on those mountain forests was still in its infancy. He cautioned Tomioka to be very sure of the nature of a forest before recklessly cutting it down. In particular, the slash-and-burn method of agriculture, as practiced by the aborigines, had significantly altered the condition of the primeval forests. This too needed to be carefully considered. Especially in the provinces of Vinh and Tanoa in northern Annam, Marcon had heard that there had been a great deal of development by the Japanese Army. In the central areas, however, the mountains ran right down into the sea, and in such steep terrain, there were few rivers down which timber could be rafted. Even though trees were felled and the areas developed, it was not easy to come by sufficient means of transport. Only in northern and southern Annam, where the terrain was gentle and gradual, could rafts be conveniently used for transportation. Marcon advised Tomioka to think carefully about that sort of poorly planned exploitation. The enterprise of forestation was something very different from, and opposed to, war, Marcon had said.

"Hey, do you remember, someplace outside Tsuran, when we visited a Japanese cemetery?"

Tomioka, feeling as if he had been wrenched back from his wanderings through the past, turned his eyes from the stains on the ceiling and looked toward Yukiko.

"That town, what was it called?"

"Heio?"

"That's it, Heio," Yukiko said. "Kano-san, me, and you, the three of us went to Heio. It was a three-day trip, right? Kano-san was in a bad mood and kept an eagle eye on us. We managed to escape his surveillance and get together in the dead of the night. We were acting crazy too. Do you remember?

"And the trees along the road were called *fukugi*? They were dense, old-growth trees. When we stopped the car for a rest, some children ran up crying, *tonbos yaponezes*, which apparently meant 'Japanese tombs';

they wanted to take us to see them. The children had no interest in me, because I was a woman. They only chattered away to you, the tall man. On the road to the cemetery, I remember, there were lots of big cactus plants. At one point, I peeked into my compact mirror and thought that it was a shame I hadn't been born a first-class beauty."

27

THREE HUNDRED FIFTY or sixty years ago, many Japanese had lived in Heio. They had come and gone in great numbers, in the ships licensed by the shogunate of the day. They brought red sandalwood, ebony, aloes, cinnamon, and the like to Japan. But later there would be many who were unable to return to Japan because of Japan's new closed-door policy. These people assimilated with the natives of Heio. The tombstones in the cemetery included some with epitaphs, such as "Here Lies Tarobei Tanaka." Yukiko thought that the spirits of the Japanese people centuries ago who had drifted like coconuts on the flowing waters, to all sorts of faraway places, were brave. She felt a certain pathos in these simple epitaphs—for example, "Hanako."

"Heio was a nice place. The roads were narrow," she continued. "Barely wide enough for one automobile to get through. There were rows of whitewashed houses that looked like two matchboxes piled on top of each other. Oh, and there was a little bridge, with a roof over it, that was called Nihonbashi, after the bridge in Tokyo. Kano-san took a picture of it, but he wasn't able to bring the photograph back here. We had it good back then. Nowadays, it would be so expensive to take a trip like that."

"Well, we were punished for it."

"Yes, that's a good way to think of it. By the way, what time is it now, I wonder."

Yukiko, turning over on her stomach, took her watch from the bedside table, and looked at it. It was a little past four in the morning. Although they had been talking so much about death the night before, Yukiko was not thinking about things like that at all now. She felt that committing suicide in a place like this would be foolish. She didn't think that Tomioka had meant what he said, either. Today, she thought, she'd like to sell this watch and go back to Ikebukuro. Their memories of Indochina were a bond between them, but those memories had given rise to very different—even opposed—dreams in each of them.

She was worried about how they were going to pay the bill, which made her think that no matter how long they stayed at Ikaho, it would be impossible to create a romantic mood. She wanted to broach this subject with Tomioka. But he seemed to be feeling quite depressed and to have no inclination to think about how they were going to leave the inn.

"Today's New Year's, isn't it?"

"Yeah."

"Are we going back today?"

"Didn't you say you wanted to stay three or four days? Have you changed your mind?"

"It's not that I've changed my mind, but we seem to have run out of memories to talk about, and besides, I think you're tired of me."

"Maybe it's you who has become tired of me."

"Silly."

Although she said "Silly" in a loud voice, as if to reassure Tomioka, the fact was that Yukiko was looking forward to going to Ikebukuro on her own. She felt that she was being fickle and unfaithful.

"If we want to get anywhere, beyond the life we're living now, we'll need to undergo some hardships," Tomioka said. "Probably you don't care one way or another about getting anywhere. We get together and talk about the old days, but time keeps on passing. Having that kind of conversation is a bad habit to get into. I don't feel the love I did in the past, even for my wife. The war certainly gave us some bad dreams. Nowadays, we try to avoid coming head-on with reality. But the problem is that, apart from reality, there's nowhere to go."

'That's right. That makes sense. But even so, don't you think it's strange that when we part and don't see each other for days, all of a sudden we want to see each other? I'm always thinking about you. Sometimes I hate you, sometimes I love you . . . There's just nothing you can do about other people. Maybe, as time goes by, I won't feel this way so strongly."

The two began to doze off again. Maybe the best thing was to let things take their course. There might be no other way.

They fell into a deep sleep, and when they next awoke, it was quite late in the morning.

In the distance, she could hear a drum being beaten. The sound awakened Yukiko, and she realized Tomioka was not in his bed. She then saw that the sound was coming from a radio. Yukiko got up, pulled her quilted kimono shut, and looked at her watch. It was already a little past ten. The maid came to put fresh coals into the brazier.

"Your husband has gone for a bath," the maid said. Taking the same hand towel that she'd used the night before, Yukiko went along to the bathhouse.

Tomioka had entered the smaller of the two baths. Sliding the glass door partially open, Yukiko peeped inside.

"Can I come in?" Yukiko asked.

"Sure."

Yukiko shed her quilted kimono, roughly slid the glass door open the rest of the way, and descended into the bath area. The reddish hot water was lapping over the edges of the cypress tub. The hot water vapor, densely steamy, filled the narrow bathhouse.

"Happy New Year," Yukiko said.

Tomioka returned the greeting. Since they were not the kind of New Year's travelers who were loaded with time and money, a deprived, lonely feeling filled their hearts even as they exchanged good wishes. When Yukiko entered the bath, the water overflowed.

"Ah, nice and hot."

"We seem to be the only guests."

So saying, Tomioka rose up from the bath. His flesh had turned red. The lighting in the room was quite bright. Momentarily averting her eyes from his naked body, Yukiko looked at the red earth that pressed close to the window outside.

"Well . . . ," she started.

"Yes?"

"We've settled in here somehow. But the maid must think we're a pretty strange pair. We don't go out, and we don't seem to have much money, and yet we're relaxed and intimate. The people here are very kind."

"Yeah, that's true."

"Are you still thinking of something else? Still thinking about death? I'm going to make you be more alive."

"No, I'm not thinking of anything in particular. When we get out of the bath, all nice and fresh, let's have some sake. Then, tonight, we'll go back." Tomioka lathered a cake of soap and began to wash himself.

"So have you given up the idea of climbing Mount Haruna and jumping in the lake?"

"No, I just can't die with you. It needs to be someone more beautiful."

"Gee, what a fine thing to say."

Laughing flirtatiously, Yukiko put both her hands to the edge of the tub and made swimming motions. Her arms were somewhat plump, and their flesh was smooth and sleek. Did a life of doing nothing but eating and sleeping have an effect on the body this quickly, Yukiko wondered, gazing at her own rosy skin.

After returning from the bath, the two sat down to lunch trays in their room. But the atmosphere was different from when they had been sitting in the warm bath. Their cold thoughts again began to seem opposed. Although two bottles of sake were brought, even that didn't help things along much. In a large bowl there were some glutinous rice cakes boiled with vegetables, which had gotten cold. Tomioka and Yukiko did not eat much of them.

When the meal was over, Tomioka went into the town by himself, to sell his watch. It was an old Omega, and he had once had it repaired. It would probably be enough, by itself, to supplement what he had to pay the inn. Leaving Yukiko's watch alone, Tomioka went out in his padded kimono. Outside, there were scattered snow flurries.

28

TOMIOKA WENT DOWN the stone stairs and emerged into the narrow street that was lined with shooting galleries and cafés. Women in fur coats were window-shopping the souvenir stores. Tomioka was cold in only his padded kimono, but he went along the streets, searching for a jeweler's. Next to a bus stop was a place that looked like a bar. A woman wearing scarlet rouge called out to Tomioka, "Hello; come on in here." Thinking that she was likely to know the area, Tomioka briskly approached her and went inside. The cramped bar was inside a flimsy sort of house that seemed to have been slapped together, with some paint thrown on. Tomioka was cold, so he ordered sake. The woman brought a porcelain brazier out from the back and invited Tomioka to sit straddling it.

"Are you from here?"

"Not far away."

"I thought Ikaho would be an old town. But it's surprisingly new."

"There was a big fire, and after that it apparently became what it is now. They say it was nice in the past."

Pouring the hot sake into a glass, Tomioka downed it in a single gulp. As he paid, he asked the woman if there was a jeweler's nearby. The woman, saying that she would go in back and ask, had started to do so when Tomioka, slipping the watch off his wrist, asked her to please take this in with her. Presently, from the back, a small bald-headed man, evidently the proprietor, came out.

"How much will you let it go for, sir?"

Tomioka was somewhat embarrassed, but he explained that he had brought a woman to Ikaho two or three days ago and they had liked the town so well that they had stayed on a bit longer than they expected. They were a little behind on the bill, and that was why he wanted to sell the watch.

"Actually, I don't want to sell it. If there is somebody who will hold it as a pledge until I come to redeem it, that would be good," Tomioka said.

"It's a nice watch."

"Yes, I bought it in the south."

"Oh? Whereabouts in the south were you, sir?"

"I was in French Indochina."

"Is that so? I myself was with the navy in a place called Banjarumashin, in South Borneo. I was repatriated last year."

'Oh, South Borneo? That must have been very difficult. Is there a navy base there?"

"Yes, there is. There's nothing there, in South Borneo. But business conditions were good. I once saw this same brand of watch down there. That's a nice watch, I thought. How much will you take for it?"

"Do you know of some place where there's a demand for it?"

"No, I want it for myself. Just once, I thought, I'd like this kind of watch. Cima and Elgin are nice watches too. I've never yet had a watch that nice. The other day I saw a Vulcan, but it was an old-fashioned version, and I didn't care for it. It wasn't smart looking, like this one. If we can reach an agreement, please let me have it."

"If you want it that badly, I can let you have it. Give me a price. I really don't know."

"Well, I'm not a businessman myself. Would one big bill do?"

"One big bill? You mean ten thousand yen?"

"Yes. How would that be? Even if you went to a jeweler's, you'd be taken advantage of. They'd only give you five thousand or so, I think."

That's so, Tomioka thought. If he took the watch to some unfamiliar shop around here, he would be lucky to get five thousand yen. Telling the woman to bring some sake, the proprietor came to Tomioka's table and turned a light on. Putting the watch on his own wrist, he scrutinized it. Holding it to his ear, he listened to it ticking for a while.

"It has a good sound. A nice, firm tick."

"You might want to change the watchband."

'No, it's fine as it is. I like the band too. Japanese leather bands aren't nice and supple like this.'

The woman brought the sake. The proprietor withdrew to the back of the shop and did not come out again for a while. But after a few minutes he shuffled back out in a pair of wooden sandals and said: "This is all I managed to scrape up."

He laid the money—in batches of ten hundred-yen bills—down crosswise on the table.

"I've heard that, unlike Borneo, French Indochina was a pleasant place. Were you a soldier there, sir?"

"No, I went there as an administrator. I was with the Ministry of Agriculture and Forestry."

"Oh, an official."

The proprietor laughingly told Tomioka that at first, when the waitress had brought the Omega to him at the counter in the back, he'd thought from Tomioka's appearance that Tomioka was dealing in stolen goods.

"In this business, you see all types. I have a sharp eye. I thought you might be an artist. I never thought you were an official."

The proprietor had a little sake himself. Every time a bus arrived or departed, the shacklike house trembled. Tomioka, secreting the bundle of bills in the front of his padded kimono, took out a business card from his card case and handed it to the proprietor.

"So you're in the lumber business?"

"I've left the ministry and am helping a friend now in his business. But what with raising capital and all the regulations these days, basically you're tied hand and foot."

"Regulations, taxes—they make it impossible to get started in business. Even when a good customer walks in, I'm not allowed to serve him rice curry. Informers are everywhere, and the bureaucrats are as strict as the bailiffs of the Tokugawa era. They're like kids fighting over who's going to be the bully of the neighborhood. After gleefully making business impossible, they harass you. Meanwhile, the black market is thriving. How's the rice situation at your inn?"

"If they didn't have any rice, they wouldn't be able to put anyone up. So they must have bought a small amount somewhere."

"Yes, that's what everyone is doing. Rice is easy to find on the black market. And to have no food to offer guests who've come all the way down to Ikaho, well, that wouldn't speak well for the place at all. But then, just when we're trying to attract the customers, the regulations and the officials step in to ruin everything. Times are certainly hard . . . Was your family in Tokyo throughout the war, sir?"

"Yes," Tomioka said. "Fortunately, my house didn't burn down, but nothing has worked out. In the end, I even had to sell the house."

"My parents moved to Honjo Narihira before I was born, and I had lived there all my life. But in the March 9 air raids, my house burned down and one of my children died. Then, after I got back to Japan, my first wife and I split up, and I got this place with my new wife. Still, I want more than anything else to go back to Tokyo. Selling fish is my real trade. But my present wife says she hates the idea of the fish business, so I'm keeping this shop."

"Your wife is that young woman?"

"Yes. She's so young she looks like a girl. I'm ashamed of myself. But everything is fate. This too, I think, is the result of some kind of chance encounter in a previous existence. These turns of fate, sir, you know, one has to be very careful with them. It's no good resisting them, that's what I believe. I live in such a way that I don't set myself against fate."

It seemed hard to believe that the heavily made-up woman was this man's wife. The man's words—that one had to be careful with the turns of fate—struck a chord in Tomioka. It seemed to him that his relationship with Yukiko was precisely another such turn of fate.

"When I arrived back at Otake Harbor in Hiroshima, on the pier there was an empty Camel cigarette package. I thought its colors were beautiful. And I thought, We have truly lost the war. Foreign cigarette packs on the ground made me realize it. Losing the war, too, was a turn of fate."

'Was buying this watch from me a turn of fate, also?'

Tomioka was drunk and had become more relaxed. As he made his mild joke, he accepted a cigarette from the proprietor and lit up. Munching on some peanuts with his buckteeth, fumbling with the zipper of his jacket, the proprietor said, "Everything in this world is a matter of fate, that's for certain. Had Japan won the war, we might very well be suffering even more now. At least we learned that war is madness. I went to the ends of the south—Borneo of all places. I have to think of it as fate."

29

WHEN HE RETURNED TO THE INN, Yukiko was at the *kotatsu*, buffing her nails with her handkerchief. Seen from behind, her figure suddenly seemed forlorn. Although the proprietor of the bar had told him that everything was due to fate, the word came home painfully to him only now. It seemed insane that until the previous day, he had fantasized about dying with this woman. Suddenly he had the feeling that suicide was out of the question. As if getting rid of the watch was a turning point in his own fate, his feelings had gradually, with the help of the sake, become lively.

"Ah, did you get drunk?"

"I had a few drinks."

With an expression that asked whether it was a good idea to drink, Yukiko looked intently into Tomioka's eyes. To her surprise, the gentle look in his eyes since Tomioka had returned gave Yukiko a sense that something good had happened. "Were you able to sell it?" she asked.

"I was. I sold it for ten thousand yen."

Tomioka told Yukiko in detail about how he had sold the watch. Yukiko, tearing up, said with a sigh, "He sounds like a wise man." There was something compelling for both of them in the proprietor's words.

It restored the flow of their attraction for one another in a way that was not counterfeit. Yukiko gazed at the bundle of banknotes that Tomioka placed on the *kotatsu* coverlet.

"It's a way out."

Yukiko said, "That man is a returnee from the south, too, and he has a young wife. He's got courage. You, on the other hand, do nothing but fantasize about death."

It was not that Tomioka had completely discarded his dream of death. He remembered how thoroughly Stavrogin had prepared for death in *Demons*, which he had read in Indochina. At the time, he had felt repugnance for the coolness with which Stavrogin had thought everything out beforehand—laying in a strong silken cord and smearing it thickly with soap, to ensure as painless a death as possible. But he felt differently now. He thought that Stavrogin's plan seemed reasonable. He too wanted to plan some convenient method of dying. Stavrogin, making a pilgrimage up and down in the earth, had found nothing to sustain his heart and had returned to his native country as an accursed man. Tomioka, returning from distant Indochina as a man disillusioned with human life, wanted to cut off his own life. For Tomioka, this world was no longer interesting or amusing.

"It would have been better not to stay on but to have gone back right away. But you wanted to stay for two or three days. What do you think now?"

As he asked this, Tomioka lit another cigarette from the previous one. Both came from the pack of foreign cigarettes he'd been given by the proprietor of the bar. Yukiko also lit one up, with a wondering air, and took a drag. She said, "I think it's interesting. I'd like to meet that kind of man."

"He likes people. He's what anybody would call a good person. A good person like Kano, whom you made a fool of."

"That's a nasty thing to say."

That evening, the pair settled the bill at the inn. They had decided to return to Tokyo that night after stopping off at the bar. The only customers were two men who looked like chauffeurs, drinking sake. The proprietor showed Tomioka and Yukiko into a narrow private room on the second floor and told them to make themselves at home. A different woman from the one who had been there at midday brought some tea up to them. The *kotatsu* in this room was sunk into a hole in the floor. A woman's overcoat and kimono dangled on the wall. Presently, the woman from midday came upstairs. About eighteen or nineteen, she had a larger build than Yukiko. She was a quiet woman, who almost looked as if she was asleep. She had a way of widening her eyes now and then, making them enormously large and shining. Although she was not a beauty, the fresh young lines of her body radiated flamboyantly.

Today being New Year's, the customers downstairs left early. Soon, the daytime woman employee also gave everyone the customary New Year's greetings and left. The owner asked his wife to close up the shop and came upstairs with a bottle of whiskey.

The proprietor was short and thickset, already in his fifties. He took some apples from the pockets of his jacket and placed them on the *kotatsu* coverlet, telling Yukiko to please have one. The men drank whiskey and began to embroider on tales of the south.

It was a six-mat room with a drop ceiling made of paper and a map of the world pasted up on the wall. The proprietor's wife, holding her hands out over the lid of the potbellied brazier, seemed to be vaguely thinking about something. She was sitting next to Tomioka, and he glanced over from time to time to look at her profile. Yukiko, peeling an apple, munched away noisily on it. She insinuated herself into the men's conversation, chattering away. There was a rustling sound of snow brushing against the window. The wind made a deep echoing sound, like the rumbling of a mountain. The woman, sitting at ease by the brazier, propped her cheek on the palm of one hand and slid the other hand under the *kotatsu* coverlet. Casually, Tomioka poked the front of his foot hard against the woman's knee, as he sat with his legs crossed. The woman's face was impassive. With his left hand, Tomioka tried touching the woman's hand under the coverlet. Then quietly, still looking at the woman's profile, he squeezed her hand, hard. In his heart, sparks flared up into a blaze. The woman, her head quietly lowered, closed her eyes. But her hand, damp with perspiration, responded any number of times to Tomioka's.

Impressed with the woman's primitive strength, Tomioka felt the blood rush to his head. With his other hand, he held the glass and drank the whiskey down. Yukiko was peeling a second apple.

Now and then, Tomioka would eye Yukiko carefully as she ate the apple in her heavily lipsticked mouth. But Yukiko was having a rambling conversation with the proprietor of the bar, whom she had said sounded like a good person—like Kano. The proprietor was wearing the watch on his wrist now, ever so proudly. On his stumpy wrist, the gold-cased watch gleamed dully.

Under the coverlet, the hands of the pair would not let go of each other. The woman, growing audacious, moved her knee so that it rested on Tomioka's foot. Tomioka let go of the woman's hand for a moment and, in a shrill, choked voice, said, "Ah, this too is a turn of fate. No better night to celebrate than the first of the year. It's a beautiful evening. Here, have another glass of whiskey. I'll have some, too, in honor of our all being together tonight."

With this, Tomioka filled the proprietor's glass up to the brim. And after reaching his hand deliberately across to Yukiko and telling her to drink, he put her glass to her lips. Thinking how changeable people's hearts are, Tomioka made Yukiko drink any number of glasses. His feelings toward her had once more gone cold. Yukiko soon became quite drunk. Perhaps because she hadn't had any supper, the alcohol spread rapidly through her system.

Yukiko thought this sleepy-looking woman, with her lowered head propped up on her hand, was an incredible hick. Hers had been a country life, spent without a youth and with this insignificant man. Even Yukiko looked at her with sympathetic eyes. Since the woman remained silent throughout, it was not clear what she was doing here. As Yukiko grew drunk, Yukiko began to tell the proprietor, with naïve enthusiasm, the story of her passionate love affair with Tomioka in the south.

Tomioka was not drunk. The other three kept on drinking until the bottle was almost empty. Then Tomioka said that he'd be back after he'd had a bath and abruptly got to his feet.

His eyes hazy, the proprietor said, "Come on, Seiko, show the gentleman the way. Take him to the bath at the rice merchant's place. Will you be going as well, ma'am?"

"I'm all right. I've had two baths at the Kindayu since the morning. Besides, I'm completely drunk. I feel dizzy."

Stuffing her cheeks with the ham that accompanied the drinks, Yukiko again raised the glass of whiskey to her lips. When Tomioka asked to borrow a hand towel, the woman took her own peach-colored one from the wall and followed Tomioka down the steep, narrow stairs.

It was dark and chilly. At the foot of the stairs, Tomioka waited for the woman to come all the way down. On the floor of the shop, where the chairs were piled on the tables, mice scampered about.

The woman came down. The two stood face-to-face, close together, their eyes glittering.

30

STANDING ON THE DIRT FLOOR at the foot of the dusky stairs, Tomioka abruptly embraced Seiko. Seiko pressed close to Tomioka, almost without breathing, and let him do whatever he wanted. But just as she was responding to his kisses, they suddenly heard Yukiko laugh loudly upstairs, and Tomioka let go. Seiko silently went over to the back entrance of the shop. "It's dark, so mind your step," she said. Tomioka grabbed Seiko again, around the waist. But she shook off his hands and went down the narrow stone stairs. The surroundings were dark, and a lamp shed a feeble light at the foot of the stone stairs. Thick clouds of steam hovered in the night air around the lamp. Near the lamppost there was a glass door, lit from within. Seiko opened it and waited for Tomioka to come down the stairs.

When he reached the doorway, a young woman clad in a kimono with a flashy flower pattern and long, flowing sleeves, fastened with a brightly colored sash, was just putting her feet into a pair of wooden sandals.

"It's terribly cold," she said to no one in particular. Abruptly shaking out a white shawl, she threw it over her slender shoulders—she was not even wearing a Japanese half-coat. She said, "Sayonara" and hurried off. Tomioka let her go by.

"She's working for us as a geisha," Seiko said.

Seiko went in first and Tomioka followed, closing the glass door behind him. They went along a chilly corridor that made many twists and turns, always going downward, until it ended at a spacious bathhouse. It was apparently mixed bathing. In the disrobing area, men's clothes and women's clothes had been tossed together in round hampers. In front of the mirror, a middle-aged woman in a kimono said, "Seiko-san, I didn't come today for a New Year's visit. But please convey my greetings to your husband. Tomorrow I will call on you."

As Tomioka started to remove his Western-style clothing, Seiko, as if she had been waiting for him to do so, opened up a cotton carrying cloth and wrapped his articles of clothing in it, one after the other.

As he took off his clothes, Tomioka looked at the hampers around him. There were two or three kerchief bundles in them. Were people's clothes wrapped up in carrying cloths as a precaution against their being stolen? It amused him.

Seiko too began to take off her clothes.

Tomioka briskly entered the bath area, where steam hovered in clouds. Six or seven men and women—who might have been young or old, it was hard to tell—were already sitting in the roomy, tiled bathtub. Tomioka felt an ease of spirit in the lively atmosphere. Seiko had also entered the bath area and, kneeling, was rinsing herself off with hot water in the corner, near the door.

When Tomioka leapt into the bath, the hot water permeated his skin, wrapping itself all around his cold body. Seiko was half-hidden in the steam, talking with someone, but soon she too entered the bath. She slowly came over to Tomioka. Her well-fleshed shoulders, her white skin floated up from the reddish muddy water. She smiled sweetly at him. Stretching out his leg in the water, Tomioka touched the flesh of her leg. Seiko, pretending to be groping for her submerged hand towel, touched her hand to Tomioka's lap. Since the water was red, no one could see what they were doing from the neck down. With a strange smile, Tomioka looked into Seiko's eyes. But she was no longer smiling. As if all her energy had slipped down to the parts of her body beneath the water, she moved invisibly below the surface, while her head, always at the same distance from Tomioka's, simply bobbed about like a buoyant watermelon. Tomioka had the feeling that this scene had been enacted somewhere, sometime before. Not trying to remember, though, and submerged to his chin, he merely let his smiling face float upon the waters. A couple of men noisily made their entrance. Tomioka, facing Seiko, let his mind run to fantasy. In the bathtub, someone began to sing the "Apple Song." Riding on the waves of the melody of the "Apple Song," casually sung by someone, Tomioka was sure that he understood the feelings of the proprietor, whose proper trade was selling fish and who, in order to live with the young Seiko, had settled in this hot springs hamlet of Ikaho. Making swimming motions, Seiko headed for the far side of the tub. All of a sudden, she heaved herself out of the water. Viewed from behind, her splendid, big physique seemed to Tomioka the most beautiful female nakedness he had ever seen. He felt an uncontrollable desire for her body. He was allured by her figure from behind. Abruptly, he swam across the tub himself and came out of the bath next to her. With a hollow roaring sound, the rough night wind off the mountains grazed the eaves of the bathhouse.

"Shall I rinse off your back?" Seiko asked. Her large-bodied nakedness as she sat on the tiled floor, with her thick thighs neatly aligned, resembled the naked body of Niu when she was bathing. Tomioka suddenly thought of Niu's face. Niu's strong, slim body and dusky skin, the smell of her breath as she chewed on a cinnamon stick—that whole life in Indochina—invited thoughts of a bitter nostalgia at unexpected moments. Now and then, when Tomioka was tired and stretched out on his bed, Niu would peel and pare some cinnamon bark, steep it in hot water, and bring it to him, telling him that cinnamon had been cherished since the old days and used by men as a restorative of youth. This youth-restoring cinnamon was apparently prized as a royal medicine. Tomioka and his colleagues had gone on outings to search for it in the uninhabited mountain areas of Nean Province. It was known as *katsura* in Annam. It grew sparsely in the mountains of the north. Since the cinnamon—a tree of middling height—was used for its bark at the Annamese royal court, it was forbidden for the common people to harvest it. The chiefs of the Mon mountain tribes, after receiving a special permit from the Annamese officials, would set out on a search for cinnamon trees. It was thought that the discovery of a cinnamon tree depended upon divine protection. The cinnamon hunters would enter into the deep interior of the mountains only after performing auspicious religious ceremonies. Tomioka had heard about this from Marcon of the Forestry Bureau. It was not unusual for the Mon tribesmen to be away a year or two. Unless they were experienced cinnamon hunters, they were usually unable to find any trees, it was said. They searched the trees out by their perfume, and on the rare occasion that they found one, they would notify the authorities. They were required to submit a sample of the bark, which would be stamped with a government seal. In the mountains around Tanoa, Tomioka had, a few times, smelled the perfume of cinnamon. As he was having his back rinsed by the naked Seiko, Tomioka recalled the scent. The child born between himself and Niu had, no doubt, learned to speak some words by now and to toddle about. Wondering how Niu, bringing up a fatherless child, was living her life, Tomioka fantasized about the lives of the woman he would never see again and their child.

The dim lights in the bathhouse flickered now and again.

"How many years have you been in Ikaho?" Tomioka asked.

"About two years. I want to go to Tokyo, you know, I'm already bored with this kind of lonely place. Business is bad, and when it's cold, nobody comes."

"It's not popular?"

"It's just no good at all. Even my husband says it's no good and that he's going back to Tokyo to set up again in his old business; but I wouldn't be able to stand a fish shop. I'd like to go to Tokyo alone and be a dancer. Remember the geisha we saw in the doorway before? I'm learning to dance from her, but . . . they say in Tokyo you can earn enough to make a living. So I'd like to try it. Here, except in summer, there's no business."

"A dancer? A dancer is all right, but you won't really be able to get along on just that. Eventually you'll be living by selling your body, most likely."

"But even so, I want to go to Tokyo. He puts up all sorts of objections. I can't seem to get away from here."

Sluicing a last bucketful of water down Tomioka's back, Seiko entered the bathtub again, to the accompaniment of noisy splashes.

When the two finally left the bath and came back upstairs, Yukiko was chattering away to the proprietor, who was still drinking whiskey. Interested and amused by her own stories, she was relating her various memories of French Indochina.

"You certainly took your time. I thought perhaps the two of you had eloped."

Yukiko was joking, but Tomioka was startled by her intuition. Seiko, without batting an eyelash, hung up her cold hand towel on a nail on the wall and crawled beneath the *kotatsu* coverlet. What had seemed to be rouge on her cheeks was in fact the redness of her natural coloring. She looked very much a woman of the mountains.

Her face seemed to shine smoothly, even without any makeup. Tomioka looked casually at Seiko's ample bosom. Already he had stopped feeling any consolation that he could cling to in Yukiko. From Seiko's strapping physique, however, Tomioka began to gain a sense of what his life could be like tomorrow. He no longer had any thoughts about death. He didn't respond to Yukiko anymore. Seiko, her eyes gleaming, glanced at Tomioka every so often. In his heart, Tomioka felt the same extravagant freedom of being under foreign skies that he had in Indochina. He was not completely free from concern for ethical questions, but deep inside he had no regard at all for Seiko's husband or for Yukiko. He wanted somehow to come back to life by means of Seiko's seduction. He even felt a sort of burning excitement. Tomioka wished that the proprietor and Yukiko would simply go away somewhere. He thought that if only the two of them weren't there, he could freely set out with Seiko on a new life. He was confident that he could cast off all the bonds of family. He even entertained the fantasy of doing time in jail with Seiko for the crime of killing these two. Both the proprietor and Yukiko were rather drunk, and the proprietor had fallen into a drunken slumber at the *kotatsu*.

Yukiko's eyes were half-closed, the whites showing. Seiko watered down the rotgut sake she had brought and poured it into Yukiko's glass. Yukiko's throat was very dry, so she gulped down the liquid. She was talking gibberish.

Seiko dragged her husband's body into their bedroom next door. Tomioka did not lend her a hand but simply poured more rotgut sake into Yukiko's glass. Yukiko burst out laughing from time to time, spraying her surroundings with sake. Her face felt as if it was on fire.

"The milk of coconuts is so delicious. When it's really cold, it has a fishy smell. I want some coconut milk."

"This is coconut milk."

Tomioka poured her some more sake. Yukiko's whole body had gone numb, and she slipped into a stupor. Tomioka, lighting up a cigarette, listened to the sound of the wind. Seiko held her hands out over the lid of the potbellied brazier and used one hand to grab Tomioka's foot, which was inching toward her knees. A pale ether seemed to flow out from her opened wide eyes. Creeping alongside the brazier, Tomioka pulled Seiko toward him, with his hand on the back of her neck.

"We can't."

"They're drunk. They won't know a thing."

"No. Your wife is still talking about something or other."

With an expression of hatred, Tomioka glared at Yukiko, who was now drunk and without any makeup on. He had the feeling that the curtain of this act of his life with this woman had fallen. Ignoring Yukiko, who was turning and tossing and still talking to herself, he drew Seiko to him by the shoulder and violently planted a kiss on her lips. Laughing, Yukiko was singing some song. It was the song about how when lovers first met, their eyes were true eyes. Thinking, You fool, Tomioka pulled away the brazier that Seiko's knees were nudging.

Every so often Yukiko opened her eyes, but it was dark all around her. The heavy snoring of a man was audible not far from her ear. She could hear the snores and, in the dark light of the streetlamp that came in through the curtains, two shadowy, whispering figures seemed to be snuggling together. Yukiko's throat was burning with thirst. She wanted to crawl to a place where coconut milk was flowing freely. The room was swinging from side to side like a hammock. She had no strength at all in her shoulders or thighs. She wanted so much to drink some water, but her parched throat seemed to be stuck shut. She could not call out. With all her strength, she finally managed to turn over on her stomach. Suddenly, though, somebody seemed to straddle her pillow as they stepped toward the paper door. Happening to open her eyes, Yukiko saw the figure of a tall woman slide back the paper door and vanish into the next room. Yukiko called out to the figure, as loud as she could, "Please, some water."

The paper door slid shut. There was no answer. Yukiko cried out again, "I want some water." Since there were no signs of anyone getting up for her, Yukiko crawled around the *kotatsu*, groping with her hands.

31

FOR THREE DAYS OR SO, Tomioka and Yukiko stayed on at the inn. But Yukiko began to press for their return to Tokyo. With a woman's intuition, she had somehow begun to have a reaction against Seiko. On the evening before they did in fact leave Ikaho, at the farewell party, the proprietor was once more tricked into drinking too much, but this time Yukiko drank sparingly. Her deep drinking on the first night had left her with a permanent headache and a heavy feeling in her stomach. Although Seiko poured out the sake with a liberal hand, Yukiko, stealthily drawing an ashtray toward her, regularly emptied the sake into it. But she acted drunk. Tomioka, closing his eyes, now and then hummed an Annamese song. Yukiko, as if spying on her, sometimes stole a look at Seiko's expression. The dim phantom that she had seen the first night seemed to Yukiko to resemble Seiko. It was a mystery why she had been standing by the sliding paper door. The proprietor, already in good spirits, talked about how he wanted to go back to Tokyo and set up in business again.

"I'd like to build a sake shop in one of the burned-out areas in Honjo. Even if it's twenty thousand yen per four square yards, forty square yards would be suitable. And then for laying in stock, I'd have to set aside three hundred thousand yen. I hear it's no easy matter to find housing in Tokyo today. And yet, I can't go on doing this kind of thing forever. I want to put the whole place up for sale, but I don't have the perseverance to hang on until summer. Instead, I'm talking about the two of us going to stay with a friend of mine in Tsukiji."

Tomioka now and then opened his eyes and chimed in with some appropriate remark. But in fact he did not care one way or another about what the others were saying. With a dried-up lack of energy, he raised the cup to his lips. The proprietor, who very much liked the taciturn, modest Tomioka, seemed to want to talk to him about everything. He said that he and Seiko were utterly bored with their present business. Although there was no wind, it was a bone-chillingly cold night. They heard the unusual sound of the flute of a passing masseur outside the window.

Tomioka, exactly as if he'd just thought of it, said, "Well now, shall I go and take a bath?"

Whereupon Seiko, immediately rising to her feet, taking a soapbox and a hand towel, said: "I'm going to warm myself up with a bath too."

"Yes, I'll go with you too," Yukiko said, casually standing up.

At this, Seiko, with a sudden look of displeasure, said, "Well, the two of you go together, then."

Yukiko, startled by Seiko's rough, angry manner, followed Tomioka as he went down the stairs.

They each shoved on a pair of wooden sandals and went out back. The cold air seemed to cut into their skin.

"Seiko-san is a strange woman. She seems quite taken with you. There's something odd."

Yukiko spoke gently, trying to trick the truth out of him. But Tomioka, his back to her, just said facetiously, "Oh, really?"

"She's a sly monkey, a faithless one, all right."

"Oh, yes?"

"You and your innocent questions. You always act indifferent to the woman, and then you end up grabbing her."

"I have no particular intention of grabbing that monkey. Come on, let's not even talk about it."

"But you're not saying that you have no interest in her, are you?"

"I'm not interested."

"I wonder. When I said I was going to the bath, she suddenly got so angry. She's infatuated with you. The service here is good—but only for you."

"Really? I never noticed until now. Should we stay another four or five days?"

"Sure, that would be nice."

Giggling, the two went into the bath at the rice merchant's. Seven or eight bathers were there, talking in loud voices about the black-market price of rice. Evidently they were a group, because a couple of geishas were mingling with them, pouring water down the guests' backs. Once in a while, one of the men having water sluiced over him was kidded by his friends. It was lively tonight. Tomioka casually looked over Yukiko's naked body. Her lack of Seiko's splendid physicality seemed sad to him. Perhaps because both the geishas were young, Yukiko's body in comparison somehow seemed to show signs of decline. And yet, her legs were smooth and willowy, and there was a pleasing symmetry between them and her torso. Yukiko willfully bathed herself, without bothering to wash off Tomioka's back as the geishas were doing for the other men.

Yukiko quickly finished and left the bath. When she went to the hamper to find her discarded clothing, she saw that Tomioka's things in the hamper next to hers had, during the last few minutes, been wrapped in a blue cotton carrying cloth. Thinking, That can't be the right hamper, Yukiko looked around, but she didn't see Tomioka's hamper. When she peeked under a corner of the carrying cloth, however, Tomioka's clothes, strangely enough, were all there. Tomioka seemed ready to come out of the bath, so Yukiko quickly got dressed and, going over to the mirror, set about combing her hair. She watched Tomioka in the mirror. He seemed just a bit puzzled by the carrying cloth, but he soon undid the kerchief as if there was nothing unusual about it. Somehow seeming to search the contents of the hamper, he turned and glanced toward Yukiko after a moment and then put on a pair of new underpants. Those pure white pants were a mystery to Yukiko. Hastily putting on the rest of his clothes, he crumpled the carrying cloth into a small ball and crammed it in his pocket. It was all unbearably strange to Yukiko.

"It's very strange how your clothes got wrapped up in a kerchief."

Saying this as if teasingly, Yukiko came away from the mirror.

"Probably someone wrapped them up for me."

"They also brought you a new pair of underpants. What happened to the old ones?"

Not answering, Tomioka briskly went into the bathhouse to wring out his hand towel. Yukiko felt a pang at her heart. But when Tomioka came back, she didn't say anything. She went out ahead of him, into the cold corridor.

Yukiko tried to tell herself that he often tried to get away with this sort of thing and that it was her fault for losing sight of that fact. She thought that she must avoid letting herself be dragged around by her memories of Tomioka. It would be unendurably lonely, but for the time being, Yukiko meant to live by herself.

The two of them went back up the stone steps without talking. The dust of the stars twinkled just like a ship's lights. To make herself feel better, Yukiko began to whistle. Now and then, she wiped away with the sleeve of her overcoat the tears that were pressing against the backs of her eyelids. The dryness that she had noticed in her heart at the time that she came back from Haiphong had finally turned to tears. How was it that returning to Japan had reduced them to this listless loneliness?

"What's the matter?"

"Nothing's the matter."

"Are you suspicious?"

"Of what?" Yukiko was overcome with anger. But before she could even express it, it faded away as quickly as it had risen. Little by little, her agitation subsided. When they had climbed the stairs, there was an alley alongside the house that led to the thoroughfare.

"Shall we take a little walk?" Tomioka suggested.

"I don't want to catch a cold."

Stopping, Tomioka said in a low, desultory voice: "Your nerves are in bad shape." Then he added: "No, I guess it's my nerves that are going. The one not at peace is me. I've gotten so I can't stand the loneliness . . . I just can't bear it. I'd like to take a walk just anywhere, at random. Even now, I was thinking of selfish things."

Tomioka placed his hand towel, which was quickly starting to freeze, over his shoulder.

"It's cold here," Yukiko said. "At any rate, I'd like to go back and go to bed right away. Because I want to leave here early tomorrow morning."

"You mean you're going back by yourself? I'm going back too. Since we came together, we have to go back together."

"Yes, I suppose, but you're a difficult person . . . I don't care anymore, one way or the other. Let's stop talking about this. My legs are shaking."

The two went up to the second floor, from the back entrance. In the next room, the proprietor was snoring away. Seiko wasn't there. Picking up a sake flask from the tea table, Tomioka placed it to his ear and shook it. There seemed to be a little bit left. Pouring it into a glass and clearing his throat, Tomioka drank it. The fact that Seiko was not in bed beside the proprietor had something of an effect on Tomioka and Yukiko, back from the hot springs bath. The two of them, each in a different way, brooded over Seiko's not being there. Yukiko, putting her chilled legs under the *kotatsu* coverlet, thought about her life after she'd separated from Tomioka in Tokyo. She had the feeling that this absence of more than a week had helped her to clarify what her life in Ikebukuro would be.

3 2

THE TWO RETURNED TO TOKYO on the evening of the fifth. Feeling even
more depressed than when she'd left Tokyo, Yukiko returned to her
hideaway with Tomioka. When she went to the main house to wish a
happy New Year to the kitchenware dealer's family, the proprietress
looked displeased—no doubt because Yukiko had been away for so
many days. She felt almost like an intruder in someone else's house as
she opened the lock of the shed. Turning on the electricity, which had
just been set up, she put the plug into the socket and fiddled with the
switch of the small electric stove. The room was somehow in a mess.
There was a letter on top of the *kotatsu* coverlet. It had been left behind
by Iba. He had stayed here for two days, it said, waiting for Yukiko. He
advised her to return at least once to her hometown. It also said Iba's
family would gather in Saginomiya for the upcoming Festival of Seven
Herbs; she should try to come that day and stay for a night. Yukiko
immediately tore up the letter in little pieces and tossed them into the
portable clay oven. Lighting a fire in the *kotatsu*, Yukiko made coffee on
the electric stove.

Tomioka, putting his legs under the coverlet and lighting up a
cigarette, ran a hand roughly through his hair.

"Hey, is there any sake around here?" he asked. Silently, Yukiko held two or three bottles sitting in a corner of the room up to the light. "No, there isn't any," she said.

Tomioka realized he had gotten to the point where he had to have sake every night. Unless he enlivened himself with sake, he rapidly fell into a deep depression. The fact that he had left Seiko in the lurch when she had asked him to take her away with him now seemed like part of the distant past. He liked her very much, but at the same time he didn't really care one way or the other. When she had asked him to give her his address, he'd handed her some made-up number. He had returned to Tokyo wearing the new underwear Seiko had provided, but he didn't think much about it.

"Do you want a drink?"

"Yeah, I would like a drink."

"Coming right up then." Yukiko said this as she prepared the coffee. She didn't feel like going out to buy sake.

"Are you still worried about something?"

"What would I be worried about?"

"Oh, nothing. So, shall we celebrate having survived?"

"It's as if we've been saved by Seiko-san."

"By that monkey?"

"She does have a beautiful body, doesn't she? At the bus stop, tears were shining in her eyes."

"I don't know, I didn't notice that."

As they drank their coffee, Yukiko thought that tonight she would like to sleep deeply, by herself. Since Ikaho, she hadn't wanted to drink a single drop of sake.

Tomioka finished his coffee and said that he would go out and buy some sake and be right back. Yukiko let him go. Maybe Tomioka's drinking habit was his fate. It was unusually cold in Tokyo. Yukiko went out to the back of the main house to get some water to wash the rice. Joe had probably come to see her, she thought, but it didn't seem to matter now. Ladling the water into a bucket, Yukiko returned to the shed. Tomioka was back, with a large, two-liter bottle of sake. He poured some sake into a teakettle and set the kettle on the electric stove.

"You're a man who loves his sake."

"Yeah. These days, it's my most important love . . . You, won't you have some?"

"I don't want any. My stomach hurts."

"Don't say that. Why not have some? It'll make you feel good."

"I'll boil the rice and eat that. I don't need any sake."

Yukiko washed the rice in a pot and put it on to boil on the electric stove. Tomioka, pouring his second drink of sake in the coffee cup, took a couple of small dice from his pocket and began throwing them onto the *kotatsu* quilt. Seiko had slipped them to him at his departure. A two and a five came up. That's no good, he thought. Those were the numbers he most disliked. Flustered, he threw again. This time, a four and a five. With a feeling close to indignation, Tomioka threw again and got a two and a five once more. He had returned to the same numbers.

"Is the rice done yet?"

"In a little while."

"Ikaho was interesting, don't you think?"

"Yes. Probably because the monkey was there."

"Hm."

"Are you in love with her?"

"Hm."

"It would be good if you could go again."

"It's too much bother, going."

"Why are you getting angry? You liked her so much."

"Yes, I liked her. She's a woman who without speaking says everything with her body. I'd like to see her again."

"You should go and see her then."

"It's too late, I've discarded her."

Yukiko was about to say something when a freight train passing through Ikebukuro Station shook the ground like an earthquake and made the shed tremble.

The glow of Seiko's eyes rose up behind Tomioka's eyelids. Brightly glittering, like an animal's, they were beautiful eyes. He thought of her big-bodied, solid white nakedness. Their breathing in the dark as they silently hooked fingers returned to him too. By now rather drunk, Tomioka was aroused by his desire for Seiko. The feel of her stiff hair done in a permanent was just like a horse's mane. Tomioka, growing desperate, tossed the little bean-sized dice on the *kotatsu* coverlet again and again. The freight train passed far away into the distance. The tremor of the earth also faded away. Tomioka raised his fourth cup of sake to his lips. Yukiko took the pot off the stove. Only now did Seiko seem unbearably hateful to Yukiko. Tomioka's words, that Seiko silently expressed everything with her body, pricked her like needles. The dim, phantomlike woman, whom she had seen when she was drunk that time—was it not, after all, Seiko? Yukiko thought.

"You're a frightening person."

Tomioka gave no answer but simply tossed the dice. It was tedious. Yet he had no desire to return to Kuniko. The figure of his wife, as she sat at home in what amounted to a vacated house, depressed Tomioka in his present state. However, it was not as though he felt any deep affection for Yukiko. Rather, the mutual craftiness with which they were trying to purify their relationship into something like camaraderie had started to become clear. The period when he had made Yukiko his mistress had receded into the distant past.

3 3

TOMIOKA HAD ALREADY drunk most of the two liters of sake.

"You used to drink a lot of sherry in Dalat."

Yukiko, finishing the rice, put some more coffee on and drank it. Observing Tomioka, who, as he drank his sake, was talking about whatever he felt like, by himself, Yukiko was flabbergasted that he had nearly emptied the large bottle. Perhaps the sake had become an anesthetic for him. No matter what kind of good work he got into, if he drank like this every day, he was not going to make more than a meager living. Yukiko was angry—since he had started indulging himself in drink, he had lost the power to think seriously about things and talk them over with her. His face had been youthful in Indochina, but now it was terribly tired looking and thin.

"What are you staring at a person's face for? Are you trying to chase me out? What am I, an impediment to business?"

"What are you talking about?"

"No, the important things are knowing when to leave and being able to settle your accounts. As long as you understand that about life, you should be able to get through without any mishaps. Although of course these days everyone is separate, everyone is going his own way.

"You're very talkative. Don't drink any more sake, and please go to bed. Although you say the parting time and the settling of accounts are important, you're going downhill by easy stages. What is this?"

"You shouldn't get so angry. Tomorrow we go right and left. We'll each be going our own way. What happened at Ikaho doesn't matter. Don't hold it against me. *Ma chère* Yuki . . . "

Yukiko watched him as he chattered away, his lips purple, his hair hanging down on his forehead.

"A person like you is a hopeless human being. And yet you seem all right to others, so you get by. You're a fop and a two-timer, yet you're timid. You become courageous only when you drink . . . you're a fake."

"Hm, fake, huh? Come on, surely you can think of worse things than that to say."

"Yes, you're someone who has a great capacity for trickiness and hides it. And you're not someone to resign yourself and just go down quietly. And although there's a part of you that's a very good schemer and tactician, in business your head simply doesn't work. Maybe that's the bureaucrat side of you. So who knows—maybe if you can ride out the waves of this rough world, you'll do all right, Tomioka-san."

"I still have a future. Hey, there's no need to treat me like a fool. Although I may seem timid, I have more desire to make a lot of money than other people do."

"Then why did you want to die?"

"What about you? I want to live, and so I also think about dying. When I think about the loneliness of dying, I drink like this. I've seen through my own lack of courage. I've even resigned myself to it. I suppose everyone in his or her lifetime has thought about death, right? Only we, even in dying, have this nuisance of self-awareness hanging over us. We can't just simply go ahead and do it. Viewed from heaven, we're the size of millet grains. But we have the ability to reason, to think well of ourselves, and to put on airs. Even at Haiphong, when the ship departed, weren't there all sorts of bad-natured people there? They wanted to return home quickly, and so they tried to get on board even if it meant shoving others aside. There were even people who said that everybody around them was a war criminal, except themselves . . . That's what people are like. And self-righteous people are the worst. It's nothing to seduce a woman. But one thing I do know—Kano was a good man. He was honest, and he always had bad luck. Although he never thought of himself as an unlucky man."

"You and I both should apologize to Kano. We tantalized him and made fun of him. We were the ones who did wrong. When he was arrested and taken to Saigon, he didn't hold it against us in the least. But although it was I who was cut by Kano, you were the one who profited by it. Because you're cunning."

"I had good fortune. I came out all right."

"All through the war, Kano said we would win. He must have been astonished when he finally got back. When we were over there, even I thought Kano-san was a bit of a fool."

Tomioka was becoming drunk enough. Sprawled out at the *kotatsu*, he rested his head on his arm. But he was thinking about Kano—the way he had devoted himself headlong to his studies. Kano had been studying under Professor Herald at the labs of the Ministry of Agriculture and Forestry in Saigon. Herald had first completed an investigation of African forestry and experiments in the use of charcoal gas and then gone on to contribute to the development of the charcoal-burning automobile in Indochina. He had vowed to devote his life to researching methods of manufacturing gas from charcoal and growing forests suitable for charcoal. But Tomioka now realized that Kano's single-mindedness was a rare and valuable thing. He had heard rumors that Kano, when he got back, had abandoned everything and become a casual laborer in Yokohama. But he would have no way to know unless he actually went to see him. With a man like Kano, it was not impossible that he would take any job he pleased. Tomioka thought he would first try writing once to Kano.

When the peace treaties had been signed, and the time came when it was possible to travel freely anywhere, Tomioka felt he would like to return to Saigon again, as a forestry employee.

"Are you sleepy?"

"No, I'm not sleepy. I'm actually becoming more and more awake. I'm doing a lot of thinking about how I'm going to live from now on. Women are women, whatever happens, but for a man it's rather difficult."

"It's hard for women too . . . I can't rely on you, so I'm thinking of going back to the country for a while. What do you think about that?"

"That would be good. Go home, and become a healthy bride. If you can make a peaceful life for yourself, that would be the best."

"Are you kidding—I can't become a bride. When I said I might go home, I didn't mean that sort of thing. Since I've found a way of living, I would be going back to say good-bye to them."

"Ah, yes, your way of living. That's right. Everybody needs a way to stay alive . . . But even so, you shouldn't do anything unreasonable. You can't spend your entire life alone."

Yukiko put some charcoal into the *kotatsu*. Blowing on the fire, she said as if angrily, "You talk as if all of this has nothing to do with you."

Every so often, a train went by, making the ground shake. It felt like a dream that they had been at Ikaho until yesterday. It was good to have Tomioka still sprawled out before her eyes. Once they had actually separated, life in this shack by herself might be a lot more lonesome. At least it was a consolation for two comrades who knew each other's life story to be together in the same place.

"Don't you have a cigarette?"

Tomioka held out his hand. Yukiko took a pack of Hikari cigarettes from her handbag and handed it to him. Then she picked up the dice that were lying on the quilt and held on to them. The thought of what sort of work she should do weighed heavily on her. Any office skills she had had were lost by now. She could hardly become a waitress. She didn't want to be somebody's wife, either. But unless she did something, she would starve. Shaking the dice, Yukiko had a secret vision of herself as a streetwalker, buffeted about by the cold wind.

34

ON THE DAY OF THE FESTIVAL of Seven Herbs, Yukiko did not after all go to the Ibas. Once Tomioka had gone back home, Yukiko holed up in the shed for four or five days. She didn't want to go anywhere or do anything. She sent postcards to Seiko in Ikaho, as well as one to the place in Yokohama where Kano was said to be staying. In the card to Seiko, Yukiko deliberately sent greetings from her "husband." It was an interesting prank for Yukiko to see what kind of reaction she would get from Seiko in her return card. To Kano, she wrote that she very much wanted to visit him in the near future and asked when would be a convenient time. Unexpectedly, as soon as she had posted the cards, Seiko's husband came by to visit Yukiko. It was a day that promised snow. The morning after Yukiko and Tomioka had gone back to Tokyo, he said, Seiko had left the house as well, and she had still not come back.

Yukiko immediately had thoughts of Tomioka. He had gone to his home after staying just one night and might well have arranged a rendezvous with Seiko. Although she had seen nothing definite between them, Seiko's tears, when she came to see them off, had not been a woman's ordinary tears, Yukiko was sure. And now, with Seiko's husband having come to see her in this way, Yukiko thought that Tomioka might have been lying about giving Seiko a made-up address. Now Yukiko somehow was beginning to regret that they hadn't committed suicide at Ikaho, as Tomioka had wanted to. Now that things had come to this, dying seemed uncomplicated and peaceful. Yukiko felt that her secret despair was like a bamboo palisade that had been built around her. She deliberately gave Seiko's husband Tomioka's address.

Early the next morning, Seiko's husband came by again.

"I saw Tomioka. He doesn't seem to know anything about Seiko. He was surprised. And I certainly don't have any idea where she might have gone. I thought I might make inquiries at a police station. Tomioka-san kindly put me up for the night, but there were no extra futons, so I slept in my clothes by the *kotatsu*. It was a great imposition on his wife, I'm sure."

So saying, Seiko's husband—who seemed to understand Yukiko's position for the first time—stepped inside the dark shed, with a slightly rude casualness.

Perhaps she had, after all, been wrong about Seiko's tears that time, Yukiko thought. But since it was Tomioka they were talking about—Tomioka who could be extraordinarily cruel—perhaps he had indeed withheld his real address from Seiko. If he had, then his cruelty seemed more and more complicated and strange. Perhaps his relationship with Seiko was just a passing affair on a trip?

After about an hour, Seiko's husband departed, with a dejected air.

Yukiko felt that she had seen into Tomioka's real intentions She even somehow felt a certain sympathy for the young Seiko, who had been toyed with by Tomioka and had now run away from home. That same day, Yukiko received a return card from Kano, saying that although he was ill and living in miserable conditions, he still felt a nostalgia for the old days. If she meant what she had said in her card, would she please come and see him. At the end of the card, he said in a short postscript that he would like to meet Tomioka too, so if they liked, they should both come. Yukiko wanted unbearably to see Kano. She felt relieved that he showed no signs of holding a grudge against Tomioka and herself.

Yukiko made up her mind and went to visit Kano in the Minozawa district of Yokohama. Carefully checking the numbers of the houses that faced onto a squalid, dug-up thoroughfare lined with such establishments as a ball-bearing factory and printing shops, Yukiko finally located Kano's boardinghouse, up a cramped alley. He had a room on the second floor of a long tenement house, at the end of a row of small, cheaply made structures. Angora rabbits were being raised inside the house. Told by some child that Kano was in bed on the second floor of the house, Yukiko intrepidly ascended the ladder-stairs. The place resembled Seiko's house at Ikaho. Passing a clay portable cooking stove and a sack of charcoal in a low-ceilinged single room, she stood at the threshold of a torn sliding paper door. Kano called from inside, in his unmistakable, shrill voice, "It's nothing to look at, but please come in."

When Yukiko slid the door open, Kano, with a dirty hand towel wrapped around his head, was lying down with a blanket over him. A naked lightbulb dangled on its cord just above his head. Kano's face was pale and dark. The changes in his features had left not even a shadow of the past.

"Well! How are you? Do you have a cold?"

Making her way to Kano's pillow, where things were so scattered about that there was no place even to put one's foot, Yukiko peered down at Kano. His face suddenly flushing scarlet, Kano looked back at her with a fond, affectionate smile. His teeth were white.

"I haven't been well. My chest is bad. Just last night I had a slight hemorrhage."

Kano signaled with his eyes toward a cushion over by the wall, with its cotton stuffing coming out, and asked her to sit down. There was a pungent smell of carbolic acid in the room.

"My body's completely broken down. I worked for a while as a longshoreman. But I caught a chill in the rain, and I've been in bed now for forty days. I'm a living corpse. Didn't you come with Tomioka-kun?"

"No, I came by myself. I haven't seen Tomioka-san in a while."

"You're not married?"

"What? Me?"

"I thought you and Tomioka-kun were living together happily."

"No, no—I'm alone. Tomioka-san is Tomioka-san. So who is taking care of you in your illness?"

"There's my mother and my younger brother. My brother works as a typesetter at a print shop just up from here. During the war, he was a kamikaze trainee. But now he's a typesetter and lives with our mother. They waited for me. Anyway, they were burned out of their house. So now they're living in this kind of place. Even so, it's basically a palace for us."

From the window that had lost its glass and was now papered over, the dull rays of the afternoon sun cast stripes of light across the soiled army blanket. The pale, unshaven face of Kano, who had had a round child's face, was thin and sharpened by hardship. He looked as if he had aged a full ten years. From his features now, it was hardly possible to remember the life in the south. As he lay there on his side, his face looked like that of someone else. She almost felt like a perfect stranger.

"You've changed."

"Are you surprised?"

"Yes."

"Well, let's talk a little about the good old days before you leave. When your postcard came, I was very happy . . . I didn't think you would write to me."

"I wanted to, as soon as I got your address from Tomioka-san. I wanted to see you too."

"Well, thank you."

Suddenly, they both fell silent, thinking about the way they had treated one another.

3 5

"MY MOTHER ALSO is out at work, so I can't even offer you any tea. On the other hand, this way, you won't catch what I have, so it may be for the best."

Kano gave a wry smile. Now and then he would cough violently, shaking his head.

"Shouldn't you keep yourself from getting a chill?"

"It doesn't matter. I don't have any energy left anyway. The only thing I can try to do is keep from being a nuisance to my mother and my brother. I'm determined to show my gratitude by not being a burden to others. I'm not afraid of dying. But since this is the life given to me by God, I would rather live even one more day than die and turn to ashes."

"Don't say such sad things. I hope that you'll get well quickly."

"I'm not going to get well."

"Why do you talk like that? It all depends on your outlook. I want you to go back to being the healthy person you were, the Kano-san I knew."

"The Kano I was back then died in the war. I put everything I had into that war. But it can't be helped. I've resigned myself. Now and then, when I think about Indochina, I think it was the most remarkable period of my life . . . Has the cut on your arm hurt since then? It was your left arm."

Kano's concern for the wound on her arm moved Yukiko to tears.

"I acted truly unforgivably toward you, I've thought."

"No! It was I who was unforgivably selfish toward you, Kano-san. We were all acting crazy."

"We all were acting crazy, it's true. I've sometimes had the feeling you deliberately leaned into my sword. It was Tomioka I meant to cut. When I went to his room, there you were, and that made me even angrier. When I think about it now, I know I acted like a fool."

"Let's not talk about it."

"Please forgive me. It's just that when I saw you, it all came back, like it was yesterday."

Yukiko, oppressed by the medicinal smell that hung in the room, stood up and slid back the paper door a few inches. A cold breeze smoothly flowed in. It felt refreshing.

"Is Tomioka-kun well?"

"Yes, he seems to be all right."

"He's a lucky fellow, that one. He understands the bad luck of others. He sits back and watches what happens to them. I'm not trying to speak ill of him. It's the reason for his good fortune, I think. Lately I've thought that I should waste no time in learning from his example."

"Well, he doesn't seem all that fortunate these days."

"Really? But you probably take a sympathetic view of him. He wasn't burned out of his house, and he's found a good business associate. It sounds as though he's flourishing."

Yukiko thought back to the trip to Ikaho where she had gone with Tomioka to commit suicide and had not succeeded. "Right now, he really seems to be having difficulties. He's sold his house and has sent his family back to the country; for the time being he's working and living as a carefree bachelor. That's his story, anyway."

"Working? He could never become a longshoreman like me for two hundred yen a day. It would seem like a farce to him that I'd reduced myself to this miserable state by hoisting hundreds of pounds onto my shoulders."

"But wait. What *were* you thinking, when you decided to become a longshoreman?"

"It was just so I could eat. There was no work I could find that required any thinking. This kind of rough-and-ready work might be good, I thought. It was certainly better than becoming a thief. But for a bureaucrat who had never lifted anything heavier than a pen, it took its toll."

"That must be so."

Opening a bag of five or six apples that she had brought as a present, Yukiko looked around for a knife and began peeling a piece of the fruit. As she peeled off the skin round and round, she thought she would like to do whatever kindness she could for Kano, who seemed as though he might not live much longer. She cut the peeled apple into small pieces and put them one by one in Kano's mouth. He ate greedily.

"Many things have happened to us, but we were, after all, able to live to see this kind of day. And we were able to see each other again, weren't we? That's why you must eat good food and become strong."

"Good food? That's right. If I only had the money, I could probably live another two or three years."

"You have to try to get better, for your mother and brother."

"Thank you so much for being kind. These days, my mother and my brother act more like they were tired of me."

"That's just your distorted view of it."

"Distorted view?"

Kano was, in fact, unable to emulate Tomioka's good luck in being able to slip through crises by using a straightforward approach all his life. Whenever he thought of Tomioka, he seemed to just get angry. Tomioka always dodged aside and escaped; he never went under. Yukiko wrapped up the apple parings in a sheet of newspaper. She almost started to say something but then stopped. It was strange to Kano how Yukiko, without displaying any signs of the passions of the past, could sit there so calmly. It was a riddle, he thought. Her intrepid spirit was a mystery to him. According to her story, she hadn't returned to her family even once. Rather, she had simply come back from abroad and settled into the life of a solitary vagrant. Kano wondered if all women had hearts as cold as the flesh of a fish.

"As for the man Tomioka, he's definitely got survival talents. He's one who can always get by. That guy . . . When I heard that he'd gotten passage from Haiphong last May and later heard about what had happened at that time, I thought to myself, That is one lucky fellow. I heard that he realized that if he told the authorities he was basically an intellectual, he wouldn't get back for a while; so he said he was a civilian employee of the army and had come to French Indochina with the Forestry Agency as a person who made tea and ran errands. That's what I hear. At the checkpoint on the pier, he was questioned by a lot of officers. He put on an act of being the dumb, honest type. He played it to perfection. Even when the officers were talking away in French and English, he didn't so much as look at them, I hear. If they thought he could understand what they were saying, he would be detained. Next, when he was shown a map of Japan and asked where Shikoku was, he immediately pointed at Kyushu. He displayed the scholarly power of a grade-schooler. How about that? So he got through the barrier and, using somebody else's name, boarded an early boat and came back to Japan. He's no dummy, that one."

Yukiko was hearing this story for the first time. But it would not surprise her if Tomioka had pulled this off. With Seiko too, he had probably done nothing more than accept her affection for exactly what it was. Seiko might have been Tomioka's way of amusing himself at the time.

"Speaking of that, I thought that you and he must have come back early together. But you weren't on the same boat?"

"No, we came back separately."

For his crime, committed at the height of the war and, furthermore, the first instance of disgraceful behavior by a civilian, Kano was said to have been treated very roughly by the military police in Saigon.

After an hour or so, finding it quite difficult to breathe, Yukiko said her good-byes to Kano and left. Feeling relieved when she got outside, she inhaled the clear air. In her heart, Yukiko thought Kano a very miserable figure. She had heard that he was from a good family of some means, and this made the drastic change in his fortunes seem even more pitiable.

As for Kano, although Yukiko's face did not really look any different from the old days, now that he had seen her again in Japan after such a long time, he found it strange that he could ever have desired her to the point of having a bloody scuffle with Tomioka over her. He thought that, like other Japanese overseas at that time, perhaps he had been intoxicated or perhaps possessed.

Even so, when Yukiko said she was going back, Kano wished she would stay a little longer. Until this meeting, he had thought of her as a goddess. Now he felt as if he had bleakly awakened from a dream to the reality of the human Yukiko.

Yukiko, for her part, was sorry she had gone to see him. She would have rather continued to think of him as he had been in the past. Tomioka had told Yukiko, when she had wanted to meet Kano, that she was being sentimental and whimsical. Yukiko felt she understood now the depths of his heart—the reason why he might have given Seiko a false address. The strength of a man who could cut through and settle a situation seemed a hateful, yet attractive power.

The Annamese folk song that Tomioka had sung in a low, natural voice—"That first time we met / Our eyes were true eyes"—now might also have been a song about herself and Seiko.

Yukiko went down into Shinbashi Station. A cold wind was blowing. As she began to walk toward the platform, there was a startled exclamation: "Well, hello there!" A woman in a flashy green overcoat came running to Yukiko's side and tapped her on the shoulder.

"Hello!"

Yukiko opened her eyes wide. It was Shinonoi Haruko, her companion on the trip to Saigon. Yukiko felt a rush of nostalgic affection.

"How are you? When did you get back?"

Yukiko wanted to hear at once about the circumstances of Shinonoi's repatriation.

"From the time you came through the ticket gate, I thought: Isn't that her? So . . . are you well? I was repatriated last June. My family had evacuated to Urawa, so they weren't burned out of their home, anyway. As soon as I got back, I took a course in typing English. I got a job in Marunouchi. What are you up to these days?"

For a typist, Shinonoi Haruko was flashily and beautifully made up.

36

Receiving this human form
We cannot tell what tomorrow will bring
Observing the great of this world
How long will they continue in their glory
The changes of the world are swift
Like the legs of the wide-winged dragonfly

AROUND A WEEK LATER, at the end of a letter from Kano thanking Yukiko for visiting, he had written this verse, as a postscript. The words branded themselves on Yukiko's heart. But she did not answer the letter.

After that, there was no word from Tomioka. It was strange to her, looking back on it, that when Tomioka had suggested suicide at Ikaho, she had felt such timidity.

The encounter with Shinonoi Haruko, also, had left her empty. But she could not drift along like this forever. She had received notice from the owner that she was to kindly vacate this storeroom shanty in the near future. It was like a kind of death. Why hadn't she died with Tomioka then and there? She lay down and actually tried putting her narrow leather belt around her neck, but she lacked confidence that she would be able to draw it tight enough by herself. She did tighten it to a certain degree, but she could not achieve the violence of going one step beyond and actually strangling herself. Letting the belt go slack, Yukiko fastened it around her waist. How good it would be if Tomioka were here now, she thought. She yearned for him. Did dying simply mean she would pass from this world? As time went by, surely no one would care that she had died. Even Tomioka was sure to forget about her eventually. Yukiko knew that even if the two of them were now to commit a lovers' suicide, they would not achieve death gracefully or wholeheartedly. No doubt, at the very moment of death each would be thinking his or her own thoughts. This was a hateful idea. She might die with her mind blank, but at his last gasp Tomioka would no doubt be muttering under his breath, Forgive me, dear wife.

Remembering the wash of colors and sights that was French Indochina, Yukiko thought, I want to see that place once more. This poverty-stricken life is suffocating me. With the thought that the life in Dalat would never return, the memory of Tomioka's skin on hers also seemed unendurably dear. Yukiko realized luxury is a beautiful thing. She remembered the voices and the music of the Ranbean highlands. These memories were not the desolate environment of the "Apple Song." The strength of a people that was relaxed and expansive, leisurely situated in the flow of history, seemed much more deeply rooted than that of her own people. It seemed to her that probably no one loved war as much as a deprived and ignorant people. Japan was beginning to seem remote and foreign to her.

37

AT THE END OF FEBRUARY, Yukiko returned once to Shizuoka to see her relatives, but she quickly came back to Tokyo. She moved out of the shack in Ikebukuro and, on Shinonoi Haruko's recommendation, she rented a room on the second floor of the home of a tinsmith in Takadanobaba. She had not seen Tomioka for a long time. Although it was near the station and the rumbling of the trains reached her ears, Yukiko liked the place because no deposit was required and the rent was a thousand yen a month. Carting the wicker suitcase and the bedding she'd brought from Shizuoka, she settled down for the first time into some kind of decent human existence. But she still did not have a job.

Yukiko was pregnant. Although she wrote to Tomioka three times, there was just one answer, saying he'd come soon. With that response, he sent a money order for five thousand yen. Yukiko sold almost all the clothes she had brought from the country and put the money toward her living expenses. But circumstances were very trying. Although her body was robust, and her morning sickness was relatively light, Yukiko worried every day about whether she should have the baby. She wanted the baby, and yet she also wanted to get rid of it right now. Except for going out to the bath or shopping, Yukiko spent each day secluded in her room. Occasionally Iba came by. He no longer blamed her for the theft of his possessions, and he was quite impressively dressed. Had he come into some money? she wondered. As for Joe, she had separated from him the year before. The only memento of his visits was the pillow. Yukiko had sold the radio to pay for the fare to Shizuoka.

Iba was still unaware that Yukiko was pregnant. She had not even been examined by a midwife. She just bound up her belly herself, with a length of bleached cloth. Yukiko had not known that her body possessed such stoical strength to live and endure. Even at the time when she had been slashed by Kano, she must have had this same fortitude.

One evening, when it had been raining for about three days, Haruko came by to visit. Apparently Haruko, who had said that she was working as a typist in Marunouchi, was a typist in name only. According to the proprietress of the tinsmith's shop, Haruko actually had a job at a bar. It stood to reason. Yukiko had suspected from the start that Haruko's clothes were too beautiful for someone making do on a typist's salary.

"Yukiko-san. People like us, on account of this war, have become the dregs of society." Peeling off her stockings as soon as she sat down, Haruko heaved a sigh as she spoke. For Haruko, the stockings were probably the most important things in her life at this point. She said that she had brought a piece of beef as a present, and she took out a packet wrapped in bamboo leaves. Yukiko felt dull and languid but began preparing to make sukiyaki. She went out to the market in the rain to buy some scallions. Haruko had given her some money, so she also bought bread and a small amount of sugar. When she got back, Iba had unexpectedly come to visit. He was chatting with Haruko.

Iba was talking away to her about religion. It felt very strange to Yukiko to hear about religion from the likes of Iba. Human beings were all prone to stumble, he was saying. Mankind, from the time of birth, is a creature that walks along looking down, always calculating the relative likelihood of stumbling. Iba was in the chips these days. This was because he had become the treasurer of a newly arisen sect called the Great Sunshine Religion.

"There are so many people who stumble that you would need a huge broom to sweep them all away. Generally, when they stumble, people look up to the sky for the first time, and pray to God. It's early days yet for the Great Sunshine Religion. But since it is the mighty God of the Great Sunshine Religion that illuminates the footsteps of those who have stumbled, we have had any number of shrine visits, thanks to word of mouth alone. Soon I believe the Great Sunshine Religion will be more powerful than the Kannon cult at Atami."

"But what should people like me who stumble all the time do?"

"God will make you get up and walk. Romans 14:23 tells us, 'And he that doubteth is damned if he eat, because he eateth not of faith: for whatsoever is not of faith is sin.' Even Christianity makes this absolutely clear statement on the matter. Still more likely is it that the Great Sunshine Religion of Japan will enter into the souls of people who are heavily laden with sin. At present, we are looking for a site for our main temple in Denenchofu."

"Is it a religion like Jikoson?"

"No, it's not like that. We don't rely on the patronage of celebrities like they do. We worship only the God of the Great Sunshine Religion. Our sole purpose is to raise up ordinary worshipers to prosperity. If we let in celebrities, we would become conspicuous midway, and there would be a danger of the work not going well. On the contrary, that sort of publicity would be a hindrance."

"Yes, but does God really exist? I wonder . . ."

"He does exist. He exists, and therefore many people have gone astray until they believed in God. First of all, you would do well to observe this mysterious body of the human being. No matter how much science has discovered, it cannot create a human being. God exists."

The sukiyaki was ready. Iba also dipped his hand into the pot. Yukiko had no appetite at all. She liked the whiteness of the raw scallions and ate that part. Haruko, taking a flask of whiskey from her pocket, also offered some to Iba. Having the two women sit in front of him, Iba got drunk on the whiskey. Poking vigorously at the beef, he said between mouthfuls that they should come at least once on a temple visit.

"In the old days, there were Buddhist temples in every town and village. The temples served as gathering places for the common people. But the temples gradually came to specialize in burial ceremonies. They lost their liveliness, and Buddhism acquired a reputation as a dark religion . . . When you go to a Christian church, they hold wedding ceremonies, it's a cheerful, busy sort of religion. It's not only department stores and restaurants that offer group weddings of many tens of couples, right? The Great Sunshine Religion also intends to follow that tradition. A religion where everything is lively and bright holds a certain glamour for those who have stumbled. Soon, at the main temple of the Great Sunshine Religion, wedding ceremonies will be conducted. We will not perform any funeral ceremonies at all.

"Priests at temples often say things such as, 'If people make a pilgrimage to our temple in Tokyo on the Day of the Tiger and then keep their account books with a brush-pen purchased at the temple, they will become rich'—there's no doubt that ideas like that increase pilgrimages by leaps and bounds. Unless everything is bright and cheerful, it doesn't work. Weddings don't bring in that much money themselves. Those religions that say that the temple visit has to be made in secret from others are no good. Religions that give people what they want—those are the religions that make money."

The talk shifted to the techniques of making use of God and of people. Iba opined that when people stumble, they all suffer the pains of despair. For everyone alike, despair is long and happiness short. It is the urgent task of religion today, Iba said, to seize upon the brevity of happiness. Because of love, men and women spend money. If the ecstasy of religion could also be used to make people spend money, religion might be more lucrative than any other business, he concluded.

Iba, taking Haruko's hand, put his ear to her palm.

"You have a hot hand. The ear is the most sensitive instrument for calculating the heat of the entire human body. There is no need for a thermometer. People with cold hearts have hot hands. The hand is the place from where the ether of the human soul is diffused. It is right and proper that the hand be hot, like yours. People with cold hands are keeping their heat shut up inside them. They are harboring an illness somewhere within them."

Iba, continuing to hold Haruko's hand, played with it and did not seem about to let go.

"But I'm disappointed in love these days. I feel depressed. Can you tell my fortune?"

When he heard that Haruko was disappointed in love, Iba again put his ear to her hand and pressed it against his cheek. He concentrated his thoughts. Haruko, giggling, nimbly withdrew her hand from Iba's ear.

"In the original vow of Amitabha, it says that one should have regard neither for old or young, nor for good or bad, but that one should make faith the sole requirement. In this vow, he prays to rescue mankind from many-layered sin and the flames of passion. Eh? With this kind of thing, unless you believe the heart that prays, nothing will happen. If, like you, one makes utter mock of it, it's no good. If you're going to make mock, make a fool of yourself once and believe in the Great Sunshine Religion. Otherwise, all is lost. In whatever slight degree, I, for you, am the opposite sex. When your hand touches the ear of the opposite sex, a delicate divinity is transmitted. You must make faith the requirement."

Iba, having emptied half of the pocket flask of whiskey, had a befuddled look in his eyes.

38

THE SECOND FLOOR had a three-mat room and a four-and-a-half mat room. The three-mat room was the bedroom of the tinsmith's three children. In the larger room there was a three-foot wall cupboard with a hinged door. The wall was made of composition board of compressed sawdust. A portable clay cooking stove and the ration of charcoal were stored in the alcove of the bay window. That is where Yukiko did her cooking. Beneath the bay window was a vacant lot where stalks of Indian corn grew tall. Yukiko was at more and more of a loss as to how to live. Perhaps she should try being a shoeshine girl. But she had the feeling that work that meant squatting on the ground would be too hard on her body. She tried sending a couple of telegrams to Tomioka, but there was no word from him. Making up her mind, Yukiko went to Tomioka's previous house in Gotanda. But the nameplate had changed, and the person who came out said that they had bought this house and moved here in May. But there was a postcard from Tomioka-san. "I'll give it to you," the person said, handing Tomioka's postcard to Yukiko. The return address was Mishuku, in Setagaya. Evidently Tomioka was renting a room out toward Takase.

Again making up her mind, forcing her weary body to move, Yukiko visited Tomioka's new home. It was an unusually big house with a stone gate. Alongside the gate—had the former owners had a car?—there was a garage. When Yukiko entered the gate and pressed the doorbell, Seiko—wearing a summer housedress—unexpectedly opened the door and came out. Shocked for a moment, Yukiko swallowed her breath. Seiko, also seeming surprised, turned red and exclaimed, "Oh!"

"Oh—have you come to Tokyo?"

"Yes . . ."

"How did you come to this sort of place?"

"Because it's the house of an acquaintance of mine."

"Is Tomioka here?"

"Right now he's out, but . . ."

"You're lying purely. What a strange person. This is completely strange. Well, I'll wait in Tomioka's room until he comes back . . ."

Seiko was silent. Yukiko felt as if her whole body were trembling. It was unclear even to her what she should say.

"He went back to his wife. He just left yesterday, so he's not likely to be back here soon. His wife is not well."

"Oh, is that so? All the better then. I'm not well either. You'll allow me to rest quietly in Tomioka's room until he gets back."

Seiko appeared to be flummoxed. When Yukiko looked at the entryway behind her, there was a child's scooter and a baby carriage. Apparently several families were living in this house. Seiko obstinately stood there and would not move aside. Yukiko also stubbornly held her ground.

"The entryway is fine. I'll explain the circumstances to the people of the house. You'll let me stay here."

Seiko, as if she'd lost the spirit to resist, silently showed Yukiko up to the second floor. At the end of a wide corridor was an eight-mat room with thin straw matting over a board floor. Along the wall there was a crude bed with two small pillows next to each other. On the wall hung Seiko's purple Meisen silk, unlined kimono, and a chemise and Tomioka's summer kimono nightclothes. In front of the diamond-paned hinged windows, there was a small red lacquer dressing table. A new dining table and a small tea cupboard stood side by side. Although all was now clear to Yukiko, she felt a burning fury rise up in her.

It was this kind of thing after all, she thought. Tomioka truly was not there. The only thing in the room that bespoke Tomioka was the man's summer kimono.

"How long have you been living together?"

"How long, you say. This is my room. Tomioka-san went to the country. Since he had no place to stay in Tokyo, he came here. At that time I was sleeping downstairs."

"No place to stay? Yes, no place to stay . . . What is your husband in Ikaho doing?"

"We've separated."

"How convenient for you."

It was already evening. The children were noisily playing in the upstairs corridor. Seiko, saying nothing, sat down on the bed. Yukiko, also fallen silent, sat by the bay window. As if she'd suddenly thought of something, Seiko went out into the corridor. Yukiko looked around her. It was a mystery how Seiko had gotten together with Tomioka. A couple of teacups on the dining table, a man's umbrella in the corner—as Yukiko looked, Tomioka's things manifested themselves. Seiko did not come back for some time. Going out into the corridor, Yukiko called to one of the children playing, a boy of about seven, and asked him, "Does the man in this room have a job?"

"Uh-huh."

"Does he come back in the evening?"

"Uh-huh."

"What time does he usually come back?"

"Soon, I guess."

"Where does he work?"

"I don't know."

"Does he stay here a lot of the time?"

"Uh-huh."

It's like a kind of apartment, Yukiko thought. She went back into the room and looked everything over with the cold eyes of a process server. A trunk and a wicker suitcase had been shoved under the bed. A wire had been strung across one corner of the plaster ceiling, and two hand towels hung from it. Behind the bed was a pile of about twenty books having to do with forestry. On the top was a pamphlet from the Forestry Bureau in Ranbean, written in French, about the area of virgin forest there under its control. Yukiko remembered that this had been written by one of the employees at the Forestry Bureau. Yukiko took the pamphlet in hand and looked through the photographs of the beautiful forests of French Indochina. There was not a photograph that did not bring back its memory. A photograph of a villa in the Ranbean highland surrounded by bougainvilleas and mimosas especially caught Yukiko's eye. The sublime scenery enclosed by mountains and facing onto the lake was, for Yukiko at this moment, an indescribable consolation . . . It had grown dark around her. Seiko did not come back. Perhaps she had gone to telephone Tomioka. From the open window Yukiko looked at the sweltering sky as it darkened toward night. She wiped away a few tears. Meaning to take the pamphlet with her as a souvenir, Yukiko put it away in her handbag and went out into the corridor. She no longer wanted to see Tomioka or Seiko. She felt as if her feelings had been decided.

They ought to have, and in a way they had, died in Ikaho. When Yukiko finally thought of it this way, she did not hold anything against anyone. She put on her shoes and stepped into the front garden outside the entryway. At the gate she saw someone coming toward her.

It was Tomioka. For a moment he looked surprised. But then, when he looked at Yukiko, standing before him silently, her eyes rimmed with tears, he asked quietly, as if he had resigned himself to everything, "When did you come?"

"I met Seiko-san." So saying, Yukiko stepped away from Tomioka and went out of the gate. Tomioka came after her.

"Hey!"

Yukiko did not turn around.

"Hey, I want to talk to you."

Yukiko didn't care one way or another. If she listened, at this late hour, to the details of his affair with Seiko, it would never end. She felt as if Kano were having his revenge. Kano must have tasted this same kind of feeling back then. Although when Kano had confessed his violent love, she had granted him a fleeting kiss, it was Tomioka with whom she had had the secret rendezvous. Kano, enraged at her deceitfulness, had brandished his sword. Only now did Yukiko realize that these things had led directly to the way she was now.

"I have never forgotten about you for a single day. I've been thinking I'd like to do something for you. It's because I've been forcibly seduced by that woman, Seiko."

"That's a good story."

"It's not good. I'm a bad person. I know I'm to blame."

"Is that so?"

Yukiko was walking in the opposite direction from Meguro Station. In the dark, burned-out areas overgrown by weeds, swarms of small bugs gathered and hovered in the air. The evening sky was lit with color, as if it was dawn.

"Is it October?"

"Is it what?"

"When the child will be born."

"If I were to have it. I plan to go tomorrow to the clinic and have it aborted."

Tomioka did not say anything. As long as there was life, Yukiko realized, passions would generate storms of desire in people. Yukiko had the urge to seclude herself in a temple and surrender herself entirely to prayer—even if it was to a god that the Great Sunshine Religion was employing to make money.

Although Tomioka did not know what Seiko had said to Yukiko, he imagined that she must have lorded it over Yukiko.

"So you must think that I'm an awful person?"

"Yes." Yukiko put great feeling into the word.

"Please let the child be born. From that day, I will take responsibility for it . . . And I intend to tell you the whole truth about Seiko, too."

"Seiko-san told me she'd left her husband."

"Actually, that room is Seiko's room. Even though it must look as if I'm shacked up there, it's just a room that Seiko rented. This May, I met her by chance at Shinjuku Station and was taken in hand by her, against my will. So naturally I ended up staying at her place. When you sent me word from Shizuoka, I knew from your letters that you'd gone back to Tokyo and found a new room. But I thought that if we met, it would just not work out. So I just sent money. I sold my house and sent my family to the country; I put my wife in the hospital and somehow managed to find work. Since it was a time when my feelings were all roiled up, I succumbed to Seiko's charms, despite myself."

Yukiko had no faith in Tomioka's reasons.

They located a barracklike coffee shop and went in. At the front there was a big blue-painted crate filled with ice cream. A woman with a child stared round-eyed at the two. Yukiko sat down on one of the rickety chairs. Her legs were stiff, and she was dead tired. She felt defeated in mind and body.

39

YUKIKO'S COLOR WAS BAD. Looking at her face, Tomioka took out a cigarette from the pack in his pocket. He ordered two soda waters. Yukiko, leaning heavily against the wall, closed her eyes. She had no energy to think of anything. And yet, a certain day in Ranbean, when she had been standing on the white diving board at the lake, floated up before her like a mirage. Tomioka was swimming in the dusky lake. She could hear the sounds of a noisy game of rugby being played in a nearby field. If she sat absolutely still, her exhaustion was just like the fatigue after swimming.

Leisurely exhaling, Tomioka said, "You're probably thinking about all kinds of things, but this is how things have turned out. I'll make it up to you. Please understand."

"At Ikaho, you had an affair with Seiko-san?"

Tomioka was silent.

"You're a person who'll do anything at all, aren't you?"

But even while she said this, Yukiko questioned herself too, about what sort of person she was. Although it had been brief, what about her time with Joe? Tomioka had not especially reproached her. Did the heart's emptiness occasionally leave one no choice but to reach out to someone's hand? It had been a kind of emptiness too that had caused the regrettable relationship with Iba in the past.

She had done the same things she accused Tomioka of. But when it was her own act, she let it pass by unnoticed.

"It's not that I don't understand, but I was startled ... I haven't forgotten how Seiko-san wept at the bus stop in Ikaho, but I believed in you. In your feelings ... I was conceited, maybe. But it can't be helped. There's nothing to be done about it. It's not that I got angry and wanted to abort the child ... Already, earlier, I've been thinking, Someday, someday. Today, I decided. I'll become strong, I thought. When I think of the various things I've suffered through, day by day, having the child aborted is easy. I want to be light and agile and to work at something. Don't you think it would be a misfortune to have our child? For example, even if you took responsibility, you couldn't do anything for it, and I myself would be at a loss to act in the matter. I was thinking that we should have a talk and agree on what to do about the child. It probably wouldn't matter even if you were together with Seiko-san. If things are going well for you. That woman, also, seems to love you from her heart ... Is there something wrong with your wife?"

"It's her chest."

"Is it bad?"

"If she rests for a long time, they say she will get better."

"From now on, it's going to be hard for you, too. You say you've found some work?"

"Yeah, with a soap company run by a friend of mine. It's not much. But he's been really good to me, and for now I'm letting him help me out."

Tomioka looked at Yukiko's beautiful hands. She had beautiful, gentle-looking hands. Yukiko was to be pitied, Tomioka thought, but Seiko was too.

"Up until now, I have not had a single child. I want very much for the child to be born. The affair with Seiko, also, is not going to last long. If I could just find a house, I'd like to move in right away. Seiko, too, has not completely broken with her husband. That room is like her hiding place. The husband hasn't had any news of Seiko yet. I don't like the situation either, and the people of the house seem to completely disapprove of me."

"Is Seiko-san doing something?'

"She's waitressing at a bar in Shinjuku, but for the past two or three days her teeth have been hurting her and she's stayed in."

"But Seiko-san is totally in love with you. You might even live with her for the rest of your life, no? Those who stay together win. As for us, our time in Indochina is already in the past, and we hardly ever remember it. I don't even have dreams about it anymore. Do you?"

"I occasionally have dreams. About you and Dalat."

"Did I write in my letter that I'd gone to see Kano in January?"

"Yeah, I know about it. Kano is in bad shape too."

"He seems to have resigned himself. He's thin, and he has no energy."

"He was such a great patriot—honest, straightforward."

"Yes, he wasn't a crafty, sly sort, like us."

Leaving the coffee shop, they continued walking without any destination. It had gotten completely dark outside, and there was a cool breeze.

"When we walk around like this, it's almost as if we were relatives. In your heart, you're probably thinking about Seiko-san more than me. But I'm thinking of you as a relative, just as I please. That's freedom. You're smiling?"

"I'm not smiling. I'm thinking I've done something unpardonable to Seiko's husband. I'm living like a fugitive too, being dragged along by Seiko's powerful pull."

"You're not planning a lovers' suicide with Seiko-san anytime soon, are you? If anything happens, she's fully capable of going through with it."

Tomioka thought so too. "Every day we quarrel."

"Why's that?"

"Because I don't follow her completely in everything. It will be extremely difficult to send her back to her husband."

"It can't be much worse than tonight was."

"Let's not talk about it. This next Sunday, I'll come visit you. Please hold off on deciding about the child until then. Thank you for understanding my feelings so well. I feel more at ease now, and cheerful. I'm entangled with Seiko, but I intend to resolve that in the near future."

"Don't worry about it, and don't make promises. I'm letting things take their course. To tell you the truth, it's all I can do right now to take care of myself. And I'm not saying that to make you nervous . . ."

Coming to the overpass, for a while they stood there leaning against the white stone parapet. Under the bridge, a train thundered by.

40

ABOUT TEN DAYS HAD PASSED since Yukiko parted from Tomioka. She decided to go to a small gynecology clinic in the neighborhood and have herself examined. It seemed that an abortion would cost at least five or six thousand yen. Yukiko became angrier and angrier as the days wore on. If this was any indication, then she was not going to have any help with the baby either.

Was she really going to have a child by a shallow-hearted man like that? Her feelings turned bitter, and she wound up telling Iba everything. If she could just get rid of the baby, she would be willing to do whatever was necessary to repay Iba. He said that he would give her the money if that was what she wanted, but once she was herself again, why didn't she come and work at the church for a while? He himself was engrossed with his work, and rather than a stranger, he preferred a trusted private secretary who understood his disposition.

Two or three days later, Iba brought along ten thousand yen in cash. Yukiko didn't care what work she did, as long as she was relieved of the baby, so she decided to try working for the religion that Iba had helped found. She also wanted to return to a life that was hers and to forget about Tomioka.

A week or so later, Yukiko entered the hospital. Each day, two or three women with this same secret visited the doctor. Two women of that sort were staying now in the narrow hospital room. After the curettage had been performed, Yukiko felt as if her body had descended into hell. She felt a sense of suffocation when she briefly glimpsed the collapsed lump of flesh and blood.

Iba came to the hospital to visit on the second day. All he asked Yukiko was when she would leave the hospital and come to work as his assistant. But at the moment her body felt weaker than ever before. Iba had become completely the man of faith. He boasted that the accounts office had been combined with the architectural-expenses department and that money was coming in like nobody's business.

The women who were also staying in Yukiko's room had at some point begun to listen to Iba's discourse.

The patient whose bed was by the wall, a woman of about forty, whose name was Otsu Shimo, suddenly asked, "Is it impossible for me, also, to enter among the ranks of the believers?"

The woman, who had come to dispose of a child she'd been impregnated with by an old, married man, was leaving the next day, she said. She made no mention of her status, but according to the nurse, she was a teacher at a grade school in Chiba or thereabouts.

Seemingly an unlikely person to have gotten involved with a man, she was a dark-complexioned, big-boned woman with formal manners.

"Is the Founder of the Great Sunshine Religion a man?"

Iba grinned.

"Yes, of course he's a man. He's a splendid personage. From the time of his youth, he has been studying in India—a man of considerable vision. To reach this point, he has passed through various ordeals. In order to spread the light in the wilderness, he has made his way back to Japan. For a long time, he served as a staff officer at the front in Burma and the Malay States, and he made a name for himself in both places. If all were as it should be, the likes of us would not even dare to approach him. Come just once. It's likely that he will dissolve all your woes," Iba said.

"Oh, then the Founder used to be a military man?"

"That's right. He's a purged member of the armed forces, so it's interesting. This kind of ex-soldier knows how to talk to the troops. You've got to take a firm hand with the rabble."

Iba added in an undertone, "He's going to buy a car soon under my name. Everything has been entrusted to me. I've got the Master right where I want him."

"How old a man is he?"

"Sixty-one, sixty-two maybe. He's a terrific character. He's had affairs with a hundred women or so. No matter where the grass grows, he says, it reaches toward the sun. He's said to have taken the name for the Great Sunshine Religion from that power of life. Now, we have more than a hundred thousand believers. From now on, there's no telling how much more it will grow. It's an article of faith with the Master that the work should go forward 'conspicuously, in an inconspicuous manner.'"

It gave Yukiko the creeps that Iba had utterly changed from the old Iba into something like a madman. Most likely it was simply that, as if Yukiko had nothing to do with Tomioka, Iba wanted to hire as his confidential secretary a woman with whom he'd had a previous relationship.

Otsu Shimo seemed to be thinking about something. Then, throwing a Japanese half coat over her unlined summer kimono, she sat up in her bed and said to Iba, "Actually, I come from Chiba, but for personal reasons, I don't want to go back home just now. If I were to be admitted as a believer in the Great Sunshine Religion and could undertake a course of study, I would like to receive a diploma as a missionary. But how much money would that take?"

Ceremoniously, puffing away at a foreign cigarette, Iba replied, "Ah, yes. At first, from the ordinary believer, we receive three hundred yen as an entrance fee. If they desire to become missionaries, we have them make a deposit of a thousand yen. After half a year, the permit to be a missionary is issued. On a daily basis, as a fee for remaining overnight in the temple for purposes of prayer, you give what your heart tells you. At the time permission is granted, we have another talk."

Otsu Shimo, saying that by all means she would enter a shrine of the Great Sunshine Religion for overnight prayer, asked Iba for his business card. Strangely, Iba told her that he didn't have one yet. He seemed to have lost all interest in her. She made him write out the address on a small piece of paper.

"Naturally," Iba said, "becoming a missionary is something quite different from becoming an ordinary believer. To become a missionary is like acquiring the capital for a lifetime. In fact, it costs a considerable amount of money."

"Yes, certainly. I would expect that. But I know someone who will give me any sum of money I need, provided I stay out of sight for a year or so. He is a person of some status, so he is willing to be quite generous."

"What's that? A person of status?" Iba had suddenly become very polite.

"Status? If you have a person of status as your backer, the Great Sunshine Religion welcomes you with open arms. This religion is absolutely not a heretical sect, of which there are so many these days. It does not raise people's spirits by telling them they are going to get well. Moreover, in the present age of scientific advances, we do not believe that sickness can be cured by religion. Isn't that so? The Great Sunshine Religion came into being based on the heart's desire to heal the ills of the soul. Although there are doctors who examine the body, there are no doctors who can examine the soul and offer it consolation. Furthermore, this religion leads the way to riches. It dispenses an extraordinarily bright optimism in these dark latter days. If you have a person of status as your backer, I myself will conduct the negotiations with great care, more than for an ordinary person . . . The Master does not like to see people, so I shall act on his behalf in all matters."

41

ON THE DAY SHE FINALLY left the hospital, Yukiko, while paying the bill at the office, happened to see a newspaper in the waiting room. A little item in it caught her eye.

> At 10:40 p.m. on the 12th, at XX address in North Shina-gawa of Shinagawa Ward, Mukai Seikichi, 48, formerly a restaurateur in Iikura, summoned his common-law wife, Tani Seiko, 21, to his room, and strangled her with a hand towel. After committing the crime, he immediately turned himself in at the Daiba police booth. According to the Shinagawa police station, Mukai, while operating a bar in the hot springs resort town of Ikaho, had lived with Seiko. Seiko, relying on her lover, a certain Tomioka, fled to Tokyo. Afterward, Mukai came to the city to take her back, but Seiko refused a reconciliation. On the 12th, Mukai intercepted Seiko on her way to the bath, and took her to his room. He urged her to reconcile, and an argument ensued. He then flew into a fury and strangled Seiko with a hand towel.

The article had photographs of both Mukai and Seiko.

Yukiko, sitting for some while on the hard seat, read the newspaper report any number of times. She found a strange logic in the fact that Seiko, whose personality was strong to the point of wrongheadedness, should finally have been strangled by her husband.

This would be a good lesson for Tomioka, she thought. She believed that now she understood the ambiguous expression he had had when she had gone to visit him at the house in Mishuku.

It seemed to Yukiko that Tomioka would never be free of the ghost of Seiko. It was not only Tomioka who had returned to Japan and gone completely to the bad. Kano had also fallen apart, so to speak. That evening, Yukiko slept in her own bed after a very long time. She felt completely exhausted and had a sense that she'd made a long journey to reach this day. While listening to the wind rustling the ears of Indian corn beneath the window and to the sounds of the crickets, Yukiko thought about Tomioka lying in his room in Mishuku.

Even as she drowsed, halfway between waking and sleep, Yukiko dreamed about Ikaho.

Yukiko felt not the slightest sympathy toward the deceased Seiko. That sort of willful behavior was the worst way to live one's life, she thought. And Tomioka's weakness, too, was despicable. Yukiko's contempt was such that she wanted to spit on both Tomioka and the late Seiko.

Even after four or five days, Yukiko's physical condition did not at all improve. Impatiently, Iba visited her, but when he saw the pale-faced Yukiko, apparently unable to make any demands, he hesitated to ask her to come to work quickly.

"What's the matter? You look terribly weak . . . Please show some energy. Some spiritual strength. Living and dying is a matter of spiritual strength. You've changed since you got back from French Indochina. You have to show more energy, be cheerful, and smarten yourself up. By the way, that woman, what's her name, Otsu Shimo, has joined us. She's spending three nights in the temple praying. She's a rather good prospect. She knows how to speak, and she has money. These days, she's really laying on the makeup and is all set to go. She's a grade-school teacher and her family runs a miso business. It seems women also, when they reach a certain age, start thinking about what's to become of them. She'll be useful. Even the Founder says she's a find."

Iba was wearing a new black suit, with a sunflower pin in his lapel.

"This is just between you and me, of course, but I tell you, the best business in this world—religion, without a doubt. It's interesting how people who feel lost hear about us and come to us. We have information booths everywhere and maps posted at the stations. People come and just gladly give us money. I finally sold that house in Saginomiya. Now I've bought a house that belonged to a banker in Ikenoue, and I'm living there with my family and the Founder. It's magnificent. It cost three and a half million yen. The house is old, but it has three hundred twenty square yards of floor space. The grounds are two thousand square yards. There's an artificial pond and a miniature mountain."

"God's going to punish you by and by."

"God? But God only looks after people who try to make their own way. People who don't grab the rope of destiny, even God has no interest in them. Hey, I must be smitten with you after all, Yukiko. I'm going to buy you a nice little house soon. Because whatever anybody says, I was your first. That's one thing I don't forget."

"Please stop talking like that," Yukiko said. "Even women, when they grow older, come to see the world for what it is. I've had plenty of reminiscing about the past. What you do doesn't interest me."

Iba grinned broadly. Although Yukiko's face was pale, she had a womanly glamour that was quite different from the unsophisticated girl of the past.

"No, I didn't mean anything bad. It's precisely because in everything I'm thinking of your happiness, Yukiko. It's better not to think too much of pursuing the ideal. Observing this world, you've probably studied the sweet and the sour in life. You probably understand that love and infatuation in men and in women are not greatly to be trusted. Heaven and hell in this world are a matter of money alone. I have come to keenly realize the blessedness of money. I was never so depressed as in the interval after the war, but today I am very different. I have felt the necessity to live all out, to make money while I can. The Founder says the same thing."

Iba left a packet of money and made a brisk departure. When Yukiko opened it, it was a bundle of crisp, new 100-yen notes, completely unwrinkled. Looking at the ten thousand yen in new banknotes, it seemed amusing to Yukiko that she had never handled anything before but wrinkled bills. For a while, Yukiko mused on Iba's financial strength.

Yukiko allowed Iba to buy her a little house and thought she would like to meet Tomioka every now and again. But the thought was passing.

She realized her violent jealousy toward Tomioka was sure to surface again. And she could not get used to the idea of depending on Iba, nor to that of becoming a worshiper of the Great Sunshine Religion.

One day, Yukiko received a letter from Kano's address in a woman's handwriting, informing her that Kano had died. Yukiko read the letter from Kano's mother several times. Kano's will had specified that he was to have a Catholic funeral service. It struck Yukiko as strange that Kano, who had been such a lover of his country and believed that Japan could not lose, should have chosen to have a modest Catholic funeral. It seemed that in his last years Kano had truly been a victim of the war. Although she wanted to write a letter of gentle condolence to Kano's mother, she was so tired that she ended up sending no response.

Since the article had appeared in the newspaper, there had been no word from Tomioka. She even worried about where Tomioka might have vanished. Was he even still in Mishuku?

During the day, invariably only thoughts of Tomioka came and went in Yukiko's heart. Surely, even with the melancholy death of Seiko, Tomioka could not have completely forgotten about Yukiko. Although he had said he was working at a soap company, what Yukiko wanted was for Tomioka to be rehired by the Forestry Bureau and sent to a forestry station in the mountains in some nice part of the country. Anywhere would do. Then, she fantasized, the two of them could quietly get married. Taking out Tomioka's pamphlet about French Indochina that she had taken from Seiko's room in Mishuku, and looking at the pages, Yukiko could not believe that Tomioka would simply vanish from her life without a word.

Making up her mind, Yukiko wrote him a letter.

> *I read about Seiko-san's death in the newspaper. I can only think that all of us are being dangled on the strings of fate. I think it was a terrible thing.*
>
> *How are you?*
>
> *For a while, I hated you and was angry with you. But finally I realized that, aside from me, there's no one else to console you.*
>
> *Kano-san died on the twenty-second. I got a letter from his mother, saying he had a Catholic funeral. I thought that you might not have heard, so I am letting you know. When you think about it, Kano also had a very sad time in his last years.*

More than ten days have passed since that incident. Your
feelings must have calmed down a bit by now. We should have
died together at Ikaho. On the other hand, I think that if we had
died in the mountains of Dalat, it would have been all the more
beautiful.

I had the child aborted. I think that you're a hateful person.
If I had depended on you, I would have been driven into a corner
and by now might very well have killed myself. You're a person
who kills people. On account of you, Seiko-san, Kano, your wife,
and me—all have fallen into misfortune. I'm not blaming you,
but that's what I think.

I'm still waiting to get well. When I do, I intend to work, for
once, at an honest, steady job. Are you well? I would still like to
see you. I'm not saying that I want to leave you. Please, by all
means, come to see me just once. Let me know how you are.

About five days after Yukiko had mailed this letter, a response came
from Tomioka, with a five-thousand-yen money order enclosed. "As for
meeting you, please wait about two weeks. Now is the worst time of all
for me, and so I don't want to meet anyone," it said. But receiving that
kind of letter was at least a consolation.

The letter continued, "Aborting the child, also, was unavoidable. But
I realize, and resign myself, that it is my fault that this happened. I will
certainly come to meet you. If it is your true wish that we not separate, I
will depend on that, and most assuredly I will come to meet you."

185

42

BUT TWO WEEKS PASSED, and Tomioka still had not come.

His lack of desire to see Yukiko, who was the person with whom he could talk the most freely, was not because of laziness. He was occupied with the court case of Mukai Seikichi, and he needed to help out in the matter of a lawyer. Mukai had no relatives to help, and Tomioka felt a sense of duty. At least, by helping Mukai he could make amends to Seiko. Meanwhile, he was struck by the calm demeanor of this man who had actually killed a woman. Was sexual passion between men and women so violent? When Tomioka learned that Mukai had killed Seiko, he learned for the first time, so to speak, of the existence of Mukai Seikichi. Tomioka felt the death as a harsh punishment by the husband for his own actions. Until that point, he had not given any thought at all, since leaving Ikaho, to the existence of Seiko's husband.

He had gone to Ikaho with Yukiko for a double lovers' suicide. On the verge of accomplishing this mission, out of a lingering nostalgia for the world, he had found a new beginning for his life, thanks to the chance-met Seiko. His own base desires had now resulted in Seiko's death and Mukai's imprisonment. Tomioka felt something coldhearted in his own craftiness that made him shiver. Tomioka was even unmoved by Yukiko's letter, which said that she wanted to see him. The fact that Yukiko had aborted the child caused him no pain. He could only think that since his return to Japan he had lost all feelings.

When he had met Mukai at the Shinagawa police station, Mukai had said that he didn't care where he spent the rest of his life. Whether it was the death penalty or life imprisonment, he only hoped the verdict would come quickly. He intended in prison to pray for and comfort the soul of Seiko, Mukai said. There was no need for a lawyer.

Kano, also, had finally died of a chest malady. Everyone was headed toward journey's end, pressed from behind by countless others. That was the one thing that Tomioka did not like—being hurried toward an unhappy end. Now that he had lost his feelings, he realized that there was no better road in life than to make the passage through the world as comfortable as possible.

He did not want to see Yukiko.

Although he'd scraped up five thousand yen and sent it to her, he meant it as a celebratory farewell gift to Yukiko for having eliminated the child from the world. In his heart of hearts, Tomioka had not wanted the child.

There had been a heavy wind and rain since the morning. He lay on the bed, without Seiko, and listened vaguely to the sound of the rain falling.

Until just recently, Seiko had lain here beside him. When she awoke, she had invariably laid both her legs over Tomioka's leg and crooned to him. It was at those times only that Tomioka felt the two had been truly close.

Now Seiko was nowhere. Tomioka did not think of her with love or nostalgia. On the contrary, he felt refreshed and relieved of her. Tomioka had already had enough of women. He seemed to appreciate for the first time the healthy relaxing feeling of lying by himself on a bed. An opportunity had come to turn his life around. How brisk and bracing it was to be on one's own.

First, he needed to leave this room and, at the same time, to get rid of his wife and his parents. If all went well, he would even like to change his name. He wanted to quit his job and find some new work.

Still, it was not a particularly good feeling to know that a man he'd felt friendly toward had been thrown in jail. Tomioka also hoped that the sentence might be handed down quickly—this would help him regain his own equanimity.

Since the incident, Tomioka had not gone in to the office. These past few days, Tomioka had been working, when he felt like it, on an article, "Memories of a Forester in the South," for an agricultural journal put out by a certain newspaper company. It would be around a hundred pages. If he could finish it, he would send it off to the journal and make some money. That was his plan.

And before writing about the memories of a forester, as a diversion, Tomioka had sent in a thirty-page essay entitled "Memories of the Fruits of the South." It was just about the time of the incident. The piece had appeared in the journal, and Tomioka received a payment of ten thousand yen. Tomioka was encouraged by this.

The essay was as follows:

> As an employee of the former Ministry of Agriculture and Forestry attached to the military, I lived about four years in French Indochina. Since I passed those four years in tropical regions, I retain the memories of various fruits.
>
> In tropical regions, various kinds of fruit trees flourish. For those who dwell in the tropics, the mellow taste of their fruits has above all else a powerful fascination. If I am to speak of my deepest impressions, I would have to mention, first of all, the banana, which is the king of all fruits in the tropical zone. At present, bananas are imported by Japan from Taiwan, but probably few people know that there are several hundred different varieties of bananas. Long, slender bananas, thick and short bananas, remarkably angled bananas, light brown bananas, bananas tinged with a slightly red color, fragrantly perfumed bananas—all shapes and flavors, truly of an infinite variety.
>
> During my life in the tropics, for the most part I especially selected the king banana and the three-foot banana for consumption. On rare occasions I was served cooked bananas, but I cannot say that they tasted very good.
>
> For planting, banana shoots from the bottom of the stem are used. After fifteen months or so, they grow to a height of ten to twenty feet. From the core, where leaves have been

grafted, an enormous flower stalk of four or five feet grows and blossoms. As it bears fruit, the flower stalk naturally curves downward, and the stem withers. The shoots that sprout from its stump turn into other stems. After one year, these bear fruit again.

Suitable to a moist, warm climate, if the soil is viscous and the drainage is good, the banana can be grown anywhere. But it is not suited to stony soil exposed to strong winds, nor for sandy soil formed from limestone.

The banana is a gift from heaven, most rejoiced over by the poor, who use it as a dietary supplement.

If the banana is the king of the fruits, should one say that the mangosteen is the queen? This fruit grows on a tree whose academic appellation is *Garcinia mangostana*. The first time I saw a mangosteen was at a fruit shop near Purachiku in the town of Hanoi. The size of a small persimmon, the top is flat, the skin is smooth, the color a purplish brown. Slicing the mangosteen reveals a cluster of seeds around which a white creamy flesh has formed. The fruit skin contains tannic acid, which is used as a dye. If one puts some of the juice on a piece of cloth, it is hard to get it out. It was said that the prime season is from May to July, but it was February when I found one in Hanoi and ate it. During my two-week stay at the Moran Hotel in Hue, this mangosteen appeared on the table at every meal. The mangosteen tastes like a mandarin orange.

This tree is of middling height, and cone-shaped. The leaves are large and grow in symmetrically opposed rows. They are shaped like a long oval, with a coriaceous surface. Malaya is its place of origin. It is of extraordinarily slow growth. It requires nine or ten years before it will bear fruit. As for the right soil, it must be in a warm, humid climate, deep and fertile and well drained. If one thinks of the mangosteen as a refined fruit, as its direct opposite, with a pungent, foul smell, one must write of a rare fruit called the durian.

Tomioka, writing about the ecology of such fruits as the *karudamomu*, the *sapochiru*, the *baramitsu*, and the papaya, added his memories of when he had eaten those fruits and records of his trips in the tropical zone. Reaching his hand under the bed, Tomioka fished out the agricultural journal and flipped through the pages, gazing at his handiwork transformed into print. Of their own accord, the scenes and scenery of Dalat floated up behind his eyes.

The five thousand yen he had sent Yukiko was half the payment for the manuscript. But it gave him a cynical feeling to know that the money had gone for the expenses associated with an abortion.

There was the sound of someone knocking at the door. With a thrill of fear, Tomioka called out, "Who is it?"

"It's me, Yukiko," said the voice from the other side of the door.

When Tomioka went to open it, Yukiko, looking absolutely thin and haggard, stood in the corridor, holding a wet umbrella.

From the bottom of his heart he thought Yukiko's visit exceedingly inconvenient.

43

THREE WEEKS HAD PASSED, and still Tomioka had not come, so Yukiko had made up her mind, despite the rain, to go see him. Observing Tomioka's expression when he opened the door, Yukiko just knew that no matter what efforts she might make, the affair with Tomioka would be over today.

"It must have been quite an ordeal for you."

Tomioka, pulling together the front of his worn-out *yukata* and sitting down by the window, did his best to turn a smiling face toward Yukiko. "It was terrible. It must have been terrible for you too? Is it all right for you to be up already?"

"Yes, I didn't have to stay in the hospital that long. I finally recovered."

In Indochina, when they were alone, the two would always immediately snuggle up to each other and hold hands. Things had certainly changed.

"I read about it in the newspaper," Yukiko said, sitting down heavily. "I couldn't wait any longer. I managed to live by clinging to your letter, in which you said you would certainly come to see me; that if it was my true wish that we would not part, you would depend on that and come to see me."

Tomioka, his face drained of expression, said, "I never forget about you for a moment, but there's this business with Seiko's husband. Everything was a mess, so I couldn't come."

"So, even if I'd died in the hospital, you wouldn't have come."

"No, that's different. I thought you were all right, so I didn't worry."

"That's such a lie." Yukiko's body was shaking with her jealousy of Seiko. The man's state of mind, like a stone that would not move, rebounded on Yukiko, infuriating her. "Wasn't it you who said, 'Please have the baby'? And yet you didn't even come once. When you leave, you're gone. I hate Seiko-san. I even hate her husband. The fact that I love you seems very sad to me."

Yukiko leaned against the bed and wept. Tomioka, looking fixedly at the driving wind and rain outside, listened to Yukiko's crying voice. What on earth does she expect of him? How long would this woman torment him, like a moneylender harassing a debtor, with the memories of the past? Because of those memories, she was still trying to exact payment from him. As he listened to Yukiko's weeping voice, Tomioka suddenly grew nauseated.

"I'm asking you, please leave me alone. I can't help you. I'm a shell of a human being."

"I don't want us to break off. Be gentle to me as you were before."

"It would have been better when we got back to Japan to have gone our separate ways. It would be good for you now to set out on your own path in life."

"If I were going my own way in life, I would have long since stopped seeing you. And yet, you're tired of me, so you just say exactly what you think . . . But you know what? If Seiko-san's ghost were to appear here in this room, I would say to her, 'I will never leave Tomioka-san.' "

"Hey, don't talk so loud. It's like an apartment house here. Be discreet. It doesn't matter about Seiko. On the contrary, I feel in the clear now that she's gone. It's Mukai-san I feel sorry for. Right now, I'm free to go wherever I want to go, but Mukai is sitting in prison. It seems very bizarre."

"Well, you know what? I don't really want to think about Seiko-san's husband. Why should I? What connection is there between those people and us anyway? This incident, which you created—it was nothing I even knew about . . ."

Her heart raging with shame, Yukiko's vision became blurry and she felt dizzy. All the strength went out of her, and she collapsed.

Tomioka shook her roughly by the shoulder. "What's happened? Don't you feel well?"

The rain became even more violent, and the wind blew fiercely. Tomioka carried Yukiko over to the bed and laid her down on it. The blue veins stood out on her temples. Her lips were white and looked dry. The flesh of her cheeks twitched convulsively. Yukiko's whole body looked like that of a sick person. With both her hands she was trying to grasp something. There was black dirt under her fingernails.

Tomioka brought over some water in a metal basin, dipped a towel in it, and used it to cool Yukiko's forehead. He felt absolutely rotten about himself. Tomioka suddenly wanted money. Since Yukiko had started to fall into a comalike slumber, Tomioka, seating himself at his writing table, applied himself to his manuscript about his memories of French Indochina, which dealt with the plants and trees of the region.

> Regarding the *binro* and the *kinma*, there is a charming Annamese folktale. It was during the reign of Fun Boon IV, the king of the Annamese. In the house of the courtier Kao, there were an elder and a younger brother, whose names were Tan and Kan. The two brothers, who had lost their father at an early age, were especially affectionate to each other. As chance would have it, in the house of a relative named Ru, who had taken them in, there lived also a certain maiden. She and the elder brother fell in love and ended by getting married—

When Tomioka had written to this point, the upland scenery of Dalat, where he had first met Yukiko, flitted through his heart. Yukiko's red-striped gingham skirt, the one she had worn when they visited the tea plantation at Ontore, came vividly to mind. He could not believe that the wreck of Yukiko, who had been a girlish and beautiful young woman, now lay stretched out on the bed in his room. But his heart grew calm in the end, and unexpectedly his pen made good progress. Soon he started feeling hungry. He took a small pot from the tea chest, and heated up some coffee on the electric burner.

When he looked at the bedside clock on the tea chest, it was already nearly one o'clock. As he stuffed his cheeks with bread, Tomioka suddenly turned around toward the bed. Underneath the towel, Yukiko's eyes had opened.

"Why don't you eat something yourself?"

Tomioka poured some more coffee into a teacup. Yukiko, her eyes open, was looking at the ceiling.

"Won't you get up and have some coffee?"

Yukiko meekly got up and accepted the cup of coffee from Tomioka.

44

WHEN EVENING FELL, the rain grew all the more violent. Tomioka made his pen fly across the page.

> The jurisdiction of the Mountain Forestry District of the Dalat region where I was stationed encompassed 15,700 cubic meters of *kacha* pines. On the army's orders, we forestry employees, in the rapid development of the resources, embarked on a course of rather reckless deforestation.

Even the faces of the various army officers at that time were fading away from Tomioka's memory.

"What was the name of the last station on the line from Dalat?" Tomioka suddenly asked Yukiko.

So that's the kind of thing he was writing about, Yukiko thought. All of a sudden growing lively, she got down from the bed.

"Tsuruchamu, was it called?"

"Ah, yes, Tsuruchamu."

For a while, Yukiko watched Tomioka at his desk from behind.

"Do you remember a hamlet called Manrin?"

"Manrin?"

"Have you forgotten already?"

"Oh, that's the place where the royal tombs of Annam were?"

"Right, four kilometers from Dalat. There was a substation of the Forestry Bureau there. We walked there through the dense forest for the first time."

Going to Tomioka's side, Yukiko peeped at the manuscript on the desk.

"Why are you writing about these sorts of things?"

"I can earn money with this."

"Those kinds of things are worth money?"

Taking the agricultural journal from the side of the bed, Tomioka handed it to Yukiko. "Read this."

Taking the journal in her hand, Yukiko looked at the table of contents. The name Tomioka Kengo caught her eye. Quickly flipping the pages, Yukiko started reading.

"I got money for it. It made me feel better about myself. The money I sent you was from this manuscript fee."

"Really? You were writing?" Tomioka had written in layman's terms about bananas, mangosteen, durians, and the ecology of the region.

The wind and rain continued violently into the night. The wind sweeping through the branches of the trees sounded like tidal waves. Yukiko agreed to stay, but actually it was all one to Tomioka.

As they were finishing the bread and coffee, the electricity abruptly went off.

The two set a candle on the writing desk and, like old comrades, related their memories of French Indochina. Sometimes their memories differed. By exchanging stories, there were moments when they worked together to bring back once more the days of their passionate love. The electricity remained off for a long time. The candle, too, flickered out. There was nothing they could do but crawl into the bed and lie there. The uncurtained window now and then lit up with a flash of lightning. The rain drove hard against the wooden doors and glass panes.

Yukiko was waiting for some response from him, and she kept talking about the forest of Manrin. But Tomioka would not enter into the remembered scenery of Manrin with her. Whenever she whispered in his ear, Tomioka thought of Seiko and the way her big body lay alongside his on this bed.

He had heard from the people of the inn that her eyes had been half open and her tongue had protruded, but Tomioka had not seen her after her death. Her large body, so firm to the touch, suddenly became dear to Tomioka. She had died and was no longer in this world . . .

"Dear, do you remember the garden of the Chinese villa below the tennis court at Dalat?"

"Mm."

Tomioka no longer cared one way or another about Dalat or the Chinese villa. Yukiko's cloying sweetness was tiresome to him. The dreams of the past didn't matter one way or the other. He yearned for Seiko's solid, large body.

Feeling that with Seiko, he had known a real woman for the first time, Tomioka felt a tear collect in the corner of his eye.

Yukiko's hand crept stealthily over his chest. Tomioka grasped it and put it back in its place.

"What's the matter? Is it no good?"

"I'm tired tonight. I just want to fall into a deep sleep."

Drawing back her hand, Yukiko, holding her breath, was silent for a while. Although she divined the change in Tomioka's feelings, it never occurred to her that he was immersing himself deeply in memories of Seiko.

"Well, let's talk about the south. On this kind of night, I somehow can't get to sleep right away."

"I'm very sleepy."

"How you can be so cold . . . You used to be a gentler person."

Yukiko, one more time, clung to Tomioka's chest and tried coaxing him. Tomioka recalled Wilde's remark that to assess the quality and method of fermentation of a particular wine, it was not necessary to drink the whole barrel. He'd had enough of this going over the same things again and again. Now, he desired no other body but Seiko's. His throat was still not dry. At some point, he had fallen sound asleep. In a strange, disturbing dream that was like swimming through dark water, Tomioka encountered Seiko. Her eyes were half open, and her tongue was hanging way out; she had a weird expression on her face, but she was indescribably alluring. When they immediately embraced in the water, she put her long legs around his waist and her hands around his neck. Seiko's cold tongue licked his cheek. Tomioka involuntarily cried out.

Tomioka awakened at the sound of his own voice.

Lying heavily on top of him with her whole body, Yukiko had placed her wet cheek closely against Tomioka's cheek.

45

THE NEXT MORNING, when Tomioka woke up, Yukiko was putting on her makeup at Seiko's small dressing stand. The rain had completely cleared, and the sky was crystal clear and blue.

Tomioka, lying in bed, watched Yukiko. He felt as though he were being dragged into a swamp.

Yukiko was using Seiko's powder and puff. He was put off by her lack of respect for the dead. But on second thought, wasn't he actually the one who was the most callous person in this situation? The Yukiko reflected in the dressing stand mirror was thin to the point of emaciation. The full curves of her hips had diminished, and she had aged markedly. Her bosom also was no longer ample. Her hair, a reddish brown, was dry and lusterless. Her forehead seemed extremely wide, and the rims of her eyes were red and swollen.

Abruptly getting up, Tomioka tiptoed downstairs so as not to disturb the family and went to wash his face. As Yukiko was putting on her makeup, a tear suddenly flowed over the edge of her eye. She felt it had been made clear to her the night before that the affair was hopeless. She could not fight back against a Tomioka who even in his sleep called out the name of Seiko. She realized that no memories of French Indochina were alive in him.

At ten o'clock, with thoughts that left a bad aftertaste, Yukiko went out. Tomioka, saying that he was tired, did not see her off. Yukiko, also, was tired. Idly, unconsciously, Yukiko directed her body, absolutely exhausted and feeling as if the air had been taken out of it, toward the station. Thinking about how she was going to live, Yukiko tasted a loneliness that was as if she had fallen into a hole. If she was unable to do anything else, Yukiko thought, perhaps she should make up her mind and for the time being go to Iba's place and work in the office of the Great Sunshine Religion.

About five days passed with nothing having been accomplished.

An urgent letter came from Iba. Its message was that he wanted Yukiko to come without a day's delay. Yukiko decided to see what kind of place the office of the Great Sunshine Religion was. There was no word from Tomioka. If he'd had the last remaining bit of love for her, he would presumably have kept his promise to visit her. So whether or not she even had a relationship with Tomioka, she thought she would try placing her trust in the Great Sunshine Religion. Her heart stirred a little.

It was a blazing hot day.

Yukiko went on a search for the Great Sunshine Religion at the address she had been given in Ikegami-kamicho. Iba had indeed purchased a banker's former residence and grounds. At the granite pillars of the gate, there was an iron latticework wicket door, and a gravel driveway had been laid down, leading to the building's entrance. The trees in the garden were perfectly trimmed, and there was even a new tin-roofed garage shed. When Yukiko entered the grounds by the side gate, a gaunt, middle-aged woman—one of the believers, she supposed—was weeding in the garden, wearing a big straw hat. A glass door was open, and many pairs of neatly aligned sandals were lined up in the tiled lobby.

A new, large, single-leaf screen, with a dragon depicted on it, stood in the front of the lobby. Behind it, seated at a desk, was Otsu Shimo, whom Yukiko remembered from the clinic. Her face coated thickly with powder, Otsu Shimo wore a dark blue half-coat over a formal, dark blue divided skirt. She was writing something. The entryway stretched far back into the house, and there was a chilly draught. At the back, a chorus of confused voices arose. Prayers, Yukiko guessed.

46

IF IT HADN'T BEEN FOR THE VOICES of people praying, which sounded a bit like animals howling in the mountains, the entryway would have seemed that of a small, country hospital. As soon as Otsu Shimo saw Yukiko, she immediately stood up and came over to her.

"Welcome. The Teacher has been waiting impatiently for you." Otsu Shimo took a new pair of slippers from the sandal box and placed them before Yukiko. Shimo's demeanor was placid, and her expression virtuous.

"You certainly seem at home here," Yukiko said, putting on the slippers.

Shimo, displaying a strange pride like that of a bride with her dowry, did not deign to answer. "This way, please," she said, leading Yukiko along a passageway toward the back. When they came to the end of the cramped, narrow corridors and turned the corner, there was a room. Shimo, putting her fingers respectfully to the floor, said, "Teacher, Yukiko-sama is here."

The scene looked quite foolish to Yukiko. In the room, Iba grunted out a reply. When Shimo slid back the wooden door, a man in his sixties was lying on an army blanket. Alongside, Iba had stretched out both hands over the man. Shimo took a thin tea-colored sitting cushion from a corner of the room, placed it in the doorway, and indicated that Yukiko should sit there. Quietly sliding the door shut behind her, she made her departure. It was all a strange new world for Yukiko. The reclining old man, his eyes closed, was opening and closing his mouth like a fish. He had a swarthy complexion, hair that was tangled like a bunch of withered grasses, and a large mole on his forehead. He was wearing a white T-shirt with gray trousers, and his feet were bare. Iba wore a loose fitting half-coat of a dark color, similar to Shimo's garment. His eyes were also closed.

"So, as I was saying, the Original Vow of the Great Sunshine Religion makes no distinction between old and young or good and evil, but it takes pity on those who truly believe. This is God's will, to save humanity from the burning evil passions. The good and evil of this world are in vain. If you will only intone the invocation of the Great Sunshine Religion, this is better than all the gods and Buddhas. Thou shalt fear no evil. Among the evils, the lightest of these is the evil of illness. Illness is something that can be seen. It is like looking at a mark in the road. The evil of the heart is not seen by the eye; it cannot be grasped by the hand. This verily is the evil of Hell. Do not say it is karma. The evil of illness is slight. If you will intone the Great Sunshine invocation, it is better than any religious austerity. It is the power of heaven, strong to save; it is salvation by faith. The Original Vow of the Great Sunshine Religion is truly this. It stretches out the hand of healing over the slight illness."

Speaking easily and well, without the least hesitation, Iba reeled off this kind of mumbo-jumbo. Then, placing his quivering hands on the old man's shoulders, he set up a terrific vibration. The old man noisily began inhaling air in an exaggerated way.

"Please inhale more, fill your mouth, and suck in the ether. The ether of the Great Sunshine Religion is flowing out through my hands . . ."

Yukiko, looking intently at all this, thought Iba must have gone mad. Iba, now and then opening his eyes, bent over the old man's face.

"The mass of humanity, with all its evil passions, cannot escape from the cycle of life and death. Take pity; take pity. Expunge and wipe away the true cause of the evil of illness. Let the compassion of the Great Sunshine Religion descend upon you."

Repeating this sort of thing for a while longer, Iba placed his hands on the old man's head. "And now, the purification offering." Lightly tapping the old man on his shoulders, Iba helped raise him up. The old man, looking as if he had just woken up from a good nap, abruptly sat up on the blanket. Iba wiped his hands with the white cloth that covered the small altar box in the ornamental alcove.

The old man arranged his clothes, kneeled properly, and bowed deeply to Iba.

"How about it? Do you feel somewhat lighter in your body?"

"Yes, I feel much better. Invigorated."

"If you continue for four or five sessions, you'll be completely cured. It's a rather serious illness, not to be healed in a day and a night. The Great Sunshine Master, unlike the swindlers of the world, never claims that a believer will immediately get better. As he observes the sincerity and perseverance of the prayers, he receives the departure of the evil of the illness."

"Yes, I intend to come and pray any number of times."

"That will be excellent."

"As for today's purification fee, what would be a suitable donation?"

"No, no, this is not a hospital. To perform free of charge is compassion. This is the central tenet of the Great Sunshine Religion. From people without money, we do not accept a cent. As for someone with money, we gladly receive any amount whatever, and we pray for the departure of all that person's illnesses."

So saying, Iba leisurely returned to his desk. The old man seemed to be at a loss. Promptly, Iba placed the temple register before the old man.

"This is what we have received so far as purification fees. Please use it as a reference."

The old man, reverentially receiving the register, opened it on his lap. A sickly looking young woman, dressed in a black formal divided skirt, brought some tea.

At the head of the register was the name of a former cabinet minister. He was down for fifty thousand yen. There was some question as to whether the autograph was his own—the calligraphy seemed dubious. The cabinet minister himself had since been hanged as a war criminal. The old man, after studying the tome for a while, presently placed the register on the blanket. Then, taking a brush from the inkstone on the table nearby, he entered the sum of five hundred yen.

Having paid, the old man asked Iba what day and time would

be convenient for his next visit and left. Yukiko, with a sigh of relief, listened to his footsteps recede into the distance.

"This is quite a racket you've got here, no?" Yukiko said smilingly.

Actually, it was remarkable that this man, who was a sort of human sloth and who until quite recently had been unable to find any employment whatsoever, had by some stroke of luck been able to make five hundred yen by vibrating his hands and intoning a spurious prayer. One had to admit it was a slick operation.

In the past, Yukiko would have kicked the cushion away and left the room. Iba, taking a pack of foreign cigarettes from the desk and lighting one, sat cross-legged in a peculiarly vulgar manner. "How about it? It's an interesting world, don't you think?" he said. "There's nothing to it. As long as you can make people believe, you can do whatever you want with them. It's sleight of hand. You blow the ether of the Great Sunshine Religion into them, and the sick person recovers his health. I can't go back to my old life as a monthly wage earner after this, can I? People have no gods or Buddhas. They cannot find the compassion of the gods and Buddhas on their own, so they save up a little money and come here to purchase it. In response to this need, we have set up the Great Sunshine Religion and are happy to fulfill demand. Everybody is satisfied."

Yukiko was appalled. Iba offered her a cigarette, so she took one and lit it. In the big ornamental alcove hung a scroll with something written on it. Here again, the calligraphy seemed doubtful. In a cloisonné flower vase, some boughs of red pine had been arranged. Right in the middle of the room of about ten mats, the army blanket was spread like a rug. By the doorway, from which a veranda was visible, was Iba's desk, with a small Chinese-style table next to it. Perhaps because the ceiling was high, there was a calm atmosphere. A breeze often blew through the room. In the narrow garden—was there even an inner courtyard garden?—clothes were hung up to dry.

"What will you do if some newspaper thinks it's fishy and sends a reporter to investigate?"

"We'd be onto it at once. We don't accept any money from anyone suspicious."

"Are your eyes that sharp?"

"When you operate this kind of business, you develop a sharp eye."

It seemed to Yukiko that this sort of phony enterprise, which almost resembled some kind of sex business, could not last long. But in a postwar period, when people in large numbers with no aim in life had been thrown out on their own, there were most likely bound to be some who possessed this sort of abnormal psychology.

"How is your health?" Iba asked.

"I should pay a purification fee too and receive an examination."

Smoking her cigarette, Yukiko smiled as she said this. Even if there were nothing that she could do to resolve her situation with Tomioka, it wouldn't be bad, as a temporary expedient, to help out in this business of Iba's. Yukiko had already lost confidence in her ability to find an honest job. Despite her qualms about the business of the Great Sunshine Religion, helping out there seemed better, in terms of securing some sort of foothold in life, than working as a waitress at a bar or a coffee shop.

"Haven't you lost a lot of weight?"

"Yes. If I could eat some good food and take it easy, I would get fat like you. It's impossible for a woman to be beautiful, if there is no one to spend money on her."

Iba, grinning, cleaned his ears with his fingertip. Prayers apparently having ended, a big drum sounded. Otsu Shimo came to fetch Iba.

Following Iba, Yukiko also went to the grand hall. About thirty believers, men and women, standing about the room, welcomed the Founder and Iba, the Teacher. This hall seemed to be the one new addition to the building. The room was the equivalent of twenty mats or so, and the floor smelled of fresh wood. A purple curtain was drawn around the three-sided altar. Behind the curtain, a mirror shaped like a crescent moon glittered. Before the altar, the Founder, Narimune Senzo, sat in a Chinese-style chair. He was wearing a black garment resembling a judge's robe. On his chest was a badge inscribed with a crest of an intertwined crescent moon and sunflower.

Iba, standing by the Founder's side and bowing to the faithful, said, "At ease. Be seated."

The worshipers sat down on the wooden floor. Yukiko also sat down, in the lowest seat. Iba lowered himself into a wicker chair. The atmosphere was like that of an etiquette class in a prewar grade school. The Founder rang a little bell that was sitting on a table. He mumbled something under his breath and spread out a piece of white paper on the table.

"Today, the Master of the Great Sunshine Religion will set forth the divine law of the third chapter. Everyone please put on their sacred garments." At this, the worshipers unfolded what looked like a purple sleeveless coat and threw it over their shoulders. Dyed with the characters for "Great Sunshine Religion," it resembled a shawl with the collar of a workman's livery coat.

"As the Lord said in the third chapter: Making all the borders of the world come together, mankind mingles with an earnest heart on the road of life. Nothing that man does is enough. He merely strays; he merely wanders. The Lord of the Great Sunshine Religion deigns to save those mortals from hell. He bestows the karma of this world. Unless you depend on salvation by faith, unless you truly possess the spirit of the Western paradise, all is lost, yea, you will perish in hell . . ."

Through the open glass sliding door, a refreshing breeze flowed. The gardener's shears could be heard snipping away.

"That each human being is blessed with fifty years of life is because He allows us to accumulate virtue by self-sacrificial studies . . ."

Growing uncomfortable from sitting on the bare wooden floor, Yukiko relaxed her formal sitting position.

47

TOMIOKA, ON MUKAI'S BEHALF, visited a lawyer. Unless he did what he could to help the man legally, there would be no way to make amends to Seiko. Tomioka felt only a terrible indifference toward Yukiko, as if she were an absolute and total stranger. Apparently Yukiko was devoting herself lately to some religious cult. Tomioka thought that was just as well. There were no indications that Tomioka would ever leave this room, with its memories of himself and Seiko. Every day, he lolled about in bed or worked on his manuscript for the agricultural journal. The magazine occasionally sent him some money. There was no need to meet anyone. For the time being, Tomioka was content. He felt that there would be something suffocating in having a job that would wring a certain amount of time out of him every day.

Taking leave without authorization from his friend's company, Tomioka was sinking into the mindset of a complete vagrant. He did not go near his people in Urawa anymore, and he even tossed letters unopened from his wife, Kuniko, on top of the tea chest. Even toward his wife, who had been sick in bed for some time now, he no longer had any feelings. Although he was well aware that his aged parents were also living in poverty, he had no energy whatsoever to deal with the question of what he should do from this point. Most of the money from the sale of the house had been lost in his lumber venture. There was enough money to scrape by on for six months or a year, and this he had sent to his family.

Lying on his bed, Tomioka spread out his manuscript of low-grade paper and was writing an essay on lacquer. All his thoughts of the South were like navigating a sea of memory.

> The lacquer tree grows only in Japan, China, Indochina, Burma, and Thailand.

When Tomioka first began to write about this subject, his mind felt curiously numb. From time to time he would have dizzy spells. Perhaps because he could not get regular meals, he felt his body deteriorating a little at a time. Thinking that he would have to make about ten thousand yen from this piece about lacquer, he was impatient to begin. But his mind would not accompany him. He got the feeling that it didn't matter one way or another where the lacquer tree grew.

He abruptly changed his way of writing.

> During the war, when I was stationed in Hanoi, the capital of Tonkin, I was summoned to a small town called Futo.

Starting from a memory, Tomioka wrote:

> Northwest of Hanoi, Futo is a hundred and thirty kilometers from the capital. Here there are world-famous lacquer plantations.
>
> The scientific name of lacquer is *Rhus sakushidana*. In our country, it is called *haze*, a tree of the sumac family (*Rhus silvestris*). In Tonkin, it is called *kaison*. In the town of Futo, as in the parts of Japan where silk is produced, *kaison* was cultivated as a subsidiary crop by the farmers. In the old days, Annamese lacquer was called jar lacquer. Its quality was poor, and the price low. In the long-established houses of the lacquer trade, there was a tendency not to deal in Annamese lacquer. During the war, however, in Japan also there was a lack of quality lacquer. Merchants competed to import Annamese lacquer. Although my experience was limited to a few days' inspection visit to the lacquer

plantations of Futo, I have thought that in today's Japan, if we could plant forests of *haze*—as a subsidiary occupation for the farmers, we could export fine quality Japanese lacquer to the West. Annamese lacquer has an extremely unsatisfactory drying rate, and unless technical advances can be made, it is likely that even the world's foremost lacquer capital will decline in the future. However, in the matter of pricing, there is no comparison between Japan and Annam. The farmers of Futo, bringing the unrefined lacquer that they have harvested into the town market, sell it to middlemen. But the lacquer market of Futo also sells all sorts of other things. On this day, there is a naive liveliness, as if a toy box has been emptied out. All the items of everyday life are set out for sale. The farm girls come to market in their best finery.

Tomioka got this far and paused. Life in Japan was dreary, and he felt that he had been dragged back to it against his will. The energy to write this article about lacquer deserted him. Even if Japanese lacquer were exported overseas, nothing would happen. The production of Japanese lacquer was meager and no match for that of foreign lacquer. Rolling over on his side, Tomioka looked intently at the blade of the knife that he used to sharpen his pencil. He felt that he was the one actually responsible for Seiko's death. It was as if Mukai was the hunting dog, but he was the hunter who had killed Seiko. Tomioka meditated on his own craftiness. He tried placing the knife against the vein of his wrist. But he could not summon the courage to plunge it in.

He had not eaten anything since morning, and the essay was not getting anywhere either. He put on a dirty T-shirt and a pair of black serge trousers and went downstairs. At the entryway, he shoved his feet into a pair of Seiko's sandals. Although it was evening, the streets were still as bright as midday in the light of the setting sun. Strolling as far as the train station, Tomioka passed in through the curtain of a small bar. He wanted to drown his cares with a bit of strong liquor. Ordering a glass of *shochu*—a low-grade alcoholic drink—he downed it with a single swallow and ordered a second. There were no other customers. The smell of dried fish being broiled trailed out from the back of the shop. A middle-aged man behind the counter, apparently the proprietor, was scolding a girl of fifteen or sixteen in an undertone. The girl—her hair done in a pageboy style that she occasionally would tuck behind her ear—was facing the wall with a sullen expression.

"Wipe that look off your face. Even though you know nothing about the world, playing around with men . . . Where did you stay last night?"

Drinking his *shochu*, Tomioka pricked up his ears at the father's harangue as he berated his daughter.

"Where did you stay last night?"

The girl, saying nothing, looked down at her lap. Tomioka ordered his third drink. A violent drunkenness came over him. His mood had lightened a little. He wanted to enjoy himself, even see a movie, which he hadn't done by himself in a long while. The girl brought him the third drink. She was a dark-complexioned girl, wearing no makeup. Her eyes were bright and clear, and overall she had a rather good-looking face. Her unshaven eyebrows were black and thick, just like straight horizontal lines. Placing the glass on the counter, the girl smiled sweetly at Tomioka.

So drunk by the third *shochu* that it was as if his world outlook had changed utterly, Tomioka left the bar. His drunkenness allowed him to forget everything. Unsteady on his feet, he wandered through the streets without a destination. He would go back tonight, finish off the lacquer discourse in a single effort, and take it to the agricultural journal.

He wandered as far as Sangenjaya and finally entered a small anonymous bar in the marketplace, not far from the station.

He staggered a bit as he entered the small building. A middle-aged woman wearing too much makeup politely placed her own little sitting cushion on Tomioka's chair.

"Glass of *shochu*, please."

"Maybe you should go easy on it. You've been drinking somewhere else, haven't you?"

Served a glass filled to the brim with *shochu*, Tomioka put his lips to it in a leisurely way. The paper lantern under the eaves, trembling in the wind, was lettered in squared phonetic symbols "Jamusu"—the name of the bar—which Tomioka recognized as the name of a place in Manchuria.

"So were you repatriated from Manchuria?'

"Yes, that's right. How did you know?"

"Because of your lantern."

The woman had dark shadows under her eyes, a high forehead, and small eyes and nose. Her neck powder was laid on thickly, and she wore an apron with lace trimming at the top, over a light summer kimono. On the counter, simmered fish, ham slices, and boiled eggs had been set out. Tomioka picked up a slice of ham with his fingers and stuffed it into his mouth.

"I'm a repatriate. I came back alone, without any money. Whatever you may take me for, I was a teacher in Jamusu for ten years. I don't understand people. Because I'm in this unfamiliar trade, everybody says I'm like a samurai descendant forced to work at some lowly occupation."

"So how old are you, if I may ask?"

"Well, now, how old do I look? I may not look it, but I'm still young. I've been through a lot, and it's aged me; but still . . ."

"I can never tell women's ages. About forty?"

"You're going to make me cry. Do I look that old, like your old granny? I may not look it, but I'm only thirty-five. From now on, I intend to do a little more with the decor, put out some new flowers, and make this place a success."

Tomioka, hearing the figure thirty-five, was taken aback by the woman's lie. Thinking that she was perhaps fifty, he'd meant to flatter her by saying that she looked ten years younger.

"Please forgive me for asking. Thirty-five, you say? That's young. From now on, indeed. You must be permanently separated from your husband, that's why you're so young and beautiful."

The woman, chuckling with pleasure, placed two slices of ham on a little plate and put them on the counter.

"We were separated by death. We split up at Jamusu. My husband was working with the Kyowakai Harmony Association at a place called Hosei, and our separation was a mutual decision. I don't think about him anymore."

A second glass of *shochu* joined the first. Tomioka was starting to become so drunk that he couldn't think clearly. From time to time, he would reach out his hand and ask the woman to shake it. "Did your husband really die?" he asked.

"He really did. I heard that he was living with a person from the Kyowakai Harmony Association in Korea. But even so, he killed himself with a shotgun."

"Really?"

Her story was complicated and interesting. But Tomioka, who was now on his third *shochu*, was having trouble listening, since he kept slumping further over toward the bar.

48

THROUGH THE FALL, Yukiko managed the accounts section of the Great Sunshine Religion. Behind the scenes of the religion, indescribable confusion prevailed. The Founder, Narimune Senzo, was nothing short of a miser when it came to decisions about expenses. He was always having violent quarrels about money with Iba. Yukiko observed the behavior of these two closely and did not neglect to squirrel away some money for herself.

Both Senzo and Iba were always saying that money was everything in life. Yukiko even commented cynically at times that it was not the Great Sunshine Religion but the Great Money Religion. She had by now completely recovered her health, and her glossy skin had a good color. She became unrecognizably young looking. Just as Otsu Shimo had become the mistress of Senzo, so at one time or another Yukiko returned to her old relationship with Iba. Iba, sending his wife and children back to the country in Shizuoka, bought a little house for Yukiko near the temple. Yukiko was not the slightest bit in love with Iba. If anything, she disliked him. With an elderly believer as her housekeeper in the small, three-room cottage, Yukiko lived alone and went to the church office from there. She had salted away about one hundred thousand yen. As time went on, Yukiko was gradually becoming skilled in the management of money. The number of believers was increasing steadily. The Great Sunshine Religion was by way of becoming a notable institution in the neighborhood, with considerable influence.

It was not that Yukiko did not occasionally think about Tomioka, but she had written to him any number of times and received no response. Thinking that no matter what she did, she would never be able to return to her old love affair with Tomioka, Yukiko knew that as far as she was concerned there was no rescue from her present life. Although her life was perfectly comfortable, Yukiko was in a perpetual state of emotional starvation.

One rainy night, coming back from the temple, Yukiko changed out of her black uniform into a kimono with a lining inside it for warmth. In the tearoom, she had supper with the elderly believer who served as her housekeeper. When she looked at the evening newspaper placed alongside the brazier, an advertisement for an agricultural journal caught her eye.

It listed an article called "A Discourse on Lacquer," by Tomioka Kengo. Yukiko remembered the agricultural journal that Tomioka had shown her, sometime ago, in Seiko's room. She immediately asked the housekeeper to go and purchase the magazine at the local bookstore.

Tomioka's article, while a bit amateurish, was written in a style that was easy to understand. Things about Annam that only the two of them knew about kindled a flickering fire in Yukiko's heart. As she read "A Discourse on Lacquer," Yukiko wanted to run and see Tomioka at once. She did not want to admit defeat at the hands of Seiko. If Seiko had truly been the heart of the matter, she thought, it is not likely that we would have planned to commit suicide at Ikaho. Anyway, more than two months have passed. It may be time for Tomioka to be liberated from that ghost.

"Look! This article is written by the man who was my lover. See, that's his name, there."

The housekeeper, who had been cleaning up and putting things away, took the magazine in her hand and gazed at the list of contents that Yukiko indicated with her finger. The housekeeper's name was O-Shige-san. She had lost two sons in the war and had been an itinerant vendor of fish. Her husband had died this spring. Because of this unbroken series of misfortunes, she had become an adherent of the Great Sunshine

Religion. Relied on perhaps by Iba as a person who could keep her own counsel, she had been hired as Yukiko's housekeeper.

"What is this article about?"

"It's about lacquer. This is the character for lacquer. The lacquer on trays and bowls."

"Did your former gentleman deal in the lacquer business?"

"No, he didn't. He was an officer in the Ministry of Agriculture and Forestry. A really remarkable man. During the war, when I was a typist at the ministry, I went to Indochina as a civilian employee of the military. I met him there, and that's where we fell in love."

Yukiko, as she talked, grew sentimental. "When the war ended, we came back to Japan separately—we became like strangers, even though we had been so much in love in the south. At one point, after we came back, we even went to Ikaho, looking for a place to commit suicide together."

O-Shige, as she wiped the tea table with a cloth, listened carefully to Yukiko's story.

"At Ikaho we ran out of money, and he sold his watch to the proprietor of a bar there. But it seems like a devil got into him. He ended up in a strange affair with the proprietor's wife. Do men, even when they are on their way to a lovers' suicide, go astray like that? My feelings of trust in him are completely broken down. Since then, I've been desperate, as if I couldn't breathe. I don't like Iba at all. But anyone, when they're starved for affection, becomes desperate. I think Iba is hateful. He's worse even than me. The Founder, also, is a bad person. People like you have been deceived by him."

"Yes, I'm well aware of that. Even so, unless I believe in the Great Sunshine Religion, I cannot go on living. I don't believe in the Founder-sama or in Iba-sama. Those people don't matter very much."

At O-Shige-san's words, that she believed in the Great Sunshine Religion but did not believe in the Founder or in Iba, Yukiko felt that the cynicism she had been priding herself on had been put to shame.

"That's how it is. I believe in an invisible Lord of the Great Sunshine."

"But it's not as if the gods of the Great Sunshine were anywhere, is it?"

"No; sometimes I look at my fingernails. No matter what marvelously convenient things are invented, just one of my fingernails is more amazing than any of them, I think. One of a person's fingernails is more awesome even than an atomic bomb. I think the gods have taken up residence in us. Scientists cannot create even one human fingernail. This was born naturally, from my parents. If there were no gods, there would be no way for human beings to be born. If I don't believe in something, I can't keep on living. What about you, Yukiko? Maybe you should go to that man and have a good talk with him. Don't just chatter away about all kinds of things. Sit real close to him; take him under your wing. That would be good."

Yukiko burst out giggling. For the first time, she felt she could laugh happily.

49

"A DISCOURSE ON LACQUER" finally brought in some money, which meant that Tomioka was just able to eke out a living. After paying a little of the back rent for his room, he was able to live on the rest of the money for about two months. He turned his hand, by fits and starts, to writing "Memories of a Certain Forestry Technician," which he hoped the same agricultural journal would take. His main intention was to write about his nostalgia for the forests of the south. Although he had compiled many research notes about his work in French Indochina, he had not brought the notes back with him. So he needed to write from memory. If he could do it well and the magazine was kind enough to print it, he meant to dedicate the article to Kano. He also secretly meant to offer it up as a tribute to the land of French Indochina and the people, now vanished, he had known there.

> The Annamese, of all classes, have a strong reverence for nature. They think of all natural and social phenomena as being under the rule of the spirits. It is an article of faith among them that the present life is influenced by the

activities of the spirits and furthermore that all good and bad fortune outcomes depend upon their instructions.

Tomioka suddenly recalled the day of his arrival at the forestry station in Dalat, when the section chief had introduced him to Kano. Kano had placed a small piece of wood on the table.

"Tomioka-san, have you ever seen any real aloes wood?" Kano had asked this, passing the little chip of wood under Tomioka's nose.

Kano had said, with a laugh, "Since coming to the south, I haven't smelled a woman's skin. So I've begun a study of aromatic trees. Clever, huh?"

Tomioka wanted to begin writing from the memory of when he had arrived in Indochina and he had seen a piece of aloes wood for the first time. Kano also told him at the time that this tree, called *kyara* in Japan, was called *jinko* in China. When he had gone to the forestry research laboratory in Saigon, he had been shown a magnificent piece of aloes about the size of a dried bonito. He had been told the French name for the tree by the department head, Monsieur Marcon. The tree had been used in China since the Han dynasty, and it had been in use for centuries in Indochina, Egypt, and Arabia. As a good illustration of Annamese spirit worship, there were temples and shrines everywhere where aloes wood was burned as incense. The aloes tree, said to be worth its weight in gold, was native to southern Annam. The aloes wood in their region was of the highest quality. Once he had placed an aloes wood chip the size of a pinkie fingertip under Yukiko's pillow. At an Annamese temple, he had bribed the priest to get that tiny chip. Tomioka felt a mysterious connection between incense burning and the Annamese religion.

Tomioka had managed to set down about two hundred pages. As he wrote, Tomioka realized that his descriptions of the various regions brought to mind nothing about Yukiko at all. Rather, it was the memory of the Annamese maid and their child that nostalgically grazed his heart. Ultimately, the piece was simply about his nostalgia for the fragrance of the land itself.

At about this time, the pace of his visits to Mukai at the detention center had started to fall off. He had not been to see him in the past month.

The strange thing about going to see Mukai was that the man was always calm and cheerful. It was somehow difficult for Tomioka to believe Mukai's lawyer's description of him as a lonely, melancholy sort of man. Tomioka felt there was almost something odd about Mukai. The reason Kano had been imprisoned in Saigon by the military police was not unlike the reason Mukai had been imprisoned. As for Kano, he was already an inhabitant of death's kingdom. But when he had been alive and sick, Tomioka had not gone even once to visit him—only Yukiko had. It was cowardice, he knew.

When night fell, Tomioka wanted to drink strong liquor. At the rate of five or six pages per day, it would be a long time before his manuscript about the forestry of the south resulted in money. When he felt the craving for a drink, Tomioka sold off Seiko's furniture and clothes. He sold her tea chest, her trunk, and all her clothes. Going seven or eight times to the bar where the young girl with the beautiful eyes worked, he got to be on conversational terms with her.

Once or twice, the girl had come to Tomioka's place to collect money. Tonight, feeling a bit bored with work, Tomioka thought he would go off to the bathhouse. It had been a while since he'd been there. Just then he heard a woman's husky laugh through the wall. For just a moment, the voice was that of Seiko. It was the full, throaty laugh of that night in Ikaho, when she had led him by the hand down the narrow stone stairs.

Right then, he also heard someone say "Mister," and he turned toward the door. It was the wide-eyed girl from the bar. Holding two or three copies of magazines, she peered into the room.

"What? Is that you?"

"Are you alone?"

"Yes, I'm alone. What is it? Have you come to collect the money?"

"I came to have some fun with you."

"Oh." What an audacious child, Tomioka thought. Quickly jumping inside the room, the girl pushed the dirty clogs she'd been holding in one hand under the bed. Completely at ease, she sat down on the edge of the bed and then rolled over in a convulsion of meaningless laughter. Thinking, Ah, was that the laugh I heard? Tomioka sat down on the bed alongside her. When he put his hand around her shoulder and drew her to him, the girl parted her lips slightly and looked up at Tomioka. Seen up close, hers was a typical face of the south. Tomioka gazed his fill at the girl's dark-complexioned face.

"My father scolded me too much. He threatened me. So I've run away from home . . ."

"You're always misbehaving. Probably your father scolded you because he's worried about you?"

"He's having a nervous breakdown. My mother is holding separation talks with my father, so every day he's in an edgy mood. Just the other night, I slept in a police booth. A police booth at night is an interesting place."

"Where was the police booth you slept at?"

"A long way from here. The policeman was awfully nice, a good person."

Tomioka could not understand the psychology of this kind of girl at all.

50

WINTER ARRIVED.

Tomioka, in the midst of his poverty, had written almost five hundred pages of "Memories of a Certain Forestry Technician." But it came to nothing. Told that because of stringent conditions in the publishing world, the book could not be published at the present time, Tomioka lost hope. He felt as if he were standing at the head of a steep slope and about to tumble down it at any minute. He could not sustain a life in which there was no stability. Tomioka tried going to employment agencies and visiting friends from his days at the Ministry of Agriculture and Forestry. None of them offered any help.

Lying in his cold, unheated room, Tomioka did occasionally think about Yukiko. But this only made him feel ashamed of himself. Unable to pay any rent on his room since summer, he had been getting eviction notices. And his aged mother, complaining about Kuniko's illness and their poverty, came from Urawa to see him every so often.

It was a snowy morning in early January. He received a telegram saying that Kuniko had died, so he sold his bedding to a secondhand dealer and returned to Urawa. Kuniko had been living a miserable existence. Fading away into a ghost of herself, she had died in what amounted to suicide. On top of her lengthy debility, she had glandular fever of a scrofulous kind. An operation was needed, but the doctor had merely recommended fresh air and cod liver oil. Perhaps he thought that an operation would be too dangerous for this malnourished and emaciated woman. An abscess had developed in the inguinal region, the only recourse for which was an operation and the insertion of rubber tubes to drain the pus. But Kuniko was adamant that she did not want an operation, and she breathed her last in that wretched condition.

There was no money even to buy a coffin. Tomioka felt not the slightest remorse, as he had when Seiko had died. But he did think it disagreeable that, having neglected Kuniko as his wife since the end of the war, their downfallen state was such that he could not even buy her a coffin.

It had been snowing since morning. Not only was there no money to have a priest chant a deathbed sutra, there was none to take the body to the crematorium. Early the next morning, wearing his father's old overcoat, he set out for Tokyo to borrow some money from Yukiko. He searched for the address she had given in her last letter. Iba's name was on the nameplate. A trim two-story house, it had a painted gate and green shrubbery whose red berries were mantled with snow. When he put his hand to the sliding door, a dog barked noisily inside. He slid open the door of the entryway.

It was Yukiko herself who descended from the second floor at the back, with a white dog in her arms. Wearing a yellow jacket and black trousers, Yukiko first stared at the sorry-looking figure of Tomioka, as if she had lost her breath.

She was completely different from the Yukiko of the summer. She had gained a lot of weight, and her figure had become young and buxom. She looked again like the Yukiko of the old days in French Indochina. The dog, longhaired and snow white, put out his red tongue and barked nervously at Tomioka. Yukiko, slapping the dog's head hard, said, "Oh! Who was it? I thought . . ."

Tomioka was surprised to see the striking change in Yukiko's appearance. She immediately took the dog upstairs, placed it inside a room, and slid the door shut with a bang. She soon came back down and invited Tomioka into the tearoom. With her back to him, she suddenly stuck out her tongue. When she thought that the down-and-out Tomioka had finally come to her, she felt exhilarated, so much that her chest hurt.

Yukiko understood at once that Tomioka had come to borrow money. Turning back the soft *kotatsu* coverlet, she turned on the electric switch. Not looking at Tomioka's face, she said in a gentle voice: "It's cold. Please sit down at the *kotatsu*."

"You've changed completely."

Meekly, Tomioka, not taking off his overcoat, sat down at the *kotatsu*. He stared with round eyes at Yukiko.

"How have I changed?"

"You look younger."

"That may be. I'm not particularly happy, but . . ."

Yukiko seated herself directly across from Tomioka. Apparently just out of the bath, she had rosy-looking hands. Over the big porcelain brazier, an iron teakettle was puffing out steam. By the door, there was a three-mirrored dressing stand. On the little shelf beside it stood a doll in a glass box.

"You probably know what I've come for?"

Getting right to the point, Tomioka had intended to say at the entryway that he had come for money. When he was sitting at the *kotatsu*, he somehow felt he had missed his chance to speak. Tomioka gazed wide-eyed at Yukiko's way of living these days. The dog was barking for all it was worth upstairs. "And Iba-kun?" Tomioka asked.

"He's gone to the church."

"Are you living here alone?"

"Yes. I have a housekeeper, but she's out shopping."

"You're set up nicely."

"Thanks."

Yukiko did not show it in her face, but she laughed inside herself. Perhaps she was in fact nicely set up.

"Since the end of the war, men are good for nothing. It's the women who have become strong."

Pouring the tea, Yukiko again said in a prim voice, "Perhaps that's true." Thinking, Was this the man I was so in love with until today? Yukiko glanced out of the corner of her eye at Tomioka's utterly changed appearance. He had aged two or three years. Her own coldness of heart gave Yukiko a strange feeling.

"Kuniko died yesterday."

"Oh—your wife passed away?"

Yukiko opened her eyes wide. The face of Tomioka's wife, whom she had met twice—it seemed so long ago—rose immediately to mind. She had not forgotten her impressions of the time when she was tailing Tomioka and had met the wife near their house in Gotanda. Unexpectedly, Yukiko burst into tears and wailed. Tomioka had come to borrow money from his old girlfriend, but when he saw her gushing tears, he was taken aback. Suddenly, memories of the hardships he had tasted with this woman in the past shook his desolate heart. He felt there was nothing he could say. He just looked at her.

Yukiko was not weeping sentimentally simply for herself and Tomioka. She was weeping for the misery of that period when she had been like a stray dog. But when she saw that her tears were having an unexpected effect on Tomioka, she began to cry much harder, as if she could no longer bear it. Taking a damp towel from the dressing stand, she covered her face with it.

Dismayed, Tomioka watched. Little by little, though, his heart began to beat more rapidly. He could smell the scent of perfume on the towel. He went over to her side, put an arm around her shoulder, and pulled the towel away from her face. Did Yukiko love him that deeply? It made him happy.

He kissed Yukiko's soft neck. It had a fresh scent, as if he were touching a new woman. Tomioka busily embraced Yukiko's big hips. Yukiko, like a patient receiving a medical examination, let Tomioka do as he pleased. Soon they were sharing, without words, their secret memories and their deepest sorrows.

51

THE CLOCK CHIMED TWELVE. Tomioka had the water run for his morning bath. He felt liberated from a poverty-stricken life in which he had not even had a bath for five or six days. The small tub lined with cobalt tiles was filled to the brim. While washing himself off with a white cake of foreign soap, Tomioka felt pity for his wife, who had been emaciated when she died. Looking out of the little window at the falling snow, Tomioka felt he was seeing a cross-section of human society and that it was vast and threatening indeed. His heart was nowhere to be found. The gas kettle was bubbling quietly.

His face caressed by the gentle steam, Tomioka shaved, peering into the mirror. The safety razor was probably Iba's, but, feeling reckless, he nevertheless drew it across his cheeks with a scraping sound that sent a thrill to his heart. People were simple creatures, Tomioka thought. For the most trivial of reasons, reality suddenly changed altogether. But surprisingly, people survived this. They soon got to their feet and smiled.

Looking up at the clock, Yukiko was relieved that the housekeeper did not come back immediately. The housekeeper always ran late on errands, and today again she was quite late. Yukiko had to go to the church and take Otsu Shimo's place in the office. Today, Yukiko decided, she was going to steal all the money in the safe.

In the bedroom of the Founder, Narimune Senzo, there was a big safe that contained the total assets of the church. But there was always a sum of two or three hundred thousand yen in the little safe in the receptionist's office. The Great Sunshine Religion was prospering more and more these days. Donations were pouring in, as were purification fees. The offerings piled high at the altar included bolts of cloth and fruits and vegetables of the season.

By the time Yukiko had prepared the noonday meal and set out Iba's private bottle of Suntory whiskey, Tomioka, with a fresh-looking complexion, had emerged from the bath. Watching Yukiko's flurry of brisk activity as if it were something strange, Tomioka felt almost like a thief at this pleasure being secretly arranged for just the two of them. Upstairs, the dog was barking noisily away. Under the warm *kotatsu* coverlet, Tomioka felt a faint dizziness. He drank two or three glasses of whiskey. The taste of the whiskey permeated his entire body and lightened his mood a little.

Finally the housekeeper returned. She was initially flustered at seeing an unfamiliar visitor. But from Yukiko's mode of entertaining the visitor, she seemed to surmise that this was the lacquer gentleman. Taking twenty thousand yen from the chest of drawers, although with a slight feeling of regret, Yukiko, with an air of cheerful generosity, wrapped the bills in a sheet of newsprint and pushed the packet just under the edge of Tomioka's sitting cushion. Tomioka thanked her with his eyes.

At one o'clock, Tomioka left together with Yukiko, who was going to the church. Walking slowly, Yukiko asked, "What do you intend to do after this?"

"What do I intend to do? It's as you see. Nothing's working out. Even this money, there's no hope of my paying it back soon. Is that all right?"

"Yes, it's all right. That kind of thing is all right, but . . . Are you still in that room in Meguro?"

"Yes."

"I'd like to see you again, you know, but . . ."

Yukiko didn't feel like it was a parting. It seemed to her that now that Kuniko had died, she could live with Tomioka without fear of anyone. But she would have to hold back from trying to speak with Tomioka about their living together while he was on his way to purchase a coffin. Told that she wanted to see him again, Tomioka understood Yukiko's feelings well enough. But somehow or other it was too much trouble to take the talk that far. Still less, given his present inability to live effectively, was there a single thing that he could seek from Yukiko.

They parted at Denenchofu Station, both feeling that there were things they had left unsaid.

Wearing Iba's boots on the snowy road, Yukiko went to the church and took over from Otsu Shimo. Today Otsu Shimo was going to Atami with the Founder. Yukiko, sitting on an electrically heated cushion, gazed entranced at the snowy garden for a while. The snow had stopped. In the leaden-hued cloud cover, there were chilly apertures of sky the color of kerosene. Although Tomioka's shabbiness was to be pitied, the glamour of a man who had no energy to live had lessened for Yukiko. Earlier she had wanted to steal the cash on hand in the safe behind her and flee with Tomioka, but now, curiously calm, Yukiko thought she would think the matter over for two or three hours. The light was on in the reception office. Iba seemed to be carousing in the Founder's room with some believers of the inner circle. In the auditorium, about twenty simpleminded believers, sitting on the cold wooden floor, were keeping a prayer vigil.

Warmed by the heated seat cushion, Yukiko smiled as she remembered the rough strength Tomioka had shown in their last time together. She knew that that time would become a keepsake of her heart and would lodge solidly in her body. But still she could not feel tranquil about Tomioka. She even had the sense that her love for him was something instinctual, primal, in the blood. Only in Tomioka could that kind of love be peacefully pursued. The surging waves of her heart were headed toward the safe behind her back. Yukiko stretched out her hand like an eagle's talon toward the safe. Money flowed like water into the safe, but for Yukiko, it was one humdrum, tedious day after another. Yukiko wanted to withdraw from this peculiar life in which nothing of what bothered her was wiped away. It was too lonely for Yukiko to hold out in this corner of the world.

In a casual manner, Yukiko looked at the registry of the day's donations. There had been an unusually large number of them. Yukiko opened the safe. It contained approximately six hundred thousand yen bound up in bundles.

It was common for amounts of this size to accumulate in the safe over four or five days. But the money that Yukiko saw today seemed to her a very substantial amount. Since Otsu Shimo precisely reckoned the amount of money and reported it to Iba and the Founder, there was nothing to be done about that. But Yukiko could not bring herself to take the money from the safe that evening. As for the big safe hidden in Narimune's bedroom, it was not opened every night. It was always opened on Sunday evening. Today was Sunday. It was the day when Iba and the Founder secretly calculated the week's take. But this evening, the Founder would be away, so perhaps the safe would be opened on Monday. In that case, one had to look at it as providing two days' margin.

Yukiko imagined various alibis. After she had fled, the housekeeper would most likely tell Iba that a strange gentleman had called. Wearied from worrying about this and that, Yukiko went into the auditorium, where electric candles were merrily burning on the altar. The keepers of vigils raised their voices in prayer.

"Making all the borders of the world come together, mankind mingles with an earnest heart on the road of life. Nothing man does is enough. He merely strays; he merely wanders. The Lord of the Great Sunshine Religion deigns to save these mortals from hell. He bestows the karma of this world. Unless you depend on salvation by faith, unless you truly possess the spirit of the Western paradise, all is lost, yea, you will perish in hell . . . *Horengekyo* . . . Amen. The Lord of the Great Sunshine Religion reigns. The dark fades away; the bright day shines. Oh, Lord, make cease the wanderings of mankind in the darkness . . ."

Listening to the chorus of the faithful, Yukiko seated herself on the wooden floor. Pressing her palms together hard, she tried closing her eyes. But her emotions were all tangled up, and she could not make herself feel calm. Before her eyes, the bundles of banknotes flickered. The image would not leave her. Neither above her head, nor before her eyes, did the figure of any god appear. Yukiko could not even pray to the "ether" of the Great Sunshine Religion that Iba talked about. God was nowhere. Iba, his face flushed with drink, entered the auditorium. In noticeably high color and, to look at him now, a fine figure of a man, Iba took a turn around the room, inspecting the faithful. Then, sliding back the glass door of the veranda, he hawked up a gob of phlegm into the garden. He roughly slid the door shut again. Observing that Yukiko was sitting near the entrance, he looked pleased. Then, walking with heavy strides, he withdrew into the interior of the building. As if he thought the faithful were just like a bunch of obedient children, his figure seen from behind seemed full of self-confidence as he disappeared from view. Yukiko gazed at the candles glittering on the altar. Behind a purple curtain, a mirror shone. Thinking that perhaps the god would make an appearance there, Yukiko looked at the mirror steadfastly, but not even an ambiguous shadow was reflected there. The snow on the lawn in the garden was melting in circles, in the manner of a painting of the classical Korin school. Perhaps because a wind had sprung up, the glass door rattled in its frame.

When she thought of Tomioka, Yukiko felt an unbearable longing for the pleasure they had taken this morning. It was as if someone was clutching her about the heart.

52

AFTER THE COMPLETION OF THE RITES for Kuniko, Tomioka stayed five days or so in Urawa. When the funeral was finally over, he felt relieved, as if he had shed a heavy burden. He had sold off Kuniko's bedding and personal articles to a secondhand dealer and so had got rid of all his memories of her. For Tomioka, his wife, Kuniko, had been a stranger for some time. His memories about Seiko were painful, but his only feeling about Kuniko was a refreshing sense of relief. At the same time as the funeral, everything to do with Kuniko was wiped clean from his heart. Certainly Kuniko had led a lonely existence as a wife. Since Tomioka's return from Indochina, she had meant nothing to him. The pleasurable time they had enjoyed after he had stolen Kuniko from her previous husband, a friend, had lasted less than two years, until Tomioka went to Indochina as a civilian employee of the military. If it were not for the war, Kuniko and Tomioka might have had an ordinary bureaucrat's family life. Between Tomioka, who had been away from his native land for five years, and his wife, Kuniko, a great distance had developed about which nothing could be done. The war had weighed heavily on both of them. Had their married life in a barren and desolate land, so to speak, living by half measures and compromises, lacked the passion to break new ground? In the end, it had passed away fleetingly, like the transient thing it was. When the farewell of the funeral was ended, Tomioka felt all the more lighthearted.

His aged parents announced that they would like to spend the remainder of their lives farming at Matsuida, in their native region of Gunma. Selling their Urawa house, which was not much more than a shack, for about 140,000 yen to a National Railway employee and giving them the money, Tomioka decided to send the two old folks back to their native clime. His father's younger brother was a farmer in Matsuida. He owned a shed that he had rented out before to an evacuee, so the old couple could settle down there.

When Tomioka returned to Tokyo, it was a bright, clear day. When he entered his room, the girl from the small bar next to the station was there, curled up in Tomioka's quilt, reading a magazine.

She was lying there completely at ease, as if she was in her own house. When Tomioka entered, she grinned broadly at him. Since she had come to play with him at the end of the year, she hadn't shown herself; but at some point or other she'd acquired a permanent and was wearing makeup. Once, casually, drunkenly fooling around, Tomioka had kissed the girl. With only that tenuous connection, the girl had come again.

"Before, you know, a beautiful lady came. I sent her away . . ."

Told that a beautiful lady had come, Tomioka for a moment did not know who it was. Then he understood: it was Yukiko.

"What kind of lady?"

"Really something. She was wearing a high-class striped overcoat and nylon stockings. She had a black shiny handbag. And she smoked a cigarette here."

"What did she say?"

"She asked me, 'How do you and Tomioka know each other?' So I told her I was on good terms with you. Then she laughed, wrinkling her nose at me. So I got mad and laid out the bedding right away and got into it."

"Didn't she leave a message?"

"She said she would come again. But she kept asking me if I was staying here all the time, so I said, 'Yes, I am . . .' She made a strange face. I don't really like her. I thought she seemed very cold. She looked all around at the room. Maybe she won't come again. Did I do something wrong?"

"You're horrible."

"Oh, was she a lady friend of yours?"

"She's my wife."

"That's such a lie. There's a rumor that your wife was murdered. I know all about it."

Giving him an unpleasant smile, the girl got up. She was only wearing a jacket, as she had taken off her skirt. Her plump knees protruded from under the hem of a short, soiled chemise. Averting his eyes, Tomioka turned on the electric portable stove. Since there was no place to lie down and it was cold, Tomioka couldn't settle himself anywhere. When he sat down at his writing table, the girl's compact had been left there, in a scattering of powder. There was a stick of cheap, hardened lipstick and a red comb with some of its teeth missing. Tomioka smiled to himself bitterly. Probably Yukiko, when she'd seen this state of affairs, had thought to herself, Same old faithless Tomioka.

"Hey. Daddy has some work to do, so get out of here, and go back."

"No, I don't have anyplace to go back to now. Until yesterday I was going to the Youth Center in Saginomiya, but I ran away and came here. It wasn't the least bit interesting. All they do is glue airmail envelopes together. That's how my hands got all chapped like this. Then I remembered Daddy-san and made my getaway. If I go home, I'll just be chased out again. This is the only place I have to come to."

"What's the Youth Center?"

"It's where juvenile delinquents like me go. They paste together envelopes with red and blue stripes on the edges. At first, I thought they were pretty, and it was interesting, but then I got bored. The pattern like a barber's pole somehow got stuck in my eyes like specks of dirt. I was afraid I might go color-blind."

Tomioka's head ached. It would be correct to say that he was exhausted by everything in life. He longed for the quiet life of a bureaucrat. The life of the past, which at the time he'd scorned as being dull, he now had come to think of as the most beautiful period of his life. Even in the uneventful existence of a clerk, there had been various worries. But the worries of that time were not the sordid ones he had now. And yet, even though his life seemed to be rotting and getting moldy around the edges, Tomioka simply observed with the cold eyes of an onlooker the choices made by the people around him who, moldy themselves, clung to him. Looking at the reclining figure of this refractory child, whose baby hair still showed through her clumsily applied powder, Tomioka felt as if he were seeing the colors of one particular corner of a defeated postwar society. This girl was tired out too.

But, for Tomioka now, even this girl was a bother.

"Hey, I'll take you back, so how would it be if you went home?"

"No. I want to stay here."

"Why don't you want to go?"

"Hey, just leave me alone. Today it's cold out. Rather than going back to the station, it's better here. I won't bother you, so it's all right to stay, isn't it?"

"No, it's not all right. Daddy will take you back, so you go home today."

Tomioka spoke curtly. The girl lay still and was silent for a while. Then, sitting up abruptly, she silently put on the skirt that she had discarded by the pillow and, carrying a little kerchief-wrapped bundle, went out into the corridor. After the door was banged shut, Tomioka turned around. As if the girl had left behind a certain melancholy, Tomioka stood there with a feeling of hopelessness after she had departed. He came to feel that the girl's youth would do her no good at all. Alone, ignorant, a low-grade neurotic prone to hysteria, what was she thinking of, running away from home and wandering the streets? He could not understand her at all. At this rate, even this young girl would wind up in prison or killing herself. Feeling as if he were about to be sick, Tomioka kicked at the quilt that had been left on the floor.

Tomioka suddenly remembered the body of Kuniko, brittle as a rice cracker, when they had placed it in the coffin. As he kicked at the quilt, Tomioka's recollections of Kuniko hurt him right behind his eyes. Like a tattered rag doll, without having known a single happiness, she had died. That time of parting, when they had placed her in the coffin and nailed it shut, only now, finally, called forth feelings of sorrow in Tomioka.

53

YUKIKO, WITH ONLY LIGHT, personal items that she could carry, and
without saying anything to the housekeeper, left the house. She meant
never to come back to this house. She felt as if she was ripping her
life up by the roots. She hailed a taxi and went to Tomioka's apartment.
But when she encountered a strange young girl there who seemed
almost crazy, she changed her mind. Leaving Tomioka's apartment, she
got back into the taxi, which she had kept waiting outside, and went
to Shinagawa Station. From there she boarded a train for Shizuoka.
She had no particular destination in mind. She simply bought a ticket
that would take her as far as Shizuoka. As if on a whimsical outing,
her feelings vague, Yukiko looked out of the train window at the wintry
dusk. Although she thought of returning to Shizuoka and visiting her
relatives, the idea did not really interest her. It was laborious to meet
people whom one knew. She arrived in Mishima at about eight o'clock.
From there, she decided to take the electric trolley to Shuzenji. Reading
the names of the inns listed on the advertisement boards of the stations,
Yukiko made up her mind to get off at a place called Nagaoka. She took
her things down from the baggage rack and got off the train.

Perhaps because it was late at night, she felt as if she were walking through a Tokyo suburb. It was an ordinary place. With an aged hotel runner leading the way, she was taken to a small inn named the Yellow Rose Villa. Relatively new, it had been built with inferior lumber. But for Yukiko, anywhere was all right. Before she even took off her overcoat, Yukiko immediately wrote out a telegram to Tomioka's place and had it sent. The inn was quiet, and there didn't seem to be too many guests. Stowing away the locked suitcase in a compartment at the top of a set of staggered shelves near the ceiling, Yukiko changed into the padded kimono of the inn and went off to the bath. But she could not at all calm down. Although she felt guilty after running away with the six hundred thousand yen, Yukiko was not frightened by either Iba or Narimune. But although there certainly was the pleasure of the six hundred thousand yen, it was a pleasure that could no longer be atoned for by such a sum. Yukiko had the feeling that it was all too late.

Even when she'd come back from the bath and sat down at the dinner tray that was brought to her, there was no way to satisfy her starving heart. Going out into the town, Yukiko walked with the cold wind blowing on her. Wherever she went, the streets were all dark. After buying some tangerines at a fruit store, she went back to the inn. Wanting desperately for Tomioka to come, she wrote another telegram and entrusted it to the maid. Not caring whether the people of the inn thought it was strange or not, Yukiko made a point of talking lightheartedly about how she was waiting for her lover. She had thought that, having obtained this huge fortune, she would immediately begin a happy life hand in hand with Tomioka, but now even the pleasure of having the money had chased her into an unexpected loneliness.

Although it was late at night, Yukiko could not fall asleep. Lying between the sheets that smelled of starch, listening to the wintry wind, Yukiko's longing for Tomioka burned fiercely. In the dead of night, she got up two or three times and slid back the door of the ceiling compartment, to make sure that the little suitcase was still there.

She dozed fretfully, on and off, until dawn. It was after her fourth telegram that Tomioka arrived at the Yellow Rose Villa in Nagaoka, just as she was having supper.

"You have a visitor." At the same moment as the clerk came to announce his arrival, Tomioka, came in right behind him, looking bedraggled in his old overcoat and without even a hat. He looked angry.

As soon as he sat down, he said, "That telegram saying you would die unless I came was crazy . . ."

Yukiko was happy that Tomioka had come, as she had asked. She wanted him to share in her uneasiness of the past two days. Yukiko immediately ordered some sake. She felt almost giddy about spending money and waited excitedly for Tomioka to come back from the bath. The maid was teasing her and Yukiko kept laughing, even at things she didn't find funny.

Tomioka came back from the bath and sat down. "So when did you come here?" he asked.

"Last night. You must have been surprised to get my telegram!"

"Yeah. The lady in the next room was surprised too."

"I wanted so much for you to come. I have so many things I want to talk about. I've left Iba's place."

"How come?"

"What do you mean? I couldn't stand it, so I left. Actually, I've done something bad."

Yukiko, with the mischievous look of a child who has done something naughty, told Tomioka that she had stolen six hundred thousand yen from the church and made her getaway.

"Won't Iba-san be reporting it to the police about now?"

"He can't report it. His whole business is shady. Because it's a profit-making church. If they hand me over to the police, they'll be giving themselves away. They're not going to stir up the snake in the undergrowth. Six hundred thousand yen, for that man, is only as if he'd smashed up a car . . . It's dishonest money, made without any outlay of capital . . ."

"You're going to suffer for it, one of these days."

"When it comes to the Great Sunshine Religion, I'm not so sure about that, since there aren't really any gods behind that religion. Even Iba—he gave me a house, after all—this amount of money is nothing to him."

"Well, that makes sense. When religion makes it, it makes it big."

Tomioka had already had two or three glasses of sake and was beginning to loosen up. Something in Yukiko also wanted to try to make light of what she had done by bad-mouthing Narimune and Iba. As for Tomioka, he was beginning to think of his long relationship with Yukiko as fate. Seiko and Kuniko had died. Only this woman had survived. She had already shown a tremendous will to live. Tomioka had the feeling that, this time, it was he who had been tracked down and cornered by this woman.

Remembering the prayer, "Nothing that man does is enough. He merely strays; he merely wanders," Yukiko thought that even if she were apprehended by Iba tomorrow, the pleasure of going astray today would still have been worth it. She was feeling reckless. After the meal was over and the maid took away the dinner tray, Yukiko had her bring several more small bottles of sake.

"Looking back on Ikaho, we've each been able to live a long time."

"But since then, it's like we've just been repeating ourselves."

"Well, maybe, but surely your life has been eventful. What with Seiko-san and all."

Tomioka did not answer.

"If she hadn't died that way, I think I would have been happier. When I look at your face, it's as if she were haunting you. I can't stand it. I'm not saying that because I've been drinking. I've wanted to say it before. I hate her. Even now, I think she was an awful woman."

"Did you call me here so that you could talk about her?"

"No, not at all. But the minute I saw you, I thought that somewhere inside you, behind your dark face, that woman's ghost was still haunting you. Why weren't we able to die cheerfully at Ikaho?"

"Are you able to die now?"

"Well, hmm, what about you?"

"Not me. I can't do it."

"Yeah, I know what you mean. I've come to feel that I can't die either."

"There's no need for us to die together now. Time has changed this, and we have a clean slate now."

"What do you mean?"

"Just what I said. There's no hidden meaning in it."

"Do you mean we could be together, if we want to?"

"Together? Sure. But I'm not sure there's any reason to. I came here with the intention of going back tomorrow."

Yukiko's vision immediately became blurred and watery. She asked, "Why? Don't you want to be with me?" Her tears began to fall, one after another.

"In the end, I've done nothing but make trouble for you. But when you ask me point-blank why I don't want to be with you all the time, well, there's no real reason why. That's just the way it is. When I heard that you had stolen the church's money, it's strange, but all I can think is that for the time being I don't need a wife or even a woman. I'm just starting to get serious about my own work. I've become used to life being hard. I'll be moving out of that apartment soon, too. Why can't we just cheerfully go our own ways?"

Hearing this, Yukiko felt a sense of dread, as if the banknotes were a heavy weight that was about to fall right onto her from a great height.

54

YUKIKO LOOKED HARD at Tomioka's face. His unfeeling words—that he didn't need a wife or even a woman—were not sentiments that needed to be expressed to her, Yukiko thought. For a while, she was silent.

At some point Tomioka had become quite drunk.

With his elbows on the table and the cup at his lips, he was looking at Yukiko, but his eyes were empty. The cold expression of his eyes, which had not been there before, was perhaps the look that was natural to him, Yukiko thought. His cheeks were hollow. Each time he raked his fingers through the hair that fell forward on his forehead, he had a habit of plucking out a hair. His eyes red around the edges, the front of his padded kimono open, even the way Tomioka slapped at his reddish-bronze chest made Yukiko feel she was seeing things that until then had not been in him. Feeling that she was now seeing him for the first time, Yukiko looked at him intently. She sensed the rank, stifling scent of a man that draws women to him. Thinking that perhaps it was that very smell—the smell of success with women—that drew women, Yukiko held out an empty cup to Tomioka. She was beginning to get drunk as well.

Yukiko wanted to get very drunk. Unless she could share the excitement of having stolen the money and come to this place, her thoughts of this morning had been frivolous and foolish. At any rate, even though she had gotten together with Tomioka, she did not think it could work out well. But she could not reconcile herself to the idea of letting Tomioka go.

She started to get drunker and to have the urge to tell him just what she thought of him, in the vilest language. Soon she found that, once again—as she always did when she was drinking—she was talking about her memories of Indochina.

"Well, I haven't lost hope the way you have. I'll show you how I can live. You can have all the women you want. At the camp in Hanoi, I read a short story called "Bel Ami," by Maupassant. You're like the hero in that story. He's a wanderer, without a roof over his head, and he uses women as a ladder to rise in the world. You use women like the rungs of a ladder too, only you don't do it to get ahead, exactly."

Tomioka had not read the story, but he did not like being told by Yukiko that he used women as a ladder. Grabbing her arm, he pulled her toward him. "Is that why you called me here—to say things like that to me? Even if you had come here with ten million yen, I'm not the sort of man who responds to that sort of thing. Stealing the church's money and then looking so self-satisfied, as if you had pulled off a great exploit . . . If I was so dear to you, anyway, why did you go to Iba's place?"

"What are you talking about? You've done nothing but one selfish thing after another, yourself."

Tomioka let go of Yukiko's arm. "You should probably try using men as a ladder too."

Rolling over on his side, Tomioka closed his eyes. By some association of ideas, he remembered the day he had stayed at the Grand Hotel by the Clemenceau Bridge, when he had arrived in Hue. He spent several days in Hue in order to visit Monsieur Marcon at the Forestry Bureau. He had gone to Hue to earnestly request a transfer of seeds. Although he had walked proudly about the Grand Hotel at that time, now he was a broken-down man, not even the shadow of his former self, secretly depending on the six hundred thousand yen that a woman had stolen for him . . . Tomioka gave a wry smile. Yukiko had said he used women as a ladder, and perhaps it was so.

Recently, with the help of a former colleague at the Ministry of Agriculture and Forestry, Tomioka had been asked if he would like to go to Yakushima Island, at the very southernmost tip of Japan—a heavily mountainous place known for its vast primeval cedar forests. Although Tomioka was not overly enthusiastic about going back to his old job as government functionary, if there were nothing else available, he had no choice but to return to his former employment. In fact, there were two other jobs on offer. One was as a technician at a forestry research laboratory at Taikake in Wakayama Prefecture. But Tomioka preferred to go to the forestry station on the lonely island of Yakushima, at the southernmost limits of the country. If the post at Kochi was not to his liking, his friend had said, there was a post at the forestry station in Kooya, in the township of Kudosan in Ito County—again, in Wakayama Prefecture. "At any rate," the friend had continued, "if nothing else works out for you, I'll put in an inquiry." With this, they had parted. Tomioka, rather than hanging around in Tokyo, thought that it would be better to make up his mind and head for the mountains again. Particularly now that Kuniko had died and his parents had withdrawn to Matsuida, there was nothing to keep him in Tokyo. As early as tomorrow he was expecting his friend to give him the written appointment to go on to Yakushima Island.

Tomioka knew little about Yakushima. He only knew that its forests were famous for the Yakushima cedar. He had the feeling that the island might be completely deserted. Only a research station was maintained there. His friend had said, "The customs and people's manners there are simple and honest, and it rains hard for one solid month. Are you ready for this?"

If he had to go back to his old job, Tomioka thought, he would rather see something completely new and unfamiliar, like Yakushima. When he looked at the map, he saw that Yakushima was a round island, not far from Tanegashima.

Closing his eyes, Tomioka thought about the remote island for a while. Yukiko had crawled over close by him and was mumbling about something, but Tomioka had trouble keeping from dozing off. Yukiko was saying, "Why has your heart gone so far away from me? Why have you suddenly grown so cold toward me? Are you angry because I went to Iba's place, Tomioka-san?"

He managed to say, "No, I'm neither angry nor not angry. Since the end of the war, like everybody else, I've lost the power to decide things for myself. Nowadays, everybody just tries to do whatever society gives us to do. Even if you and I were to try to pursue the dreams of the past and to live it up on the money you have for a while, it wouldn't do any good. We're like floating weeds with no roots. I don't think it will work out for us . . ."

"We should die, then. Because we couldn't die when we should have at Ikaho, when we run out of money we should die. Weren't you just telling me to please die?"

"Dying is painful, though."

Tomioka thought about the methods of suicide detailed in Dostoyevsky's *Demons*. If a gigantic rock the size of a large house fell onto one's head, would it be painful or not? Imagining an enormous rock, Tomioka was overcome by the fear that standing under it and being crushed by it would be painful indeed. There was no agony in the encounter with the rock itself, but there was agony in the fear of the rock. Tomioka saw that he would feel that same fear toward any method. "Dying is definitely painful."

"But if one is able to choose to die, then it must not be so painful, right?"

"No, if you can die skillfully, that's all right. But if you cannot die skillfully, that would be painful."

"I can stand its being painful. What I can't stand is not being loved by you."

Yukiko, seizing the collar of Tomioka's padded kimono, shook it as if to lift it off.

"I don't dislike you. I like you, and that's why I'm talking about changing our ways of life. You should go back to Iba's place and get yourself into some kind of work with that money. Yukiko-san, that's how much the world has changed. Our romance disappeared with the end of the war. It would be good, at the age you are now, if you abandoned your girlish dreams. Even I, when I'm apart from you, sometimes have dreams about you and feel a sort of ecstasy. Human beings are like that. Now, turn to me. Let's spend the night talking things out leisurely. Neither of us wants to have some kind of horrible parting. I won't part from you disliking you. If I disliked you, would I have come out here about this?"

Tomioka sat up, and poured himself a small cup, from the cooled-off bottle of sake. The maid suddenly came by to lay out the bedding. Tomioka asked her to bring some warmed sake. While the maid was laying out the bedding, the two sat in chairs on the veranda. The roofed corridor, open to the elements, was quite cold.

While the maid was busy inside, the pair sat silently facing each other at a table. Presently, the entire floor space of the room was covered with bedding. The brazier and the tea table were put aside in the ornamental alcove. There the arrangements for sake were made. The brazier, replenished with charcoal, sent up a blue flame.

The two sat with the brazier between them.

"Please feel free to talk about anything."

"But I don't really have much to talk about. We should get beyond all this talk about living and dying."

"What a selfish person."

"What do you mean?"

"It's not something you can casually ask 'What do you mean?' about. I came out here with every intention of dying."

"Every intention of dying? That won't do. In the Book of Matthew, it says: 'Enter ye in at the strait gate: for wide is the gate, and broad is the way that leadeth to destruction, and many there be which go in thereat. Because strait is the gate, and narrow is the way, which leadeth unto life, and few there be that find it.' Both you and I have already passed by the gate that leads to destruction. Because like I said before, the fear of the rock is great."

'"Well, then, I'll die by myself."

Tomioka, scoffing, with a dismissive look, said quietly, "Do as you like."

55

WHEN THEY AWOKE THE NEXT MORNING, it was nearly noon. Tomioka lay in bed for a while, reading the newspaper. A strike by the National Railway Union scheduled for the beginning of February was featured prominently. Tomioka quickly lost interest, tossed the newspaper off to the side of his pillow, and gave a big yawn. Yukiko looked fixedly at a dirty stain on the white curtains. When she thought that Tomioka could just go back to that room, but she herself had nowhere to go, Yukiko grew forlorn. Bathed in the yellow morning light, she took her hand from under the quilt and looked at it. Cradling the pillow, Tomioka turned over on his stomach and, taking a cigarette from a pack, lit it up.

"When are we leaving here?" she asked.

"There's a trolley leaving around two o'clock."

"Do you have to go back?"

"And you?"

"Where should I return to? I don't have anyplace to go back to, do I?"

Tomioka puffed at his cigarette, intently watching the smoke rise from it. Yukiko did not want to go back to Iba's place. If she had come out here with the feeling that she could go back anytime, there would be no need for her to cling to Tomioka like this. If she could go back to Iba's right away, all frivolous and demure, that would be best. It weighed on her that although she didn't feel like committing suicide, she also didn't want to go back to Iba. She didn't want to talk about anything. She would like to stay here for at least one more day. But Yukiko had secretly given up on Tomioka. When she thought that today's parting would be their real parting, she naturally began to cry.

Although Tomioka knew Yukiko was crying, he pretended not to notice. The feelings of Yukiko's heart were reflected in his own. Stubbing out his cigarette in the ashtray, Tomioka went to Yukiko's side and took her in his arms.

The night before, they had been drunk in a curious way and so had talked the night away. But after all, their abstinence was because they were unable to execute a decisive parting.

"Now, we're embracing this way. But in another two or three hours, it's going to be an awkward parting, worse than if we were strangers."

Yukiko, her face pressed against Tomioka's chest, spoke in a lonely voice. They were a wretched pair, with pangs of nausea like seasickness.

"You, too, do your best."

"Yes."

"I thought I wouldn't tell you, but I'm about to go back to work myself."

"Really!"

"In around a week's time, I'll be going to my post."

"Your post? Where?"

"It's a boat ride from Kagoshima. It's called Yakushima Island, at the very southernmost tip of the country."

"Yakushima Island? What sort of job?"

"There's a job there at the forestry station. I intend to go there for five or six years, or perhaps the rest of my life, to live in the mountains . . ."

Gripping Tomioka's shoulder, Yukiko cried, "I don't like it. Going to that sort of faraway place. Well, then, take me with you."

"That won't work. It's a lonely island. First of all, you're not the kind of person who can live in a place like that for five or six years. I'll probably be able to come up to Tokyo once a year, so we can meet then. But for the time being, I don't know whether I can do it or not, but I want to go back into the mountains."

Yukiko did not know what to think. But she found it easiest to imagine herself following Tomioka and going to Yakushima Island.

"I bet you're going to be getting together with that girl who was at your place?" Yukiko asked suddenly.

"Girl?"

"Yeah. There was a nice-looking girl in your room. In your bed."

"Oh, that one. She's the daughter of the owner of a bar in the neighborhood. She's a juvenile delinquent."

"Didn't you care about her? Like Seiko-san?"

"No, she's just a kid."

"Going by yourself to that kind of faraway place. I can't—see you doing it."

"I'm going alone. I'm going there by myself."

"Alone. But that's fine for you. What's the saying? A man will always find a place to stay, but a woman doesn't have a dwelling in the three worlds."

"Go back to Iba's place . . ."

"Do you think that's the best thing for me?"

"What other choice do you have?"

"I am absolutely not going back to Iba's place. If I were, this would be nothing but a frivolous outing on my part, wouldn't it? Please don't make a fool of me. Wasn't it because you were alone now and thinking this time, at last, we could get married, that I made up my mind and ran away here? Since coming back to Japan, we've each had all kinds of obstacles in our paths. We've acted desperately, and done things we shouldn't, but we've been committing the same offense. If after so much trouble we have passed the wide gate, then we shouldn't separate; we should try and seek out together the strait gate. Although you say that I shouldn't dwell on the dear memories of the past, you have dreams about me when we're apart. Doesn't that mean that you too are a romantic, a man who can't forget the things of the past? I don't understand why, now that you're finally alone, you're leaving me. If you don't like me, just say so, directly. On that basis, I may go back to Iba, as you say I should, or I may not. But it's still a mystery to me why we can't get married."

Tomioka was silent. He could not say outright that the matter of Seiko had not been settled in his heart. If he went to Yakushima Island, he could divide his salary and entrust it to Seiko's husband's lawyer. When he thought it over, Seiko had been the sacrificial victim of the affair between himself and Yukiko. Tomioka understood that if he stated the case as clearly as that, Yukiko would get upset. There was no other way than to let his feelings flow away into ambiguity.

Presently the two, having had their bath, sat down to a late breakfast. It was exactly one year since their stay at Ikaho. Tomioka, squatting in front of the mirror stand, combed his hair. In the depths of the mirror, he came up against the fierce eyes of Yukiko, who was looking fixedly at him from behind.

"You look happy."

"Ah, yes?"

"Cutting the connection with me, you'll be fancy-free, no?"

"That's right."

"You've always been a cold person."

"Me?"

"Yes, you. Now that things have come to this, I feel so sorry for Kano-san."

"He must be dear to you."

"Yes, he's dear to me. Why did he die, I wonder. It's such a loss."

"That's why, even though it may be difficult, it's better to live."

"It's too late to seek out the strait gate."

"It's not too late."

"How about money? Do you have a hundred thousand yen?"

"Are you going to give me a hundred thousand yen?"

"That's not too little?"

"No, that's all right."

"I can give you two hundred thousand."

"Considering it's other people's money, you sure talk big."

"This is just money off the top. There are a lot of believers around."

"Probably it's the entrance fee for the strait gate."

"That's right."

When Yukiko dragged out the suitcase from the ceiling compartment, Tomioka, laying his comb on the mirror stand, said, "I don't need any of it. If I have a job, I don't need anything. The money will be important for you."

"How is it important for me? I don't need any money."

"That's not true. Money is the biggest ally a person has."

"I understand exactly your feelings in going to Yakushima Island by yourself. I don't know whether it will work or not, but that's surely it.

The affair with Seiko-san is still caught in your heart, isn't it? Or perhaps you can't get over the matter of your wife?"

Tomioka sat with his back to the ornamental alcove. The maid came by again, bringing hot tea. Tomioka sent her to check on the times for the trolley.

56

IF TOMIOKA WAS GOING BACK, Yukiko did not want to linger behind at the inn by herself. Leaving the inn, the two went by trolley to Mishima, where they boarded the train for Tokyo. Tomioka could not just discard Yukiko, who had no place to go. There was no choice, really, after all, but to take her back to his room. The two got off at Shinagawa.

On the platform of the Yamanote Line, they smiled at one another and Yukiko went to Tomioka's room.

More even than in Izu, the cold in Tokyo chilled one to the very marrow. The storm of life was raging furiously. Both Tomioka and Yukiko sank again into dark moods.

When they got to the room, they saw that there was a postcard from the agricultural journal. The journal wanted to publish "Memories of A Forestry Technician" as a serial. Tomioka's spirits brightened. Since the electric stove was not functioning properly, Yukiko deposited her luggage, went to the neighborhood charcoal ration distribution center, and bought some expensive charcoal. Tomioka, taking out his manuscript, began flipping through it and reading choice passages. The lady from next door came over to say that a gentleman named Iba-san had called, and she passed Tomioka his card.

Tomioka put the card away in his pocket. He did not want to show it to Yukiko. Soon Yukiko returned, her face red with cold. She had bought some other items besides the charcoal, including a large bottle of sake. Tomioka thought Yukiko was to be pitied.

The heart of a woman—with its capacity to embrace childish illusions—made Tomioka blanch. It flew in the face of various contradictions. Tomioka himself did not fully understand the path whereby he was naturally betraying the woman. He knew that he had a fear of women's ways. And that this was a fear of something within himself. Thinking this, he felt a guilt like that which a criminal must feel.

A woman, no matter what happened, never looked back. Earnestly, with a simple innocence, she seduced the man. If Iba had come here, even this room was no longer safe. He would have to make arrangements quickly to proceed to Yakushima Island. But he was unsure what to do about Yukiko.

"Don't you want to return to your old job? I could make inquiries for you. You could rent a room and live a life of ease. You could study, too. And you might find someone you could marry."

Yukiko stared at him, her eyes wide.

Her expression seemed to say, Don't even touch on that subject, please. Yukiko had lost the sense, after spending all night on the road, of yesterday or tomorrow. There was just herself now. The fact that she had stolen six hundred thousand yen had made her bold. The money would somehow enable her to fight free of her situation. If worse came to worst, she would go to Yakushima Island on her own. She could not, now, separate herself from the scent of this man's body.

Like a madwoman, Yukiko wanted to cling to the manly odor that neither Iba nor Kano had possessed. If she had been going to part from Tomioka, she would probably have done so at Shinagawa Station and gone straight back to Iba's place.

With an easy familiarity, as if she had been living in this room for a long time, Yukiko made preparations for a meal. Feeling that he had to, Tomioka took the card from his pocket and showed it to her.

"Oh, did Iba come here? When did he come? How did he know about this place?" Yukiko was surprised.

"It's strange."

"God told him where to look."

"But, joking aside, how did he know? I didn't tell anyone where you were."

"Didn't he find out when there was that big fuss about Seiko?"

"No, I doubt it. Even if he did hear about Seiko, it's not likely he would have found out about this place."

The appearance of Iba was mystifying to Yukiko. Tomioka, meanwhile, felt as if he were being hunted down by something.

"Anyhow, I'm physically strong, so I think I can live anywhere. Couldn't you just take me along with you, to Yakushima Island? If I get tired of it, I'll come back alone. Please take me with you, for a month or two. If you do that, I think I'll be able to reconcile myself."

Although Tomioka did not want to take Yukiko with him to the ends of the South, he thought that perhaps he should, given that Iba was obviously looking for them.

The next morning, he immediately went to his friend's place to ask his friend to get started right away and helped arrange the posting to Yakushima Island. On his way back, he took his manuscript to the editorial department of the agricultural journal, whose office was in Marunouchi.

Tomioka waited there about an hour for a reporter, whom he knew by sight, to put in an appearance. When the reporter did arrive, he had something strange to say. He said that yesterday morning somebody had come and asked for the address of the person who had written "A Discourse on Lacquer." Ah, so that's it, thought Tomioka. Yukiko had told him that she had purchased a copy of the agricultural journal that had carried his article about lacquer and read it. Clearly, because of that copy, Iba had gotten the idea of finding out his address from the journal.

Yukiko had decided to stay out for the whole day. Taking her valise with her, she went around and saw two or three movies. She knew that during Tomioka's absence, Iba might descend on her and try to force her to go back with him.

If she went off to Yakushima Island with Tomioka, there would be nothing at all for Yukiko to worry about. Now that she had given over the money for Seiko's husband's lawyer, there was really nothing that she wanted.

Late that night, she returned to Tomioka's place. Again, the next day, valise in hand, she spent the day out of the house.

This went on for about a week. During that time, a special-delivery letter came from Iba to Tomioka, saying that he would like to see him somewhere and to please name a meeting place. However, Tomioka's appointment came through that very day.

Tomioka tore up the special-delivery letter and threw it away. Yukiko was a little worried but not overly so—after all, it was just Iba who was making the threats. Tomioka went around to see various clients and acquaintances and to formally tell them of his plans; he also worked on his manuscript. In the second week after their return from Izu, he finally vacated the room. He assembled his baggage and sent it on ahead.

Until the day he left Tokyo, Tomioka still thought that he would like somehow to leave Yukiko behind, but since he had allowed her to pay the money to retain the lawyer for Seiko's husband, leaving alone was no longer a possibility. All he could do was let things take their course. During his life in the south, this spirit of letting things take their course had become a habit. The Malay lumber porters, when they came up against some unlucky turn of events, would say, "*Apa bore boatto.*" But this "it can't be helped" attitude was not easy to maintain in Tomioka's present circumstances.

He was not pleased with the way things were going. He had not laid a hand on Yukiko's money himself, true, but it was shameful just the same to have allowed her to pay for everything. The railway strike that the newspapers had predicted for February had been forbidden, but still the world was in more and more of a mess. Tomioka had learned how difficult it was to survive in Tokyo with nothing but a point of view. He did think that living somewhere other than Tokyo might be easier. There were even signs that a third world war might break out.

With all this uneasiness in the world around him, Tomioka was glad to be removing himself to a remote place. He only wished that the move were not with Yukiko. She was like a mold that that had gotten under his skin.

It was the middle of February when the two left Tokyo. They boarded the night train.

57

THE DEVIL IN THE FLESH. It's as if there's a demon inside me. These were phrases that Kano had often used at Dalat. When asked who that devil was, Kano would point his jaw at Yukiko.

The train journey was long and tedious. Tomioka was flabbergasted at the way Yukiko, who did not seem at all bored, kept eating sloppily.

They arrived at Kyoto in the morning. If Yukiko had not been there, Tomioka would have liked to spend a day in the city.

Perhaps because Yukiko had money to spare, even at Kyoto she went down to the platform and bought some things to eat. When Tomioka leaned out the window to look, Yukiko's figure—seen from the back, in her overcoat—was that of a woman well past her prime. He noticed she was buying some cigarettes for him. As she turned toward him for a moment, her face was terribly pale and dry looking.

They passed Osaka and Kobe. When they were going along the seashore at Maiko, the sea, which shone a dull leaden color, made the train windows glow white.

Yukiko, with the collar of her overcoat turned up, had fallen into a profound slumber. The third-class car, where they were riding, was rather crowded. Some passengers were even sitting in the aisles.

What with the various husks and rinds and skins left over from people's meals, and the stuffy smell of humanity, the interior of the car at midday was rather warm even though it was unheated. Tomioka gazed vaguely at Yukiko's face as she slept deeply. In these four or five days of their living together, the skin under her eyes had grown slightly darker, and her lips had developed tiny cracks in which her lipstick had hardened. The hair of her eyebrows stuck out, and oil was shining on the bridge of her nose. Now and then, her eyelids twitched nervously.

The "demon" was asleep. Except that in fact she was awake and was aware that she was being watched. With eyes closed, Yukiko gave a little smile. Tomioka, flustered, turned his eyes away.

Opening her eyes suddenly, with a knowing look that said, Did you want to say something to me, Yukiko picked up a tangerine and began peeling it. Outside, the landscape was dotted with factories—smokestacks, wintry rust-colored fields, rice paddies, mountains, rivers, and the sea raced backward into the distance, punctuated by the roaring rhythm of the train's wheels.

It was late at night when they arrived at Hakata in the northern part of the island of Kyushu. They needed to transfer there to the train that would take them much farther south, to the city of Kagoshima. From there, it would be an overnight boat ride. Rain was falling. Although the two were tired, they immediately made their transfer. They wanted to be even wearier—completely exhausted—so that everything in them would be numb and paralyzed. Yukiko gradually grew forlorn. The shining night rain streaked down the dirty windowpanes. Any number of times, Yukiko had scraps of dreams. It was as if she could feel the shaking of the car driving to Dalat in the Ranbean highlands, by way of Jirin, from Saigon.

Every time she woke to the reality of the night train driving through rain, Yukiko grew more depressed. It seemed that Japan was a lot larger than she had realized. Tomioka was plunged in heavy slumber.

It was a long journey. They were far from Tokyo now, and Yukiko felt as if her memories of life with Iba had been cut up and shredded into little pieces. At Kumamoto, the rain let up a bit. The faces of the passengers around them kept changing. The language, too, turned into the Kyushu dialect. Everything that they felt any connection to had vanished. Yukiko, shoving her tired legs between Tomioka's legs, closed her eyes. While thinking that there was nothing to fear anymore, from anywhere, Yukiko had amusing thoughts about Iba's furious face. He could no longer drag her back with him. She felt like telling Iba that she would pray for the prosperity of the Great Sunshine Religion. As for Otsu Shimo, she no doubt would be sitting, every day from now on, wearing her thick makeup, right in front of the safe. Every now and then, Yukiko checked to make sure that the valise was still on the baggage rack above her head. Now, all she had to depend on was that one Boston bag.

They arrived in Kagoshima in the morning. It was raining hard. Letting a pedicab driver lead the way, they were taken to a neighborhood called Sengoku, near the harbor, where they put up at a small inn.

When they entered their room on the second floor, they saw the gigantic volcano of Sakurajima looming outside their window. The mountain smoldered a purplish color.

Exhausted, Yukiko stretched out her legs on the tatami, which smelled of the sea.

Tomioka asked the maid about the departure times of the boat for Yakushima Island. She answered that when there were stormy conditions, the boat might not leave for any number of days. Asking the maid to check the schedule, Tomioka, still in his overcoat, sprawled out on the tatami.

As he lay there, he could see Sakurajima. Below it, the sea had a color that was like blue lacquer. A motley array of little boats jostled alongside the piers. Tomioka ordered some beer from the maid who had brought the tea.

"We've come to a very faraway place. And from here, it's still an overnight trip on a boat. It's like going into exile. I could never come out all this way by myself."

"We're going to live here for four years, five years."

"That's so . . ."

"How about it? If you are going back, this would be a good spot to go back from."

"Are you still talking about that?"

"Because you just said you wouldn't be able to come out here by yourself."

"Yes, right, so I came with you, didn't I? Don't you have any sympathy at all?"

"I can't bear it if you're going to put the blame on me."

Somewhere nearby, a radio was playing noisily with a sizzle of static. Yukiko took off her overcoat, slipped the padded kimono of the inn over her shoulders, and looked out at the veranda and the driving rain.

"I'm not putting the blame on you. I don't have that sort of petty feelings. But even for you, isn't it better than being alone? If I couldn't live on Yakushima Island, I would have wanted to come here anyway and work as a waitress in a restaurant. That's how women are. If I were discarded, I would have wanted to come out this way, anyway."

"No one's saying anything about discarding you."

The maid came with the beer. Swigging the foamy brew at a single go, Tomioka seemed to come alive for the first time.

The maid told them that the boat would not be leaving for two days. Although the prospect of two more days in this place was daunting, there was nothing they could do about it. Stepping out onto the veranda, Tomioka looked at the sea under the driving rain.

"Did you tell the magazine that you were going to Yakushima Island?" Yukiko asked.

"Ah."

"Iba must be furious."

"Is he going to come after you?"

"Surely not. It's not that much money, is it?"

"No, it's quite a bit of money. It's possible he might just report it to the police."

"It's all right."

Despite saying it was all right, Yukiko went back into the room and drank some beer herself. She could feel the cold beer soaking into her stomach. But somehow her mood took a turn for the worse.

"Will you be having your bath, madam?"

The maid had come to tell them about the bath. Addressed as madam, as if she were Tomioka's wife, Yukiko, who had never been called that by anyone, stared intently at Tomioka, wide-eyed.

"Please go ahead and take your bath ahead of me, madam," Tomioka said teasingly. Tomioka was totally exhausted. He didn't feel like taking a bath at all. Saying that he would go to the shipping company's office, find out what time the boat was leaving, and buy the tickets, Tomioka borrowed the inn's coarse oilpaper umbrella and went outside. The people at the inn had told him where the shipping company was. He walked along a wide, dreary avenue, toward the sea. At first, perhaps because he was by himself, he felt lighthearted. If he had been told that the ship was leaving right away, he would have liked to board it all by himself. When he got to the shipping company's office—a simple, blue-painted structure—he was told, just as they had said at the inn, that there would be no departure until the storm ended, but that the ship would probably leave the day after tomorrow. He bought two second-class tickets for Yakushima, writing down Yukiko's name on the passenger list as his wife.

On the way back, along one of the lively thoroughfares, Tomioka bought some whiskey. When he got back to the inn, Yukiko was lying on the bedding, her face pale. She was trembling violently.

"What's the matter?"

"I'm cold. I can't stop trembling. Can't you call a doctor?"

Yukiko gripped Tomioka's arm. There were fine shudders going through her body. She didn't look so bad—she only looked like she had a cold. But he noticed some blood on her lips. Tomioka put a hand to her brow, but she was not particularly feverish. It would be bad if she were to become bedridden at this inn, he thought. He asked the people of the inn to call for a doctor. He laid three quilts over Yukiko, but even so she said she was cold. Her trembling continued. The doctor did not come for some time. Tomioka went out to buy some cold medicine.

Making her take one dose of the cold medicine, Tomioka tried giving Yukiko some hot tea. The trembling still did not stop. After an hour or so, the young doctor finally arrived. The maid helped him to remove Yukiko's clothing, and the doctor examined her. He gave her injections of camphor and vitamins. With rest, he said, she would recover in a couple of days. Tomioka guessed that he should be relieved, but somehow he had the feeling that Yukiko's condition was similar to that of his wife, Kuniko. He could see the signs of it in Yukiko's face.

After she had taken a sedative, Yukiko fell into a slumber that was like a coma. Tomioka began to have the feeling that one by one the things happening around him were like a series of solid, heavy doors being closed against him, sealing his fate. When Kuniko had taken to her bed, the doctor had also said she would be well in two or three days. But she was not. The inn where they were staying, evidently put up quickly after the bombings, had only five rooms or so. Surprisingly, it was full. In the next room, guests were laughing boisterously. Only his and Yukiko's room was silent and gloomy.

Without even changing into his padded kimono, Tomioka sat by Yukiko's pillow. He uncorked the bottle of whiskey and had a drink. The wind and rain drove harder and harder. Now and then the building shook in the wind. The electricity did not come on, and as evening drew on, the darkness of the room became oppressive. Perhaps because Sakurajima loomed so hugely in the window, there was a sense of pressure in the room, as if the volcano were about to topple over and come crashing through the window.

58

SINCE THEY HAD GOTTEN THIS FAR somewhat thoughtlessly, Tomioka felt a considerable shock at Yukiko's becoming ill.

The second day, the weather was fine.

The rain had ended. The day was windy. When the maid came at daybreak, bringing charcoal for the brazier, she kindly informed them that a ship called the *Terukuni* would be leaving that morning at nine. But Yukiko's condition had not improved. Deeply asleep, she was still coughing. When he heard those coughs, Tomioka felt a pain as if his own skin was being scraped off.

Seen from the veranda window, Sakurajima was lost in the kerosene color of the cold daybreak sky. Along the seashore, flimsy-looking wooden warehouses stood in a line, and above them the ships' masts made an intricate latticework. The lamps along the streets were still lit, and the moon was in the sky. Tomioka gazed intently at the dawn harbor, where as yet everything was quiet. He thought that it would be difficult to leave this morning, with things as they were. He decided to delay their departure. Going to the brazier beside the pillow, Tomioka squatted and lit a cigarette. Yukiko opened her eyes.

"Well, how do you feel?"

Yukiko, perhaps trying but unable to smile, her eyes opened wide, looked up at Tomioka's face. Tomioka put his hand to Yukiko's forehead. It was unexpectedly cold. In Yukiko's wide-open eyes, there was an expression that Tomioka was unused to, of inexpressible loneliness. In a sudden rush of pity, Tomioka knelt and brought his face close to hers.

"I've put off our departure, so everything's all right. I'll have the tickets changed, so rest easy and don't worry about anything. There's nothing to get upset about. All right? Your tiredness has caught up with you; that's all. You shouldn't have exposed yourself to the rain."

Tomioka spoke slowly, biting off each word. Yukiko, her eyes still open, nodded acquiescence. Taking her hand, he placed it against his cheek. Yukiko had the exact same look in her eyes as when he'd been at her bedside in the French clinic where she was operated on after she had been cut by Kano, Tomioka thought. His memories of French Indochina ached in his heart. He remembered experiencing a nausea approaching terror, as he gazed at the dawn sky over the lake from the clinic, when he had thought about the sort of travel weariness the two shared. Since she was a woman he had met by chance under foreign skies, this was the way things had turned out, Tomioka admitted to himself. But his transient affair with the Annamese maid was the result of travel weariness as well, wasn't it, he thought ruefully. Niu's naive and trusting face, and her skin the color of wheat, burned fiercely in Tomioka's breast. Simply because she was a woman whom he would never be able to meet again, she had become as dear to Tomioka as the dead Seiko. But when he thought back on it, his life in Indochina did not seem to have been based on a simple thing like a lonesome journey. A keen sense of loneliness, a tenderness toward all others, like the attitude of a man who has just been condemned to death, made Tomioka treasure others' feelings. Within the rigid hierarchical power of the army, not even the freedom of loneliness was allowed. His own selfishness, which had sought to quench a thirst of the spirit by means of Yukiko's body, had eventually come to this, he thought. Wanting to make it up to her, Tomioka gripped Yukiko's hand firmly.

"Aren't you going to board the boat yourself?" Yukiko asked weakly.

"You fool! Did you think I would go without you?"

Yukiko shrugged faintly, like a child. As if he were family, Tomioka wiped away the tear that had gathered in the corner of her eye. Seeking to convey the feeling that everything was all right, he squeezed Yukiko's hand two or three times. Letting go, he asked the maid, who had come up with the tea, what time it was.

"About seven o'clock, isn't it?" Looking at her wristwatch, the maid held it to her ear.

When Tomioka went downstairs, it was a little past seven, according to the clock in the entryway. Tomioka went to the shipping company and requested that their tickets be changed. He decided to take the *Terukuni-maru* that would leave here at the same time four days from now. Since he was there, he took a stroll around the harbor, to see the *Terukuni-maru*. The white ship, sending up smoke from its big funnel, was hoisting a cargo of timber with its crane. All along the wharf was a line of stalls selling fruit to passengers. Coming here to the ends of Kyushu, seeing the piles of fruit on the stalls, Tomioka had a strange feeling. He bought about eight pounds of apples for Yukiko and had them packed in a green basket. He then went alongside the ship. The passengers were already standing in line. Every single passenger was holding a little glass bowl of goldfish. This was exactly the kind of ship that plied the Indochina route. Tomioka had the illusion that if he could board the ship with Yukiko this morning, just so, it would be an incalculably pleasurable voyage. But now this ship of pleasure sailed only as far as Yakushima Island. Beyond that, its route had had its boundaries set by war. This ship could not proceed a foot farther than Yakushima Island. It had no route to those yellow seas of the south. On the wharf, passengers and porters milled about. Scraps of straw and wood and apple peel were scattered over the pier. Tomioka gazed vaguely at the cable of the crane being wound up. A steam whistle went off, signaling the ship's imminent departure. Another whistle was blown. Women and children made their way through the crowd that had come to see the boat off, selling streamers. Tomioka bought a roll of red streamer. The purser, wearing a prewar uniform, walked along the gangplank and descended to the pier. People began to board. Alongside the gangplank, a white uniformed cabin boy and a policeman stood by.

The passengers, each with a considerable amount of baggage, were jostled from behind as they boarded the boat.

Presently, at a little past nine, the ship's whistle went off again. The boat began slowly to move away from the pier. Those left behind on the pier made a great deal of commotion as they saw the passengers off. The passengers, setting down their baggage on the deck, lined up one by one along the ship's railing. Rolls of streamers, like so many little birds, flew from the pier onto the deck. Red, white, cobalt, yellow, green, the rainbow of streamers, billowing in the wind, described large arcs. Tomioka tossed his red streamer toward a child of seven or eight, who was waving at the people on the pier. But the tape hit the head of a woman who looked like an office worker. The woman grabbed Tomioka's tape with both hands. She was wearing a shabby dark skirt, but she had a sweet face. She wore a faded blue jacket. She held the tape up high, so that it wouldn't snap off. Tomioka, having perhaps lost patience because the ship was moving so slowly, let go of the tape midway and went back along the pier toward the shipping company's office. Without any destination, he didn't feel there was any particular road he should take. As if suddenly remembering it, he turned and looked back at the sea. The ship was unexpectedly small, off in the distance. On the pier littered with streamers, some people were still waving their hands and hats and handkerchiefs at the boat. In the turbid seawater, strips of red and yellow streamers floated, their bright colors imprinting themselves on Tomioka's eyes.

After getting directions from a passerby, he went off to the post office. He sent a telegram to the forestry station on Yakushima Island and bought a postcard. He addressed the postcard to his parents in Matsuida, writing simply that he had arrived in Kagoshima and was waiting for a boat. The spacious post office was quite empty. Making himself comfortable at a wooden writing table, Tomioka grasped the pen provided by the post office. Just then, he noticed a young woman seated next to him, writing the word "Tokyo" on a telegram form. Tomioka grew nostalgic. That great city called Tokyo, which this woman also was writing to, seemed as far away as the ends of the earth.

Tokyo was now a realm of nostalgia for him. If it had not been for the affair of Seiko, he would likely never have come to this region of despair, of a person turning his back on the world, equivalent to committing suicide. In the clean, well-kept post office at this early-morning hour, the light was as quiet as the bottom of the sea and as peaceful. The woman next to him went up to a window with a grill, to send her telegram. The heels of her shoes were quite deteriorated. Her black overcoat was worn and wrinkled also. Dropping his card into the mailbox, Tomioka left the post office.

59

DISCOVERING A SMALL WATCHMAKER'S SHOP not far from the inn, Tomioka went up to the display window and looked at the watches for a while. All of them were imitations of Swiss watches, but one with a price tag of 3,600 yen caught Tomioka's fancy. Thinking he would like such a watch as a memento of Yakushima Island, he entered the store and asked the shop clerk to show it to him. He had sold the watch he had purchased in Indochina in Ikaho to Seiko's husband. After that had followed a period of deprivation, when he had had no watch. So he wanted to have one again. Taking the watch, he held it to his ear. The second hand made a clear, steady ticking. The dial was round and thin. He decided to go ahead and buy it.

When he returned to the inn, Yukiko seemed to have worn herself out waiting for him. Although her face was tear-stained, when she saw the basket of apples that Tomioka had brought her, she looked relieved and reached out her hand from under the quilt. Tomioka, immediately sitting down by her pillow, peeled an apple for her with a knife.

"While I was at it, I had a look at the boat," he said. "It seems rather nice. It's probably the best boat on the line to Yakushima Island. The people boarding the boat all had bowls of goldfish. I wonder if there aren't any goldfish on the island."

As he peeled the apple, Tomioka talked about the boat he had seen.

"It's a white boat. Since you're sick, it may seem like a luxury, but I had our tickets changed to first class. I hear they don't serve meals, so we should take enough food for a couple of meals. Only, they say that there are lots of good doctors at Tanegashima, on the way, but none on Yakushima Island itself."

"No doctors?"

"Ah. It's a little worrisome."

"If I start feeling ill on the boat, please leave me there, on Tanegashima, and go on."

"If it's a matter of getting off at Tanegashima, it would be more convenient to have a doctor see you in Kagoshima. If conditions are absolutely no good for the next boat, you can go to the hospital here and find a small inn and take your time in coming after me. Whatever you say, Kagoshima is a city and it's a convenient place."

Yukiko watched Tomioka's hand as he peeled the apple. Her eye lighted on the watch with a new leather strap that he was wearing on his wrist.

"Have you bought a watch?"

"Yes, I bought it just now at a shop near here."

"Let me see it."

When Tomioka held out his left arm, Yukiko looked avidly at the dial. Somehow it was like the watch that Tomioka had sold at Ikaho. "It's nice," Yukiko said. Since she didn't particularly ask about the price, Tomioka said nothing. Since he had bought the watch with the money left over from the magazine company, he didn't at all feel guilty. But Yukiko seemed a little uncomfortable. Had she thought that the watch was very expensive?

"If we had boarded, we'd be on the open sea about now. Were the waves rough?"

"The wind was strong, but the sea was calm. It was just like the departure of a foreign ship. People threw lengths of tape at each other."

"Really? It must have been pretty."

"No, it was a little strange. Strange that the boat wouldn't be allowed to go to foreign parts. There was a kind of nostalgia about it . . ."

The tapes, which were a decoration for the so-called human feelings of loneliness and sentimentality, flickered behind Tomioka's eyes. Yukiko, curiously, could not seem to get over the watch. Tomioka's state of mind, in which he could buy an expensive watch, came to seem to her like a shallowness of heart. Tomioka peeled the apple and gave her half.

Her gums smarting from the sour taste, Yukiko nibbled at the apple. But it was unexpectedly soft and tasted bad. Tomioka also munched away at the apple.

"This apple is no good." Tomioka spit out what was left of his. Nearby, they heard the noisy squawking of a hen—it must belong to the inn. It began to rain lightly again.

In the morning, the doctor came to give Yukiko an injection. Examining Yukiko's chest and back, the young doctor said to Tomioka, "It will be best if we take an X-ray."

Yukiko felt a chill of fear. As she was now, it was more than she could bear to fall ill on a journey. She had come so far. If she did have to separate from Tomioka, it would have been better simply to have remained in Tokyo, she thought. She felt an oppression of heart, as if the illness this time would somehow prove to be her last. If she had had to battle a difficult illness, she almost wished she had succumbed to the scabies she had contracted at the time of her repatriation. Yukiko thought it would be just as well if the young doctor did not say a lot of unnecessary things to Tomioka.

For Tomioka and for Yukiko, the next several days were very difficult to bear. During those four days far from home, the young doctor, with an extraordinary friendliness, became a familiar figure to them. During the war with Nationalist China, he had served at the front in central China as an army doctor. In age, surprisingly, he was not that far removed from Tomioka, but he was still single, assisting at his father's hospital. Perhaps because he was a bachelor, he looked extraordinarily young. Tomioka knew that he was a graduate of a medical university in Fukuoka. He liked music and had put together an electric phonograph himself. His hobby was collecting records for it, the maid at the inn said. The young doctor's name was Hika, and his family came from the Ryukyu Islands. One day, listening to a radio playing somewhere in the neighborhood, Hika said, intently, "I like this piece." His eyes narrowed with pleasure. Tomioka thought, I've heard this somewhere and listened attentively. Massaging herself from outside the sleeves of her coverlet after her injection, Yukiko listened to it as well. Neither Tomioka nor Yukiko knew what the piece was.

"What symphony is this?" Yukiko asked.

"It's Dvorak's *New World Symphony*."

The doctor spoke leisurely, putting the injection apparatus away and washing his hands in the basin.

Tomioka, envying the doctor's taste in music, thought it a happy coincidence, to have come across a good doctor here at the remote ends of Kyushu. Although he was stocky and did not particularly look like a doctor, he had gentle, narrow eyes and his white, beautifully aligned teeth were striking. Tomioka, saying that he was on his way to a new post at the forestry research station on Yakushima Island, talked for a while about his having gone to the Agriculture Ministry in Indochina in the employ of the army.

Hearing that Tomioka had a job at the forestry station, suddenly seemed to increase the doctor's goodwill. Saying that he had intended to attend the Imperial University in Hokkaido, he talked about the ideals of his youth.

Yakushima Island had no doctors, which was worrisome, Tomioka said, but in case of an emergency, if they sent him a telegram, would he possibly be able to come to the island and examine Yukiko? The doctor said that he would come out to them, under any circumstances.

"I've also heard that there is no doctor on Yakushima Island. There probably is a doctor connected with the forestry station up in the mountains. I myself have thought of opening a practice there, but there's no electricity and I've heard it rains year-round. It made me a bit afraid of the place. It would be lonely not to be able to listen to my records. These days, at the forestry station, they seem to get electricity once every few days. People think that doctors are selfless, benevolent souls, but in fact, a life of being exiled to an island where I can't listen to a single record is, for me, impossible.

"I'll look for a chance to come out and visit you. But, speaking frankly, what effect will such a damp place have on your wife's health? If it's your job, I guess it can't be helped, but if possible you should select a residence somewhere high in the mountains. You should establish a methodical daily regimen. At any rate, there isn't time for me to give her a thorough examination, but once you're out there, please do keep me informed on how she is doing from day to day. A postcard will suffice."

Hika, in a tone so as not to cause uneasiness in the patient, limited his advice to these matters. Although Yukiko had already forgotten the melody of Dvorak's *New World Symphony*, just the name of the symphony itself resonated strongly with her. Feeling that they had received an augury of their new departure, Yukiko felt respect and affection for Hika's straightforward, artless manner.

Tomioka, remembering Dostoyevsky's words in *Crime and Punishment*, was it, that no one can live without sympathy from others, felt this doctor to be a character out of prerevolutionary Russia. Tomioka and Yukiko had a packet made up of emergency medicines and materials for injections. On the morning of the fourth day, when they took a car to the *Terukuni-maru*, Hika unexpectedly came running—without even a hat or coat—to see them off. For Tomioka and Yukiko, who didn't have anyone to toss a length of tape to them, this was a very touching surprise. Neither had guessed that they would receive a farewell visit from the young doctor.

In the first-class cabin, there was an upper and a lower bunk. The blankets, too, were white and new. There was a sofa and, in front of it, a table and a chair. There was a mirror on the wall, and a water jug in a niche in the wall. It was a spacious, leisurely stateroom of about four-and-a-half mats. When Yukiko lay down on the lower bunk, Hika, who had come aboard, took a syringe from a case and, swabbing the needle with alcohol, gave her a shot of vitamins in the arm. Yukiko never forgot the cold touch of the doctor's hand. A feeling of faintness came over her, like first love.

Yukiko was unable to go up on the deck, but Tomioka left the cabin to see Hika off. Even when the ship started to move, Tomioka did not come back down to the cabin for some time. On the first-class deck, he kept holding the green tape that Hika had tossed to him. The messily strewn pier, like a toy box turned over and emptied out, was far in the distance, as Tomioka still held over his head the snapped length of tape. Hika, standing at the end of the pier, waved a white handkerchief. Finally, though, bent over slightly from the hips, he left the pier with long strides. Seen from behind, the doctor's figure as he swung his case to and fro seemed trustworthy and endearing.

Perhaps because the boat was now at sea, it did not seem odd that Sakurajima looked surprisingly small in the faint morning sunshine. The Sakurajima they had seen from the window of the inn had appeared huge, as if a great curtain had been drawn across the scene; but viewed from the sea, Sakurajima seemed as small as an objet d'art for an ornamental alcove. The third-class passengers crawled out of their cellarlike cabins and came up to sunbathe on the wooden chairs of the broad deck. Here and there on the deck, people had placed goldfish bowls—apparently purchased as souvenirs—and in every bowl a goldfish gleamed.

The sea was halcyon calm.

In the shade, the wind was cold enough to penetrate one's overcoat, but elsewhere the rays of the sun were quite hot. From the great funnel right overhead, dirty smoke trailed off to the west. On the sea that shone white in the sunlight, Tomioka scattered to the wind the green tape he'd held in his hand. Out on the open ocean like this, the air was bracing and seemed to blow away the chains of fate that he had felt coiling around his shoulders and ankles for some time now. As he looked over the waters of the silent sea, Tomioka was put in mind of the proverb that silence brought only one regret, while speaking brought ten regrets. He thought the same could be said of being on the ocean and being on land.

Yukiko enjoyed the way the ship seemed to vibrate through her spine. The sense of leaving everything to the ship as it moved steadily ahead was exactly the same way she had felt coming back from Indochina. She found it difficult to forget the doctor's gentle actions and words, as well as the medicinal smell of his body. His face was reminiscent of Kano's. Although she did not approve of these irregular feelings of her heart, Yukiko for the longest time entertained a fantasy of a dangerous encounter with Hika in the mountains of Yakushima Island. She happily painted the scene to herself over and over in her mind.

60

THEY ARRIVED AT TANEGASHIMA at about two o'clock.

The yellow, flattish island came into view suddenly in the porthole window. Tomioka, while smoking a cigarette, gazed at the long, lonely-looking island. Yukiko was fast asleep. For no particular reason, Tomioka thought how far she had come to reach this place.

In the little harbor, far in the distance, many small boats were moored together in a jumble. The black and white roofs of the houses along the shore, like paper cutouts, were unlike anything Tomioka had seen before.

Taking its time, the boat entered the outer western harbor of Tanegashima. The ship would anchor here in Tanegashima until nine that night. When one of the crewmen told him this, Tomioka thought that the prospect sounded quite boring. Rather than idling here, he would prefer to proceed quickly to their ultimate destination.

But Tanegashima, viewed from afar, seemed almost like a desert island. Yet Tomioka had heard that among the archipelago of islands that dotted this Sea of Osumi, only Tanegashima had its own culture. Thinking that he was on his way to an island even more deserted than this one, Tomioka gazed vaguely at the harbor as it drew nearer. It was an island like a bare mountaintop. Although extraordinarily long and wide, it looked, perhaps because it had no high hills, as if it were about to start sinking into the sea at any minute.

"So have we arrived somewhere?" Yukiko made a rustling noise from her pillow as she spoke.

Tomioka, still resting his cheek against the porthole, said, "We've arrived at Tanegashima."

"Is it a nice harbor?"

"Yes, it's a tidy little place. Would you like to get up and see it?"

"I don't really need to. Anyway, aren't all harbors the same?"

"It's surprisingly lively. There are a lot of little boats. I saw a seaside village similar to this one once; maybe it was somewhere in Indochina."

"Is it like Indochina?"

"No, it's not, but I have the feeling that there was the same kind of hamlet there, too. Harbors that Japanese have made, wherever they are, tend to be lonely and gloomy . . ."

With a violent rattling sound, the ship dropped its anchor. Little by little, it approached the small jetty of the harbor. On the sunlit jetty, many people—waiting to meet the boat, Tomioka supposed—were milling around like ants. As the boat drew closer to the pier, each person who had come to meet the boat was clearly visible. Their clothing was no different from that of Tokyo or Kagoshima. There were some young women who wore the red jackets fashionable these days. Every single woman had her hair done up in a permanent, and the young men sported Regent haircuts that gleamed with oil.

Soon the gangplank was lowered and the lower-class passengers streamed ashore with their apples and bowls of goldfish. The narrow pier trembled in the waves, and the people swarmed hurriedly along it. Tomioka, hitching his overcoat over his shoulders, went out onto the first-class deck.

As he looked on, the crowd of people gradually moved in the direction of the town, which sat on a knoll. The road of white sand gleamed dully in the setting sun. Along the breakwater, there was a miscellaneous array of buildings, a wooden building that looked like a town office, a forwarding agency, a tilting, three-story inn, and some bars.

Why would the ship cast anchor in a place like this for so many hours? Tomioka wondered. It didn't seem that the stop was intended for picking up cargo, since there were not many boxes or bags on the pier.

Tomioka and Yukiko spent the time until night on board. Neither of them went on shore. Toward nightfall, the deck was lit up and a loudspeaker played popular songs, as the passengers milled about. All along the deck and the corridors, the lovely voices of the women from the drinking shops could be heard, accompanied by the faint clip-clop of sandals. Any number of times, one of these women would open the door of Tomioka's and Yukiko's room and peer inside. Both Tomioka and Yukiko were surprised by their bad manners.

"Is Yakushima like this?" Burrowing under the blanket, Yukiko spoke disconsolately. The same popular blues song about throwing a lover's heart away played again and again up on deck.

The next day, at about eight in the morning, Yakushima Island began to appear on the horizon.

Tomioka and Yukiko were to set foot on land at the harbor of Anbo. The ship arrived near the island. The waves were rough along the coast. As the harbor was too small, the ship anchored offshore, and a small boat took the passengers to the shore. Tomioka, when he saw this thickly wooded solitary islet, like a mole at the end of the Osumi Archipelago, thought, So this is the dwelling place I was headed for all along, and felt a rush of emotion.

From a blue sea that seemed to saturate one's eye, the dense, dark velvety green mountains soared into the clear sky. Thirty-two nautical miles southwest of Tanegashima, with a land area of five hundred square kilometers, the island was round in shape, with virtually no access to it at sea level. In the middle of the island, the highest mountain in Kyushu, Miyanoura Peak, towered 1,935 meters high. With it, Nagata Peak, Kuromi Peak, and others formed the so-called Yae Peaks mass. The island abounded in a variety of vertical configurations. From a thousand to fifteen hundred meters above sea level, the Yaku cedar flourished.

In Tomioka's pocket notebook, he had written a simple description of Yakushima Island. It was a dark, round island, completely unlike Tanegashima. Gazing at the dark green color of such an island after such a long time, Tomioka felt exhilarated. He didn't have the slightest sense of having been banished to a solitary island. On the contrary, he was struck by the beckoning charms of the forest, as if both his body and mind were being cleansed. Tomioka went up onto the deck. He felt the cold ocean wind on his skin and gazed hungrily at the island that now towered before his eyes. Tanegashima was an island that lay sprawled out on its side, but Yakushima Island stood right up out of the sea. For those who visit here, suddenly encountering this kind of island on the dusky sea at daybreak must be an eerie experience, he thought.

Just the fact that on the bright, deep blue sea there was this densely forested island was a mystery of nature. The ship, when it had let the lighter go, once again busily started up its engines. Out at sea, the waves were fairly rough.

The small lighter was tossed to and fro like a leaf on the waves, but it continued to work its way toward the lonely seawall of Miyanoura.

Yukiko, getting up slowly, was combing her hair. With a resigned air, propping up her compact in a fold of the blanket, she tried to restore some order to her hair. As if the hair—lusterless these days—was an inconvenience, she bunched it in a ball at the back of her head and tied it with a handkerchief. She rubbed cream into her face. On the white painted board wall, reflections from the sea coming in through the window wavered and shimmered like a heat mirage.

Yukiko stubbornly refused to look out of the window. She had not looked out at Tanegashima either, and now she made no attempt even to glance at this Yakushima Island towering before her. For Yukiko, it might not have mattered what kind of place she set foot on. The boat seemed to be close to arriving. But Yukiko felt little inclination to get ready to get off. Tomioka thought that Yukiko's languor was probably an effect of her ill health.

At about ten o'clock, the ship arrived at the offing of Anbo, at Yakushima.

A small lighter, rocked by the large waves, came rowing out toward the ship. At some point, a fine rain had begun falling.

Tomioka, cradling Yukiko's shoulders, made his way down the steep angle of the gangplank. The ship's boy stood at the foot of the gangplank, in his white jacket, ready to receive Yukiko. The gangplank, heaving high up in the air and dipping down low in the troughs of the waves as if about to be swallowed by them, was extremely dangerous. With a final desperate thought, Yukiko grabbed at the boy's hand and slid down into the small lighter. Yukiko squatted down among the straw-wrapped bales and bundles. Suddenly, ahead of her on the sea, between the bales, the heavily wooded little island, towering like some kind of sea monster, rose up out of the depths. Yukiko, her eyes widening, stared for a while. It's like a desert island; there's no one there, she muttered to herself.

Presently, the lighter, riding a big wave, abruptly left the side of the ship. It swayed and pitched in a nauseating way. The rain, which had been fine and misty, was now hard and driving. The passengers in the lighter got soaked to the skin. Yukiko was wearing Tomioka's overcoat pulled over her head. From the knees down, her legs felt freezing cold. Under the dark shelter of the overcoat, she was coughing violently.

Once the lighter slipped inside a narrow inlet, its pitching and rolling abated. A white sandbar looked as if it had been washed clean by the rain. Inside the inlet, the water was an absolutely clear green. On the bottom, rocks, seaweed, and even bright tin cans could be seen clearly.

There seemed to be a stream going up from the white sandbar. Above a tall embankment, a large mechanical suspension bridge hung like an archway.

On the beach, four or five people had come to meet the lighter. Two of them were employees from the forestry research station, who had come to welcome Tomioka. One had a coarse oilpaper umbrella, and the other a raincoat pulled over his head. Tomioka paid the lighter's fee and jumped down onto the white sand. When he'd lifted Yukiko, overcoat and all, out of the lighter and set her down on the sand, the two men who had come for him from the forestry station came running toward him, the dense sandy beach crunching under their feet.

"Are you tired? Madam, are you not feeling well? So sorry to hear that."

Completely different from a city type, the middle-aged forestry employee, with an honest, trustworthy expression, held his oilpaper umbrella out over Yukiko. The sand continued all the way to the top of the embankment. Quite exhausted by now, Yukiko stopped on the sand and caught her breath any number of times. She had difficulty breathing, and her whole body seemed aflame with fever. The mountains that towered ruggedly above the suspension bridge were enveloped in a milk-white mist.

Climbing the embankment, crossing the long suspension bridge, Tomioka and Yukiko were taken to the one inn in Anbo, advertised by a sign reading Lookout Pavilion. The inn stood at the top of a small knoll. Along the narrow concrete sloping road, several ferroconcrete stanchions held up the thick ropes of the suspension bridge. The inn, which doubled as a rice distribution center and a forwarding agency, did not really look like an inn. It was more like a dark and gloomy store.

Taking off their shoes in the dark entryway, going up the wooden stairs sticky with dampness from the rain, they passed into a parlor on the second floor.

No matter where one looked, the walls were without any plaster. The entire place was a primitive wayfarer's refuge built simply of wooden boards. Tomioka called for the young maid and immediately had her put down bedding for Yukiko. The rain had become as violent as if solid cords of water were being sluiced through the air. To anyone looking out from the veranda, it was as if the sea and the mountains had vanished behind a veil of mist. It was a completely impenetrable wall of white mist.

The bedding having been laid down, Tomioka exchanged business cards in the brighter part of the room with the men who had come to meet him. Tepid tea and brown sugar sweets were served.

"They say it rains a lot around here."

Lighting a cigarette, Tomioka pulled the portable brazier in a wooden box toward him.

"Yes, for a month now, it's almost nothing but rain. There's a saying that Yakushima Island has thirty-five days of rain a month," the man in the raincoat said. When he took off his coat, he turned out to be unexpectedly young. He had the air of a scholar.

61

THE MAN WEARING THE RAINCOAT was named Tatsuke. The middle-aged man who held the oilpaper umbrella went by the name of Noborito. Both were employed in the office and did not work on the mountain. Every day, a handcar made two round trips from the mountain. A small official residence had been fixed up for Tomioka, but since Yukiko was ill, she would probably find it uncomfortable. It would probably be better if she stayed at the inn for five or six days. Tomioka agreed with this decision. But it was likely to be lonesome for her.

The rain continued to fall so hard that it was difficult to breathe. It was a thick white rain. After the two men had left, Tomioka took a bath in the dirty water of the old-fashioned tub. For a while, he too burrowed into the bedding. He was extraordinarily tired. Yukiko's face went red with convulsive coughing. As she drank her cough medicine, Yukiko opened her eyes in the darkened room. Feeling as if both of them had been flung there as some kind of punishment, Yukiko had a premonition that this was where she was going to die. If she was going to die, she wanted to die at once, with one simple thought. Life on this island where it rained all day every day did not seem bearable. When she listened intently, rain was falling, even inside her ear.

The room had no glass door, only a translucent sliding paper door, which sagged heavily, frame and all. There was just one quilt each. Some of the bedding smelled of seaweed. The pillow was as hard as the base of a tree. Although hot water boiled and bubbled over from a battered aluminum teakettle on the brazier, the ashes did not hiss or smoke, perhaps because they were as hard as a shell. Watching the steam from the kettle, Yukiko gazed around the room as if to drink in its loneliness. In the ornamental alcove, a flower that looked something like a chrysanthemum had been set out. Three hanging lamps dangled from above. There was a wretchedness about the room, as if one had returned to an empty life of the past. Tomioka was sound asleep, snoring. Yukiko envied him his peace of mind.

With no place to go or return to, Yukiko gave a heavy sigh that was lost in the sound of the rain. Even if she had kept her strength, wasn't everything hopeless here? Even if she went back to Tokyo, there was nothing to hope for there either.

At nightfall, the lamps were lighted.

Supper was brought. It consisted of red hard-boiled crab, with no vegetable in sight. Yukiko, who was running a fever of nearly forty degrees centigrade, soon became drenched in sweat. Since she had nothing to change into, she borrowed a light summer kimono from the inn and changed into that.

Tomioka, his gestures clumsy, gave Yukiko her injection in the arm. For the first time, he sat down at ease by her side and drank some sake.

There was nothing with the dinner that might serve as a relish. Only rice, heaped high in a lacquer tub and bulging out from under the lid. Thinking this strange, since Yakushima Island was not a place where rice was plentiful, Tomioka smiled wryly.

The sake was rotgut sweet potato sake, which had a pungent odor. Two flasks of it had been placed in the teakettle before Tomioka realized that it was rotgut. When he asked the maid whether they didn't have regular white rice sake, she said that there was none on the island.

If there was none to be had, he would have to put up with the rotgut. Tomioka drank himself into a stupor. He was taken with the illusion that he could go on living in this place by drinking enough to forget everything that had happened up to yesterday. The rain was falling almost with the force of a storm. The wild sound of the water as it coursed along the gutters rang out like a percussion instrument. Here, all thought was unnecessary. Feeling that he was in this place to do nothing but live, without thinking about a thing, Tomioka drank the sake. God ruled everywhere in the world. Whether the rain fell or the wind blew, it was all according to the will of God. Under this pelting rain, the inhabitants of this island lived and fought in their simplicity. If the rain defeated them, they could not live. And yet, even so, how the rain did fall! The rain was so loud that it seemed to penetrate one's heart. The woman, suffering with her fever, was now frothing at the mouth. It was the world of a cold-hearted and cruel deity, but one could not allow oneself to be defeated by that power. Now that he had drifted to and arrived at this distant corner, this place would have to be Tomioka's best of all possible worlds. Now that he had crawled this far, there would be no miracle. But perhaps this woman was going to die here.

Thinking of their hardships over a long period of time, Tomioka felt the tears creep into the corners of his eyes, even in his drunkenness. Where in the world had there been a woman who had given a man like himself as much passionate love as this one? Seiko, pleasing herself, had willfully sought out her death. Niu had not faithfully followed him. Kuniko had succumbed to poverty. Yukiko alone, even while fighting her illness, had shared his journey with him as far as this place. At the moment Yukiko had been addressed as "madam" by the forestry employees who had greeted them at the pier, Tomioka had suddenly recalled his healthy family life as a bureaucrat that had continued for long. The face of the child that Yukiko had willfully aborted was now, at this late hour, as though to punish him, unbearably dear in his imagination.

Yukiko, now and then, afflicted by some nightmare, called out the doctor's name. Tomioka could do nothing but occasionally turn over the moist towel on her forehead. He would wait until tomorrow and, if it still seemed serious, send a telegram to Hika. The damp and sticky tatami, the wooden wall that seemed to breathe forth a mist—everything seemed ominous.

The next day, the rain had stopped, but the morning was dark and dusky, as in the rainy season. Tomioka went to the forestry office to make a formal call upon taking up his new duties. The office chief was away on a survey in Miyazaki, so Tomioka had Noborito show him the forestry charts and documents and take him to see the official residence nearby, alongside a grade school. This was a small bungalow with a layout of four rooms like the character for rice field:

田

In the garden, a banyan tree with a trunk so large that many people could have stood around it with their hands joined, hung down its branches like pendulous breasts. Banana plants too, flourished in the garden, putting out their small green fruit. There was a beautiful greenness about the garden that did not seem at all like winter. Making arrangements to go up the mountain tomorrow, and asking Noborito to send a telegram to Kagoshima, Tomioka returned to the inn at about noon.

Yukiko's fever had not yet abated, so Tomioka tried giving her a shot of penicillin as Hika had taught him. Yukiko seemed in robust good spirits.

She said, jokingly, "If I die by your side, you realize that that's my long-cherished ambition, anyway."

"Dying is nothing. One can die anytime. After coming all this way, are you still going to complain?"

"This rain is tiresome."

"Yes, and it's already showering again."

"Just once, I'd like to see some clear blue sky."

In the next room—was there a party of some sort there?—the voices of four or five people could be heard through the opaque sliding paper door. During the shower of rain, the mountain range was clearly visible. The mountain stood up, sheer, like an inkstone. Each time he removed the towel from Yukiko's forehead, Tomioka was shocked at how hot the towel had become. When the people of the house kindly suggested that he make a mustard plaster and lay it on Yukiko's chest, Tomioka had the maid go out for some mustard seed. Dissolving it, he spread it out on a piece of paper and laid it on Yukiko's chest. When he peeled it off after a few minutes, Yukiko's skin had grown red.

Putting his face close to her skin, Tomioka prayed to the gods: One more time, let us be born.

62

EVERY TIME THAT YUKIKO drew another labored breath, Tomioka, who was holding her sweaty hand, put his face near the tatami and counted the breath. "But God said unto him, thou fool, this night thy soul shall be required of thee: then whose shall those things be, which thou hast provided?" As if he were praying, Tomioka suddenly remembered a passage to that effect. He had a bad feeling. Although he had forgotten where he had read them, now, suddenly, those lines came to mind. Now and then he cried out Yukiko's name. Her eyes were unfocused, but she opened them once in a while and gazed weakly around the room. Tomioka tried putting his ear to her heart. It seemed to be beating fairly strongly. He took her pulse by the vein in her wrist. It had been a curious relationship between this pair. Tomioka felt as if during the past several years of this worldwide war he had lost his humanity somewhere. It seemed to him that the person with his name had become someone whose heart was empty. He might look like a living person, but in fact he was just making the gestures.

From evening on, Yukiko slept profoundly. Her fever seemed to have abated just a little. Perhaps the penicillin shots given to her every four hours were starting to have some effect. Tomioka was happy that the medicine had benefited Yukiko by even that much. He was exhausted. When night fell, he once again drank some of the rotgut sake by her pillow. As he went on drinking and started to become drunk, the slovenly figure of Yukiko as she lay there asleep with her mouth open began to seem disgusting to him. His thoughts of the two of them—who had now been driven by circumstance into this corner of the world, as if they were eloping—had begun to take on a lunatic tinge. The woman held her memories dear always. She would always mistake memories for destiny.

Tomioka drank down great quantities of the ill-smelling sweet potato rotgut sake. He became more lively than usual. When the maid asked whether he was all right, Tomioka said he was just fine. His drunkenness allowed him to forget completely about such amorphous things as destiny and memory.

Perhaps I should never have come to a place like this, he thought. But I didn't want to hang on in Tokyo, like a beggar. They say that art saves the soul, but could I really have gone into the mountains and become a hermit and a sage? If Yukiko had her way I would have been a small player in her endless memories. Even the money that she made off with might have had a certain charm. At any rate, it's God's money, so no doubt it will miraculously multiply tenfold. God is fair to the point of cruelty. As he listened to the sound of the rain that overflowed from the gutter, Tomioka felt like drinking all night long.

My ability to love women has disappeared completely. Thinking this, he lined up the seven or eight sake flasks in the ornamental alcove, with a lighthearted feeling, as if he had comprehended once and for all what trivial nuisances women were. He sprawled out exhausted at the edge of Yukiko's bedding. Late at night, he awoke feeling parched, as if his throat was on fire. I've got a nosebleed too, haven't I, Tomioka thought. Groping in the dark, he took the cooled teakettle from the brazier and put his mouth to it. The rain sounded as if it might have dwindled to a shower. It made a dripping sound.

When he looked at his watch, it was nearly four o'clock. Lighting the spirit lamp, Tomioka took out an injection needle.

His head swam.

This too had become a habit. Tomioka thought this must be the psychology of nurses the world over. By force of habit alone they got up in the middle of the night, without really caring one way or the other about the patient. That was all it was. But still Yukiko would frown with annoyance or make a bitter face.

"How do you feel?"

"I feel all right."

"It's stopped raining."

"How can it rain this much? I can't believe it."

"Yeah, it never seems to stop."

"Sort of like your fondness for memories."

"I guess so."

"The two of us are like rabbits with their skins off," Yukiko said with a smile.

Readying the injection needle, Tomioka, lighting his damp cigarette and drawing on it without much apparent pleasure, reached out his hand toward the empty bottles in the ornamental alcove.

Seiko's phantom flickered before his eyes. Tomioka put his mouth to the empty bottles one by one.

"Do you want a drink that badly?"

"Yes, I'd like a drink."

"If I weren't sick, I'd like to drink too. Why did we ever want to come here?"

"I got a job here, so I had to come."

"Why did you have to get a job in this kind of faraway place?"

"It's because we couldn't eat in Tokyo. If you get a little better, go back to Tokyo. Eh?"

"What would I do if I went back?"

"I don't know. What would you do?"

Yukiko closed her eyes. She felt as if a painful wound had been touched on. She also came to feel that her illness was somehow unique. Hika had strenuously urged her to have an X-ray taken, but Yukiko had not allowed him. Hika had made the suggestion because there was a portable X-ray machine available, but Yukiko did not want to have the inside of her chest examined.

"What time is it?"

"It's already daybreak. Five o'clock. Does it rain all year-round on this island?"

"Hmm, maybe so."

"There's no choice, really, for me here, but to go up and work on the mountain. Yesterday, I had a look at the official residence, but are you really going to be able to stay there by yourself? If I go up on the mountain, I'll be away for as long as a week."

"Can I go up on the mountain too?"

"It's so hard to get there, I don't think it's possible."

"You're probably right. If it just didn't rain so much, I think this would be a very nice place. It can't rain like this every day . . . At times like this, it would be nice if Kano-san were here."

"Are you going to summon him from Hades?"

"If I went to summon him and didn't come back, you'd be relieved, wouldn't you?"

"I would be relieved. Because there are women everywhere."

"Ha. That's how women are, for men. Even the most splendid woman, as seen by a man, is replaceable. It's because women and men are fundamentally different. It's sad to hear you say that."

"If it's so sad, then get well quickly. Get well and fight back against me. Use woman's ultimate weapon."

"There you go again, saying hateful things. You've had a poisonous tongue from way back. But if a member of a women's congress were to hear you, she'd be very angry with you."

"A member of a women's congress? I don't think the members of women's congresses are particularly women. I'd forgotten that such people even exist."

Amen. That's certainly the case, she thought. Though she was angry, Yukiko, reaching out her hand from her chest, sought for Tomioka's hand.

63

THEY COULD NOT STAY AT THE INN FOREVER, so on the fourth day, Yukiko was taken on a stretcher to the official residence during an interval of clear weather. The islanders, wondering what was going on, peered at the stretcher as it was carried past.

The sun, visible again after so long, shone down from the blue sky. The trees and shrubs, pressing in from both sides, sparkled with raindrops in the sunshine. The color of the sky was so dazzling that it was impossible to look at directly. It was a blue, warm color—such that it could not possibly be considered a winter sky.

The stretcher was borne along the winding road. When Yukiko opened her eyes at one point, in a place along the way where there were no human voices, a hen clucked raucously and fled into a hut. The houses, scarcely enough to be called a village, all had their rain shutters opened just a little. It was exactly like an Annamese hamlet in French Indochina. Yukiko, turning her face toward the left and right, gazed wonderingly around her. All the rain shutters were now closed. When they had gone through a tunnel of big trees that resembled banyans, suddenly there was the voice of Tomioka.

"Oh, thank you very much."

The door of the entryway opened with a creaking sound. The stretcher, its bearers stumbling, entered the house. The ceiling boards were stained all over, and the wooden wall had its cracks stuffed with newspapers. Was this the official residence? Yukiko opened her eyes wide.

At noon today, Tomioka was to go up into the mountains in a handcar. Sleeping overnight on the mountain, he would return in the evening tomorrow. He had requested the services of a war widow with one child as housekeeper, so in his absence the woman would take care of Yukiko.

A rather nice striped cotton quilt—where it had been obtained?—had been laid down. A blanket bought in Kagoshima served as the under bedding. The bare, worn tatami mats had no edging. On the portable brazier, a new aluminum teapot sent up puffs and wisps of steam.

After finishing the noonday meal that had arrived from the inn, Tomioka put his boots on, made preparations for going up the mountain, and departed. In his rain hat, his dirty raincoat, and with a wrinkled rucksack on his back, Tomioka looked the part of a mountain forester skilled in such preparations. Noborito, who had armed himself against the elements in a ski outfit, came to meet him. Having given instructions to the housekeeper, Tomioka left with Noborito. It was absolutely unusual, beautiful weather.

"We hardly ever have beautiful days like this. It refreshes the spirits. Madam, there's some rice gruel. Will you have some?"

The housekeeper's face had an unhealthy color. Her eyes were muddy and unclear. Perhaps she had bugs in her stomach. Her name was Towai Nobu. Her husband had died in the war nine years earlier, she said.

Yukiko had no appetite at all.

She looked at the blue sky through the cracks in the rain shutters. She brooded over Tomioka's joking remark about there being women everywhere. That man would no doubt shamelessly survive her and go on living just like this. But she herself would not be able to go on living many more years, Yukiko thought secretly. On the nearby mountain, a turtledove was singing. The mountainside—purplish and chiseled like the surface of an inkstone—was visible through the cracks of the rain shutters.

"Is it far to Kosugitani?" Yukiko asked Nobu.

Nobu said, "Yes, it takes two and a half hours. It's an hour just to

Tachu Peak. But they say there's an awful lot of snow at Kosugitani now. So your husband will probably be cold."

Kosugitani was a forestry harvest area about seven hundred meters above sea level. The temperatures there went down as low as sixteen degrees centigrade. From December to March, it was deep in snow.

The area was a rugged, towering mountain range and, throughout the day, fair, cloudy, and rainy periods followed one another. It lay in the route of typhoons, and Yakushima Island was visited by heavy rains all year long. The economy of the village was dogged by poverty, and riparian works had not been carried forward.

The island's main sources of income were the flying fish of May, the sweet potato, sugar cane, and forestry.

Although Yakushima was famous for the Yaku cedar, the rivers could not be used for carrying the logs down to the rivers' mouths. Everything had to be taken down by handcar.

The cedars, enveloped all year round by rain and mist, did not float—perhaps because of the many years they had lived. If a log of the pulpwood transported down the mountainside by handcar fell into the sea as it was being loaded onto a boat, it stayed at the bottom with a weight that no power could raise.

"It's so warm here—does much snow fall?"

"Yes, you can ski until March at Kosugitani."

"Have you gone up there yourself?"

"No, I've only gone as far as Tachu Peak."

The sky had suddenly grown dark. Mist had begun to envelop the peak of the mountain. As Yukiko watched the mist wrap around the mountain, she felt an unutterable sadness. This was not the sort of landscape in which someone like her could live all the time. For Yukiko, who had once known luxury, the stains on the ceiling and the board wall stuffed with newspapers were unendurable. If she went back to Tokyo, she would be able to return to all kinds of civilization. But what about life in the storage shed in Ikebukuro? She finally remembered the American soldier, Joe, at this late date:

My dearly beloved, now it has withered
but this flower which yesterday was the color
of lapis lazuli, bright and vivid, today

is like a pleasant memory, telling me
of past days spent with you.

Tomioka—his eye lighting on the small radio that Joe had brought her, which played her that song—had asked Yukiko to let him listen to dance music, but Yukiko had deliberately turned the dial to the war-crime tribunals.

"At that time, what were your thoughts?"

The American-accented Japanese of the Nisei interpreter was politely couched. But when it flowed out from the radio, Tomioka felt an ache in his heart and badgered Yukiko to play some American jazz. But Yukiko had said angrily, "You and I are involved too, in these trials. I don't want to listen to them either. But when I think there are people who are actually being tried, I want to hear the facts about the war."

The time she had begun to know Joe seemed ten years in the past. By now, he had perhaps returned to his homeland. Their words had not been sufficient. But their bodies had understood each other's hearts. When Tomioka had made sarcastic remarks about the affair with Joe, Yukiko had answered back, "In Indochina, you loved Niu."

As she thought about it, the past became dear to Yukiko. Her relationship with Joe had had a brightness about it that needed no searching of each other's souls. She remembered that there had been an ease of spirit that had dispensed with seriousness and solemn chitchat about responsibility.

64

RIDING IN THE LOCOMOTIVE CAR, next to the engineer, Tomioka felt as if his body were suspended in air as the train, with a formidable hollow roar, pushed its way up along the narrow gauge railway. Below him, the Abo River, blue and clear, shone as it wound its way deep through the dense forests. Tomioka somehow felt awkward about the business cards in his breast pocket, printed just today, with his title of technical official.

"You're not having a smoke?" The engineer looked at Tomioka with some surprise.

Below them was a sheer precipice. The plants called *hego*, which resembled ferns, were unfamiliar to Tomioka. In the interior of Dalat, a similar kind of fernlike plant had also flourished everywhere. They resembled the devil's ferns back home. Tomioka, lighting a cigarette, transferred it to the fingers of the engineer who was gripping the handle of the controls.

Along the river on the right, the hamlet of Awa vanished among the trees, little by little. The handcars seemed to be gliding through the air. Behind the locomotive, four open handcars were being drawn. They were piled with sacks of rice, vegetables, mail, and salted barracuda.

Five or six sawyers from the Agriculture Ministry on Yakushima Island were sitting on top of the sacks. They looked cold. Noborito was also riding back there, talking with them in a loud voice. The area under the jurisdiction of the Forestry Bureau was about twenty thousand hectares, but all of it was national forest. It was a small area, not as large as the private properties held by individuals in French Indochina. But for present-day Japan, stripped of its territories, even these meager twenty thousand hectares on a small island must be a precious storehouse. In this defeat, Japan had lost Korea, Taiwan, the Ryukyu Islands, Sakhalin, and Manchuria, and had been reduced to its four main islands. Nowadays, it had to feed a great family, digging into the very corners of the kitchen, so to speak.

"It's probably cold on the mountain."

"This year they've had a lot of snow all over the country, I hear. But the mountain has had really a lot of snow. Everybody says it's extraordinary."

"You've come prepared for winter."

"When one goes to the mountain, one wears the appropriate clothing."

"How long is this island from east to west?"

"Well, let's see, from east to west it's fifteen miles. From south to north, it's about seven and a half miles, they say . . . From Kagoshima, it's ninety-seven miles. It's warm in the village of Awa, but up on the mountains it's pretty cold."

In a military accent, the engineer gave the statistics. The mountain range on the left had broad patches of red earth that seemed to sink into the eye. The line of handcars laboriously ascended toward the top of the mountain. The air one breathed out was white.

At the mountain's top, a dark rain cloud like overhanging eaves began to envelop the mountain. Big drops of rain came down. When Tomioka looked behind him, the group in the handcars had put on raincoats and opened up oilpaper umbrellas.

When they arrived at Tachu Peak, the rain was falling steadily. The train stopped, which meant that tarpaulins could be put over the cars. By now, the cold was rather harsh. It was evening when they arrived at Kosugitani. The mountain was growing dark, and something like sleet was falling. The lofty, towering cedars flourished densely. There was a cluster of sheds in the felling area.

Tomioka hurried into the Forestry Bureau office and warmed himself at the stove. Noborito introduced him to the office staff. Unfortunately, there had been a power outage today, they were told. A large lantern had been hung from the ceiling.

An old man called Sakai, the office chief, whose hair was already white, said, "In the old days, almost all the workers were Korean, but now they're all Japanese, repatriated from Manchuria and Korea. It's gotten so that five copies of the Communist paper *The Red Flag* are sent here. Even on this island, things have become somewhat democratic. It's become difficult. The world has changed, changed completely. It's so lively now. Everybody is talking at the top of their voices. We old men are no longer necessary on this mountain. Even you, Tomioka, you shouldn't be felling trees. You should become a political orator."

Old man Sakai, saying this with a smile, took a cigarette from Tomioka and lit it at the stove. The glass sliding door grew dark. Here and there, icicles hung from the low eaves.

65

THE ROAD LEAVING THE HEART of Saigon entered a neighborhood called Kyaden, where there were many Japanese soldiers. Traveling from Kyaden to Bienhoa, one passed through fields of sugarcane, orchards, coconut groves, and betel palm groves, all flourishing, as well as several little hamlets. The road went over two long iron bridges stretched across the Donai River, and then went through the beautiful neighborhood of Bienhoa. Yukiko, Kano, and Tomioka had spent one night at a small hotel here. A French hotel, it was called the Maison Poisson. The signboard was just a picture of a large fish tail. There had recently been an air raid, and the power plant had been damaged. The three of them had their supper in a shadowy garden where flame trees were in full bloom. In the shrubbery, a strange wild bird was singing. The perfume of the flowers was almost suffocating. The garden lawn was a wet-looking green. Beneath the wooden table, Yukiko rubbed Tomioka's feet with the tips of her white shoes. In the sultry night, it was difficult to get to sleep, and the eerie croaking of the bullfrogs resonated in the distance. Yukiko found it difficult to breathe under the weight of Tomioka's body lying on her chest.

Yukiko had heard the sound of a key being stealthily turned outside her absolutely silent room. Then the door had opened. From the light outside the doorway, the tall Tomioka had presently vanished into the darkness. Inside the white mosquito netting, Yukiko deliberately made a slight whirring sound with her fan. Between the lips of the pair, there was the fragrance of the sherry, which the two had drunk earlier on the lawn. Two groups of Japanese soldiers were also lodged at this hotel. Yukiko and Tomioka, without saying a word, stared at each other in the darkness. In the depths of their eyes that gleamed with an animal light, far away from the war, a secret love, one between the two of them alone, spoke its thoughts eloquently and in silence.

Outside the window, there was the sound of a large fruit dropping from a tree. The sound startled them for a moment. That one quiet night, at the hotel in the upland of Bienhoa, like being at the bottom of a well, had permeated even Yukiko's dreams. Even now, if she concentrated, she could remember the feel of Tomioka's bushy hair and smell the perfume of it in the palm of her hand.

The next day, the two of them, with innocent expressions, had gone on the bumpy ride from Dojiai by way of the crossroads at Jirin, for about forty kilometers along the ribbonlike government road. Yukiko had sat with Kano in the back, while Tomioka had sat in the passenger's seat next to the Annamese chauffeur. Kano was in a very bad humor. The car, driving through orderly rubber tree groves that formed a tunnel of greenery pierced by the rays of the fiercely hot sun, sped through the Jirin uplands.

Stopping briefly at Torangubomu, where there was a forestry research station, Tomioka and Kano had attended to some business. Then the car once again sped along the winding, lonely government road. Hereabouts, the Annamese driver said, were places where wild elephants often came charging out of the brush. It was a weird, sinister forest region, where huge banyan trees clustered darkly.

In her dream, Yukiko gave a bitter smile and continued to follow the dream. That springtime of her life would not come again. She could not go back to things as they were then. Although Yukiko and Tomioka had now come to Yakushima Island at the far end of the south, they had aged many years since then. Yukiko listened to the rustling sound of the rain in her ears, hearing it as the wind through a sea of forests.

She felt as if she were in Noah's flood; as if the building itself had been submerged. When Yukiko closed her eyes, she could hear clearly the sound of her own heart, passing through muscles, sinews, and skin. Now and then, her heart would stop briefly and then begin to beat again. When she put her ear to the pillow, the beating of her own heart resounded like someone's heavy footfalls.

It was an intensely irritating rain, so thick that one wanted to cut through it with a sword. Yukiko stretched her arms and legs out as far as she could. She was wondering what size her coffin would be. Then, secretly, in her heart, she concentrated her whole body on eagerly awaiting the return of Tomioka, who had gone up to the mountain the day before.

Hika had not been kind enough yet to come. For some reason, Yukiko wanted to send a letter to Shizuoka. Although she thought at first that she would like to write a letter to her stepmother, she soon changed her mind. The housekeeper, Towai Nobu, did not seem ready to put herself out at all in making meals for Yukiko. Bad-tasting seaweed gruel, a single pickled plum, and from time to time a raw egg rolling about on a plate—such was the extent of her efforts. Yukiko was seized with the idea that Tomioka might be in cahoots with this Towai Nobu. She felt that she had to be free of this woman. She began to have the feeling that she would be murdered.

Now and then, raising her eyes, Yukiko looked over at Towai Nobu, who was intently reading a book. Having lost her husband in the war, she had apparently sustained a solitary life for nine years. She must be a strong-willed woman. And yet, around her breasts and her jaw, her skin had a voluptuous oiliness and a delicious-looking beauty. Wondering what she was reading, Yukiko wanted to ask the title of the book, but she did not have enough energy to speak. Placing her sweaty hands loosely on the blanket, Yukiko gazed at them. As she did, she had the feeling that in this same way she would be able to quietly perceive the end of her life. Towai Nobu put her book down and went out to the entryway. The book was an old manual on household medicine that Tomioka had borrowed from the Abo inn. Perhaps because the air was filled with rain and mist that obscured the atmosphere today, Yae Peak was not visible. The white soles of Towai Nobu's bare feet as she went out to the entryway caught Yukiko's attention. The women around here all went about barefoot. Perhaps because they walked through so much fine sand, the soles of their feet were extraordinarily beautiful. Not even particularly bothering to rinse their feet off first, the women came right into the house, just as they were.

Perhaps, Yukiko thought, if she were to die this way, Tomioka would marry Towai Nobu and settle down here . . . She could conjecture a future in which that occurred. As she imagined the process by which the two would come together, Yukiko violently coughed up a slimy gob from the depths of her chest. With a pain in her chest that left her breathless, Yukiko rolled around on the bedding. She held both hands over her mouth and nose, but the slimy vomit kept coming up. She could not breathe. She could not cry out. The blanket, the under bedding, and the pillow were soiled with clotted blood.

Yukiko thought, I must be going to die just like this. A cold, divided other self sat by Yukiko's side. This other self clung with all her might to the god of death. The god of death was there, before that other self. Proclaiming, Everything is departing this woman's body, he was dancing a dance of triumph. Among the thoughts coming and going in her heart, Yukiko felt as if she could faintly hear Kano's voice calling to her. She shook her head weakly. In her life up till now, there was not one thing that Yukiko thought back on with regret. What was more, even if Tomioka had been sitting by her side, the train on which she was the only passenger was already racing away with her toward the underworld. Where had it come from—this rapid dissolution of her flesh that was coursing through her now with a thunderous roar of collapse? Yukiko wanted to know when her death actually began. She gasped painfully. She wanted some water. Memories of the long journey, when she had been in good health, floated up at random to her mind's eye. She felt as if her blood was muddy, and overflowing in her lungs.

There was someone, a flickering shadow, at the side of her pillow. Irritated, Yukiko raised her bloodstained face, trying to avoid the shadow. But the shadow, accompanied by a dark lightning flash, flickered across Yukiko's brow.

The judgment of Noah and Lot approached thunderously in the sound of the rain. Beyond its cavernous rumbling, Yukiko saw a sad figure, of a wasted life of a woman who had been loved by no one, return to her as an echo. There was no way now to recover that failed self of hers. What had become of that self? Too weary to even try to recall memories of

French Indochina, Yukiko pushed the slimy gobs of blood back down her throat and, like a person being buried alive, moaned, I want to live. She did not want to die. Her mind was as clear and cold as ice, but her body was beyond her control.

66

UP ON THE MOUNTAIN, there was an unusually heavy downpour. Tomioka put off his return to the town for a day and, warming himself at the office stove, drank some sweet potato sake with five or six of the mountain workers. He didn't have the courage to go back down to the town to the official residence. Telling himself that Yukiko's illness was nothing to worry about, he became more coldhearted as he got drunk from the sake.

Tomioka, thinking that the shape of this mountain resembled the Buddhist temple at the heart of Angkor Tom in French Indochina, talked with the others about that time.

"There's a soaring tower that shows a huge human face in the stone of the mountain. The stone pillars of the rooms are beginning to lean, and the stone beams are beginning to fall. In the front courts of these mountain ruins, big trees hold up the retaining walls, which have started to collapse. What's more, they're exactly like the fossilized cedar trees here. In the royal palace, male and female sexual organs joined in copulation were celebrated as symbols of Siva. They're called *linga* or something . . . Civilization goes on developing in various ways, but this heavenly nature of Siva is the ultimate of human civilization.

Probably even the atomic bomb was born from the secrets of this supreme being, Siva . . ."

The mountain workers all liked to talk. Listening to the reminiscences of Tomioka, who had seen the forests of faraway places, they kept on bringing flasks of sake from the kettle boiling on the stove.

Tomioka had by now gotten used to the smell of the sweet potato rotgut sake. Different from the low-grade alcohol that one drank in Tokyo, it did not go to one's head, and it tasted unexpectedly good. The talk at some point turned to women. The old woman and the young girls waiting on them giggled as they sliced up squid and poured soy sauce over dried mackerel. Tomioka was getting fairly drunk. Even when he put his wristwatch to his ear, he could no longer hear the ticking of the second hand. Unless he got drunk, he was not able to endure his feelings. Perhaps it was not his heart's feelings that he could not endure but his body's. His eyes flickered over the sallow flesh of the plump wrist of the short girl who was serving him. Tomioka had not touched a woman's flesh for some time. The girl's thick neck and the fullness of her hips, her ankles and the soles and toes of her feet, almost purple, tingled in his belly. The girl was wearing baggy workpants, dark blue with a white splash pattern, and a green jacket. On the mountains, the snow lingered. When one stepped outside, the sleet stung one's cheeks. In that life on the cold mountain, the young girls, without even any socks, scampered about their errands, moving from shed to shed. The girl's firm, springy body made Tomioka ache. If no one else had been there, he would have liked to have flung his arms about her and forced her to the floor. It was a long time since he had even had this kind of feeling. The girl's face somehow resembled Seiko's. But the past had already turned to ashes, and I have come this far, Tomioka thought. After climbing up to his third-story bed, which was located in the attic, just as a rack for raising silkworms would normally be, Tomioka stripped off his leather jacket and lay down on the blanket. On and on, the girl's playful, laughing voice sounded in his ear.

Tomioka woke up at about five, wishing that he could have a few more hours' sleep. A lantern had been lit. A voice was calling up to him from downstairs. Peering over the handrail, Tomioka was told there was a telephone call from the town for him. His wife was seriously ill. Tomioka, putting on his jacket, went down the ladder stairs. He put his mountain boots on by the side of the stove.

"Is there a handcar going down?"

"Yes. You should go down quickly. Someone will drive you," the old supervisor said.

It was completely dark outside. Lanterns glimmered in all the mountain sheds. The rain at some point had turned to snow. Tomioka put a shawl that the girl had lent him over his rain hat and wrapped it around his cheeks and neck as well. He got into a handcar about the length and breadth of a tatami mat. With a student who was returning to Kagoshima by a boat that was calling at the island the next day and a young lumberjack who handled the controls, Tomioka squatted in the handcar. Between the two of them, Tomioka and the student took turns holding the metal hand lamp by whose light the lumberjack worked the controls.

The handcar raced down the steep mountain track, making a noise like thunder. Now and then it would actually float off the rails. Cutting back on his speed, the young lumberjack would say, "It's really straight down here," alarming both the passengers. The light of the metal hand lamp raced smoothly along the rails of the dark valley track. There was absolutely no visibility. In the town of Awa, they encountered a driving rain.

It was already about ten o'clock by the time Tomioka reached the official residence. There he was told that Yukiko was dead. Seven or eight people, unknown to either Tomioka or Yukiko, crowding into the room, had witnessed Yukiko's last moments. Tomioka, greeting the people around him, sat down by Yukiko's pillow. By the light of a lantern, he stared for a while at Yukiko's face. Someone made Tomioka take off his rain-drenched jacket. Yukiko's hands had not yet been folded on her breast. Just as he had done for his wife, Kuniko, Tomioka quietly folded her hands together. Her hands were beginning to stiffen, and they were soiled with dried blood. The housekeeper had wiped clean only the face, it seemed. Tomioka, looking at the blood on Yukiko's hands, found his eyes suddenly filled with tears. There had been the death of Seiko, the death of Kuniko, and now the death of Yukiko. Tomioka violently shook Yukiko. There was no response. Several people now started to leave. He could hear them outside, below the window, opening oil-paper umbrellas and starting to return home.

"About when did she take a turn for the worse?"

Towai Nobu did not exactly know when Yukiko had taken a turn for the worst. At the time, she was reading the medical manual—she couldn't remember just which section. Yukiko had suddenly, with a weird expression in her eyes, as if seeing through everything, started to stare in Towai Nobu's direction. Towai Nobu was pregnant. She did not want to have the child, and so by chance she had taken up the medical manual that she found lying by Yukiko's pillow. The manual described various legal methods of abortion. She was deep in thought, calculating the cost of going to Kagoshima and seeing that kind of doctor. When she finally glanced back down at Yukiko, she was amazed to see how fearsome looking her face had become. She was startled and afraid. The woman on the bed was no kin of hers. Barefoot, she had bolted and run through the pouring rain to her own house.

Towai Nobu tried to deliver a plausible story. Tomioka could tell that it was fabricated, but he resigned himself, thinking that there was nothing to be done about it now, now that things had come to this pass. It was as if Yukiko had come to this island to die. Tomioka asked everyone else left in the room to withdraw. He meant to have only Nobu stay, but Nobu seemed to be feeling uncomfortable, so Tomioka sent her on her way.

Yukiko seemed to have suffered considerably. The bloodstains scattered about her caught Tomioka's eye. Tomioka had no energy at all. Transferring some water that was boiling on the brazier in the next room to a metal washbasin and dipping a towel into it, he wiped Yukiko's face. From the handbag that had always been at her pillow's side, he took the lipstick and applied it to Yukiko's lips, but her lips were so dry that it was difficult. When he wiped around her eyebrows with the towel, he accidentally opened her eyelids. He had the feeling that Yukiko's lips were moving. They seemed to be saying, Leave me alone. The rain pounded against the wooden roof, so hard that he felt he could barely breathe. What on earth should he do now? Tomioka felt as if he were being pursued by the sound of the rain. Yukiko's eyes gleamed like those of a living creature. Drawing the lamp near, Tomioka looked fixedly into them. They were eyes of entreaty, of protest. Taking a comb from the handbag, he combed Yukiko's rather bushy hair and bound it up in a bun. At this point, Yukiko was not asking for any further consideration from the living. She was done unto as she was done unto, and that was all.

His wristwatch indicated that it was twelve o'clock.

The rain, not slackening for even a moment, made a fierce sound that filled the night. Tomioka became afflicted with violent diarrhea. He squatted in the small, stuffy privy and, burying his face in his hands, cried like a little child. What was a human being, anyway? Who was he? Human beings kept on vanishing abruptly from the world. Was it a procession of the children of God or a procession of a company of devils?

Through the window of the privy, which only had wire netting over it, raindrops came splashing in. The pain in his abdomen, which, along with the stench of the privy, made Tomioka feel he was in some sort of earthly hell, seemed about to rip his skin open.

The impossibility of his life—this narrow frame from which he could not take even one step away—was his punishment, Tomioka thought. It was an impossibility that had led him to a sort of Gethsemane. Yukiko's death had the quality of a casual accident. Her aim in dying seemed to Tomioka unexpectedly piteous and forlorn. There was no difference between this and being hit by a car in Tokyo. If she had died after a long illness, one would still have been able to harbor a dream about the dead person's gallant suffering . . . Clutching his abdomen, Tomioka crawled back into the room and wrapped the blanket around his waist. Although he hadn't even known which way was north for the dead person's head, now her pillow had been shifted alongside the wall and slapped flat. On a new quilt, a pair of scissors of Tanegashima make had been placed.

Although the two had had no acquaintances on this island, a number of people whom they had gotten to know since their arrival had been kind enough to watch over Yukiko's death while Tomioka was away. Tomioka felt that there was something strange about this. People might suffer this kind of disaster anywhere. The disasters in turn of those people who had stood witness to his disaster were part of the mystery of the world. Bringing from the kitchen the low-grade sake that he had had the housekeeper, Towai Nobu, buy this evening, Tomioka heated it in the bottle and drank it. Drinking by himself with Yukiko dead in the next room made Tomioka feel merry, with a sort of religious lightheartedness.

Soon he himself, one day or another, would also come to that end. Nevertheless, he did not want to die with Yukiko. As he drank, his feelings began to grow wilder. This human wildness of spirit seemed to Tomioka like his salvation. His drunkenness filled and overflowed his body. Tomioka felt the excitement of having found a good thing, to be thankful for, in his life itself. Now and then, he had the feeling that the ghost of Yukiko was shimmering through the empty air. Tomioka looked hard at the flattened bedding. Yukiko was silent and did not move.

Of his three women, it had been Yukiko who had followed him the most faithfully, Tomioka felt. But now, from her cold body, there was no response.

The memories of their past flitted through Tomioka's drunken brain. His drunkenness was becoming almost violent. Tomioka drank off the hot sake until his stomach burned. Since he had had nothing to eat, the alcohol circulated rapidly through his body. He talked to himself as he drank.

A wind sprang up. The flame of the candle set by Yukiko's pillow went out. Staggering, Tomioka lit a new candle and went to set it by the pillow. Yukiko's face, as expressionless as a mask, was one that had been thrown away into loneliness. Tomioka, not wishing to look at her face any more, put a hand up to her brow. But at once, the inanimate flesh of the dead person seemed to repel his hand. Since he had neither a new towel nor any gauze, Tomioka took a sheaf of common rice paper and, opening it so that it formed a little roof, placed it over Yukiko's face.

67

ONE MONTH PASSED. Tomioka took a week's vacation and went to Kagoshima. In early spring, completely dried out and with very little rain, Kagoshima was an utterly different world. First, Tomioka arrived at the inn where he had stayed before. In just a short time, all the maids and waitresses had changed. He was led to the front room where he had stayed with Yukiko, which seemed like a strange coincidence. He thought that he would have his rain-damaged watch repaired, so he went to the shop where he had bought it. He was told that the proprietor had injured himself and was laid up in bed, so he had to try to go elsewhere. On his way back, Tomioka stopped in at Dr. Hika's office. Hika was in. He remembered Tomioka and, ushered into the room with its medicinal smell, Tomioka reported the death of Yukiko. Hika, for his part, said that her condition had somehow seemed disquieting to him and that he had wanted to take an X-ray of her chest.

Tomioka somehow felt uncomfortable with the doctor, without Yukiko there. Tomioka had spent the past month completely saturated with alcohol, and he knew that his face had changed so much that he looked like a different person. He smoked one cigarette after another. The room grew smoky. Coffee was brought in. Tomioka, feeling as if he had returned to civilization after a long time, brought the cup of aromatic coffee to his lips. The doctor, saying, "I'll play Dvorak's *New World Symphony*, which your wife liked so much," set the record on his homemade phonograph.

While they listened, the doctor casually asked Tomioka whether Yukiko had not ruined her health a long time ago without knowing it.

"How about yourself? Shall I examine you as well? You've been drinking a great deal, haven't you?" Hika smiled as he spoke.

Tomioka felt the music calming his spirits. Hika had a social engagement that evening. Tomioka, promising he would call again, left the dispensary. But he had nowhere to go. Even the nostalgic affection with which he'd thought of Hika on the distant island, as of a man who went his own way in life, weaving an arabesque in which he brooked no interference from others, had now turned just a little cold. He was an honest, methodical doctor. *On ne se soigne jamais trop* (There were no limits in taking care of oneself). Tomioka, approaching a secondhand bookstore, thought he would like to buy a novel and go back and read it. He thought that he would like to read some Zola. He recalled that the mixed-race typist who had worked at the forestry bureau in Dalat had once lent him Zola's *The Tavern*. Passing through the dusky streets, Tomioka emerged on the lively Tenmonkan thoroughfare. He went around looking at the movie houses, one by one. Along the narrow avenue, mixed-race humanity flowed and jostled like a river of waters. This sort of civilization seemed oppressive to Tomioka, as he felt at the moment. Entering a back street, Tomioka entered a small eating place where they had women. The women's makeup had an oily gleam. Tomioka liked one woman who was wearing a red evening gown. She served him a beer. He had not known that beer could be this delicious. The dry, fragrant night air was exhilarating since it was, finally, not raining. The woman's eyelids were as thin and slender as a thread, but the eyes that peeped out from under them shone alluringly. The backs of her hands were milky white. The woman's red dress, seen under the colored lights, was rather dirty. A guitar player, wearing a red neckerchief, stepped into the cramped entryway.

The woman, speaking rapidly in the local dialect, sent the guitar player packing. Her accent was somehow like Yukiko's. Yukiko's face, as she was interred in the rain-soaked earth, burned itself into Tomioka's heart. And yet, that strong individual life had perished. And here once more, he could feel the roots of enchantment starting to grow. Untaught by experience, Adam, seduced by sexual charm . . . God sowed innumerable seeds. The harvest, growing on the strength of its own accord, came to fruition. That was all.

Tomioka threw back six bottles of beer, one after another, before he was dragged upstairs by the woman.

Late at night, Tomioka returned to the inn. The woman was an unexpectedly honest person, it seemed. He had left most of the money at the inn for safekeeping, but the money he had been carrying in his purse was still there. It was all the money that Yukiko had left him with. Tomioka, burrowing into the dried-out bedding in his street clothes, pursued his thoughts that went on becoming as heavy as a stone.

He did not have the energy or the heart to return to Yakushima Island. But he could not bear to leave, either, with Yukiko buried there all alone. What waited for him in Tokyo, anyway? Tomioka realized that he was nothing but a floating cloud. He was just a floating cloud—appearing, disappearing, then appearing again—it did not matter when or where.